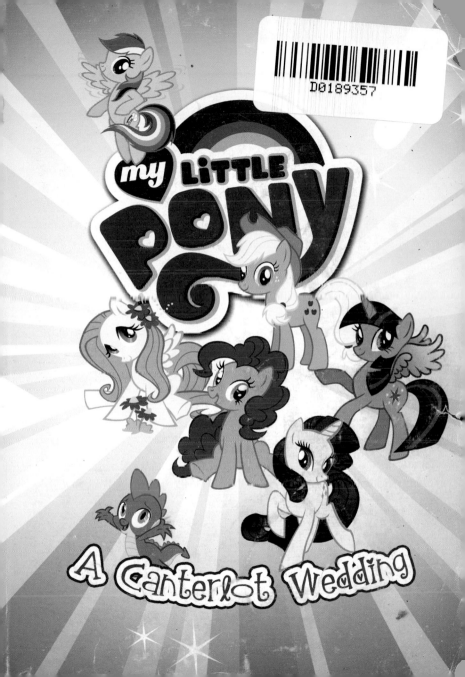

my LiTTLE PONY

A Canterlot Wedding

Special thanks to Brian Lenard, Ed Lane, and
Michael Kelly for their invaluable assistance.

ISBN: 978-1-63140-487-0
18 17 16 15   1 2 3 4
www.IDWPUBLISHING.com

Licensed By:

Ted Adams, CEO & Publisher
Greg Goldstein, President & COO
Robbie Robbins, EVP/Sr. Graphic Artist
Chris Ryall, Chief Creative Officer/Editor-in-Chief
Matthew Ruzicka, CPA, Chief Financial Officer
Dirk Wood, VP of Marketing
Lorelei Bunjes, VP of Digital Services
Jeff Webber, VP of Licensing, Digital and Subsidiary Rights
Jerry Bennington, VP of New Product Development

My Little Pony

A Canterlot Wedding

Written by
Cindy Morrow

Adaptation by
Justin Eisinger

Edits by
Alonzo Simon

Lettering and Design by
Gilberto Lazcano

MEET THE PONIES

Twilight Sparkle

TWILIGHT SPARKLE TRIES TO FIND THE ANSWER TO EVERY QUESTION! WHETHER STUDYING A BOOK OR SPENDING TIME WITH PONY FRIENDS, SHE ALWAYS LEARNS SOMETHING NEW!

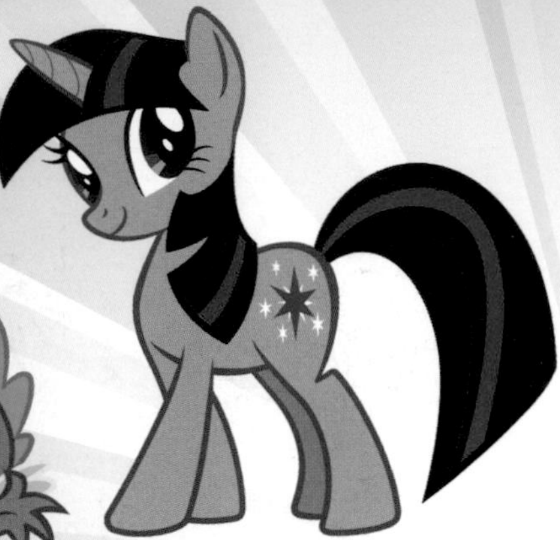

Spike

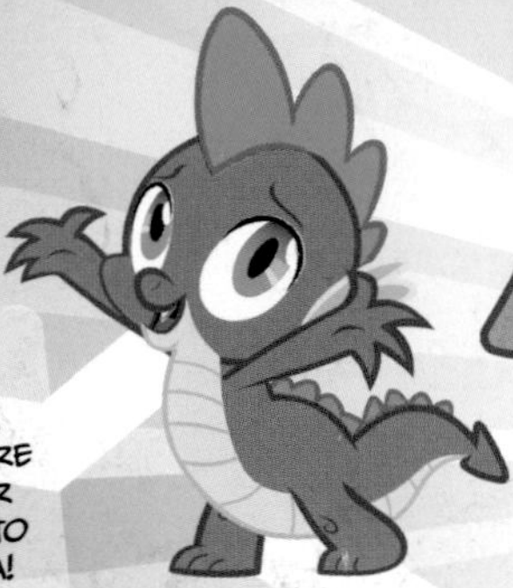

SPIKE IS TWILIGHT SPARKLE'S BEST FRIEND AND NUMBER ONE ASSISTANT. HIS FIRE BREATH CAN DELIVER SCROLLS DIRECTLY TO PRINCESS CELESTIA!

Applejack

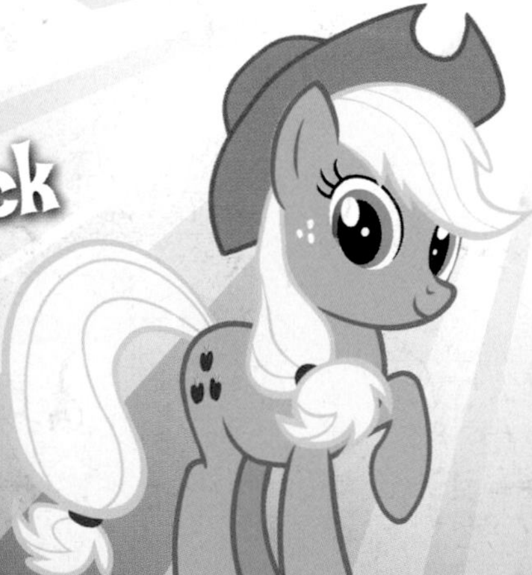

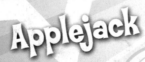

APPLEJACK IS HONEST, FRIENDLY, AND SWEET TO THE CORE! SHE LOVES TO BE OUTSIDE, AND HER PONY FRIENDS KNOW THEY CAN ALWAYS COUNT ON HER.

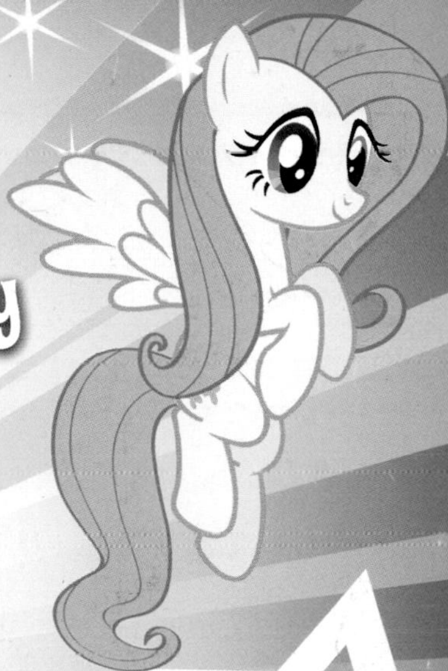

Fluttershy

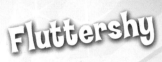

FLUTTERSHY IS A KIND AND GENTLE PONY WITH A BIG HEART. SHE LIKES TO TAKE CARE OF OTHERS, ESPECIALLY HER LITTLE ANIMAL FRIENDS.

Rarity

RARITY KNOWS HOW TO ADD SPARKLE TO ANY OUTFIT! SHE LOVES TO GIVE HER PONY FRIENDS ADVICE ON THE LATEST PONY FASHIONS AND HAIRSTYLES.

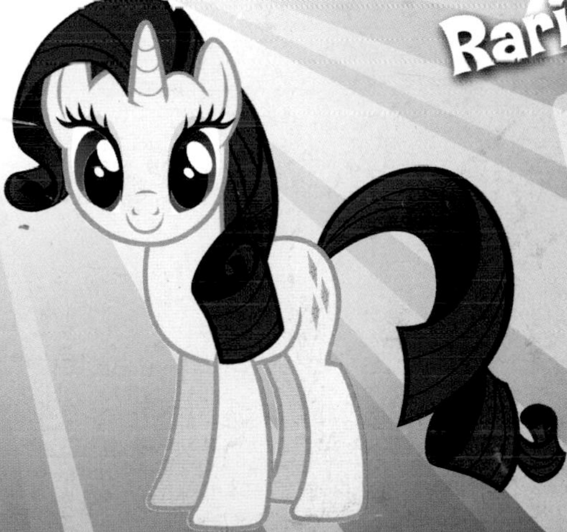

Pinkie Pie

PINKIE PIE KEEPS HER PONY FRIENDS LAUGHING AND SMILING ALL DAY! CHEERFUL AND PLAYFUL, SHE ALWAYS LOOKS ON THE BRIGHT SIDE.

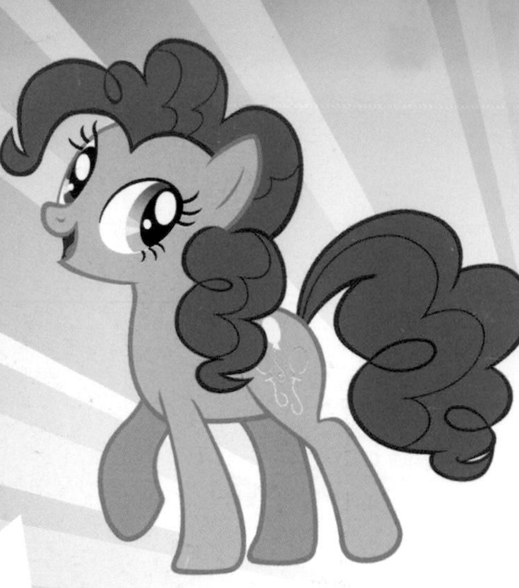

Rainbow Dash

RAINBOW DASH LOVES TO FLY AS FAST AS SHE CAN! SHE IS ALWAYS READY TO PLAY A GAME, GO ON AN ADVENTURE, OR HELP OUT ONE OF HER PONY FRIENDS.

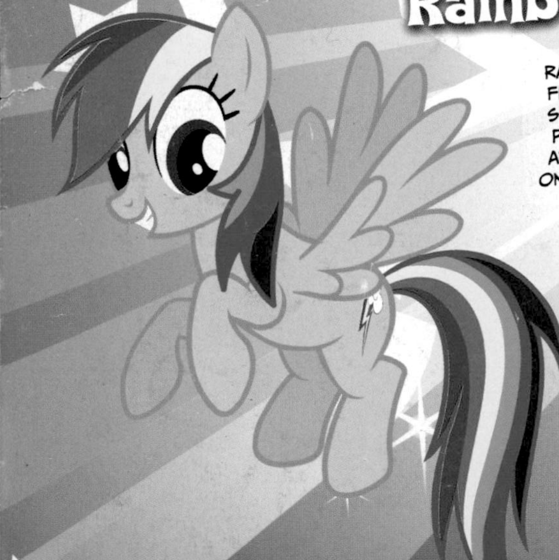

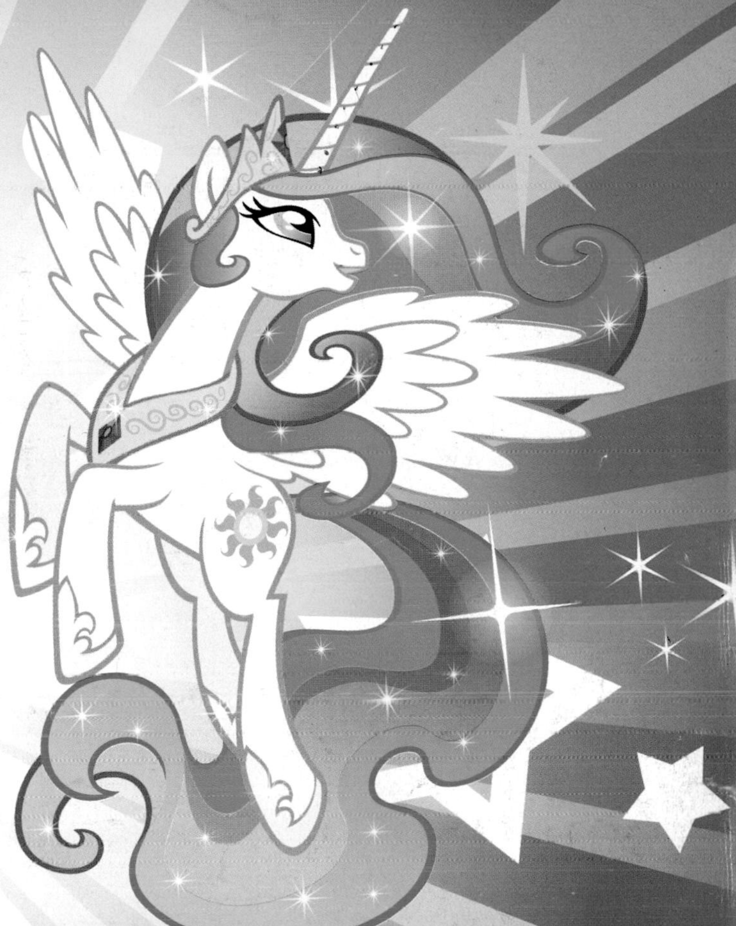

Princess Celestia

PRINCESS CELESTIA IS A MAGICAL AND BEAUTIFUL PONY WHO RULES THE LAND OF ESQUESTRIA. ALL OF THE PONIES IN PONYVILLE LOOK UP TO HER!

A Canterlot Wedding

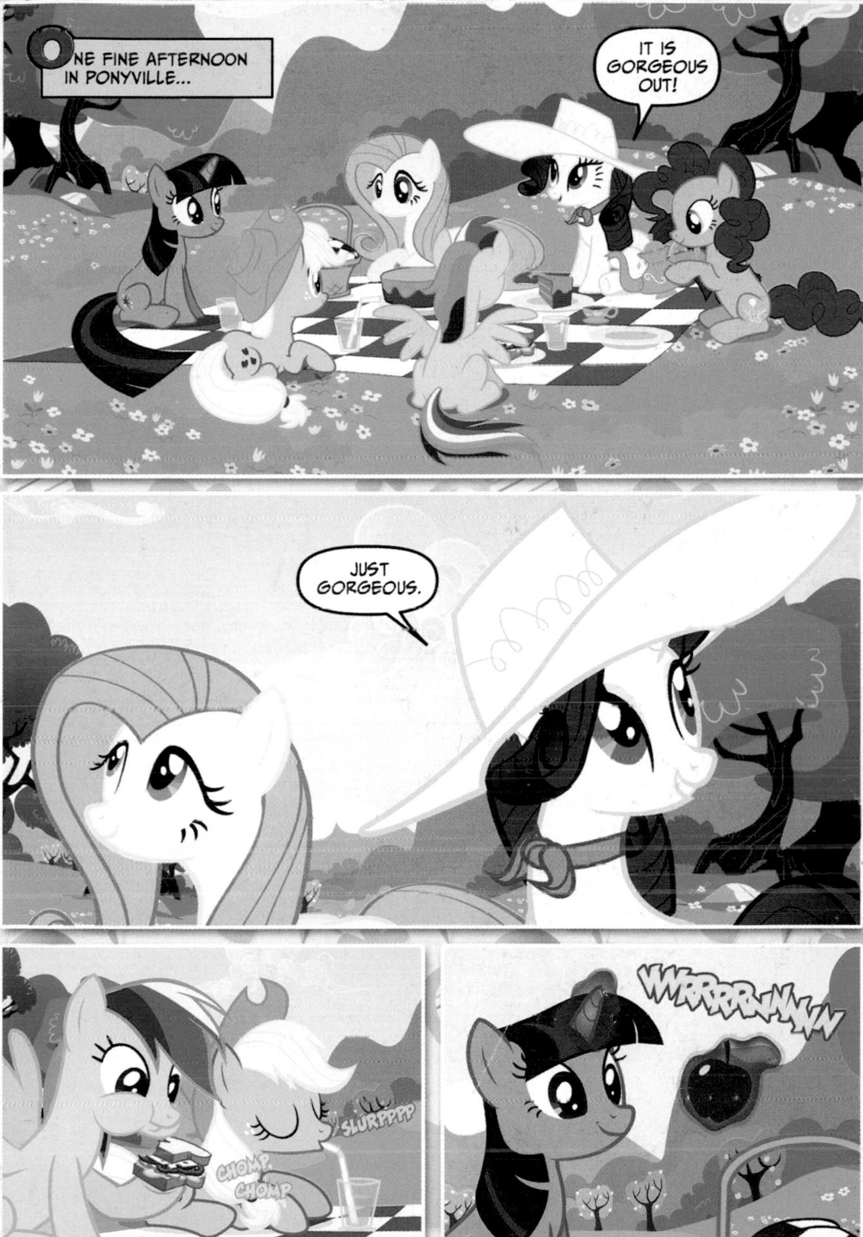
ONE FINE AFTERNOON IN PONYVILLE...
IT IS GORGEOUS OUT!
JUST GORGEOUS.
CHOMP CHOMP
SLURPPPP
WWRRRRRNNNN

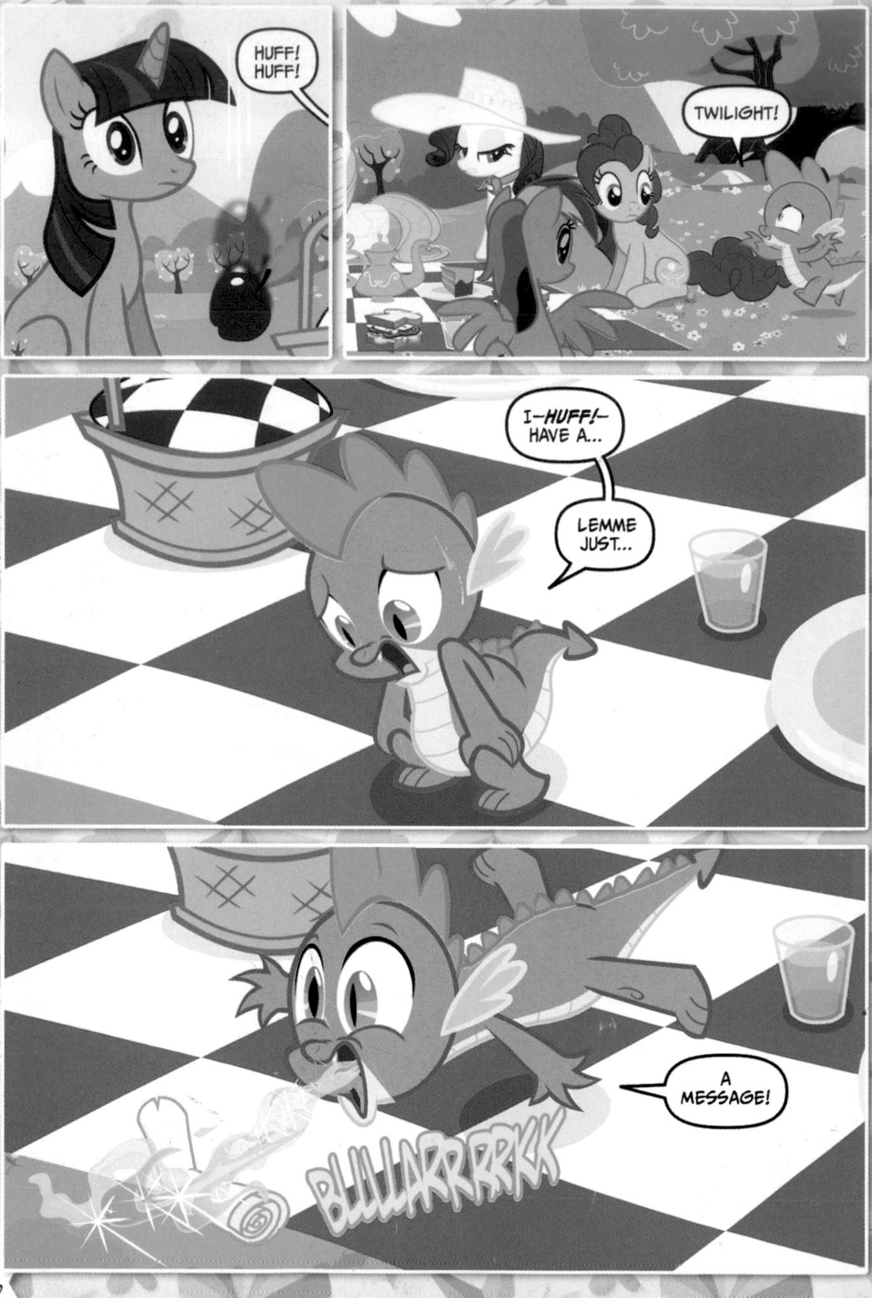
HUFF! HUFF!
TWILIGHT!
I—*HUFF!*— HAVE A...
LEMME JUST...
A MESSAGE!
BLLARRRKK

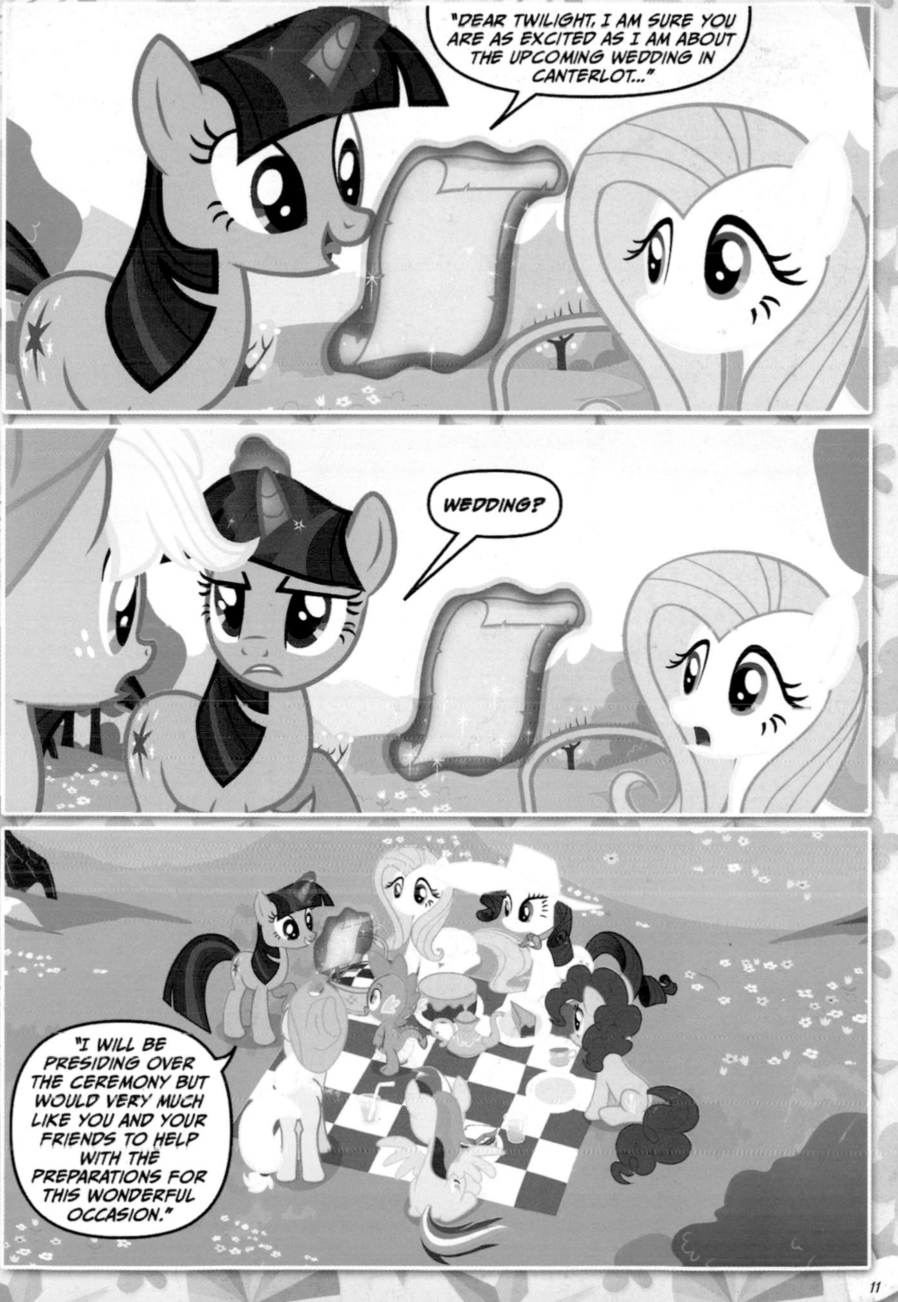
"DEAR TWILIGHT, I AM SURE YOU ARE AS EXCITED AS I AM ABOUT THE UPCOMING WEDDING IN CANTERLOT..."
WEDDING?
"I WILL BE PRESIDING OVER THE CEREMONY BUT WOULD VERY MUCH LIKE YOU AND YOUR FRIENDS TO HELP WITH THE PREPARATIONS FOR THIS WONDERFUL OCCASION."

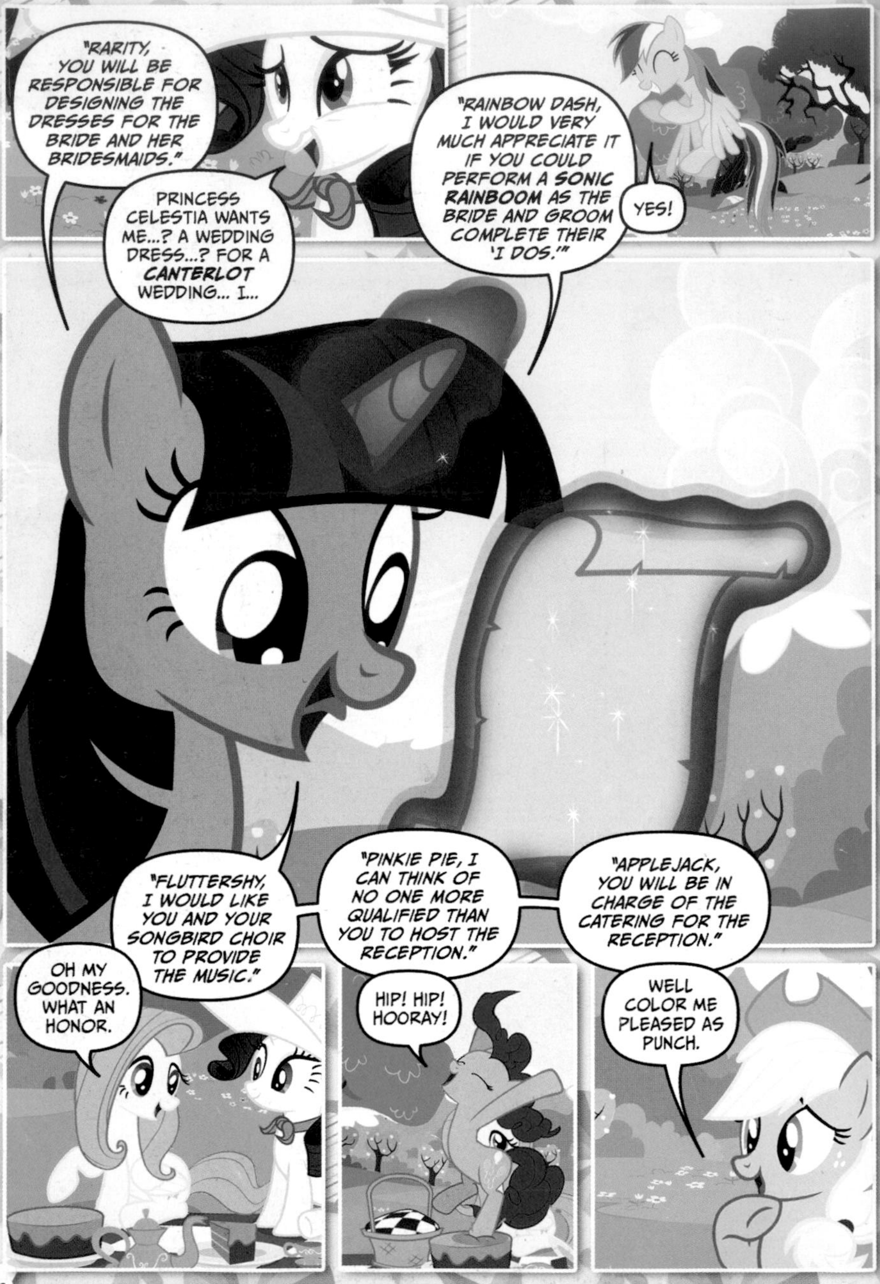
"RARITY, YOU WILL BE RESPONSIBLE FOR DESIGNING THE DRESSES FOR THE BRIDE AND HER BRIDESMAIDS."
PRINCESS CELESTIA WANTS ME...? A WEDDING DRESS...? FOR A CANTERLOT WEDDING... I...
"RAINBOW DASH, I WOULD VERY MUCH APPRECIATE IT IF YOU COULD PERFORM A SONIC RAINBOOM AS THE BRIDE AND GROOM COMPLETE THEIR 'I DOS.'"
YES!
"FLUTTERSHY, I WOULD LIKE YOU AND YOUR SONGBIRD CHOIR TO PROVIDE THE MUSIC."
"PINKIE PIE, I CAN THINK OF NO ONE MORE QUALIFIED THAN YOU TO HOST THE RECEPTION."
"APPLEJACK, YOU WILL BE IN CHARGE OF THE CATERING FOR THE RECEPTION."
OH MY GOODNESS. WHAT AN HONOR.
HIP! HIP! HOORAY!
WELL COLOR ME PLEASED AS PUNCH.

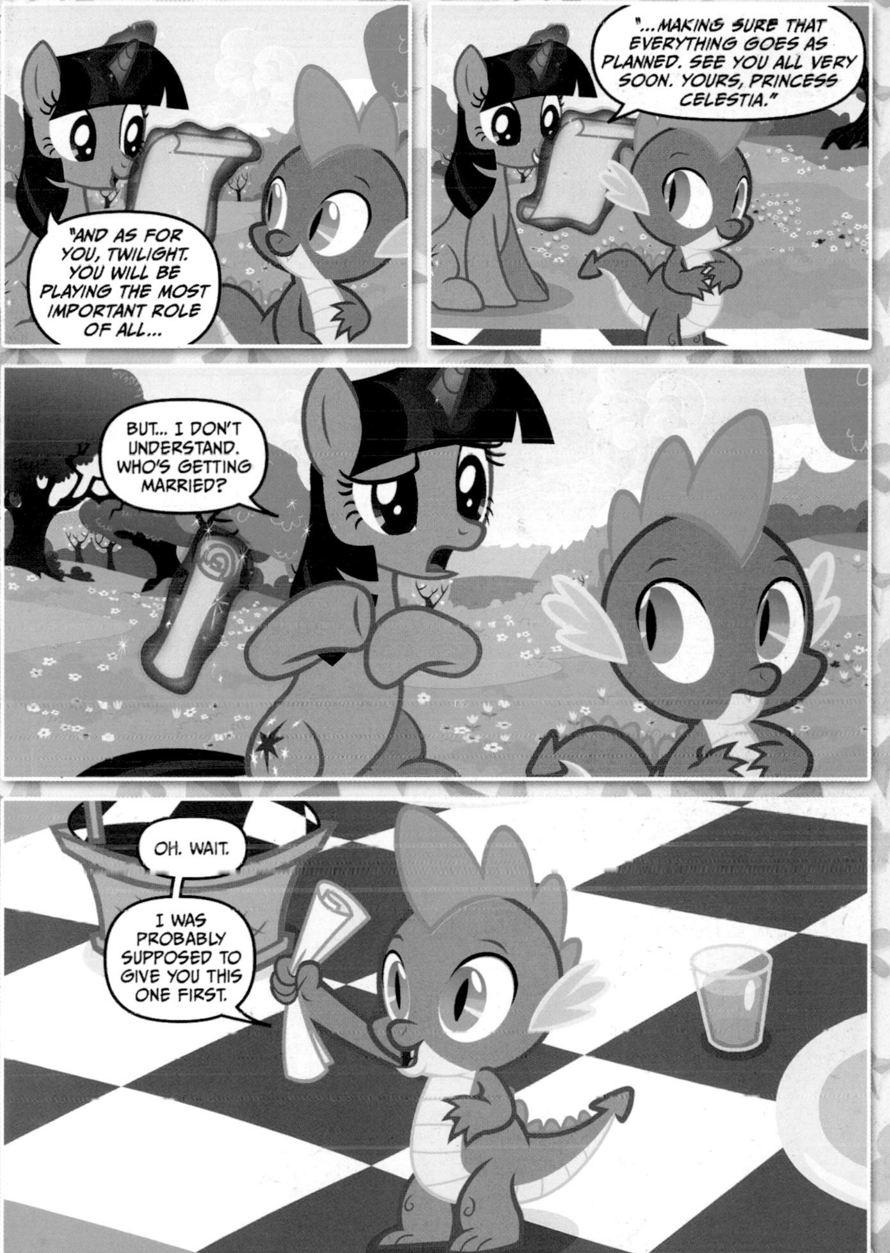
"AND AS FOR YOU, TWILIGHT. YOU WILL BE PLAYING THE MOST IMPORTANT ROLE OF ALL...
"...MAKING SURE THAT EVERYTHING GOES AS PLANNED. SEE YOU ALL VERY SOON. YOURS, PRINCESS CELESTIA."
BUT... I DON'T UNDERSTAND. WHO'S GETTING MARRIED?
OH. WAIT.
I WAS PROBABLY SUPPOSED TO GIVE YOU THIS ONE FIRST.

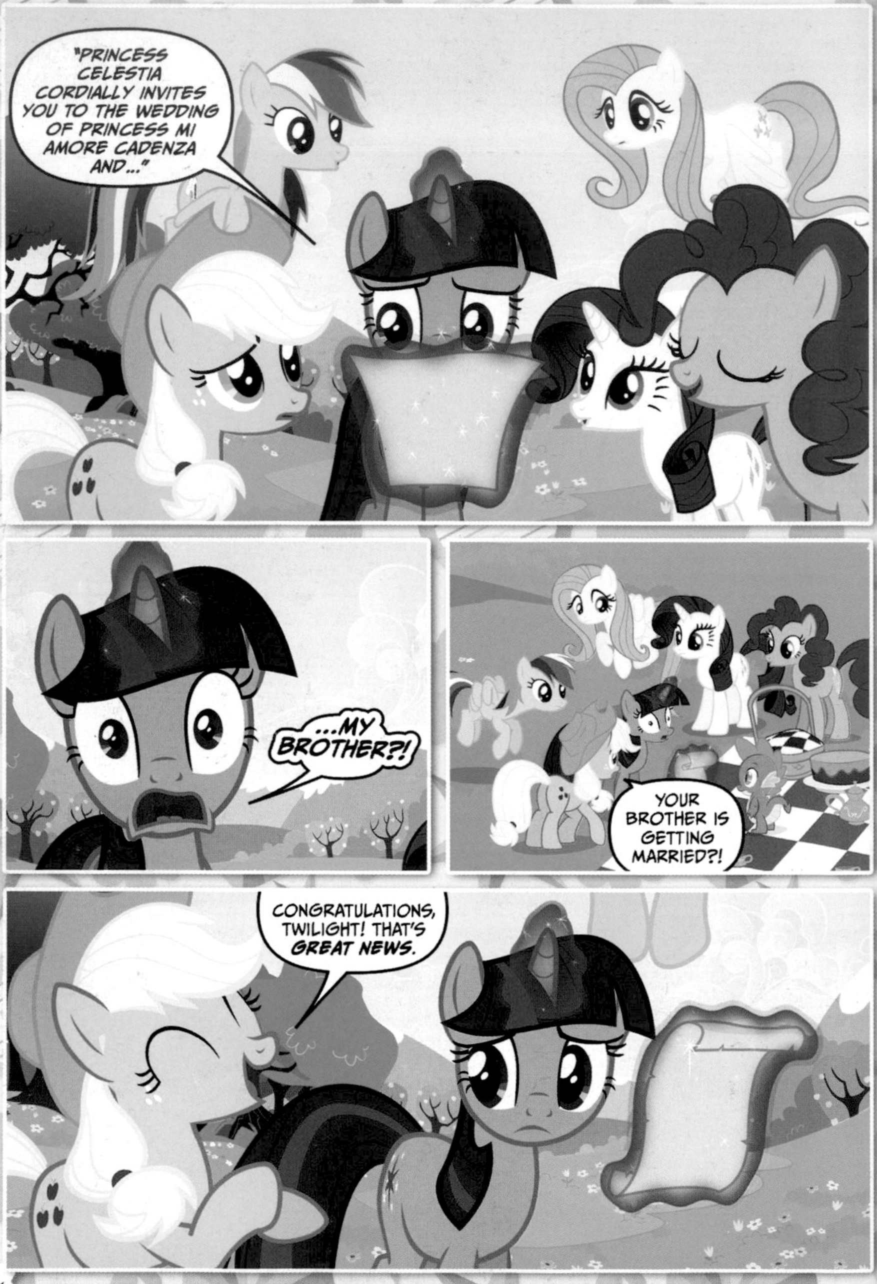
"PRINCESS CELESTIA CORDIALLY INVITES YOU TO THE WEDDING OF PRINCESS MI AMORE CADENZA AND..."
...MY BROTHER?!
YOUR BROTHER IS GETTING MARRIED?!
CONGRATULATIONS, TWILIGHT! THAT'S **GREAT NEWS**.

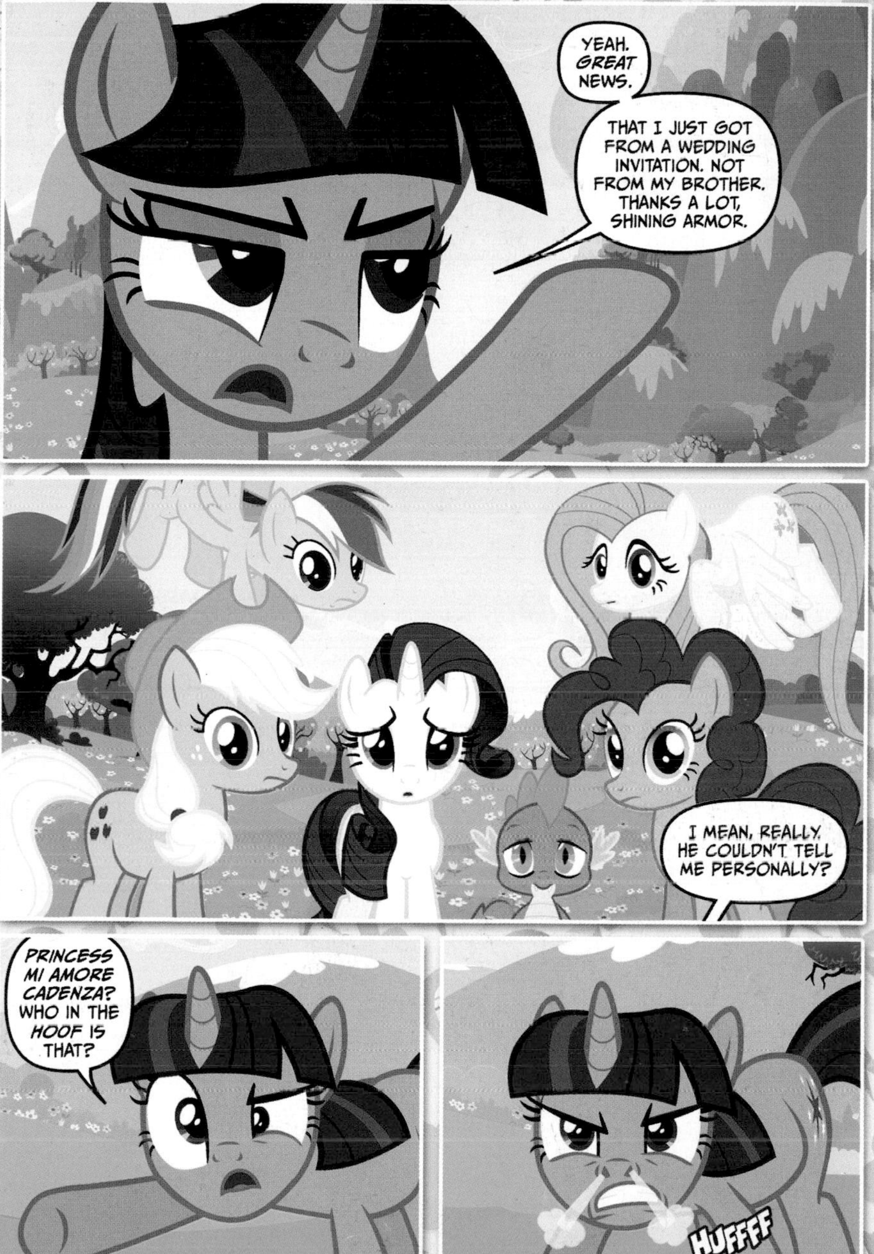
YEAH. *GREAT* NEWS.
THAT I JUST GOT FROM A WEDDING INVITATION. NOT FROM MY BROTHER. THANKS A LOT, SHINING ARMOR.
I MEAN, REALLY. HE COULDN'T TELL ME PERSONALLY?
PRINCESS MI AMORE CADENZA? WHO IN THE *HOOF* IS THAT?
HUFFFF

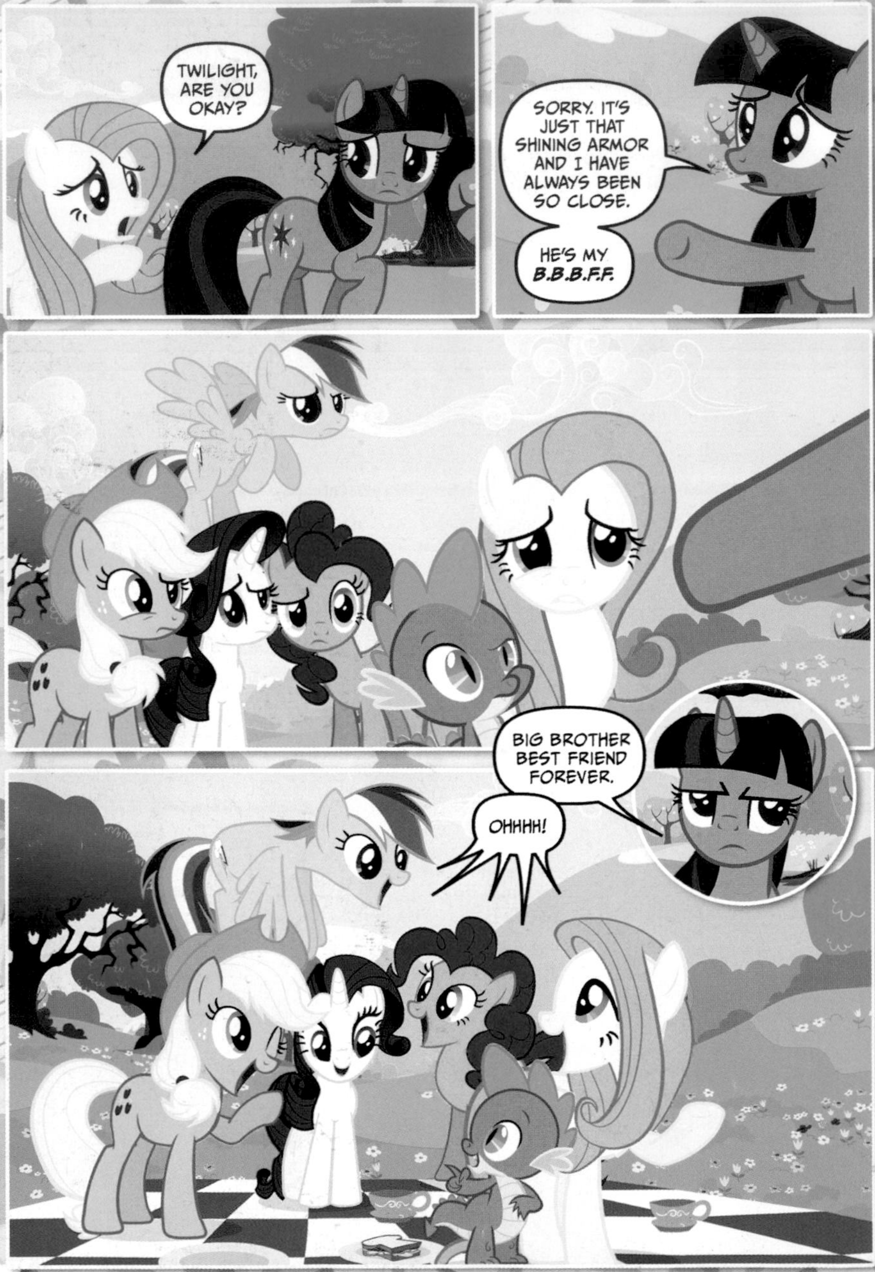
TWILIGHT, ARE YOU OKAY?
SORRY. IT'S JUST THAT SHINING ARMOR AND I HAVE ALWAYS BEEN SO CLOSE.
HE'S MY B.B.B.F.F.
BIG BROTHER BEST FRIEND FOREVER.
OHHHH!

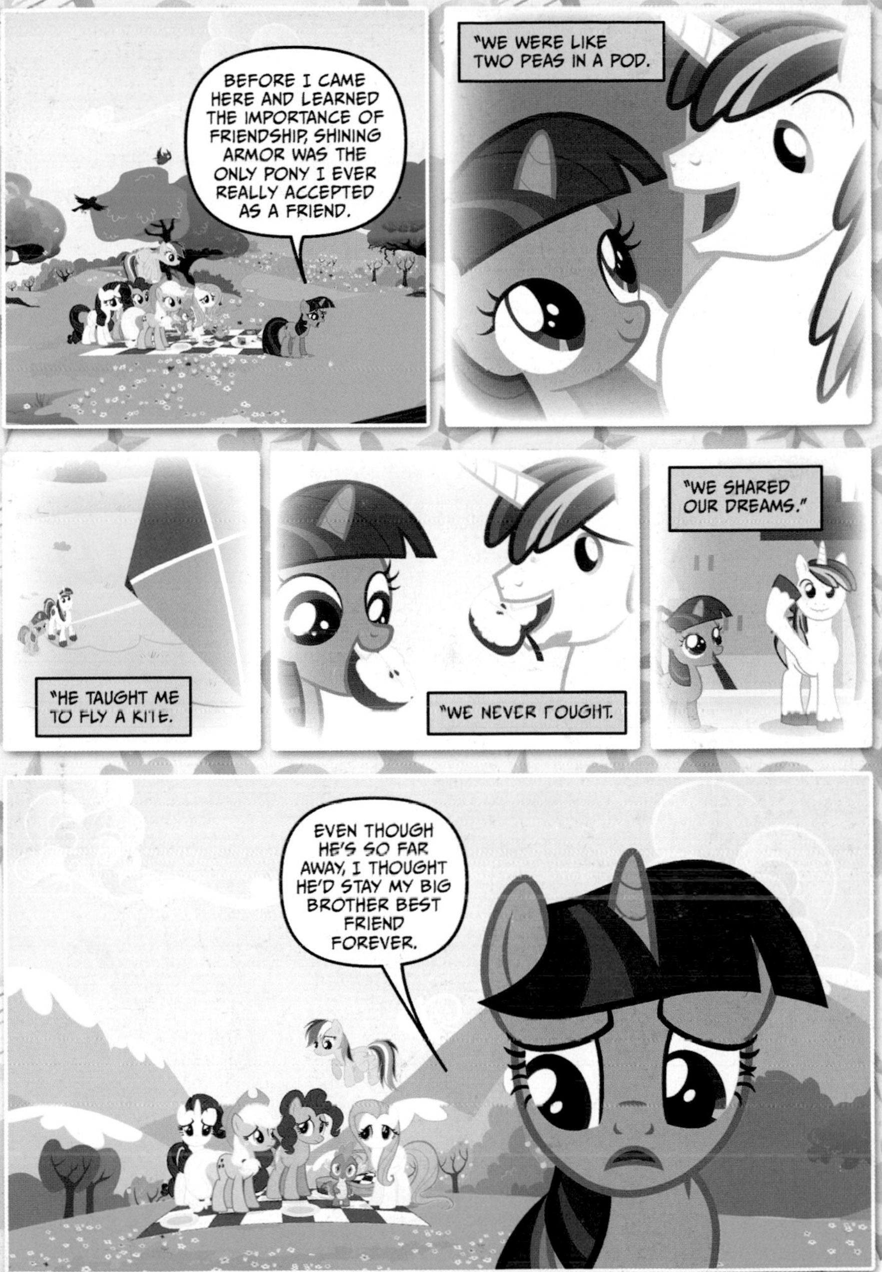

BEFORE I CAME HERE AND LEARNED THE IMPORTANCE OF FRIENDSHIP, SHINING ARMOR WAS THE ONLY PONY I EVER REALLY ACCEPTED AS A FRIEND.
"WE WERE LIKE TWO PEAS IN A POD.
"HE TAUGHT ME TO FLY A KITE.
"WE NEVER FOUGHT.
"WE SHARED OUR DREAMS."
EVEN THOUGH HE'S SO FAR AWAY, I THOUGHT HE'D STAY MY BIG BROTHER BEST FRIEND FOREVER.

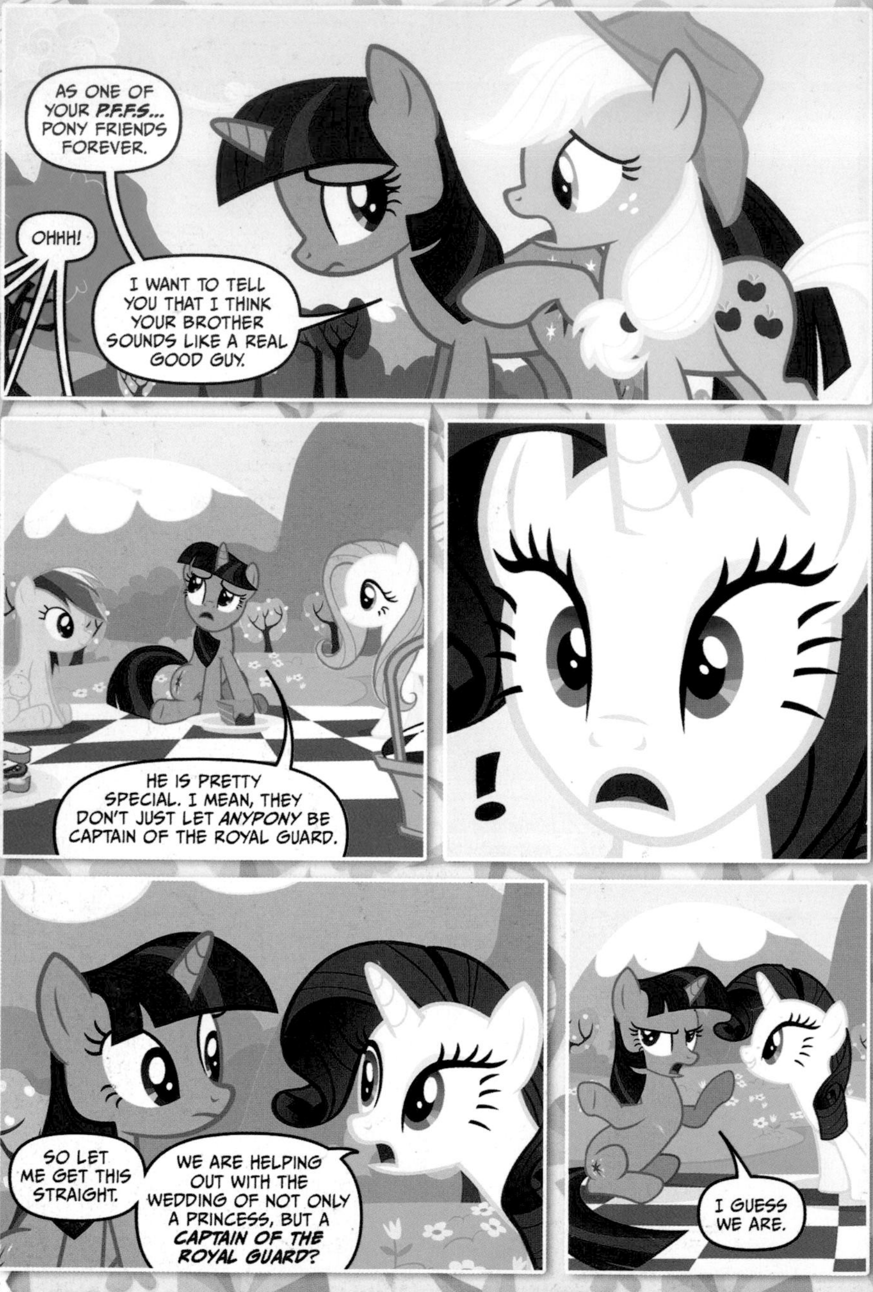
AS ONE OF YOUR *P.F.F.S...* PONY FRIENDS FOREVER.
OHHH!
I WANT TO TELL YOU THAT I THINK YOUR BROTHER SOUNDS LIKE A REAL GOOD GUY.
HE IS PRETTY SPECIAL. I MEAN, THEY DON'T JUST LET *ANYPONY* BE CAPTAIN OF THE ROYAL GUARD.
!
SO LET ME GET THIS STRAIGHT.
WE ARE HELPING OUT WITH THE WEDDING OF NOT ONLY A PRINCESS, BUT A ***CAPTAIN OF THE ROYAL GUARD?***
I GUESS WE ARE.

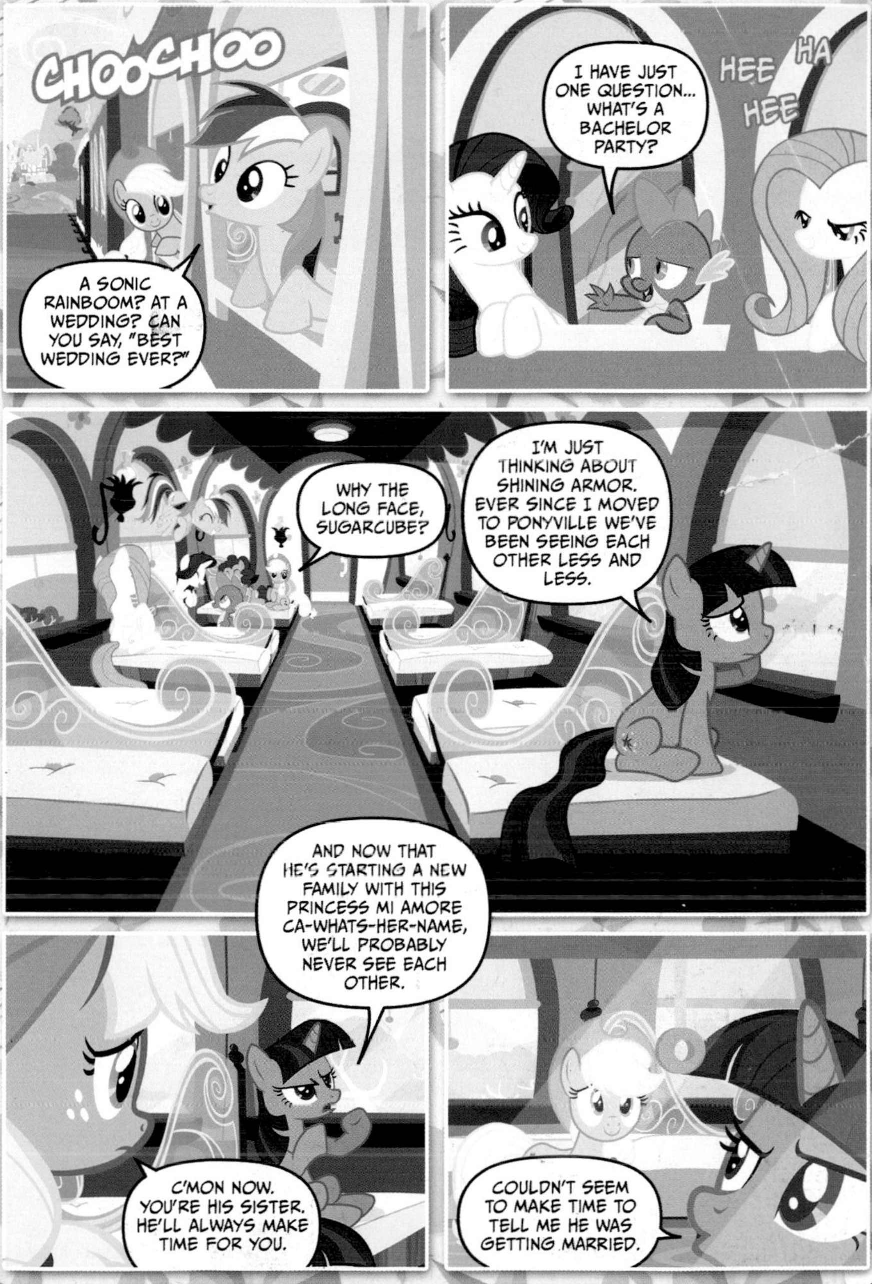
CHOOCHOO
A SONIC RAINBOOM? AT A WEDDING? CAN YOU SAY, "BEST WEDDING EVER?"
I HAVE JUST ONE QUESTION... WHAT'S A BACHELOR PARTY?
HEE HA HEE
WHY THE LONG FACE, SUGARCUBE?
I'M JUST THINKING ABOUT SHINING ARMOR. EVER SINCE I MOVED TO PONYVILLE WE'VE BEEN SEEING EACH OTHER LESS AND LESS.
AND NOW THAT HE'S STARTING A NEW FAMILY WITH THIS PRINCESS MI AMORE CA-WHATS-HER-NAME, WE'LL PROBABLY NEVER SEE EACH OTHER.
C'MON NOW. YOU'RE HIS SISTER. HE'LL ALWAYS MAKE TIME FOR YOU.
COULDN'T SEEM TO MAKE TIME TO TELL ME HE WAS GETTING MARRIED.

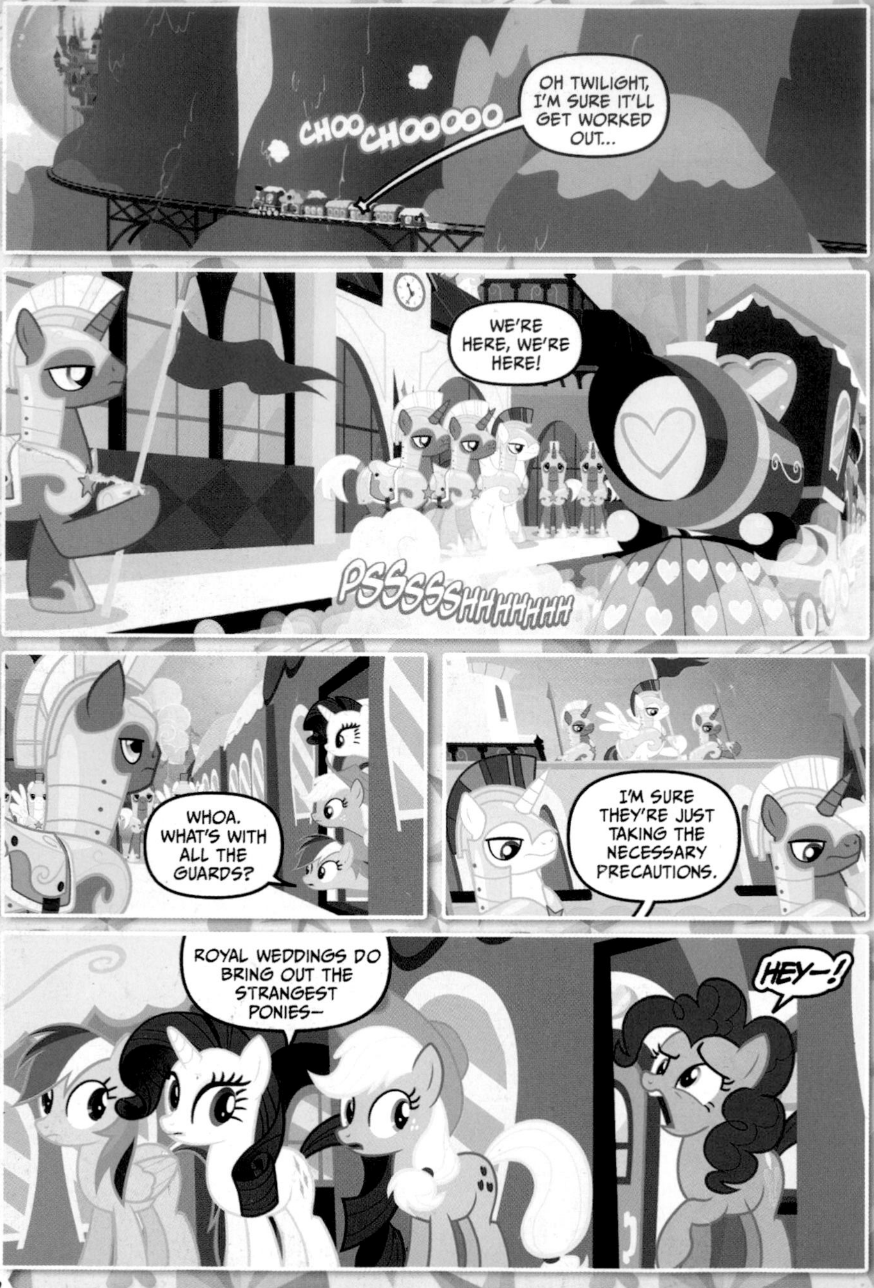
CHOO CHOOOOOO
OH TWILIGHT, I'M SURE IT'LL GET WORKED OUT...
WE'RE HERE, WE'RE HERE!
PSSSSSHHHHHHH
WHOA. WHAT'S WITH ALL THE GUARDS?
I'M SURE THEY'RE JUST TAKING THE NECESSARY PRECAUTIONS.
ROYAL WEDDINGS DO BRING OUT THE STRANGEST PONIES—
HEY—!

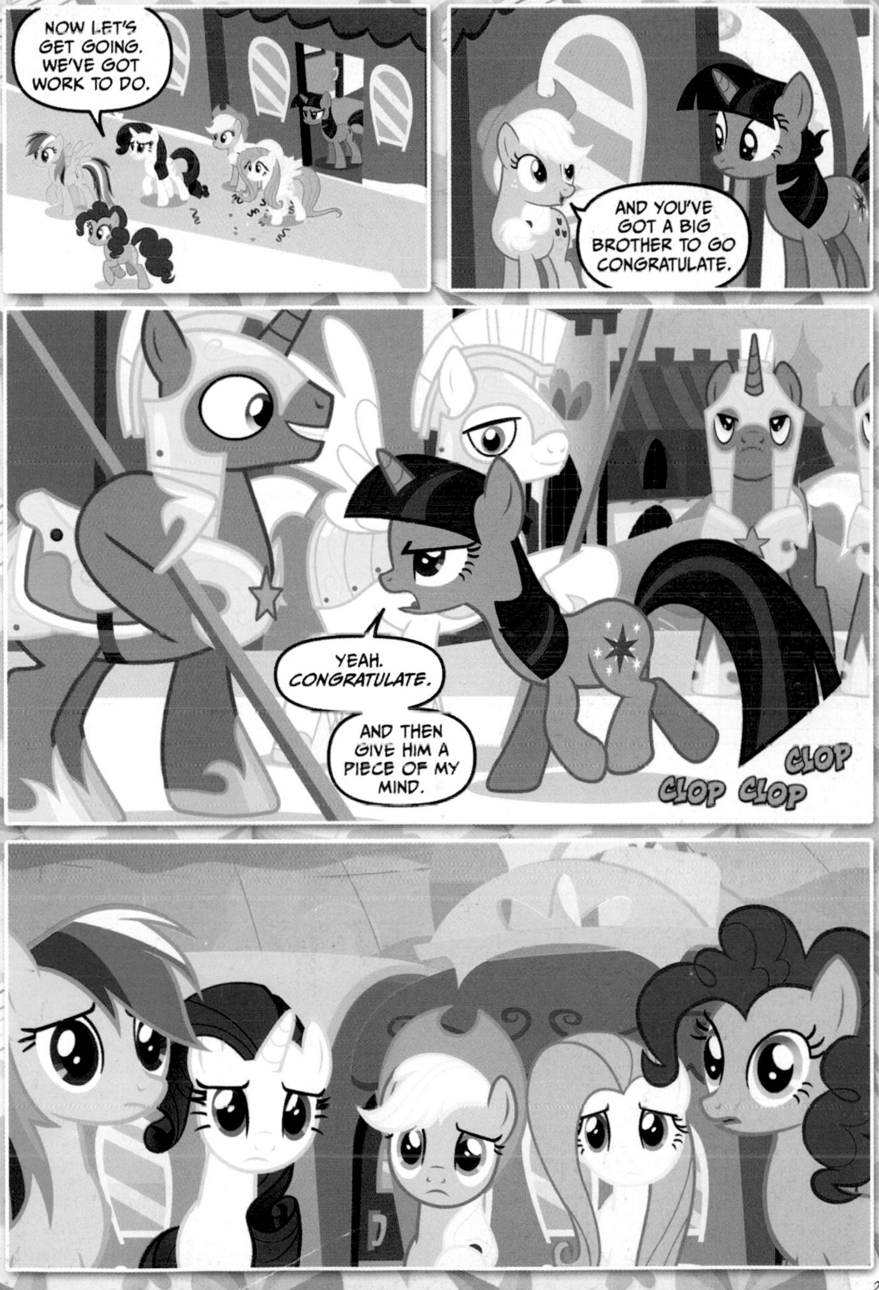
NOW LET'S GET GOING. WE'VE GOT WORK TO DO.
AND YOU'VE GOT A BIG BROTHER TO GO CONGRATULATE.
YEAH. CONGRATULATE.
AND THEN GIVE HIM A PIECE OF MY MIND.
CLOP CLOP CLOP

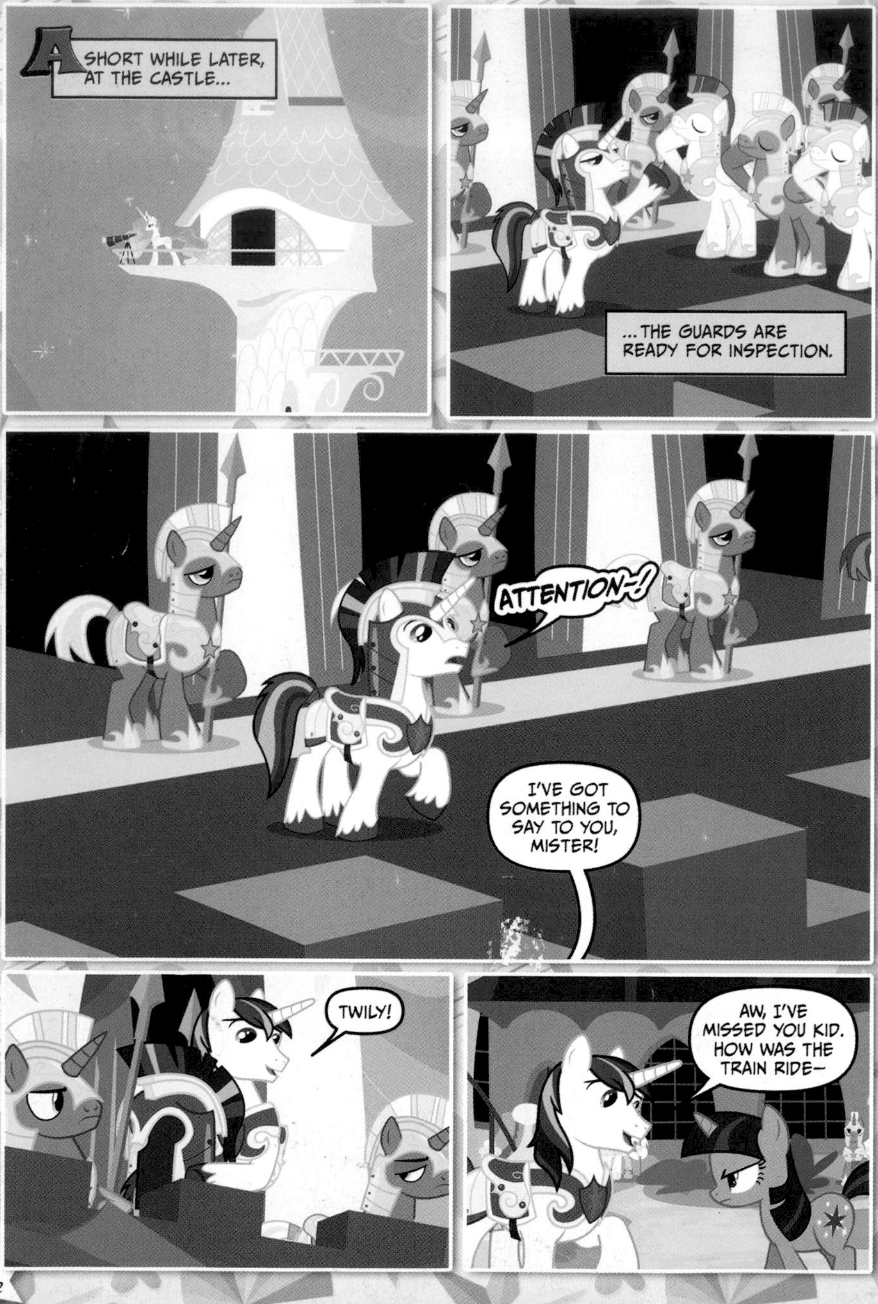

A SHORT WHILE LATER, AT THE CASTLE...
...THE GUARDS ARE READY FOR INSPECTION.
ATTENTION-!
I'VE GOT SOMETHING TO SAY TO YOU, MISTER!
TWILY!
AW, I'VE MISSED YOU KID. HOW WAS THE TRAIN RIDE—

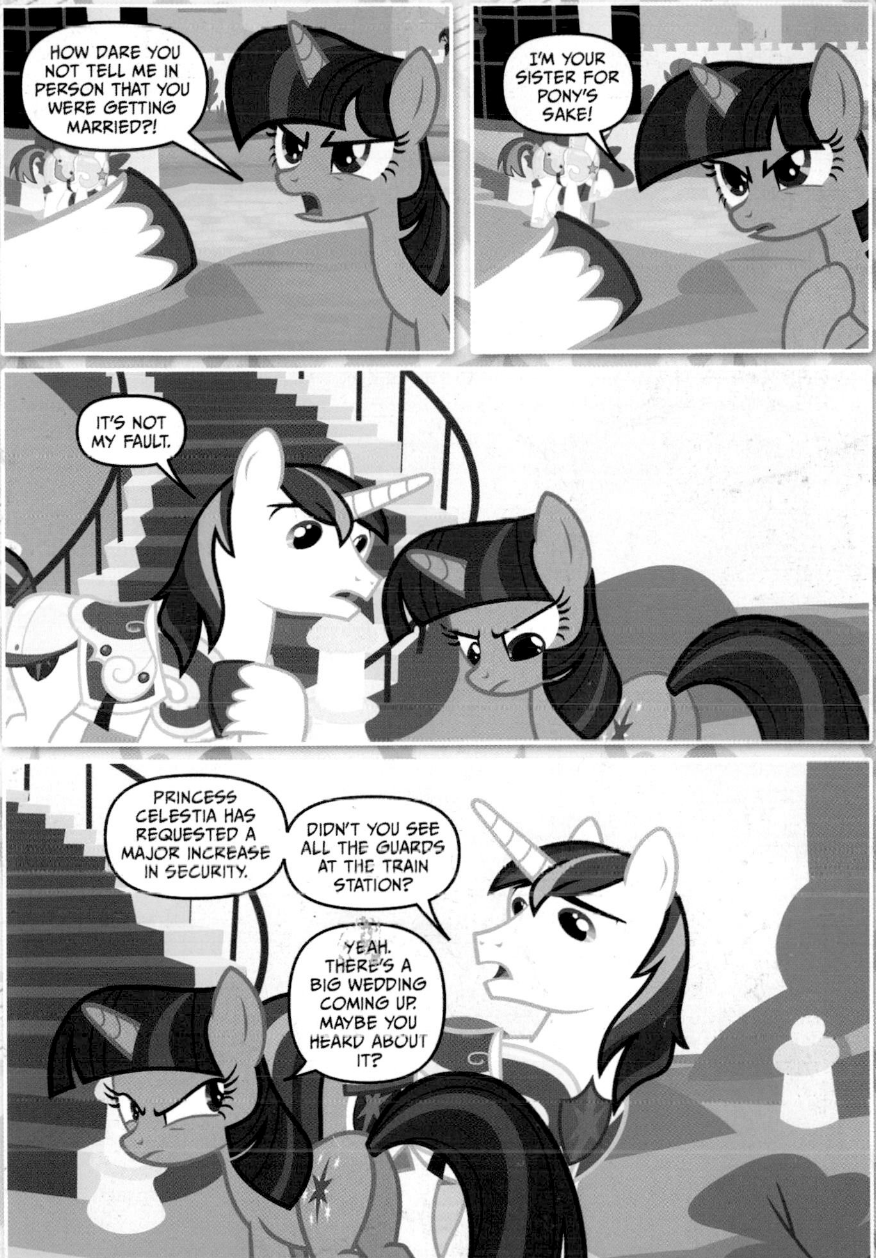
HOW DARE YOU NOT TELL ME IN PERSON THAT YOU WERE GETTING MARRIED?!
I'M YOUR SISTER FOR PONY'S SAKE!
IT'S NOT MY FAULT.
PRINCESS CELESTIA HAS REQUESTED A MAJOR INCREASE IN SECURITY.
DIDN'T YOU SEE ALL THE GUARDS AT THE TRAIN STATION?
YEAH. THERE'S A BIG WEDDING COMING UP. MAYBE YOU HEARD ABOUT IT?

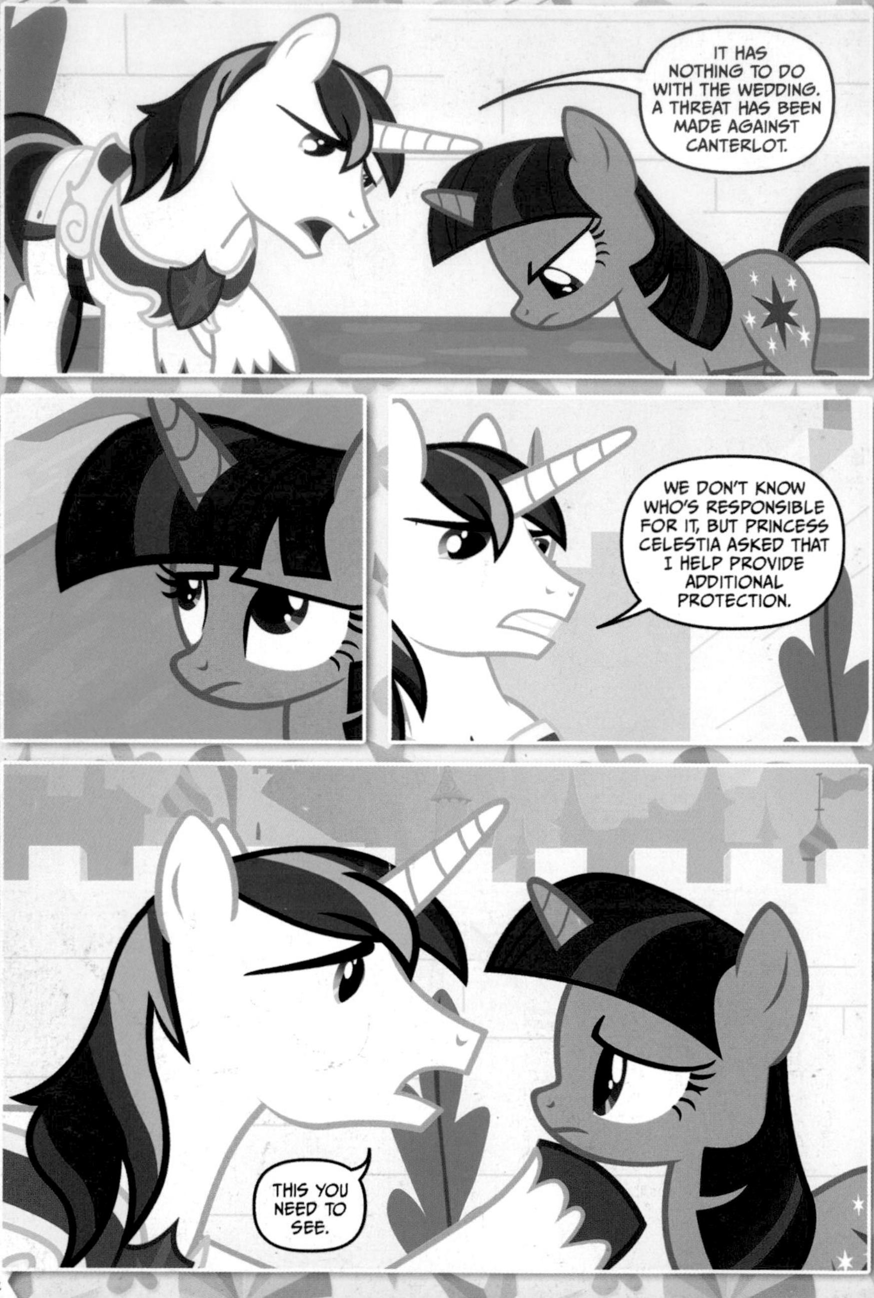
IT HAS NOTHING TO DO WITH THE WEDDING. A THREAT HAS BEEN MADE AGAINST CANTERLOT.
WE DON'T KNOW WHO'S RESPONSIBLE FOR IT, BUT PRINCESS CELESTIA ASKED THAT I HELP PROVIDE ADDITIONAL PROTECTION.
THIS YOU NEED TO SEE.

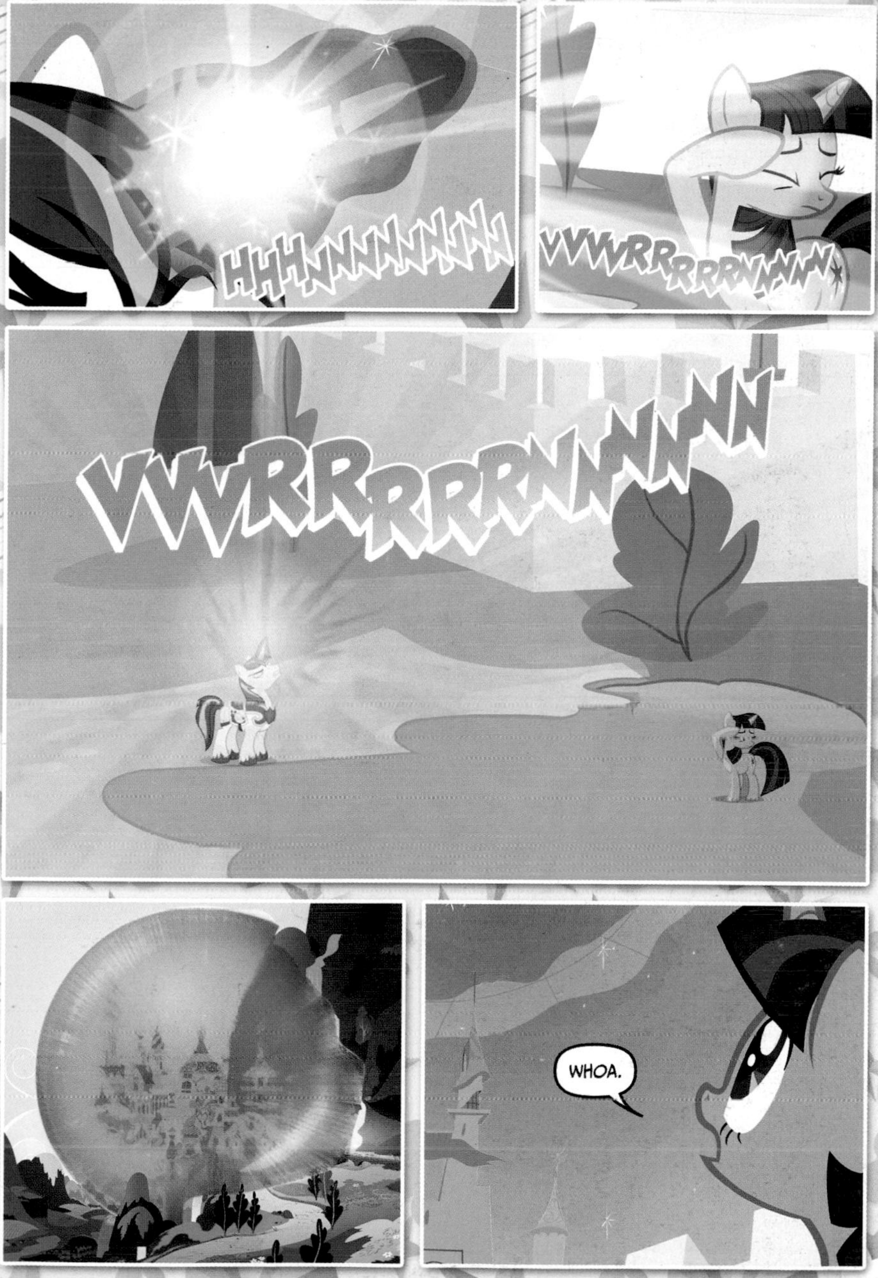
HHHNNNNNNN
VVVWRRRRRNNNN
VVWRRRRRNNNNNN
WHOA.

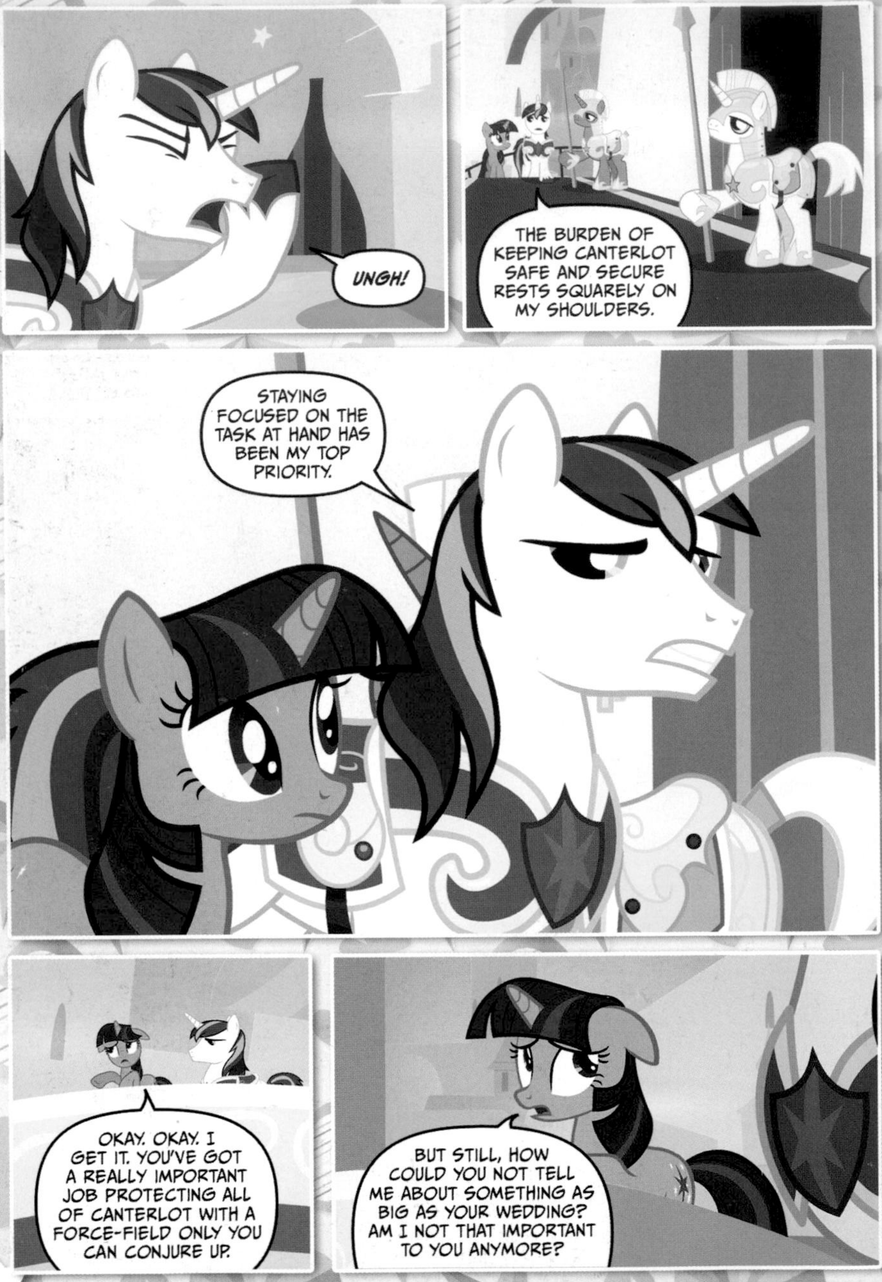
UNGH!
THE BURDEN OF KEEPING CANTERLOT SAFE AND SECURE RESTS SQUARELY ON MY SHOULDERS.
STAYING FOCUSED ON THE TASK AT HAND HAS BEEN MY TOP PRIORITY.
OKAY. OKAY. I GET IT. YOU'VE GOT A REALLY IMPORTANT JOB PROTECTING ALL OF CANTERLOT WITH A FORCE-FIELD ONLY YOU CAN CONJURE UP.
BUT STILL, HOW COULD YOU NOT TELL ME ABOUT SOMETHING AS BIG AS YOUR WEDDING? AM I NOT THAT IMPORTANT TO YOU ANYMORE?

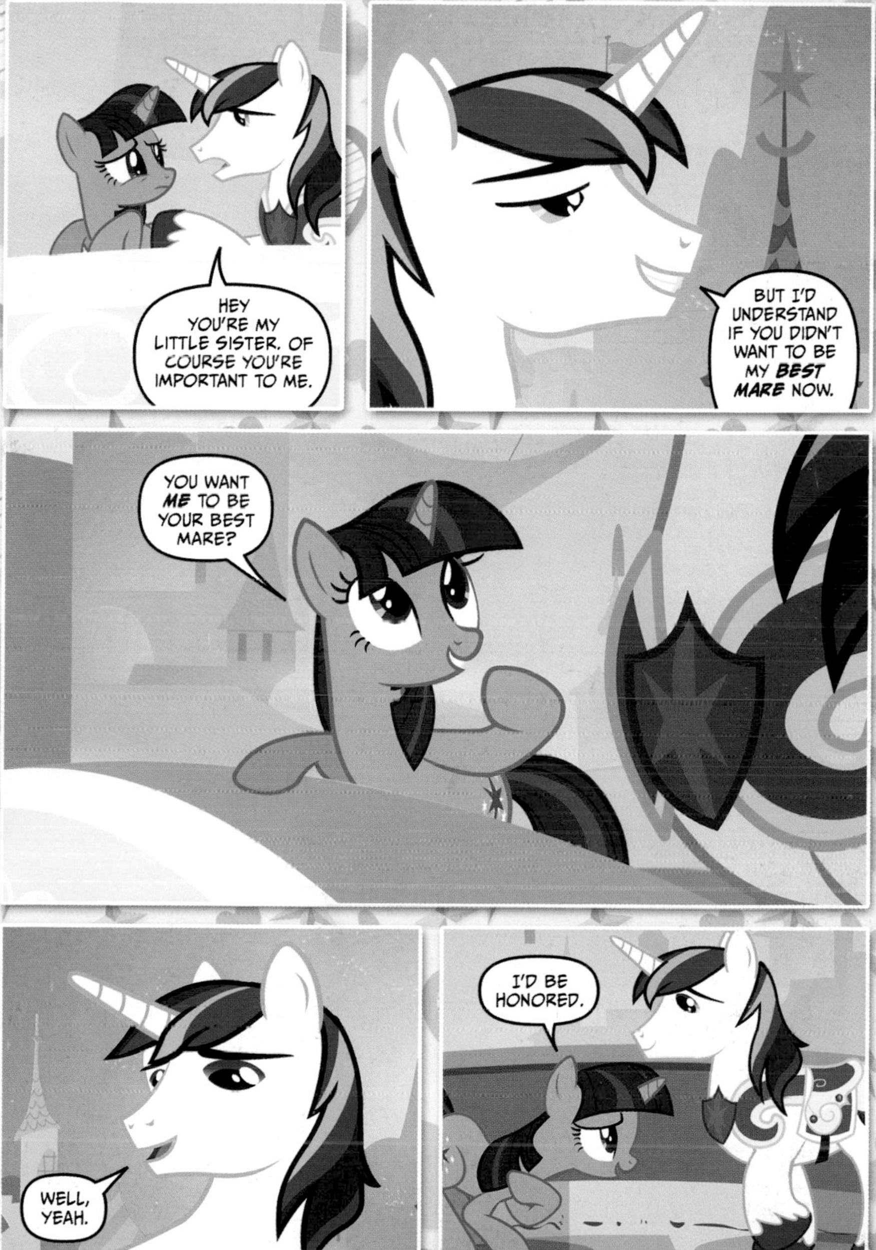
HEY YOU'RE MY LITTLE SISTER. OF COURSE YOU'RE IMPORTANT TO ME.
BUT I'D UNDERSTAND IF YOU DIDN'T WANT TO BE MY BEST MARE NOW.
YOU WANT ME TO BE YOUR BEST MARE?
WELL, YEAH.
I'D BE HONORED.

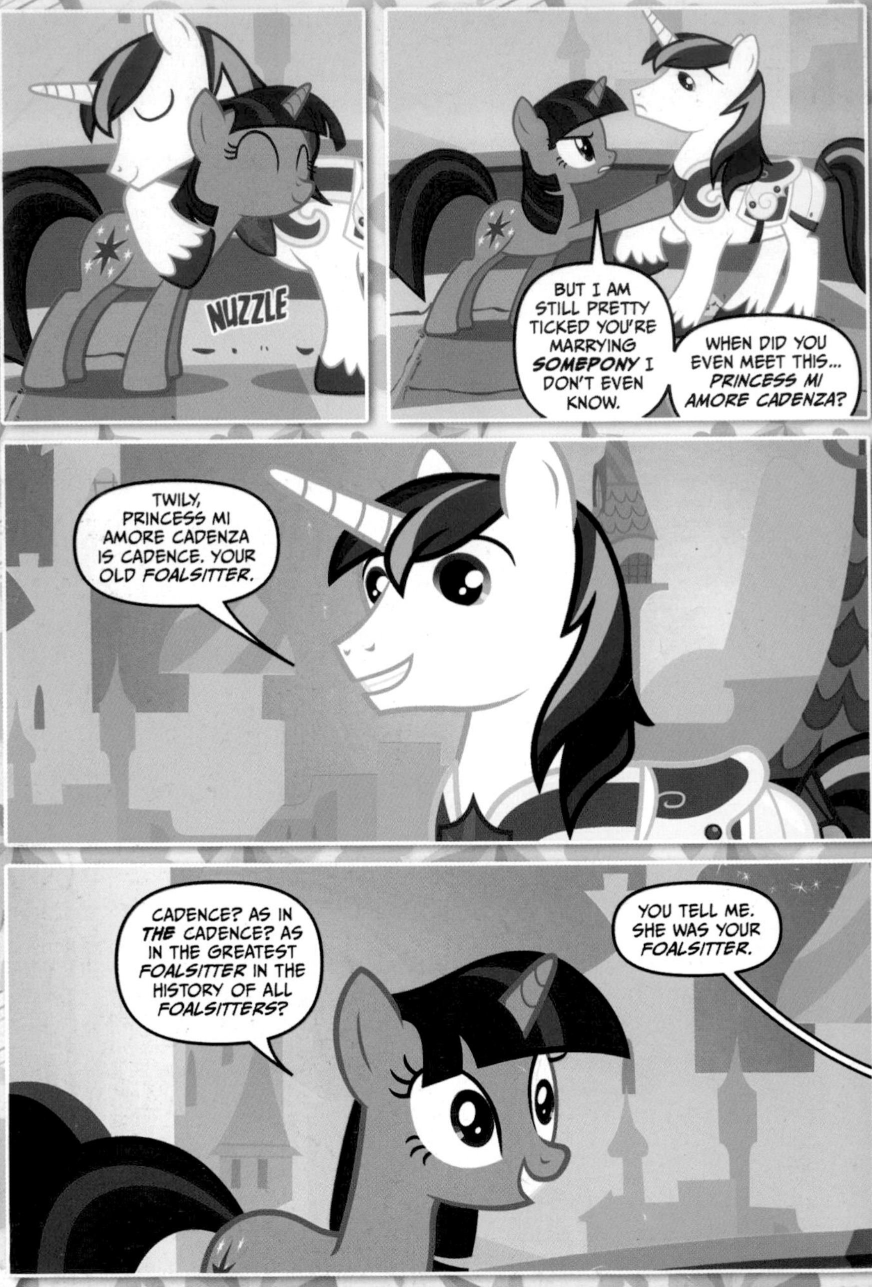
NUZZLE
BUT I AM STILL PRETTY TICKED YOU'RE MARRYING *SOMEPONY* I DON'T EVEN KNOW.
WHEN DID YOU EVEN MEET THIS... *PRINCESS MI AMORE CADENZA?*
TWILY, PRINCESS MI AMORE CADENZA IS CADENCE. YOUR OLD *FOALSITTER.*
CADENCE? AS IN ***THE*** CADENCE? AS IN THE GREATEST *FOALSITTER* IN THE HISTORY OF ALL *FOALSITTERS?*
YOU TELL ME. SHE WAS YOUR *FOALSITTER.*

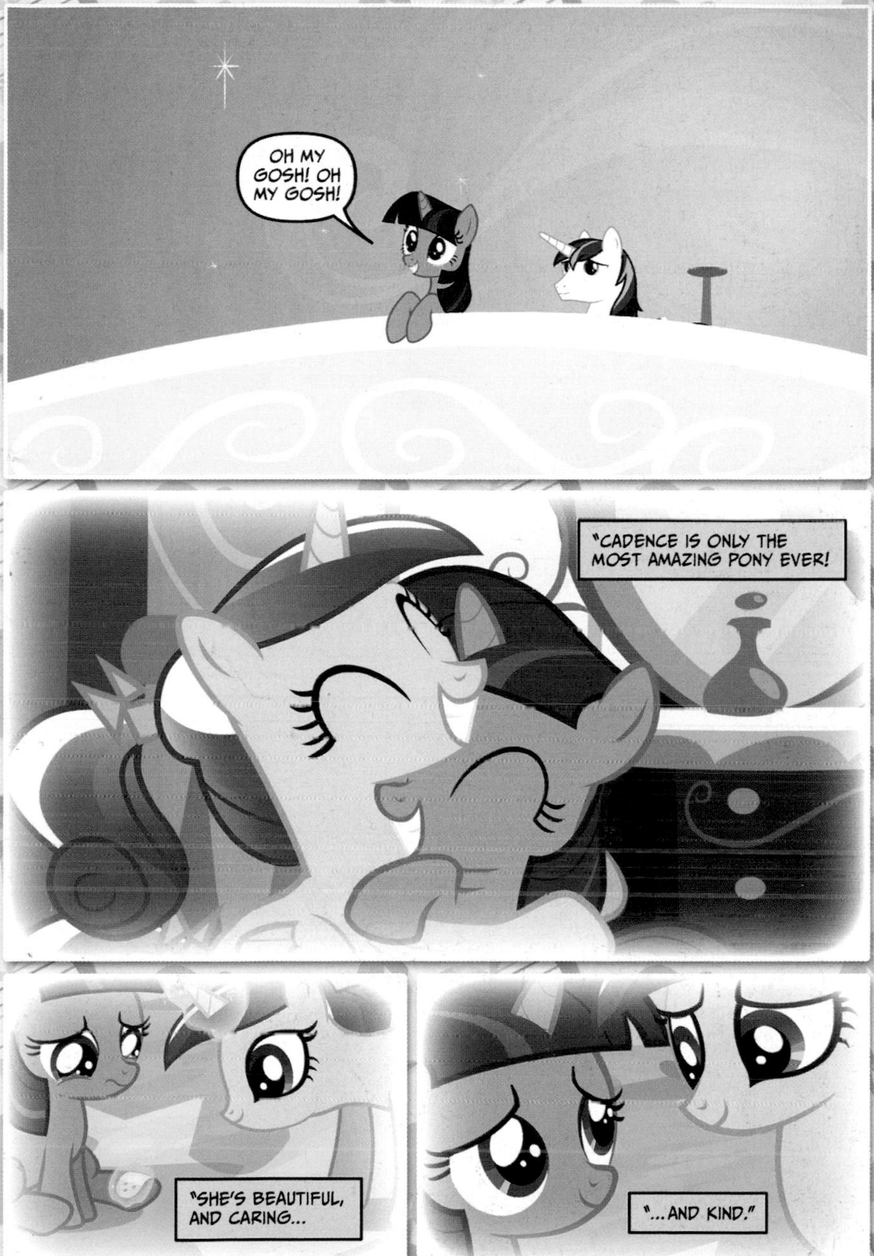
OH MY GOSH! OH MY GOSH!
"CADENCE IS ONLY THE MOST AMAZING PONY EVER!
"SHE'S BEAUTIFUL, AND CARING...
"...AND KIND."

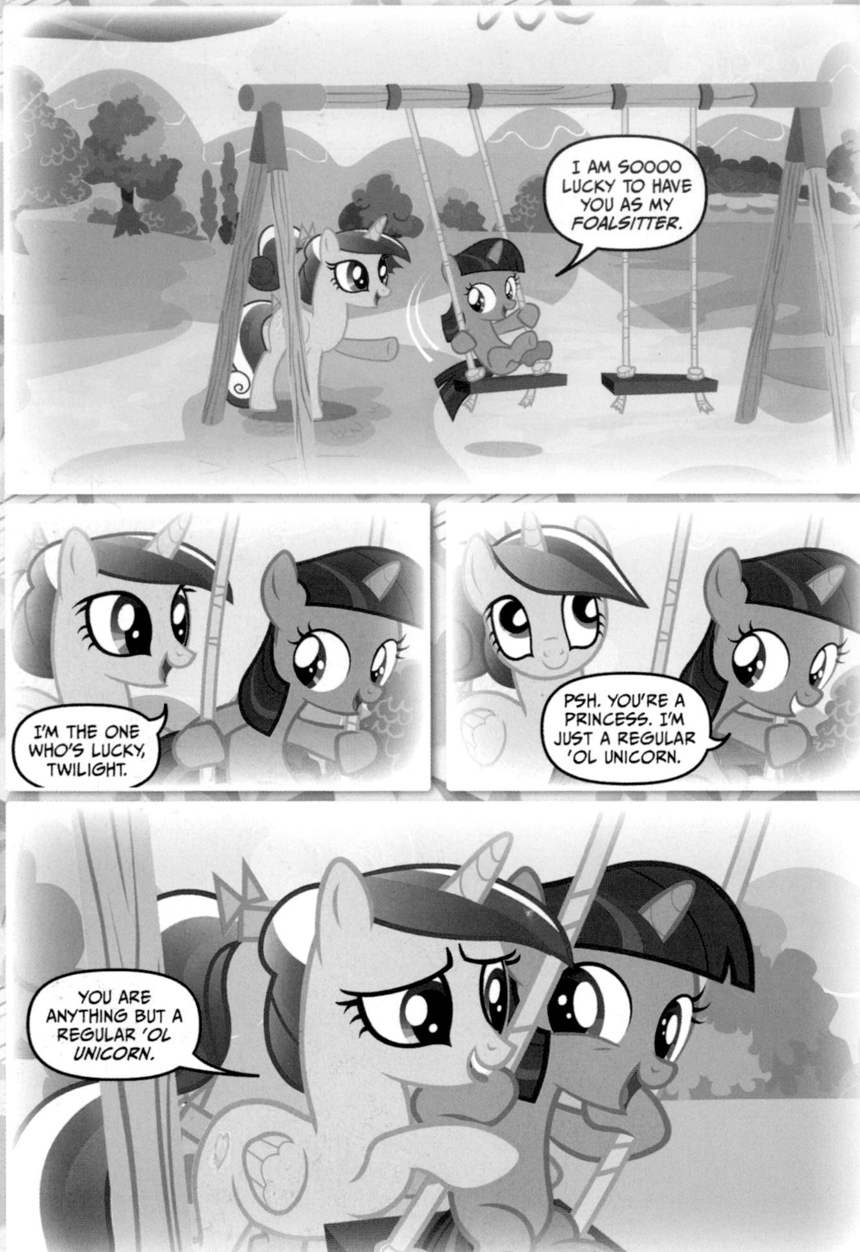
I AM SOOOO LUCKY TO HAVE YOU AS MY FOALSITTER.
I'M THE ONE WHO'S LUCKY, TWILIGHT.
PSH. YOU'RE A PRINCESS. I'M JUST A REGULAR 'OL UNICORN.
YOU ARE ANYTHING BUT A REGULAR 'OL UNICORN.

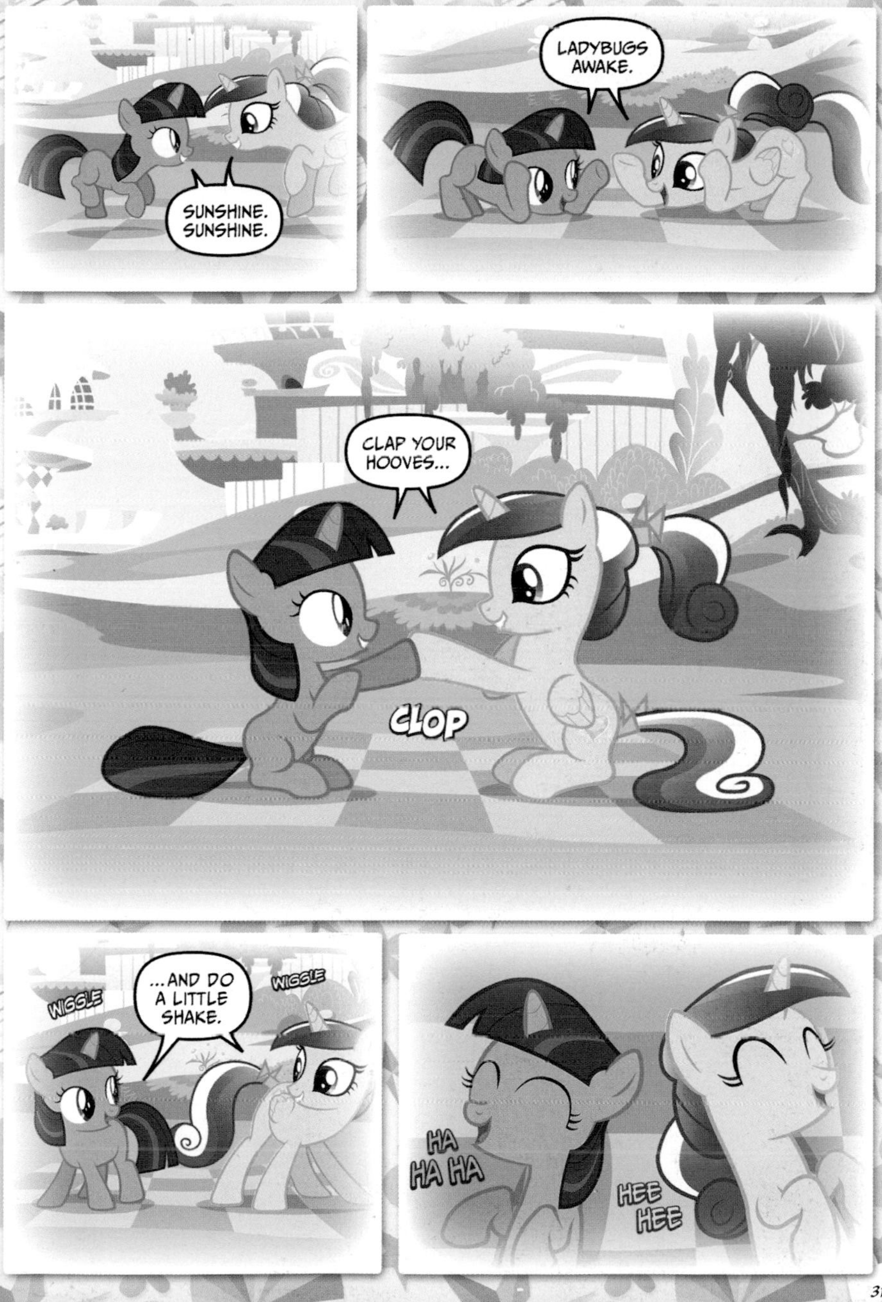
SUNSHINE. SUNSHINE.
LADYBUGS AWAKE.
CLAP YOUR HOOVES...
CLOP
WIGGLE
...AND DO A LITTLE SHAKE.
WIGGLE
HA HA HA
HEE HEE

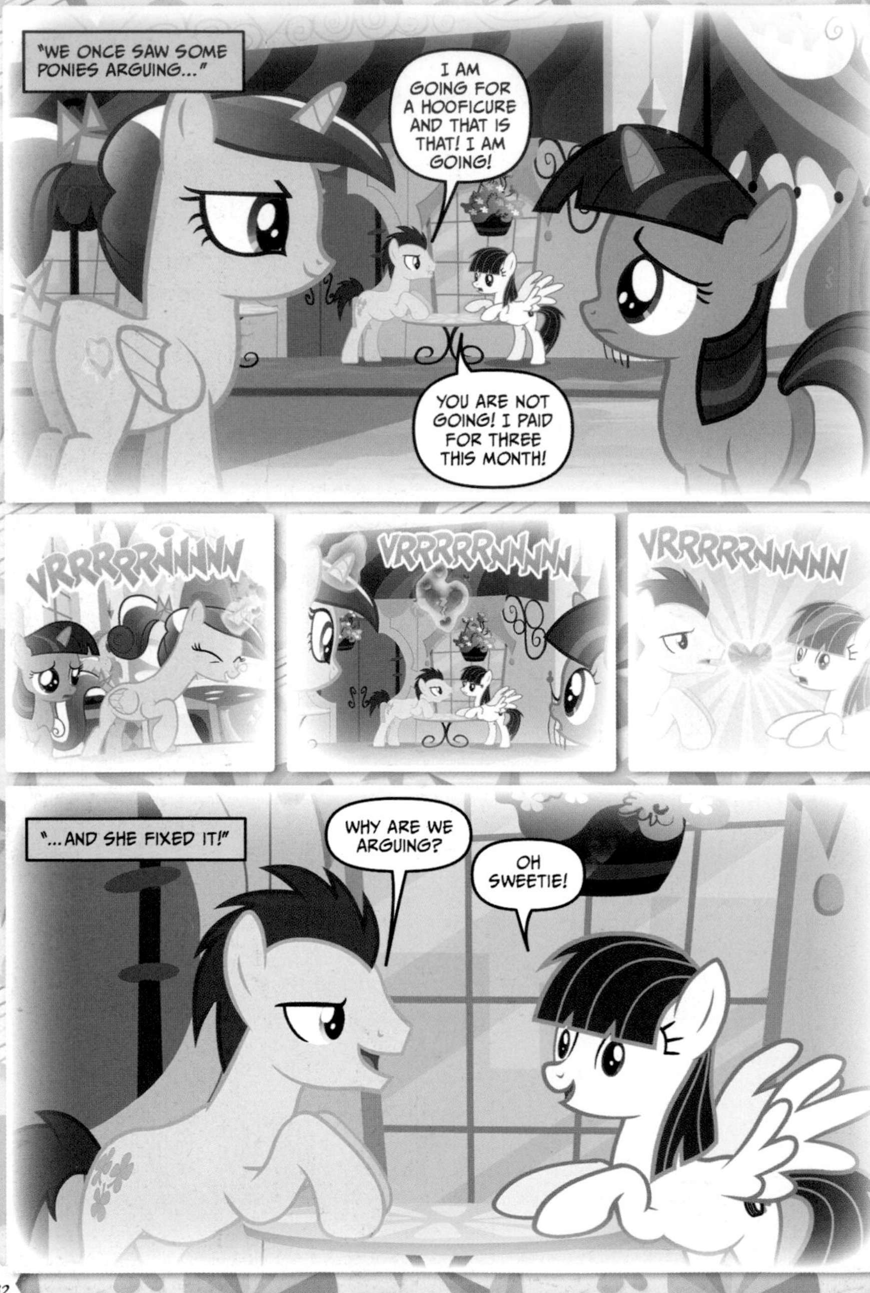
"WE ONCE SAW SOME PONIES ARGUING..."
I AM GOING FOR A HOOFICURE AND THAT IS THAT! I AM GOING!
YOU ARE NOT GOING! I PAID FOR THREE THIS MONTH!
VRRRRRNNNNN
VRRRRRNNNNN
VRRRRRNNNNN
"...AND SHE FIXED IT!"
WHY ARE WE ARGUING?
OH SWEETIE!

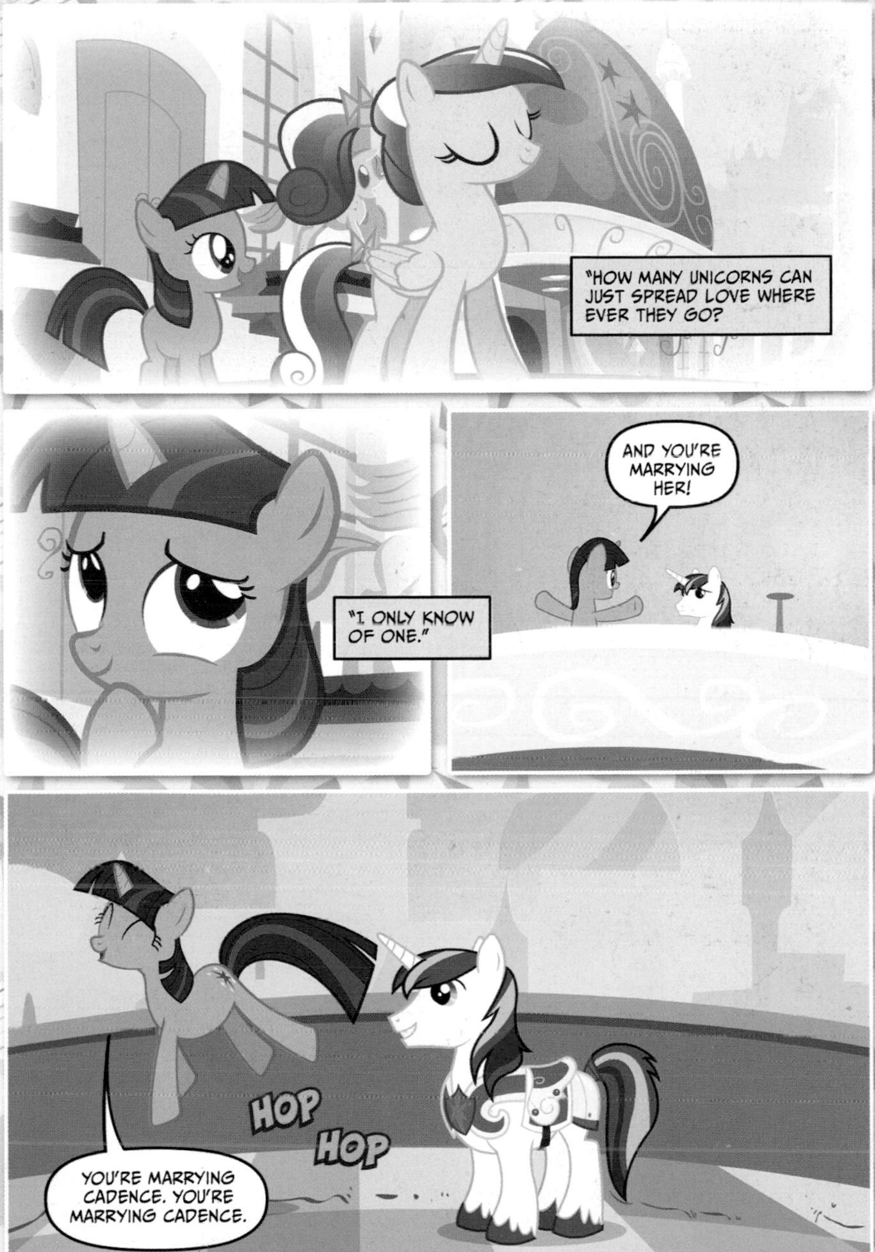

"HOW MANY UNICORNS CAN JUST SPREAD LOVE WHERE EVER THEY GO?
"I ONLY KNOW OF ONE."
AND YOU'RE MARRYING HER!
HOP
HOP
YOU'RE MARRYING CADENCE. YOU'RE MARRYING CADENCE.

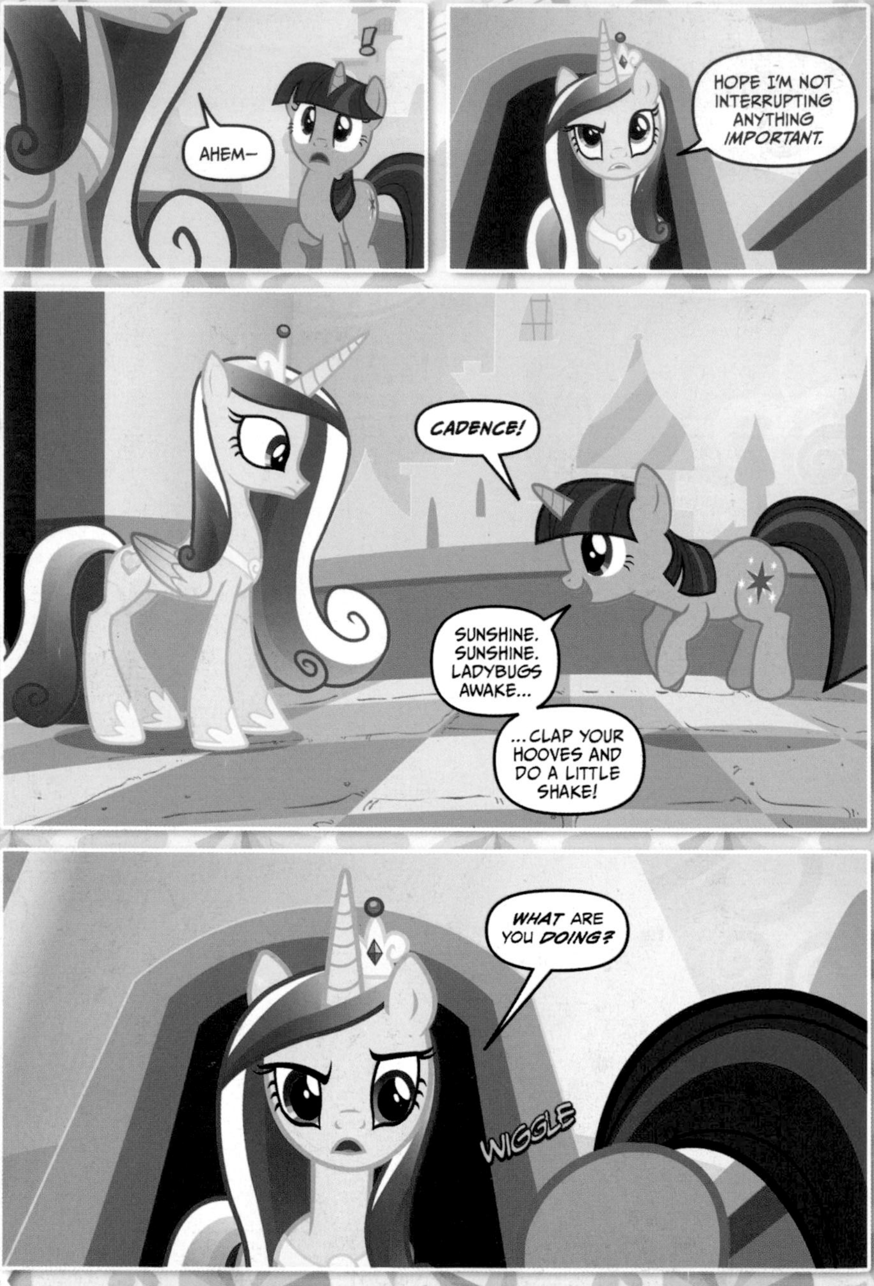

AHEM—
HOPE I'M NOT INTERRUPTING ANYTHING *IMPORTANT.*
CADENCE!
SUNSHINE, SUNSHINE, LADYBUGS AWAKE...
...CLAP YOUR HOOVES AND DO A LITTLE SHAKE!
WHAT ARE YOU ***DOING?***
WIGGLE

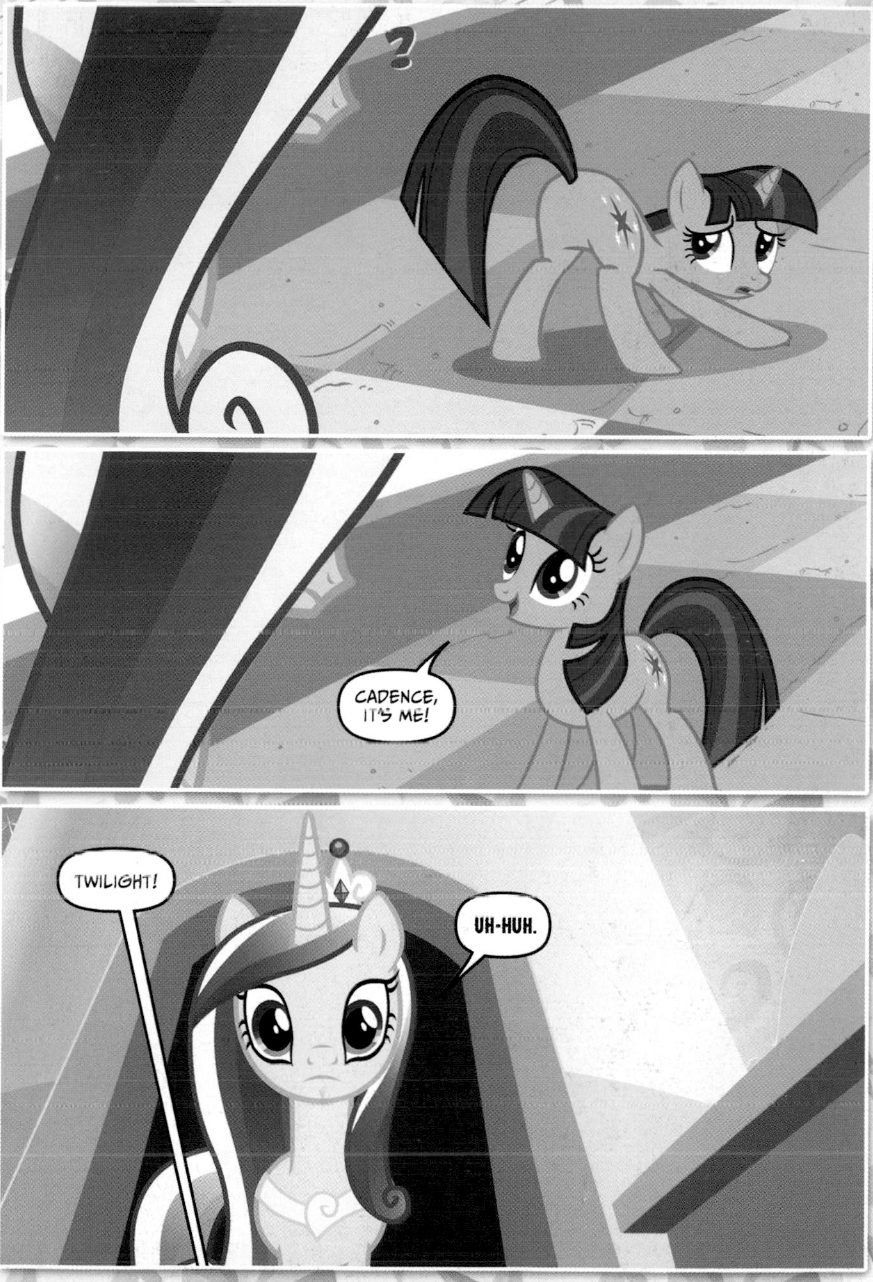
?
CADENCE, IT'S ME!
TWILIGHT!
UH-HUH.

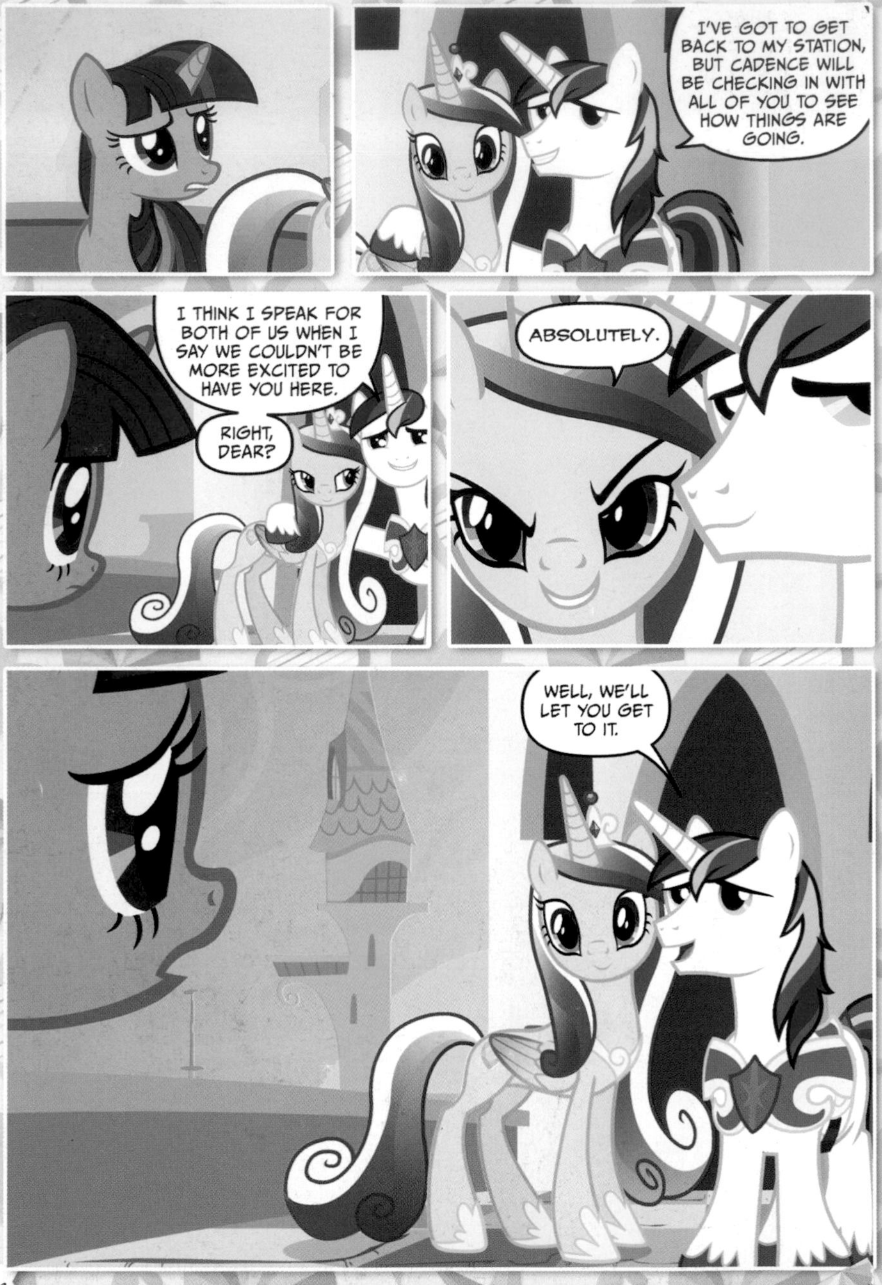
I'VE GOT TO GET BACK TO MY STATION, BUT CADENCE WILL BE CHECKING IN WITH ALL OF YOU TO SEE HOW THINGS ARE GOING.
I THINK I SPEAK FOR BOTH OF US WHEN I SAY WE COULDN'T BE MORE EXCITED TO HAVE YOU HERE.
RIGHT, DEAR?
ABSOLUTELY.
WELL, WE'LL LET YOU GET TO IT.

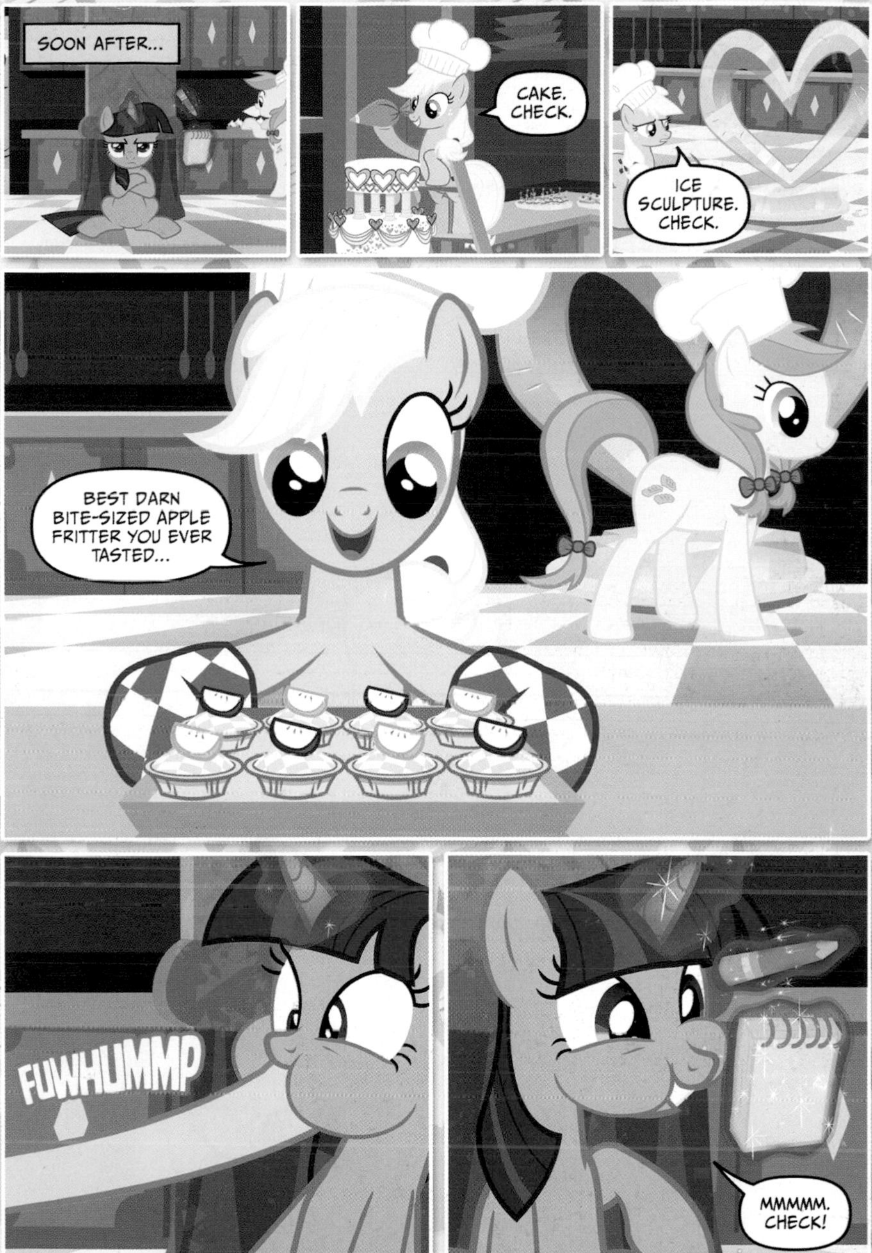
SOON AFTER...
CAKE. CHECK.
ICE SCULPTURE. CHECK.
BEST DARN BITE-SIZED APPLE FRITTER YOU EVER TASTED...
FUWHUMMP
MMMMM. CHECK!

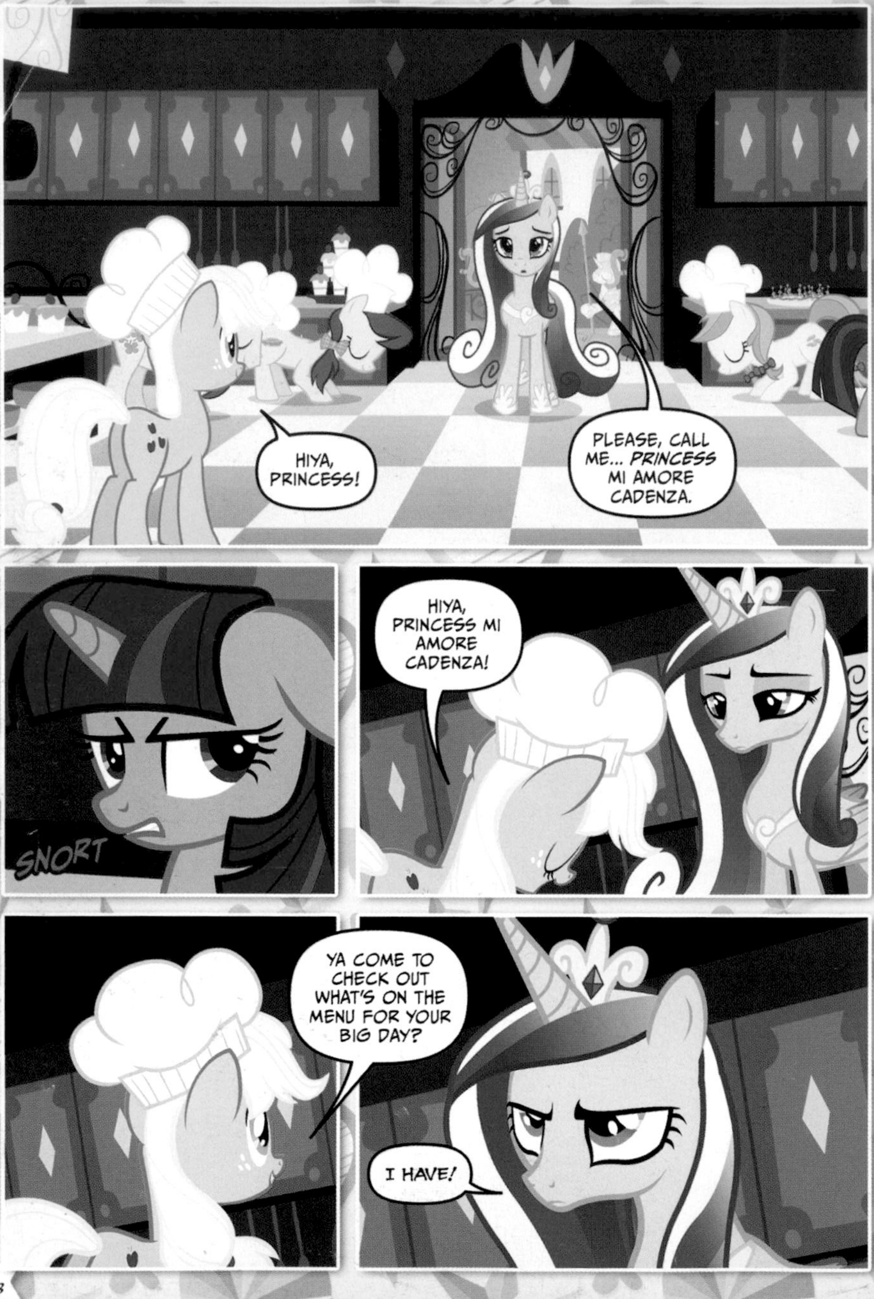
HIYA, PRINCESS!
PLEASE, CALL ME... *PRINCESS* MI AMORE CADENZA.
SNORT
HIYA, PRINCESS MI AMORE CADENZA!
YA COME TO CHECK OUT WHAT'S ON THE MENU FOR YOUR BIG DAY?
I HAVE!

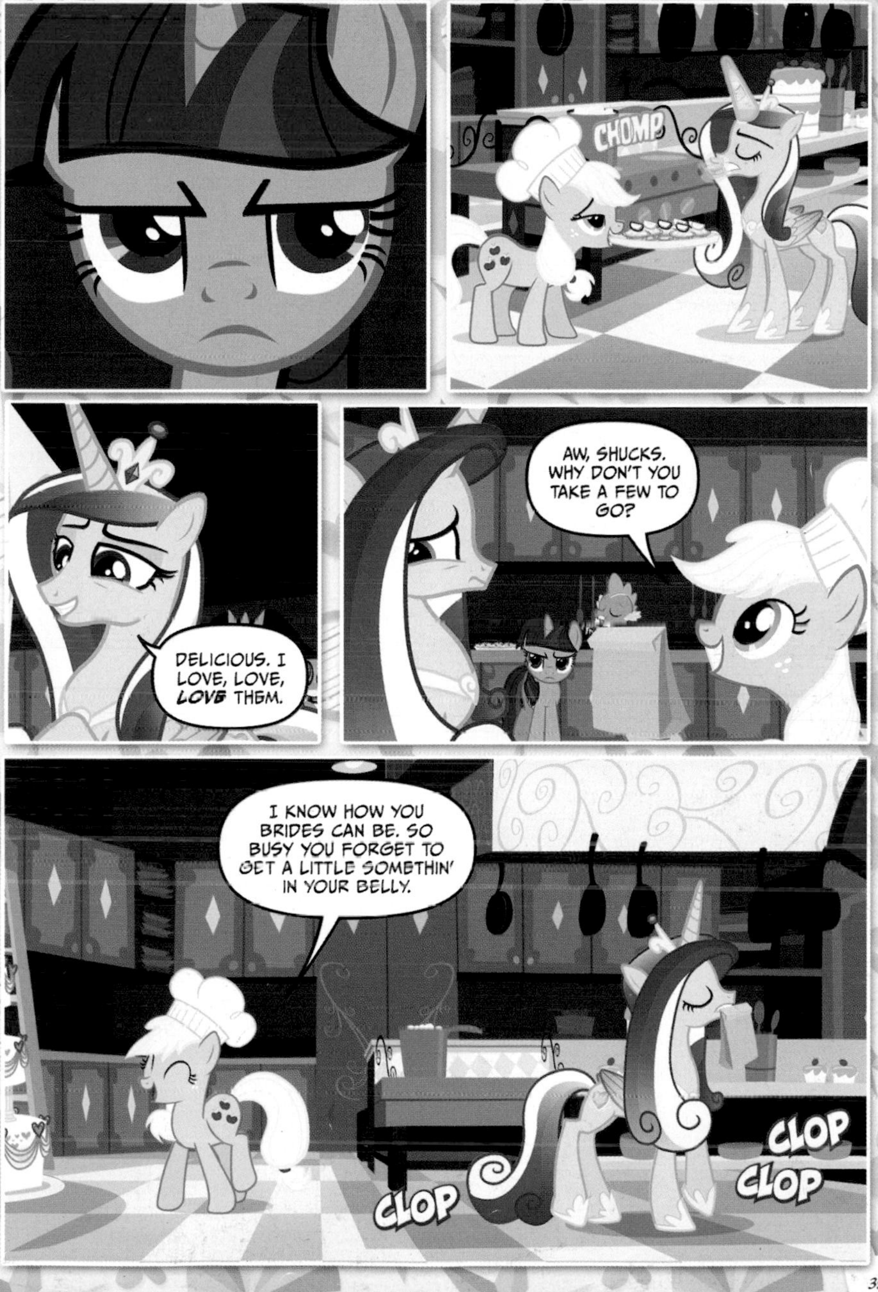
CHOMP
DELICIOUS. I LOVE, LOVE, LOVE THEM.
AW, SHUCKS. WHY DON'T YOU TAKE A FEW TO GO?
I KNOW HOW YOU BRIDES CAN BE. SO BUSY YOU FORGET TO GET A LITTLE SOMETHIN' IN YOUR BELLY.
CLOP
CLOP
CLOP

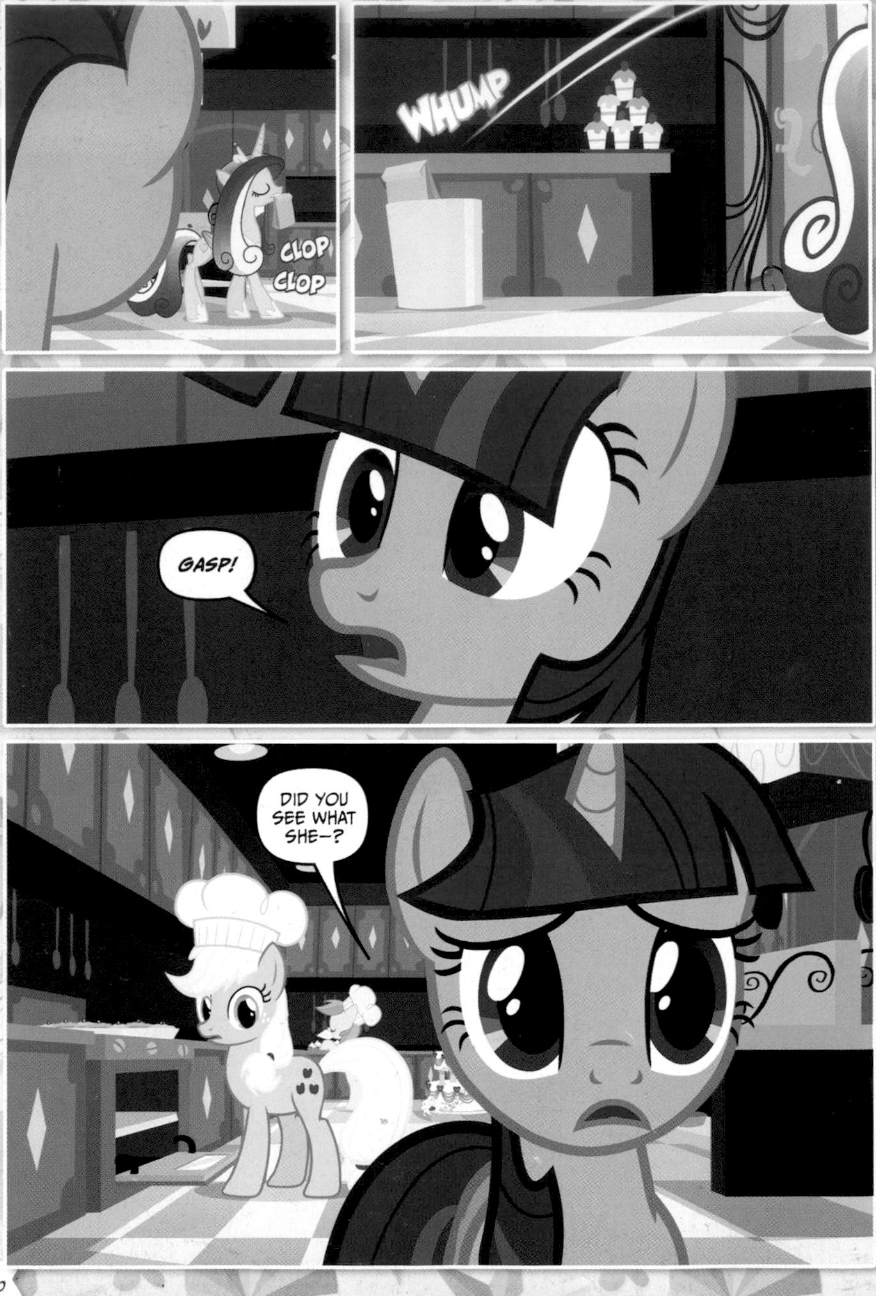
CLOP
CLOP
WHUMP
GASP!
DID YOU SEE WHAT SHE--?

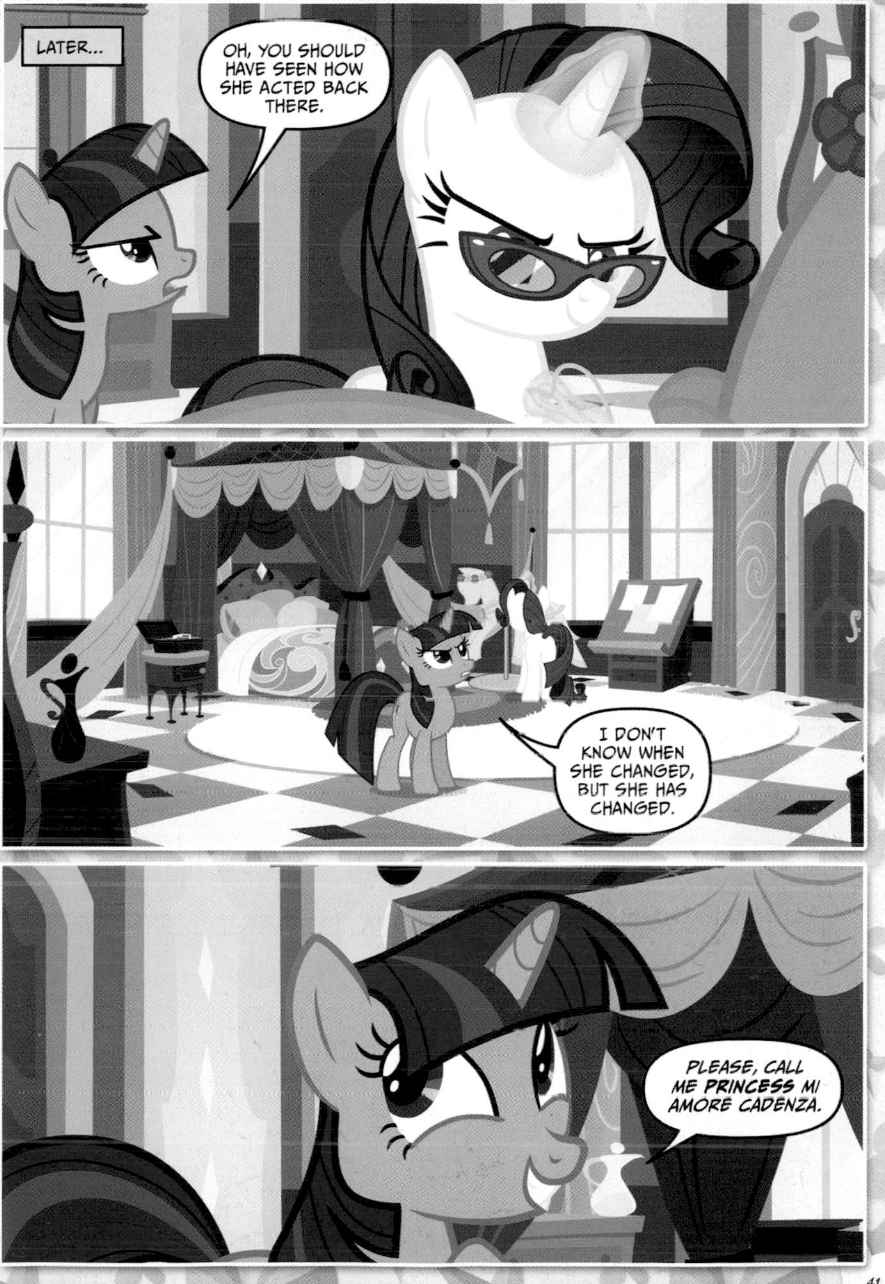
LATER...
OH, YOU SHOULD HAVE SEEN HOW SHE ACTED BACK THERE.
I DON'T KNOW WHEN SHE CHANGED, BUT SHE HAS CHANGED.
PLEASE, CALL ME **PRINCESS** MI AMORE CADENZA.

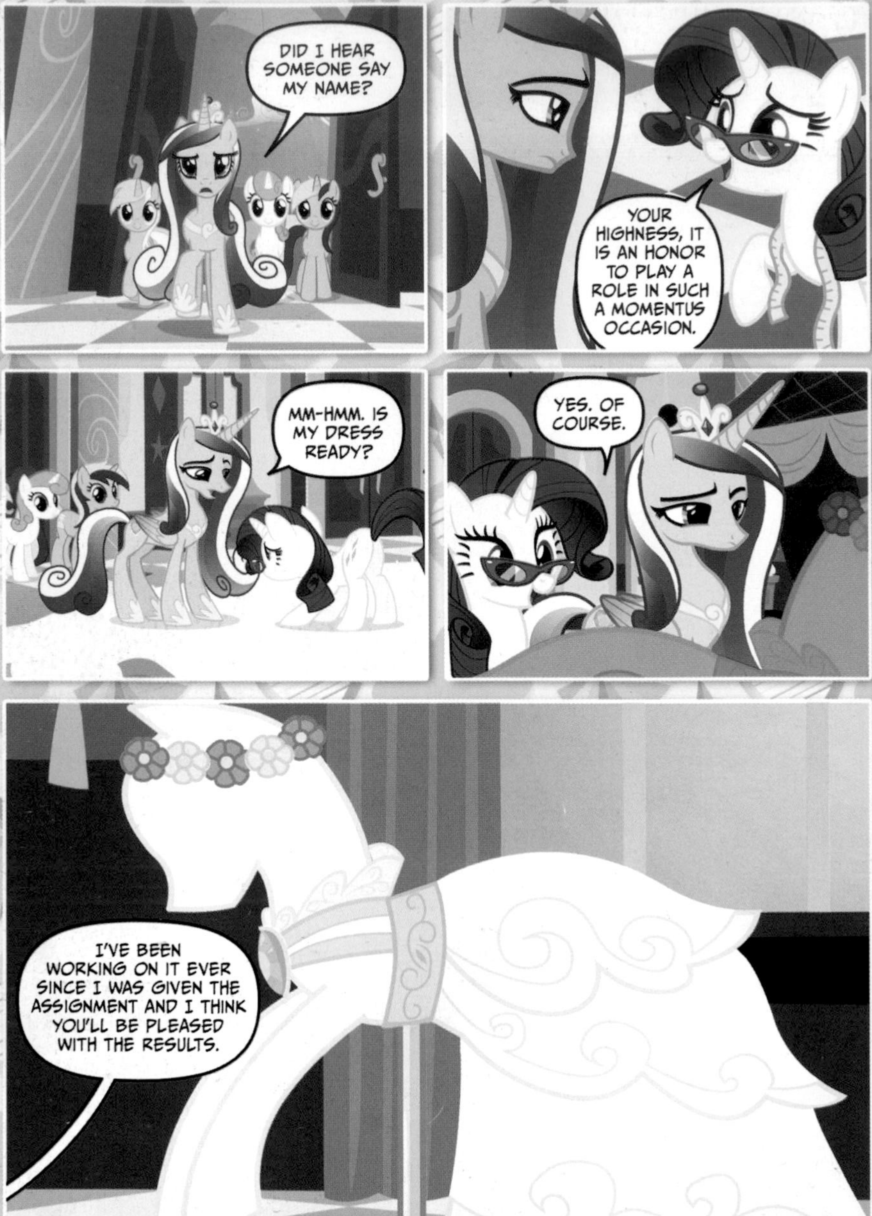
DID I HEAR SOMEONE SAY MY NAME?
YOUR HIGHNESS, IT IS AN HONOR TO PLAY A ROLE IN SUCH A MOMENTUS OCCASION.
MM-HMM. IS MY DRESS READY?
YES. OF COURSE.
I'VE BEEN WORKING ON IT EVER SINCE I WAS GIVEN THE ASSIGNMENT AND I THINK YOU'LL BE PLEASED WITH THE RESULTS.

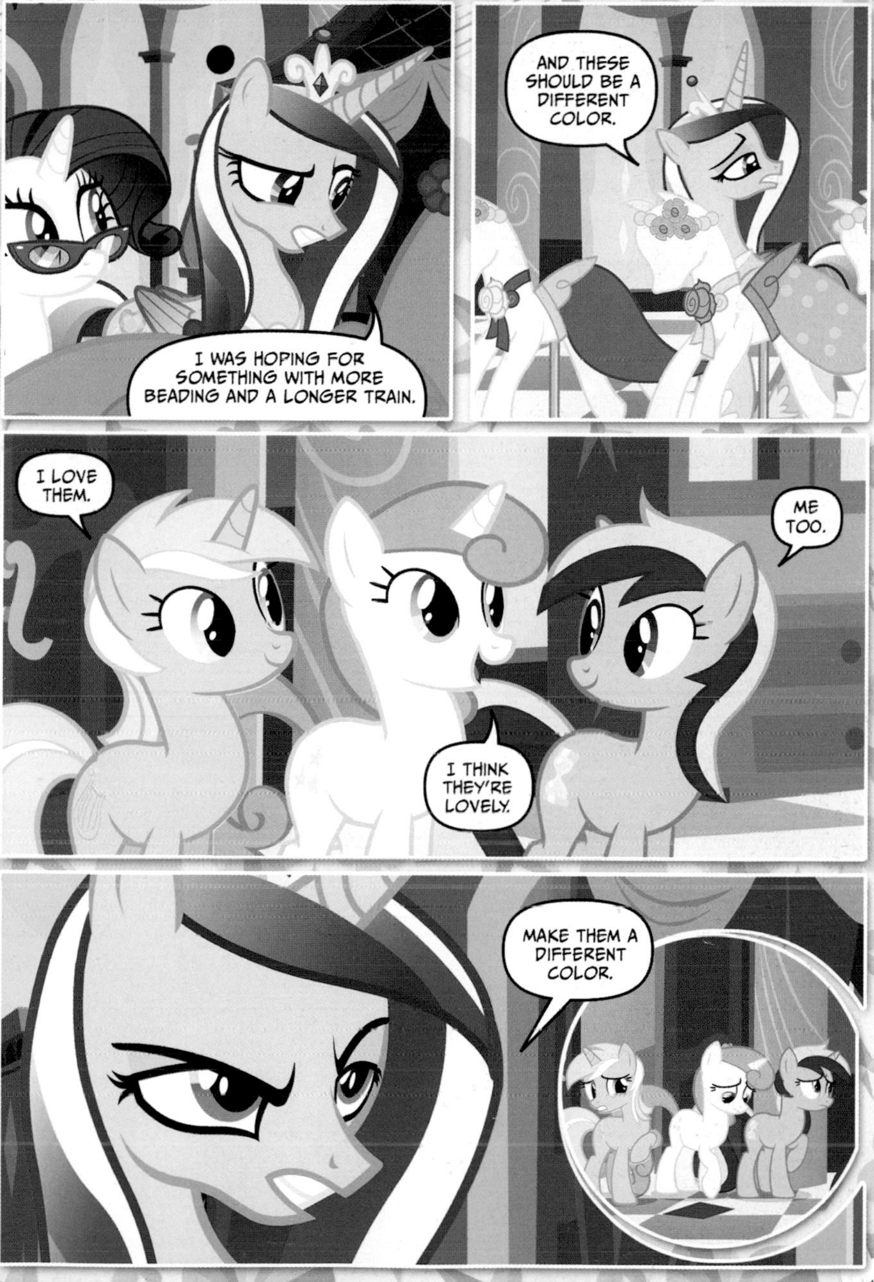
I WAS HOPING FOR SOMETHING WITH MORE BEADING AND A LONGER TRAIN.
AND THESE SHOULD BE A DIFFERENT COLOR.
I LOVE THEM.
I THINK THEY'RE LOVELY.
ME TOO.
MAKE THEM A DIFFERENT COLOR.

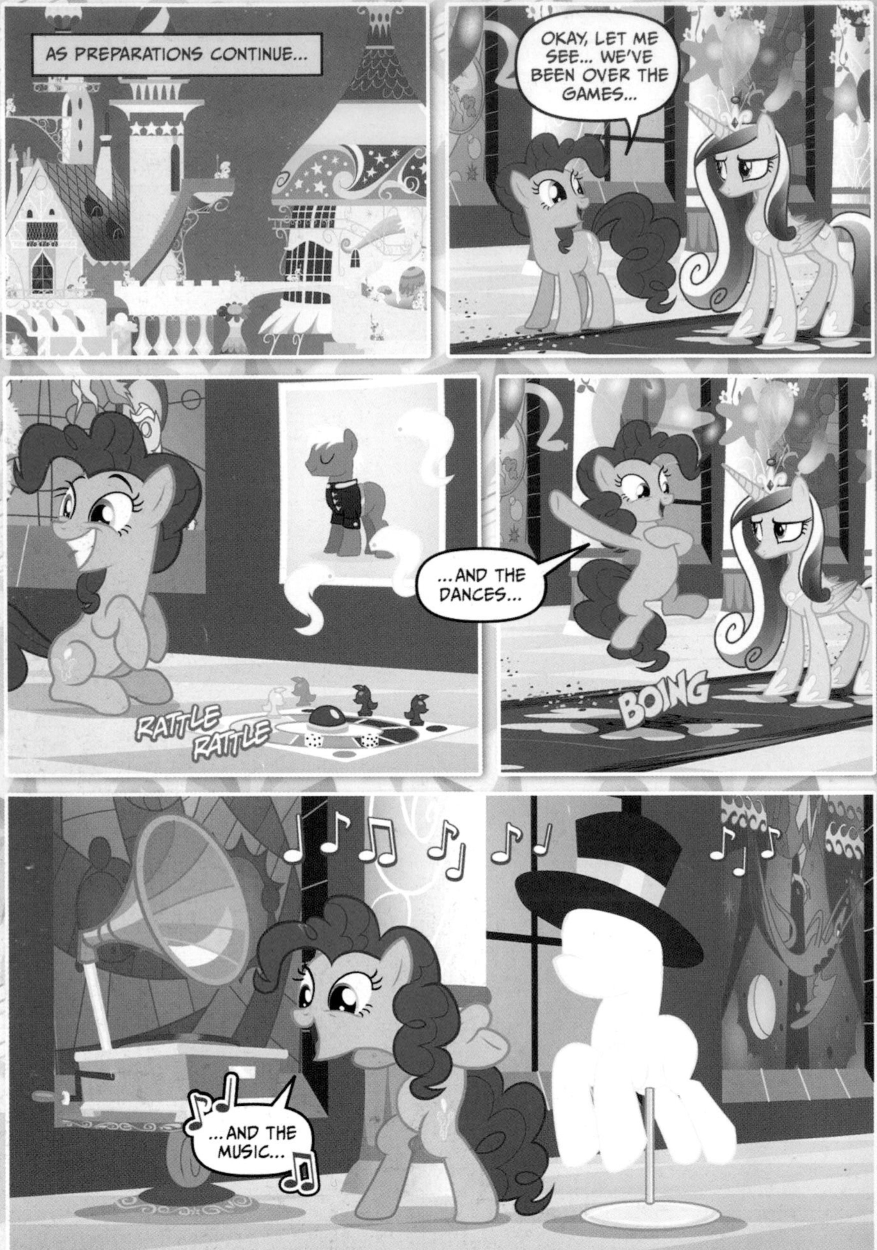

AS PREPARATIONS CONTINUE...
OKAY, LET ME SEE... WE'VE BEEN OVER THE GAMES...
RATTLE RATTLE
...AND THE DANCES...
BOING
...AND THE MUSIC...

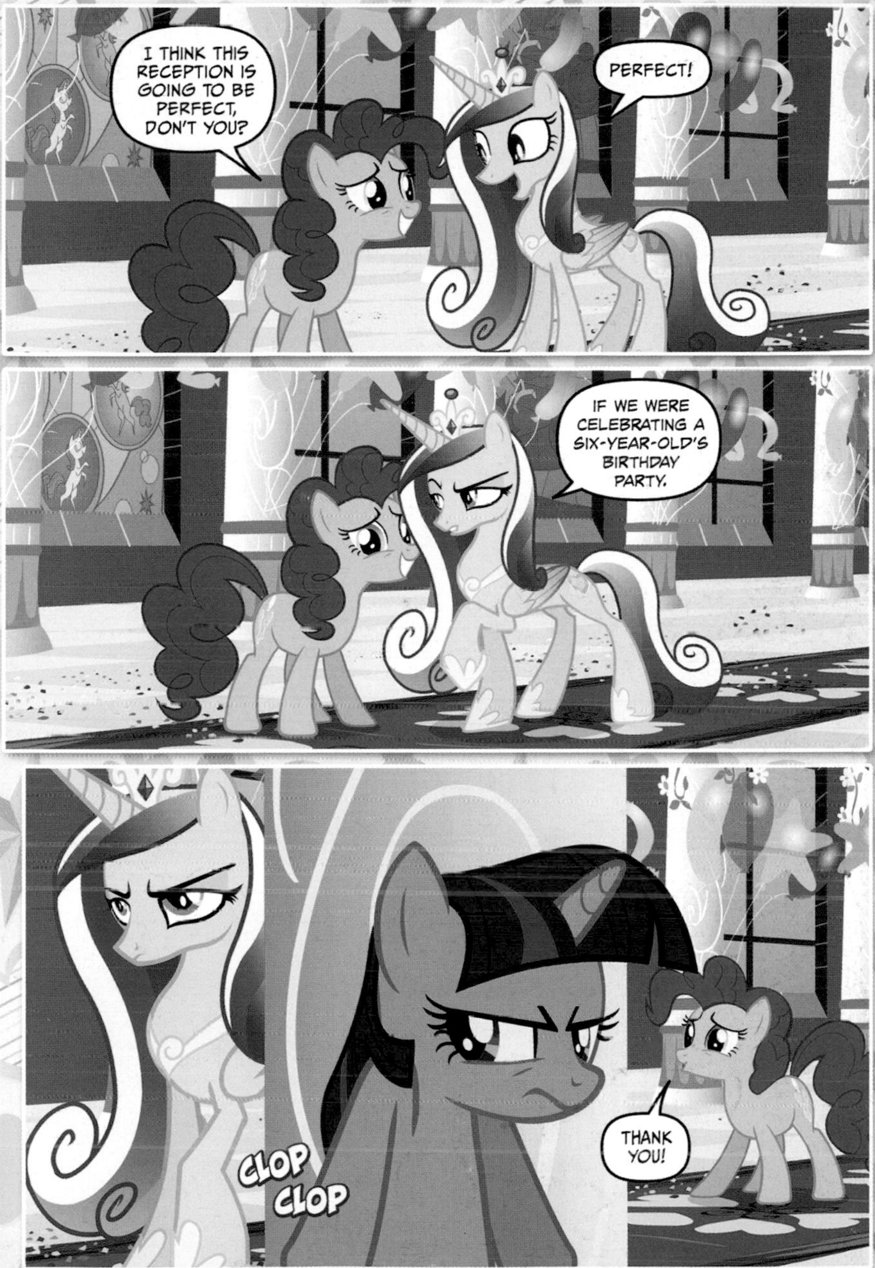
I THINK THIS RECEPTION IS GOING TO BE PERFECT, DON'T YOU?
PERFECT!
IF WE WERE CELEBRATING A SIX-YEAR-OLD'S BIRTHDAY PARTY.
CLOP CLOP
THANK YOU!

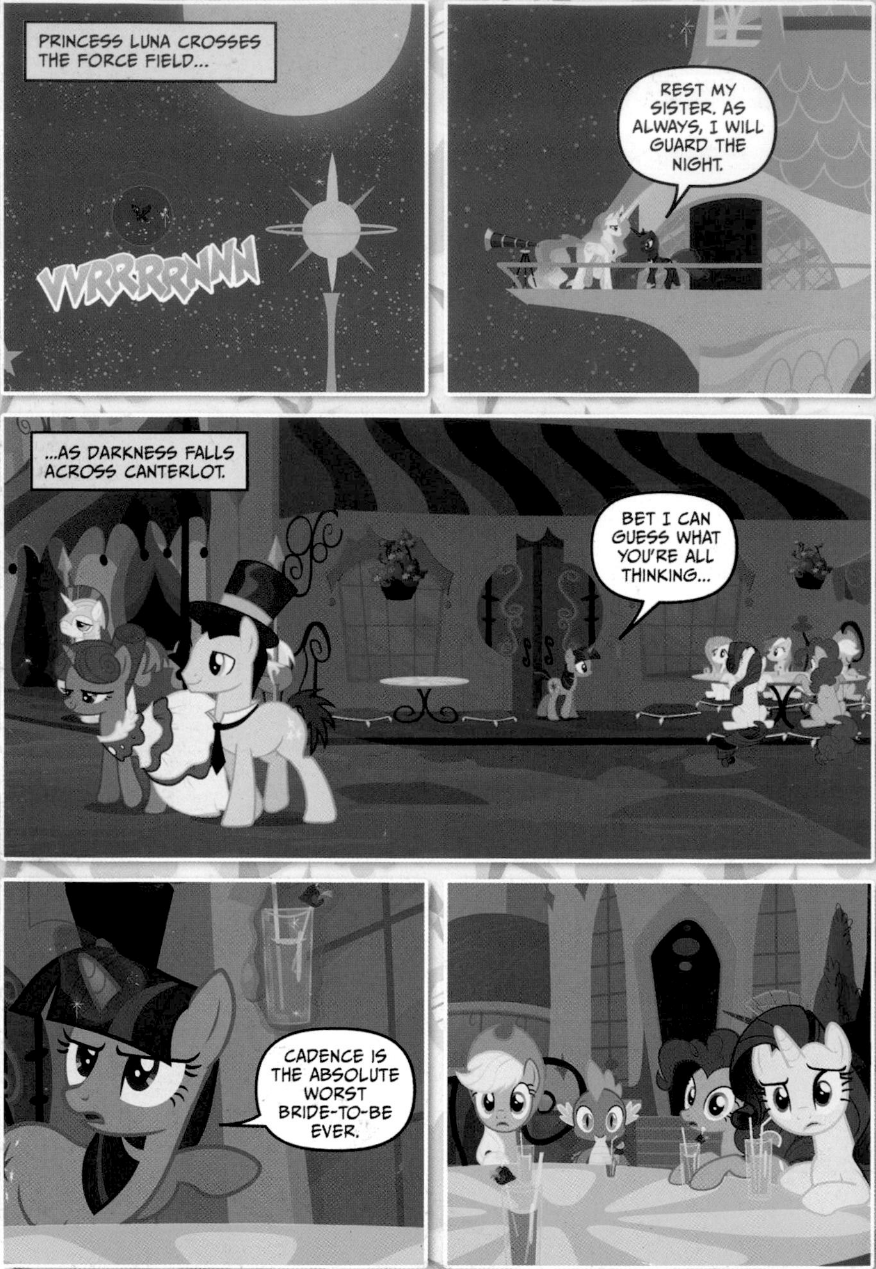
PRINCESS LUNA CROSSES THE FORCE FIELD...
VVRRRRNNN
REST MY SISTER. AS ALWAYS, I WILL GUARD THE NIGHT.
...AS DARKNESS FALLS ACROSS CANTERLOT.
BET I CAN GUESS WHAT YOU'RE ALL THINKING...
CADENCE IS THE ABSOLUTE WORST BRIDE-TO-BE EVER.

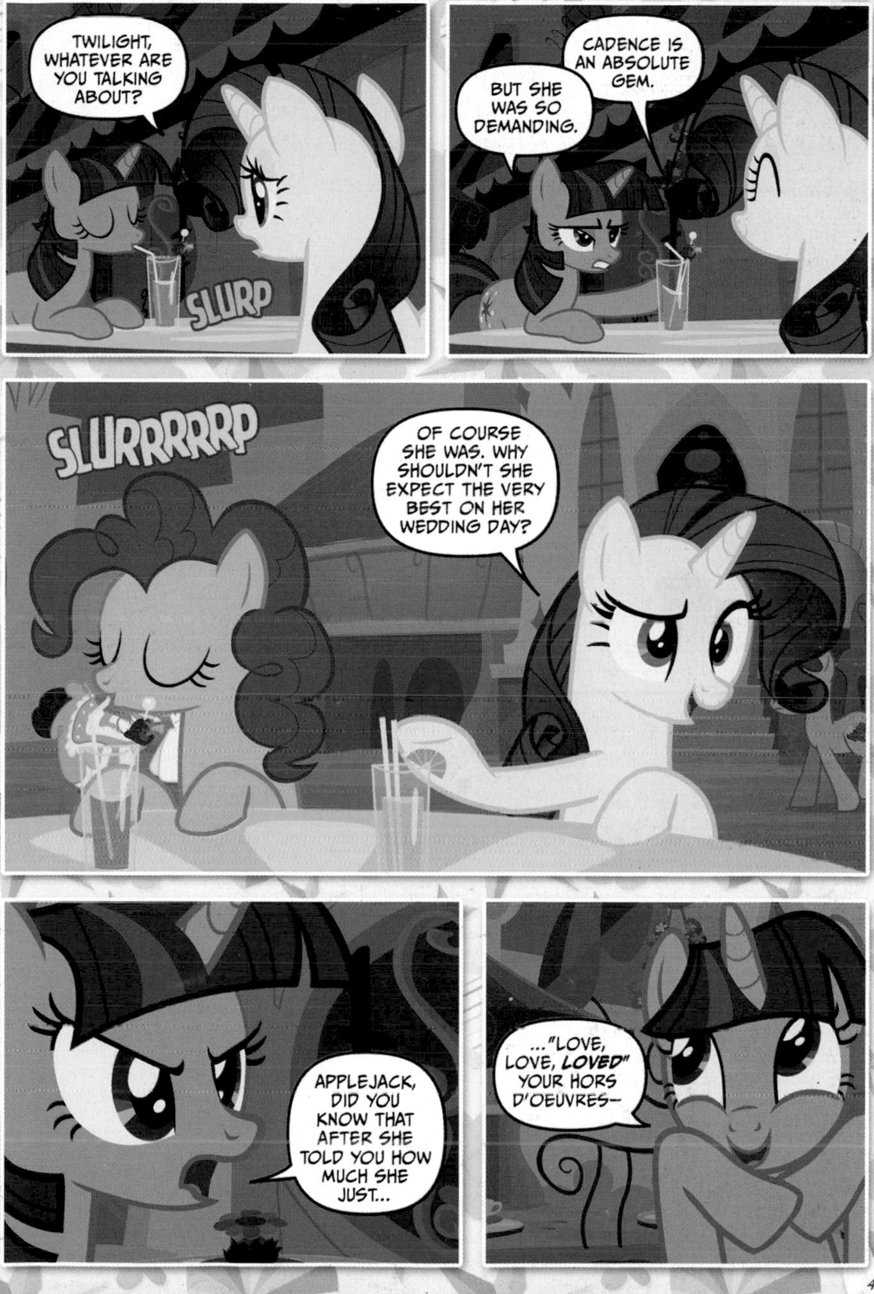
TWILIGHT, WHATEVER ARE YOU TALKING ABOUT?
SLURP
CADENCE IS AN ABSOLUTE GEM.
BUT SHE WAS SO DEMANDING.
SLURRRRRP
OF COURSE SHE WAS. WHY SHOULDN'T SHE EXPECT THE VERY BEST ON HER WEDDING DAY?
APPLEJACK, DID YOU KNOW THAT AFTER SHE TOLD YOU HOW MUCH SHE JUST...
..."LOVE, LOVE, ***LOVED***" YOUR HORS D'OEUVRES–

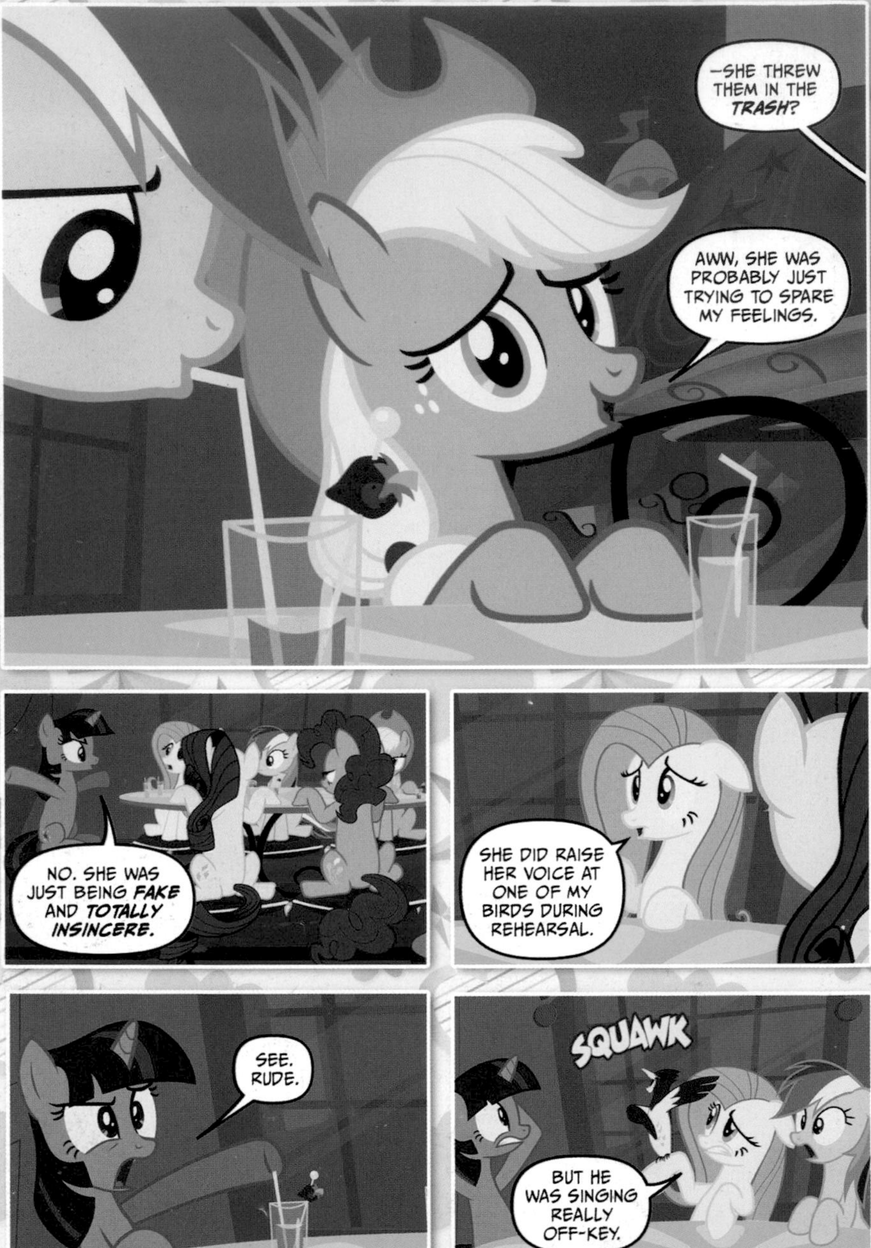
—SHE THREW THEM IN THE *TRASH?*
AWW, SHE WAS PROBABLY JUST TRYING TO SPARE MY FEELINGS.
NO. SHE WAS JUST BEING *FAKE* AND *TOTALLY INSINCERE.*
SHE DID RAISE HER VOICE AT ONE OF MY BIRDS DURING REHEARSAL.
SEE. RUDE.
SQUAWK
BUT HE WAS SINGING REALLY OFF-KEY.

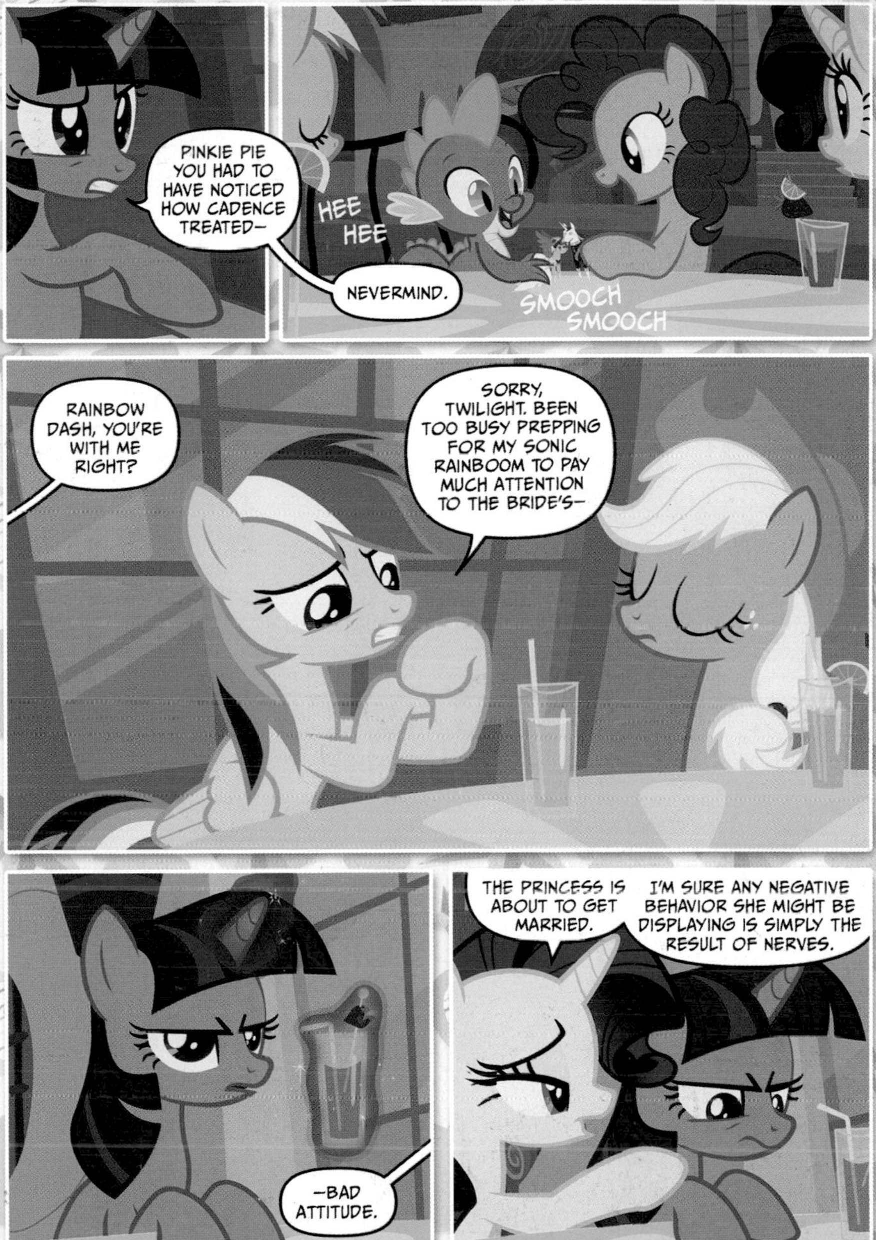
PINKIE PIE YOU HAD TO HAVE NOTICED HOW CADENCE TREATED–
HEE HEE
NEVERMIND.
SMOOCH SMOOCH
RAINBOW DASH, YOU'RE WITH ME RIGHT?
SORRY, TWILIGHT. BEEN TOO BUSY PREPPING FOR MY SONIC RAINBOOM TO PAY MUCH ATTENTION TO THE BRIDE'S–
–BAD ATTITUDE.
THE PRINCESS IS ABOUT TO GET MARRIED.
I'M SURE ANY NEGATIVE BEHAVIOR SHE MIGHT BE DISPLAYING IS SIMPLY THE RESULT OF NERVES.

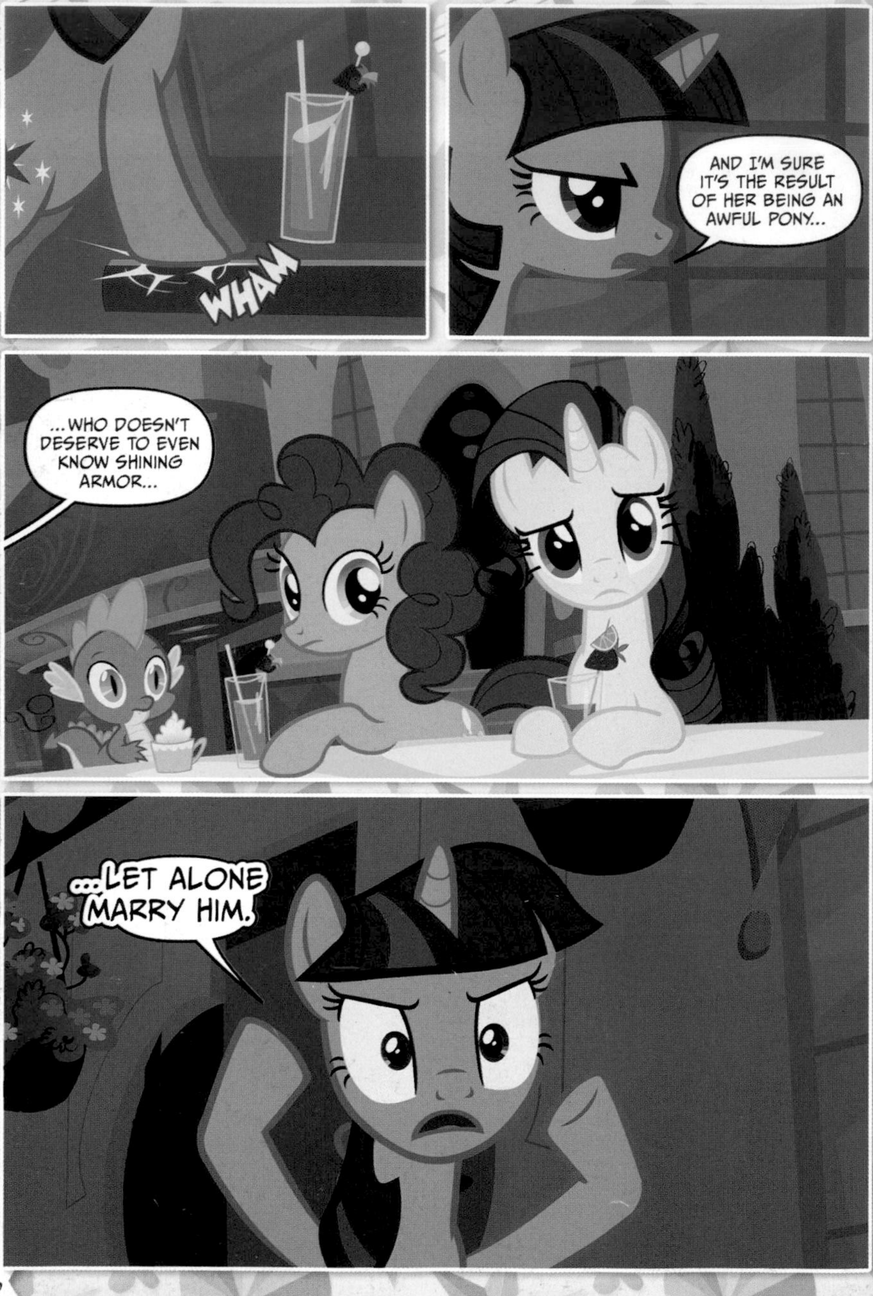
WHAM
AND I'M SURE IT'S THE RESULT OF HER BEING AN AWFUL PONY...
...WHO DOESN'T DESERVE TO EVEN KNOW SHINING ARMOR...
...LET ALONE MARRY HIM.

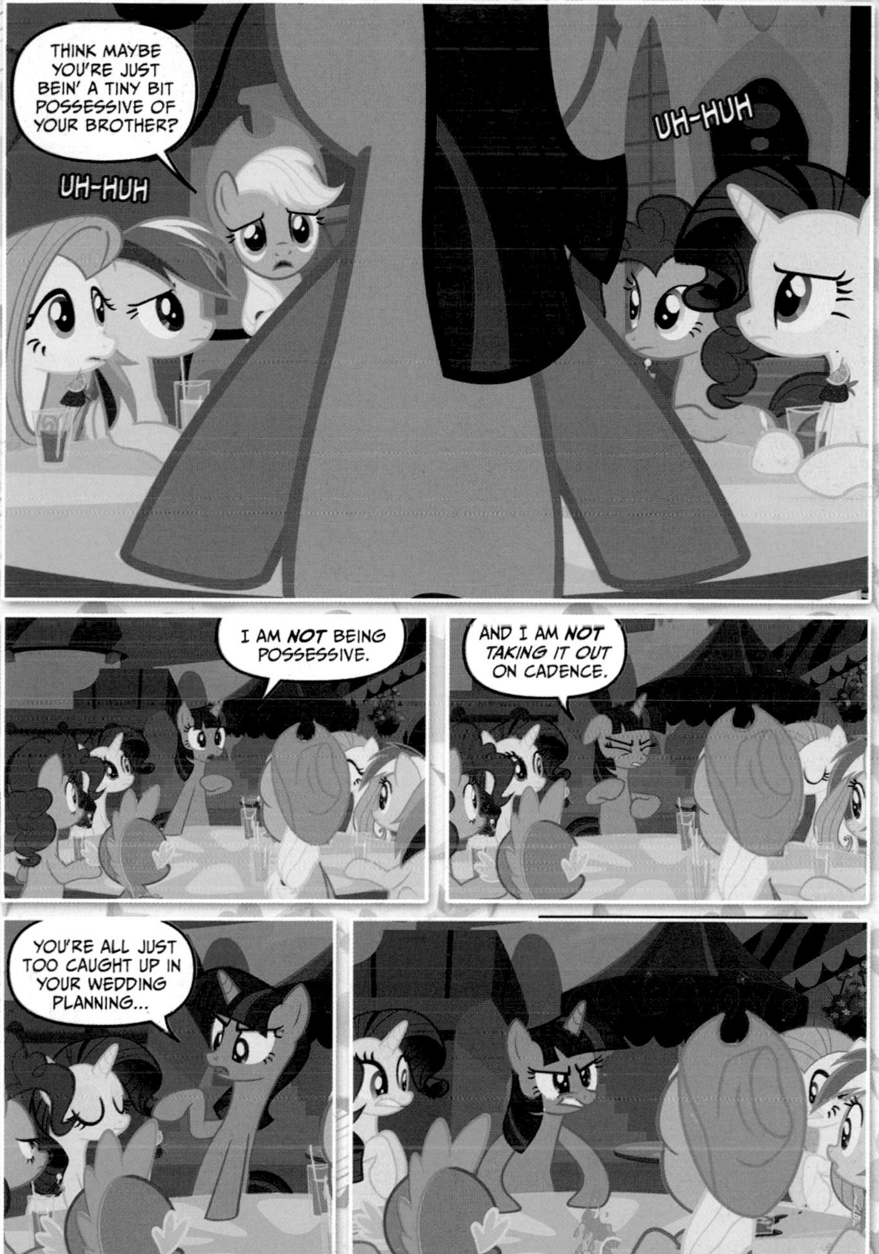
THINK MAYBE YOU'RE JUST BEIN' A TINY BIT POSSESSIVE OF YOUR BROTHER?
UH-HUH
UH-HUH
I AM *NOT* BEING POSSESSIVE.
AND I AM *NOT* *TAKING IT OUT* ON CADENCE.
YOU'RE ALL JUST TOO CAUGHT UP IN YOUR WEDDING PLANNING...

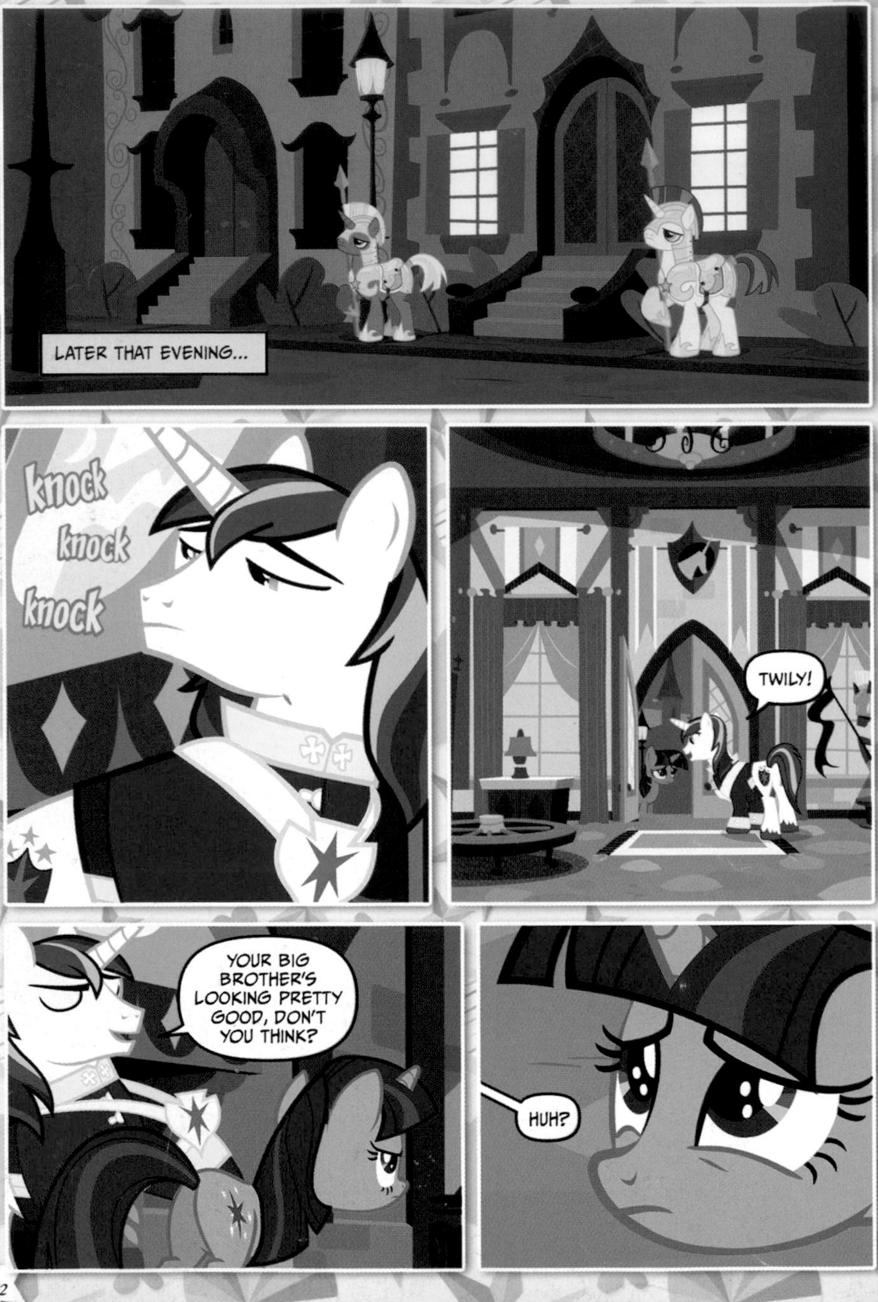
LATER THAT EVENING...
knock
knock
knock
TWILY!
YOUR BIG BROTHER'S LOOKING PRETTY GOOD, DON'T YOU THINK?
HUH?

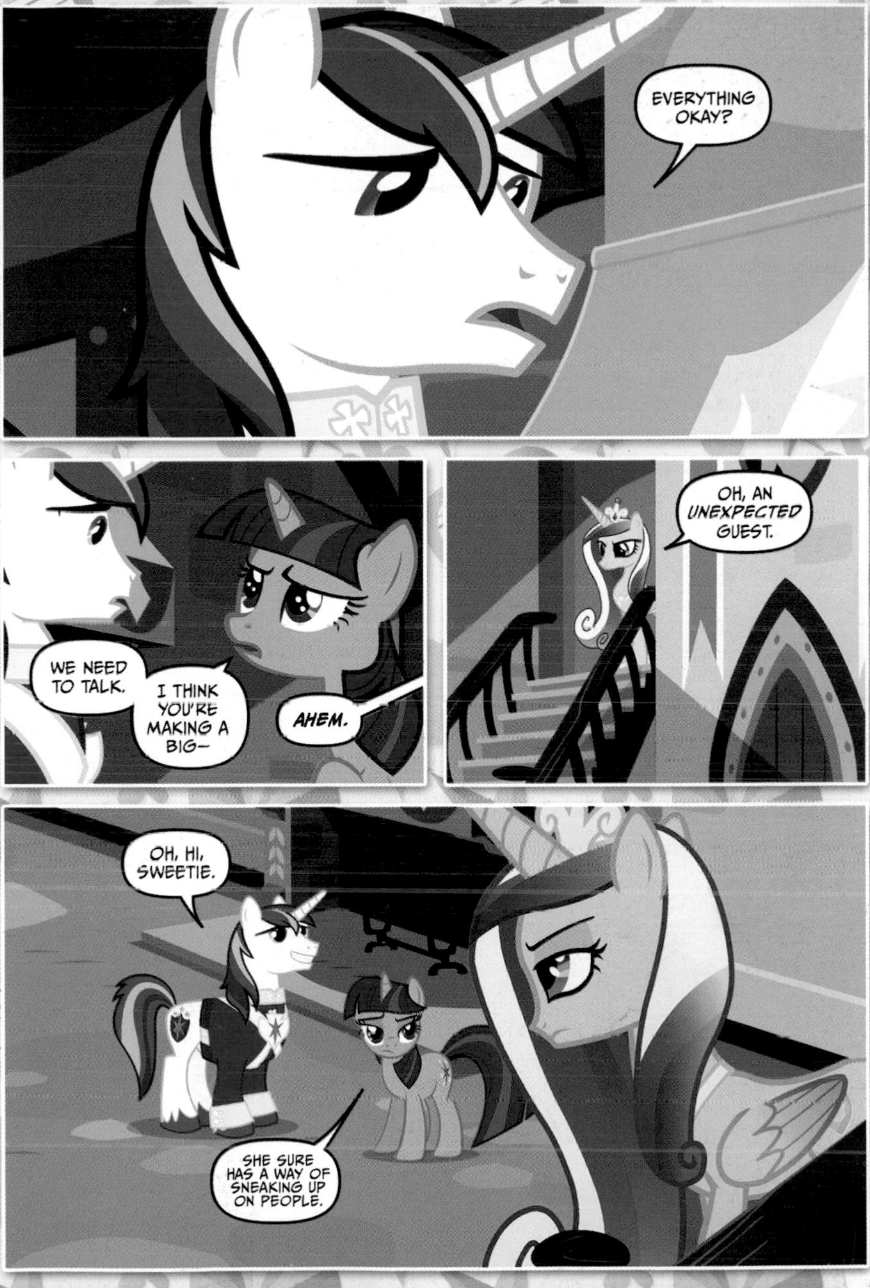

EVERYTHING OKAY?
WE NEED TO TALK.
I THINK YOU'RE MAKING A BIG—
AHEM.
OH, AN UNEXPECTED GUEST.
OH, HI, SWEETIE.
SHE SURE HAS A WAY OF SNEAKING UP ON PEOPLE.

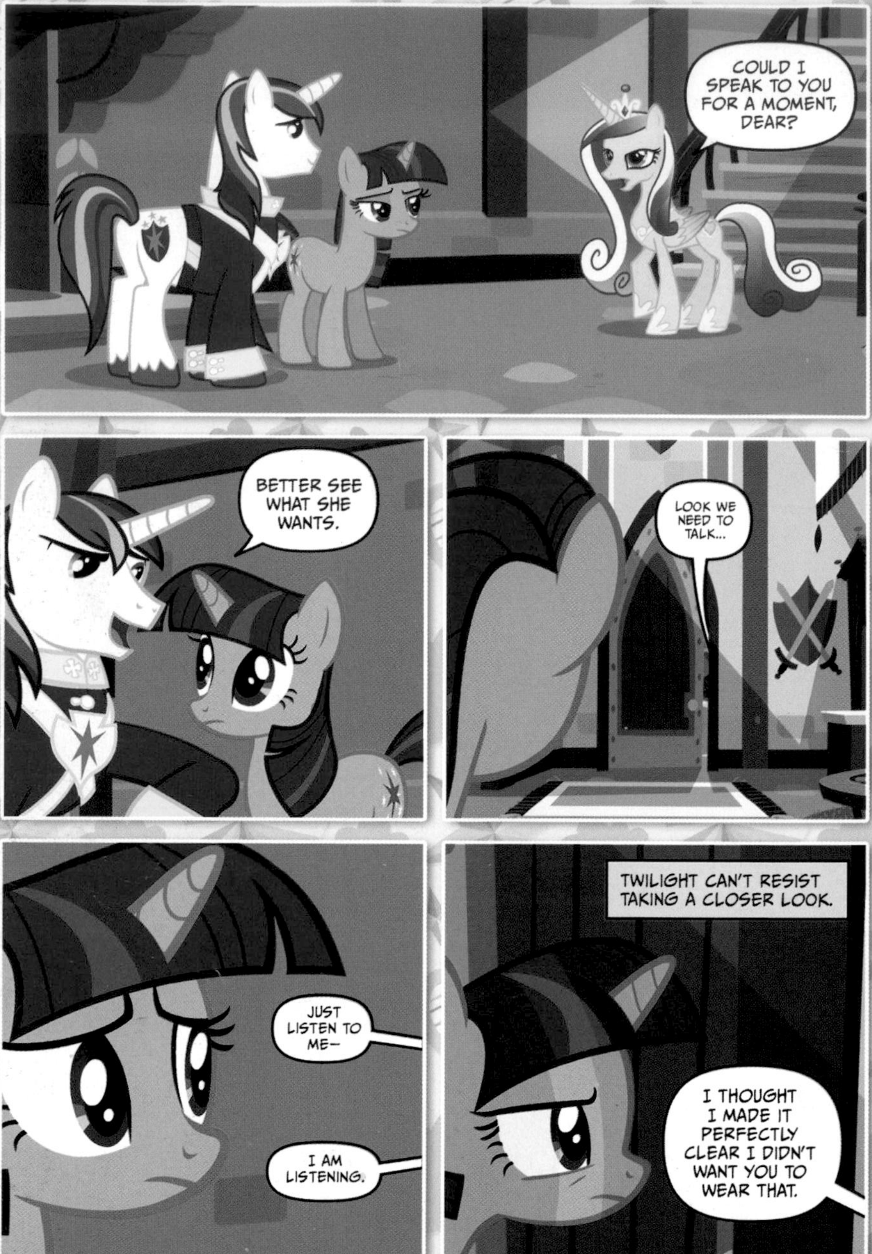
COULD I SPEAK TO YOU FOR A MOMENT, DEAR?
BETTER SEE WHAT SHE WANTS.
LOOK WE NEED TO TALK...
JUST LISTEN TO ME–
I AM LISTENING.
TWILIGHT CAN'T RESIST TAKING A CLOSER LOOK.
I THOUGHT I MADE IT PERFECTLY CLEAR I DIDN'T WANT YOU TO WEAR THAT.

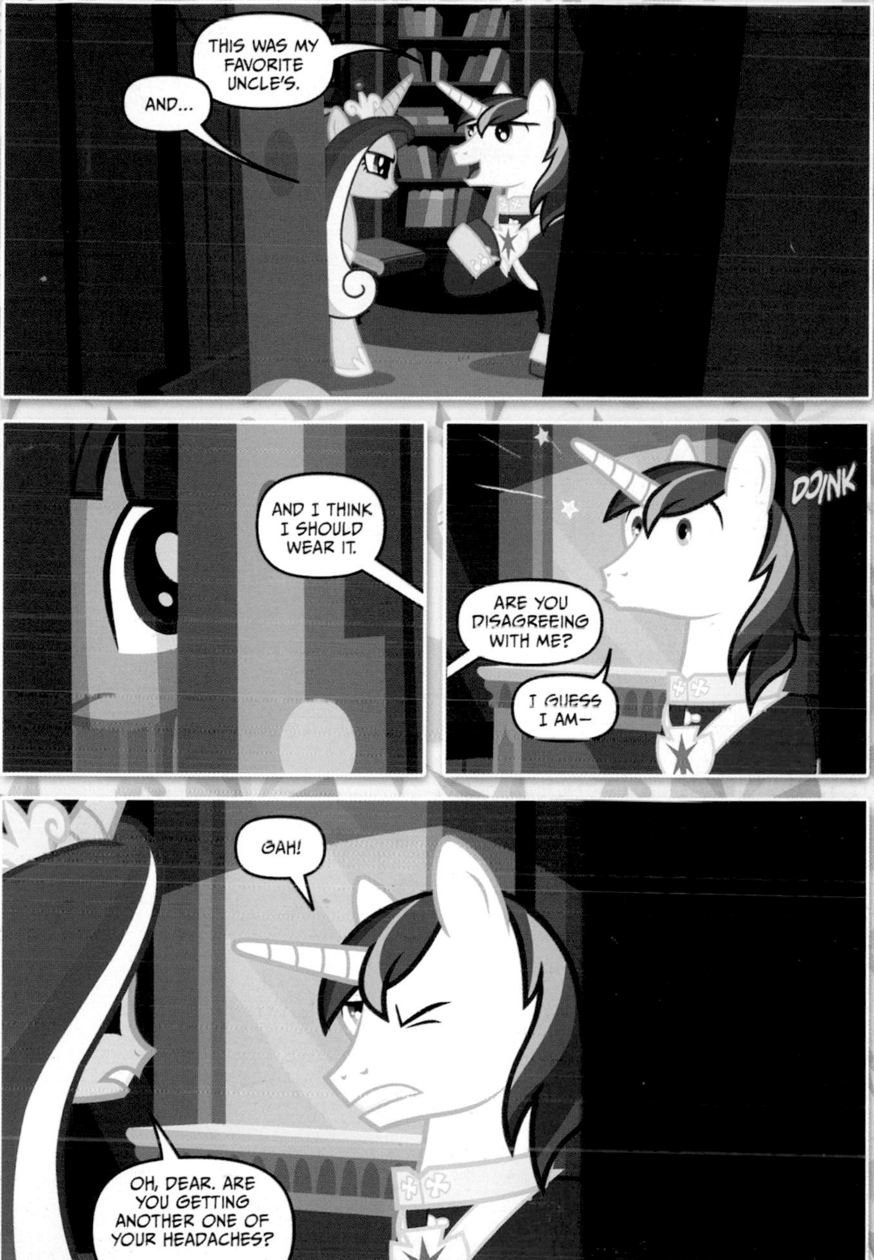
THIS WAS MY FAVORITE UNCLE'S.
AND...
AND I THINK I SHOULD WEAR IT.
DOINK
ARE YOU DISAGREEING WITH ME?
I GUESS I AM—
GAH!
OH, DEAR. ARE YOU GETTING ANOTHER ONE OF YOUR HEADACHES?

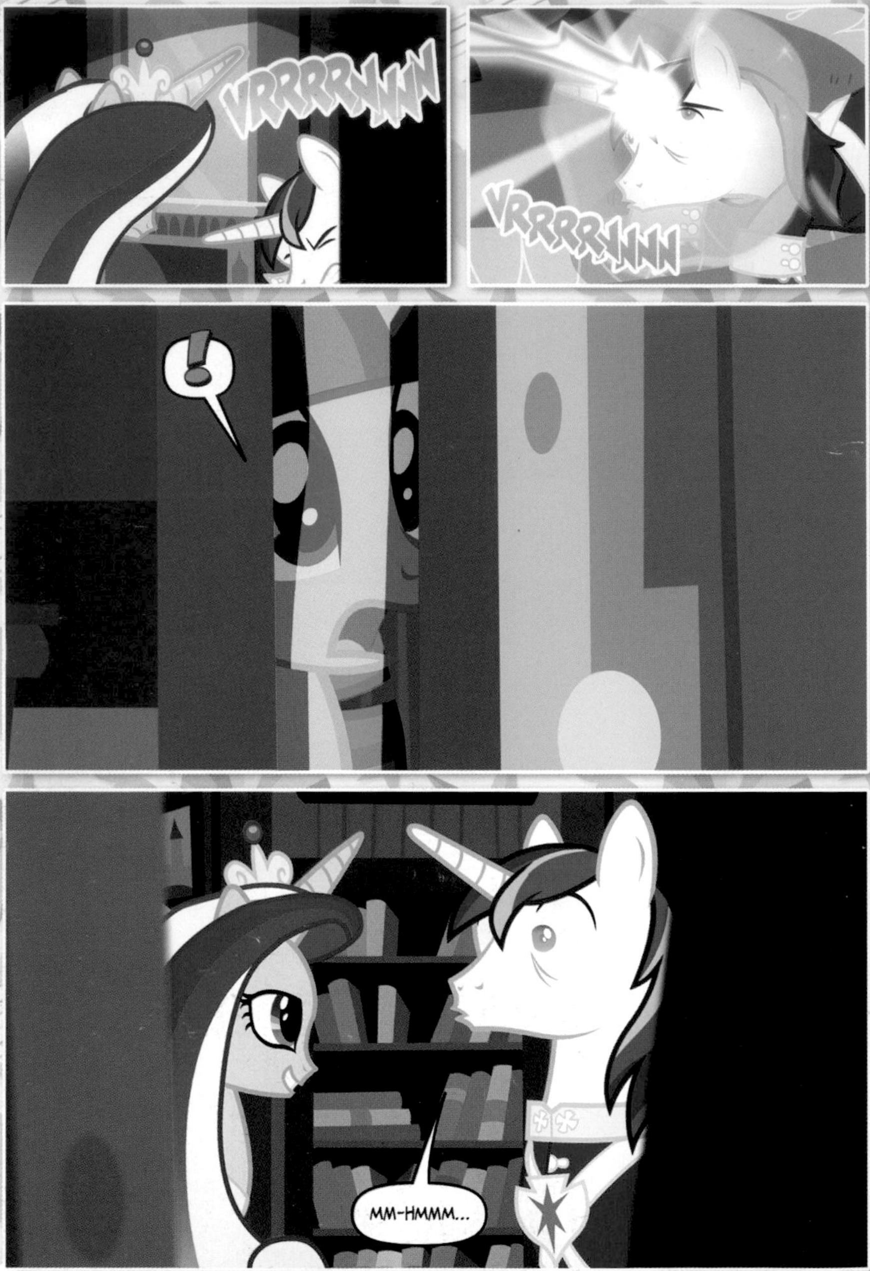
VRRRRNNNN
VRRRRNNNN
!
MM-HMMM...

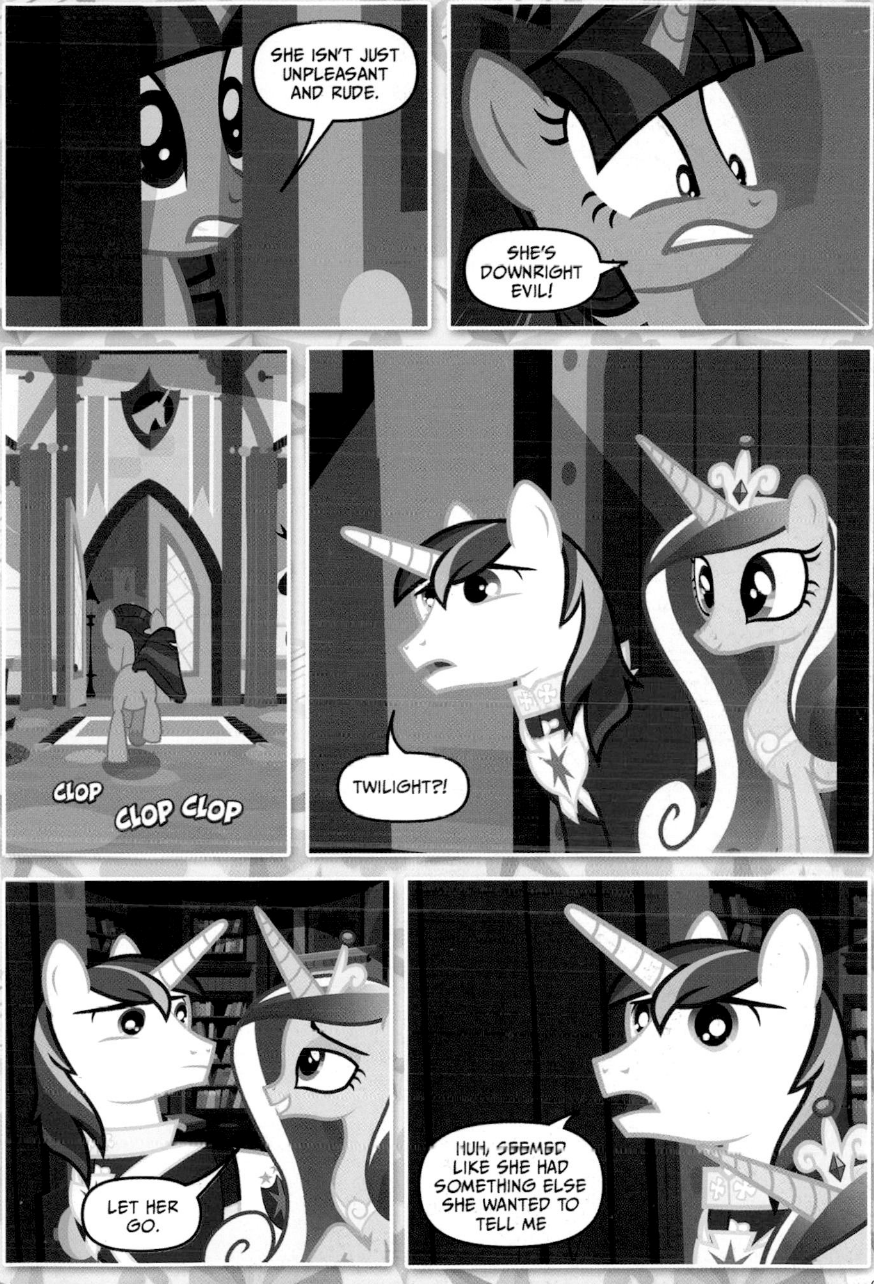

SHE ISN'T JUST UNPLEASANT AND RUDE.
SHE'S DOWNRIGHT EVIL!
CLOP
CLOP CLOP
TWILIGHT?!
LET HER GO.
HUH, SEEMED LIKE SHE HAD SOMETHING ELSE SHE WANTED TO TELL ME

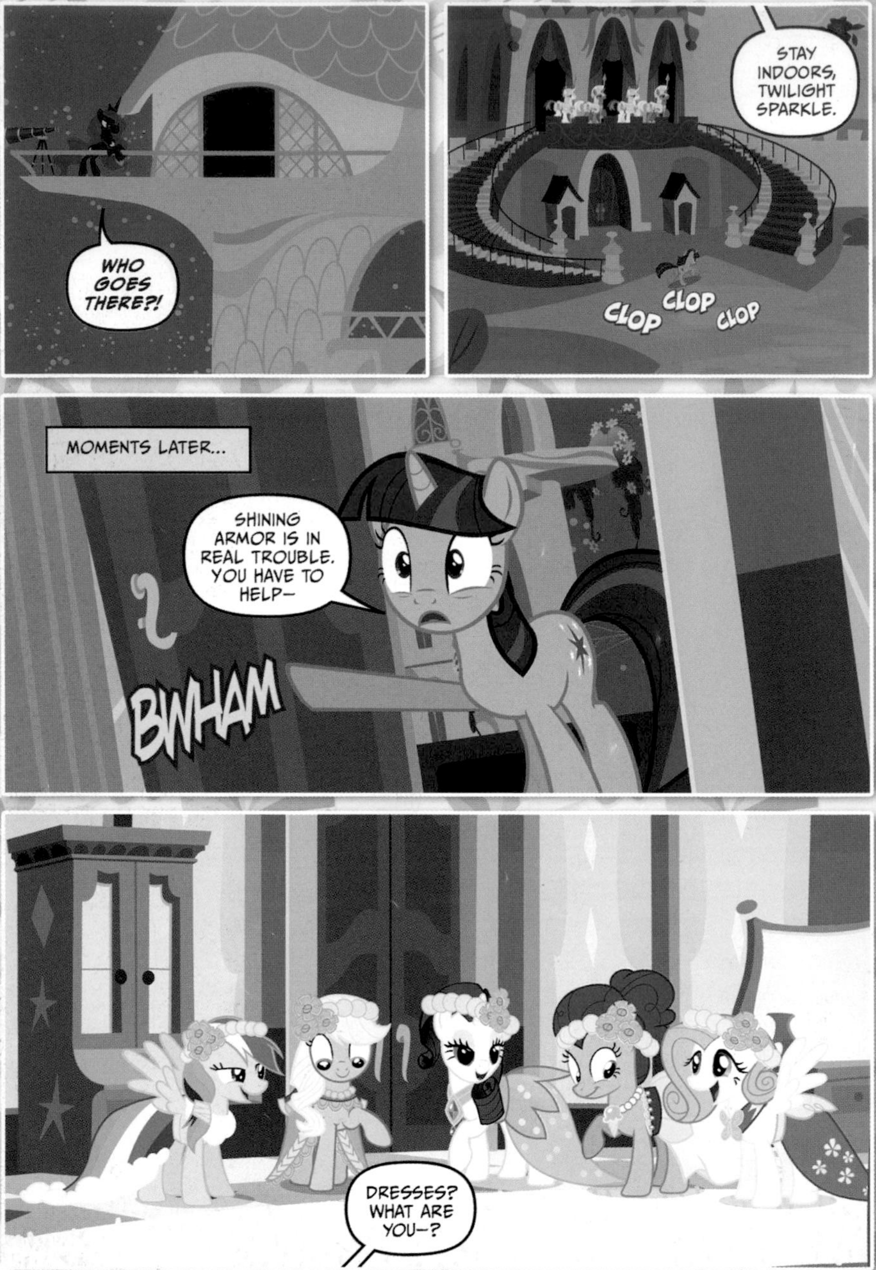
WHO GOES THERE?!
STAY INDOORS, TWILIGHT SPARKLE.
CLOP CLOP CLOP
MOMENTS LATER...
SHINING ARMOR IS IN REAL TROUBLE. YOU HAVE TO HELP—
BWHAM
DRESSES? WHAT ARE YOU—?

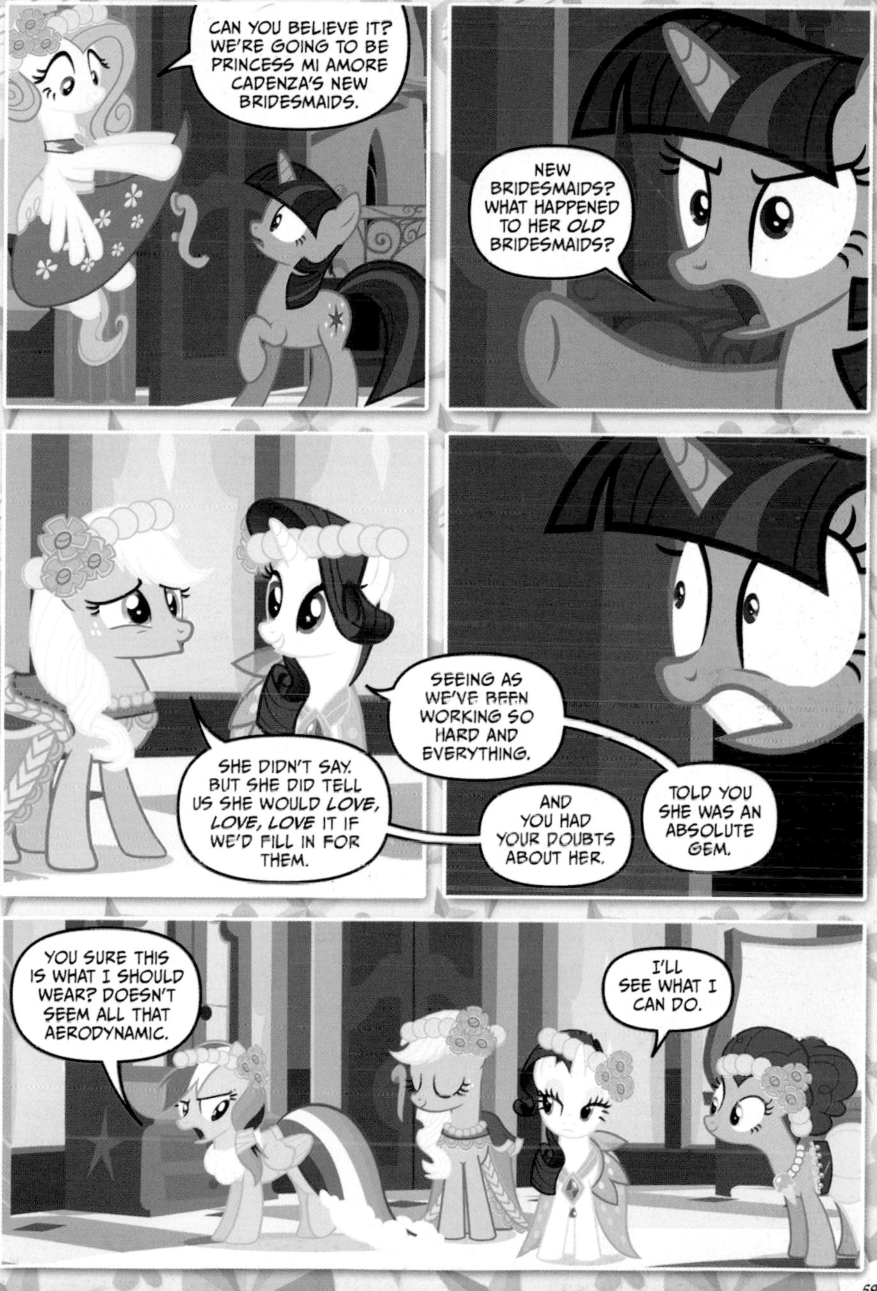
CAN YOU BELIEVE IT? WE'RE GOING TO BE PRINCESS MI AMORE CADENZA'S NEW BRIDESMAIDS.
NEW BRIDESMAIDS? WHAT HAPPENED TO HER *OLD* BRIDESMAIDS?
SHE DIDN'T SAY. BUT SHE DID TELL US SHE WOULD *LOVE, LOVE, LOVE* IT IF WE'D FILL IN FOR THEM.
SEEING AS WE'VE BEEN WORKING SO HARD AND EVERYTHING.
AND YOU HAD YOUR DOUBTS ABOUT HER.
TOLD YOU SHE WAS AN ABSOLUTE GEM.
YOU SURE THIS IS WHAT I SHOULD WEAR? DOESN'T SEEM ALL THAT AERODYNAMIC.
I'LL SEE WHAT I CAN DO.

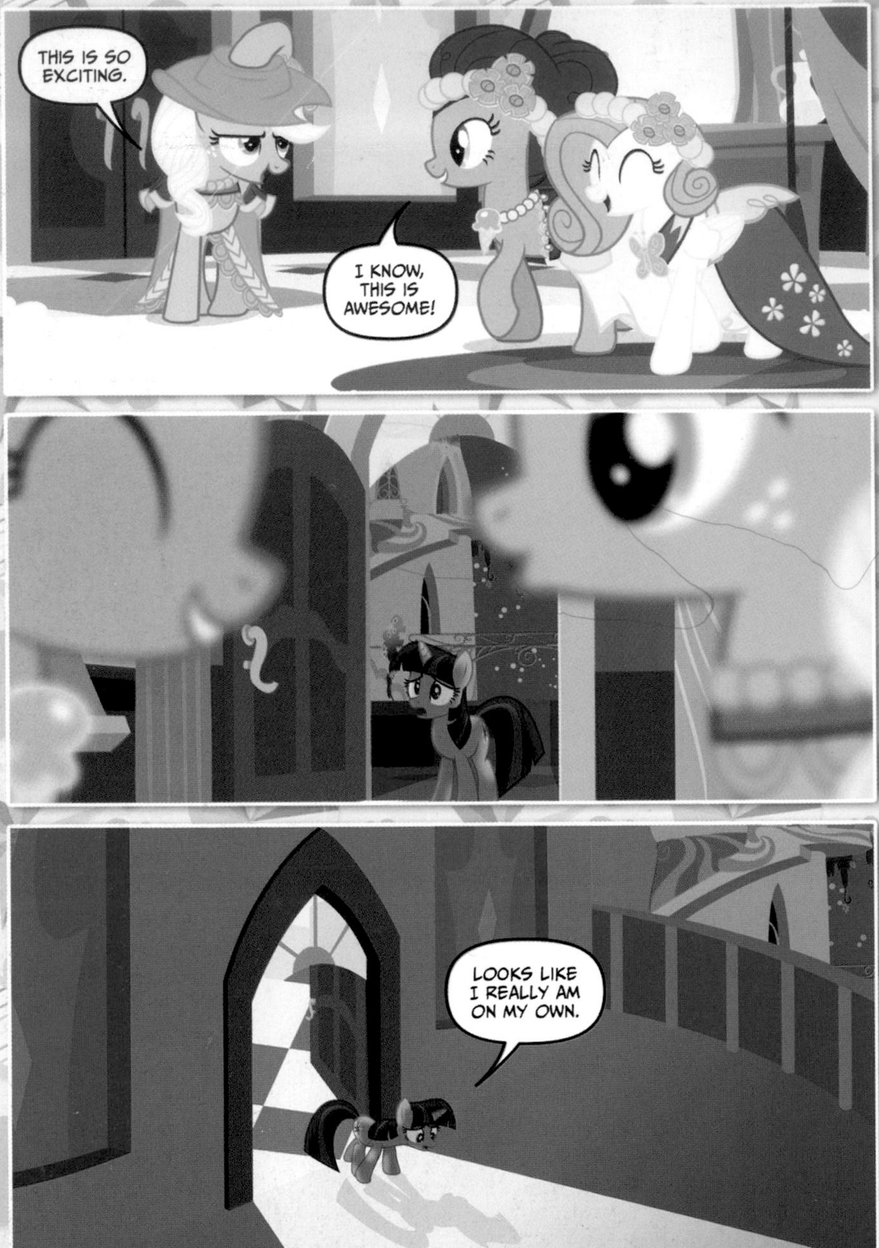
THIS IS SO EXCITING.
I KNOW, THIS IS AWESOME!
LOOKS LIKE I REALLY AM ON MY OWN.

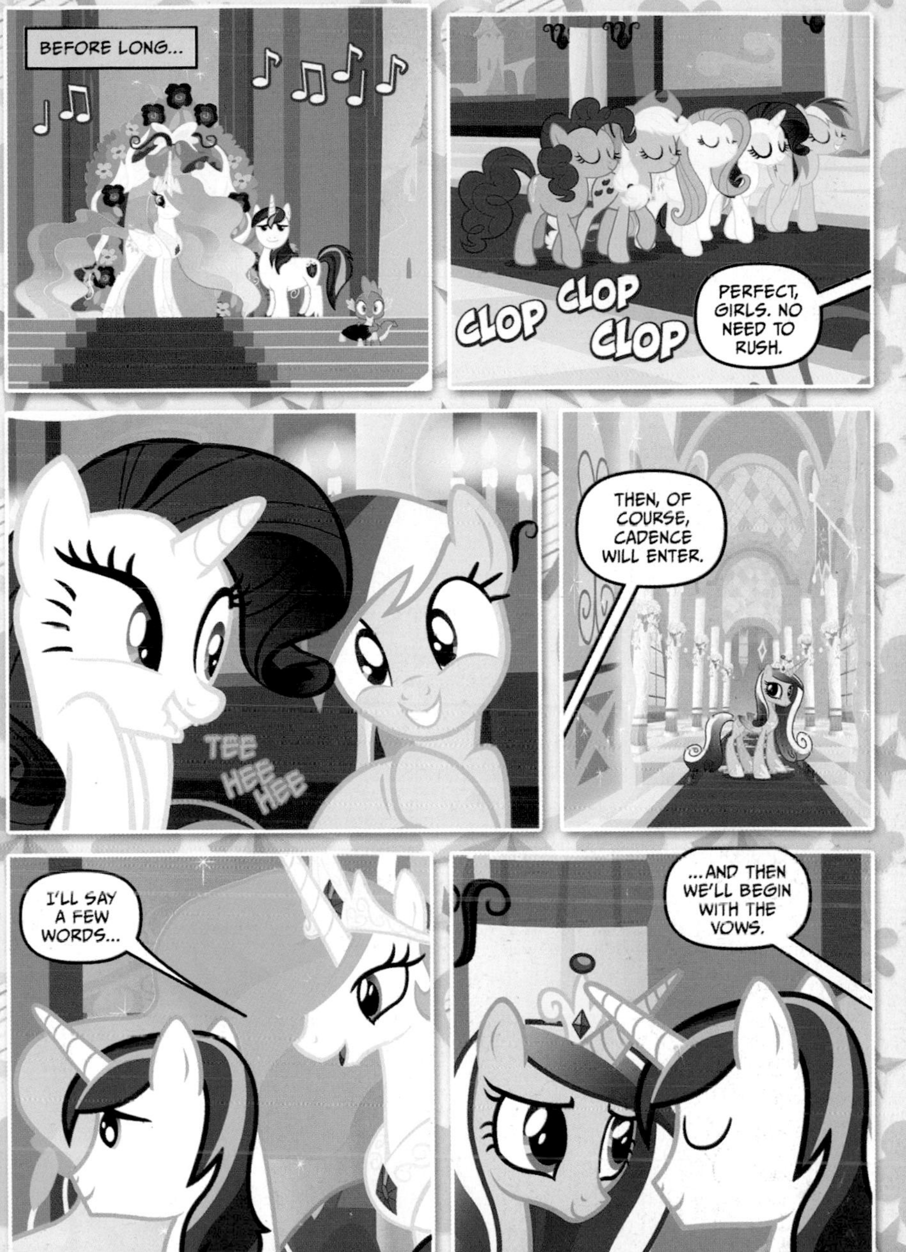
BEFORE LONG...
CLOP CLOP CLOP
PERFECT, GIRLS. NO NEED TO RUSH.
TEE HEE HEE
THEN, OF COURSE, CADENCE WILL ENTER.
I'LL SAY A FEW WORDS...
...AND THEN WE'LL BEGIN WITH THE VOWS.

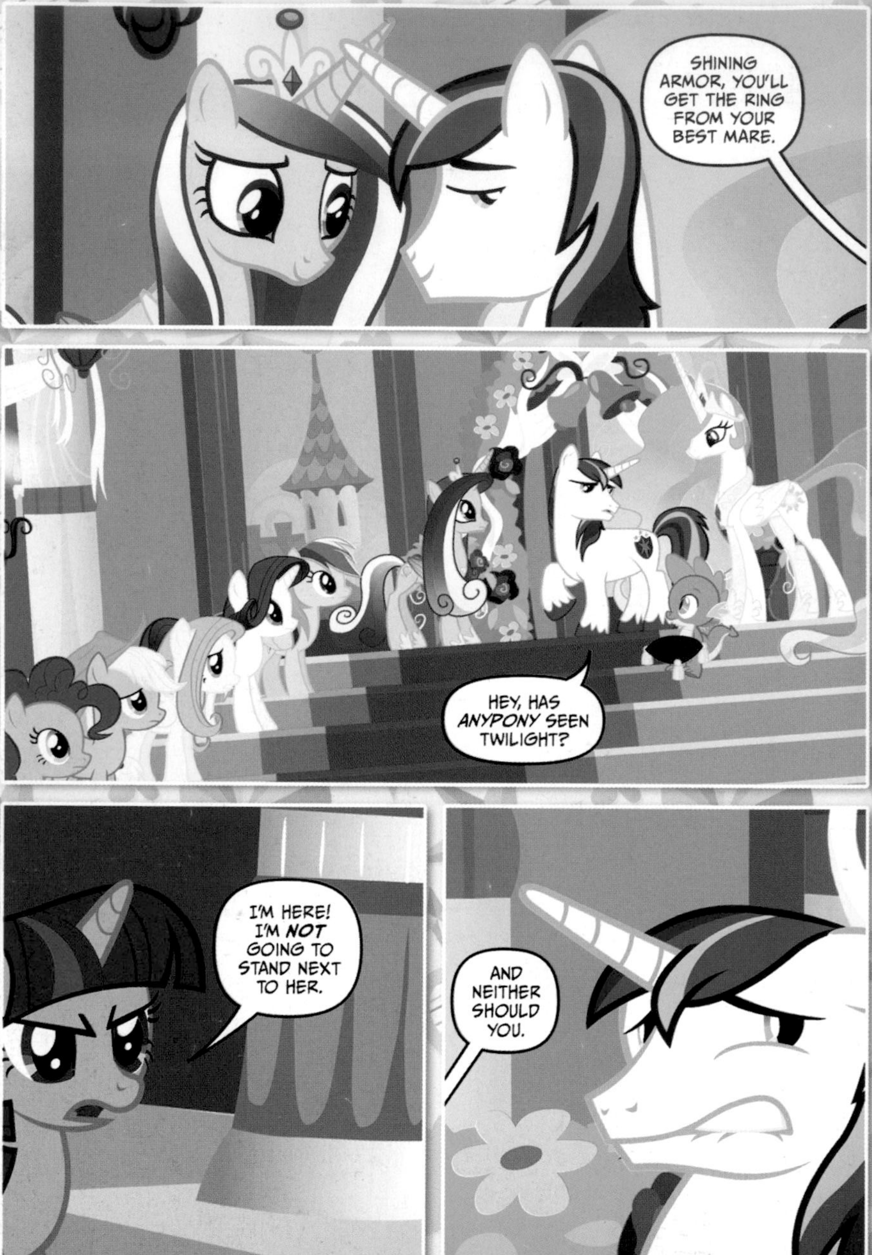
SHINING ARMOR, YOU'LL GET THE RING FROM YOUR BEST MARE.
HEY, HAS *ANYPONY* SEEN TWILIGHT?
I'M HERE! I'M ***NOT*** GOING TO STAND NEXT TO HER.
AND NEITHER SHOULD YOU.

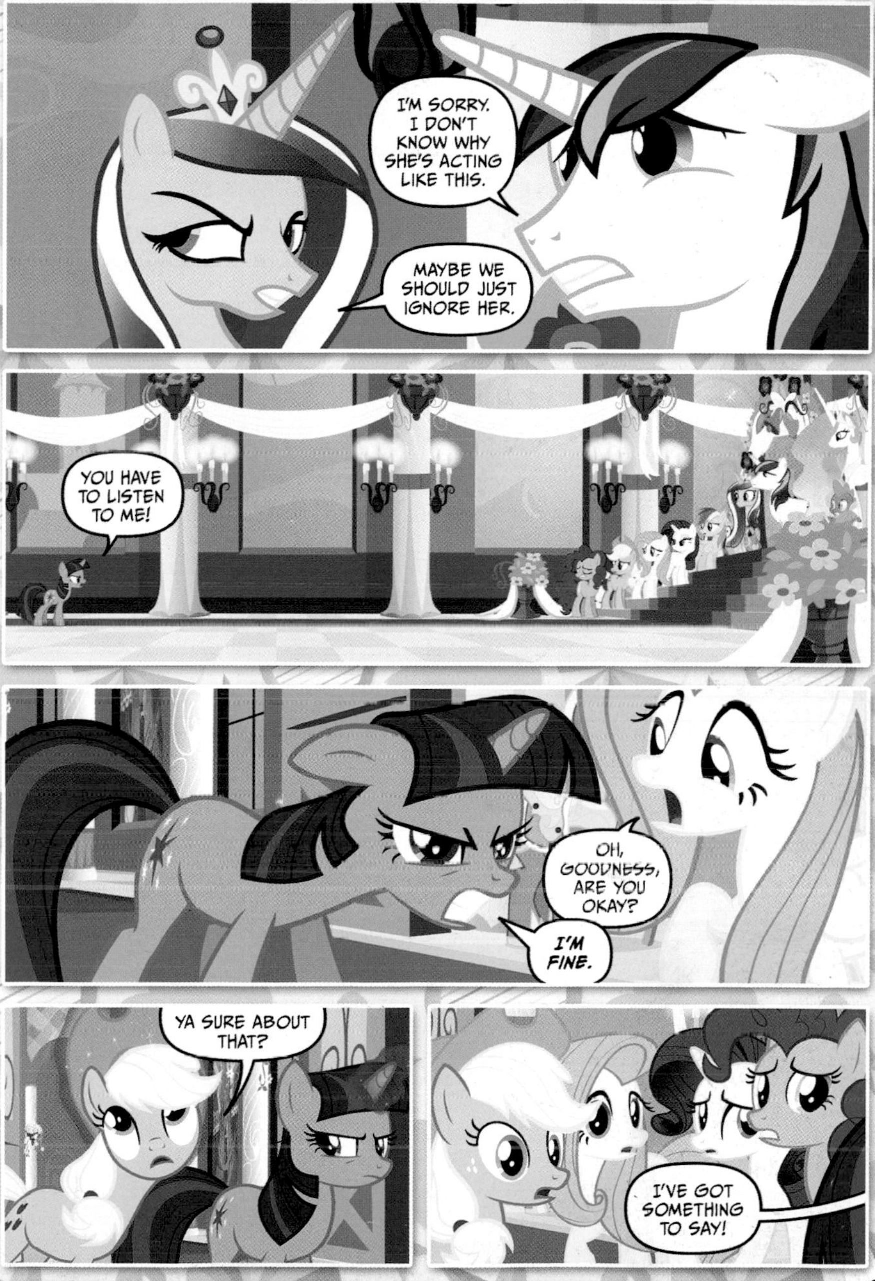
I'M SORRY. I DON'T KNOW WHY SHE'S ACTING LIKE THIS.
MAYBE WE SHOULD JUST IGNORE HER.
YOU HAVE TO LISTEN TO ME!
OH, GOODNESS, ARE YOU OKAY?
I'M FINE.
YA SURE ABOUT THAT?
I'VE GOT SOMETHING TO SAY!

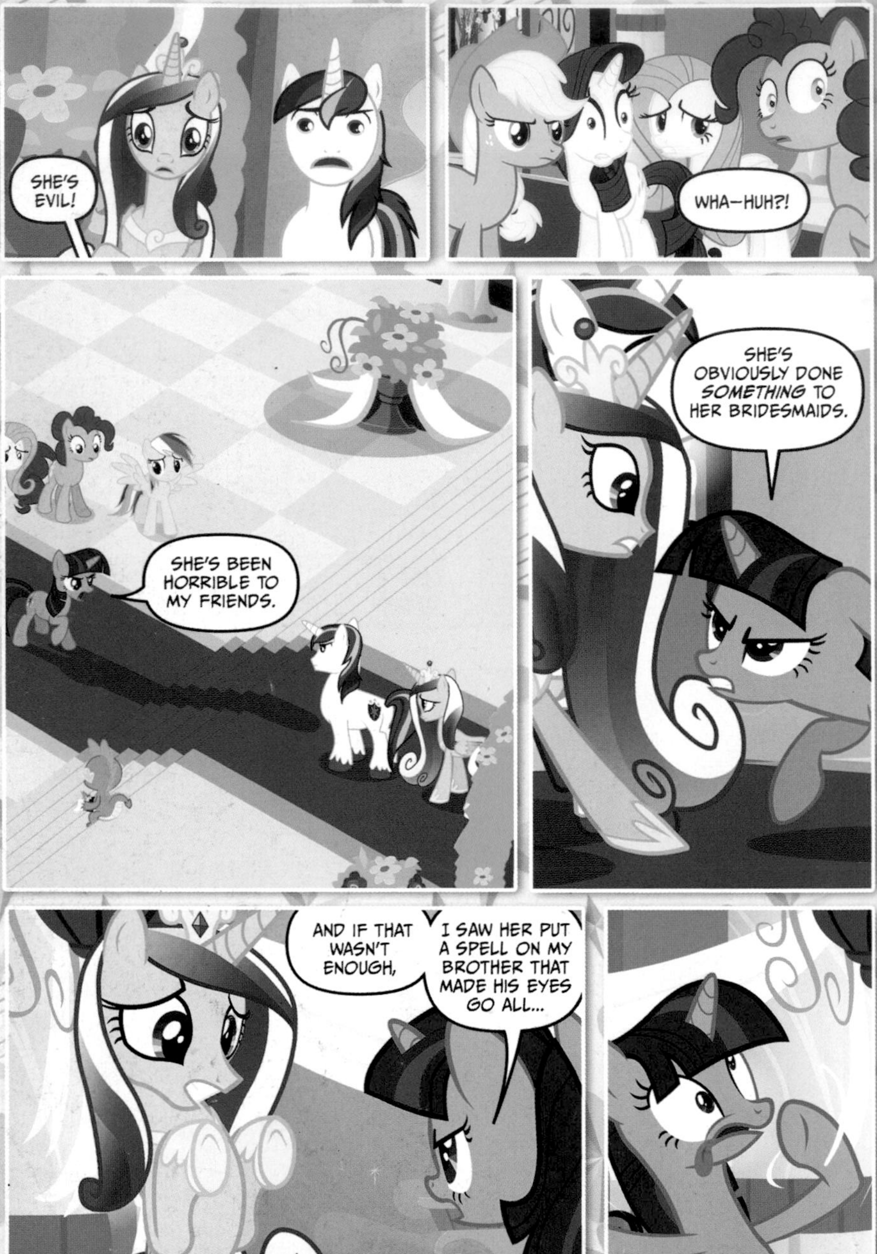
SHE'S EVIL!
WHA-HUH?!
SHE'S BEEN HORRIBLE TO MY FRIENDS.
SHE'S OBVIOUSLY DONE *SOMETHING* TO HER BRIDESMAIDS.
AND IF THAT WASN'T ENOUGH,
I SAW HER PUT A SPELL ON MY BROTHER THAT MADE HIS EYES GO ALL...

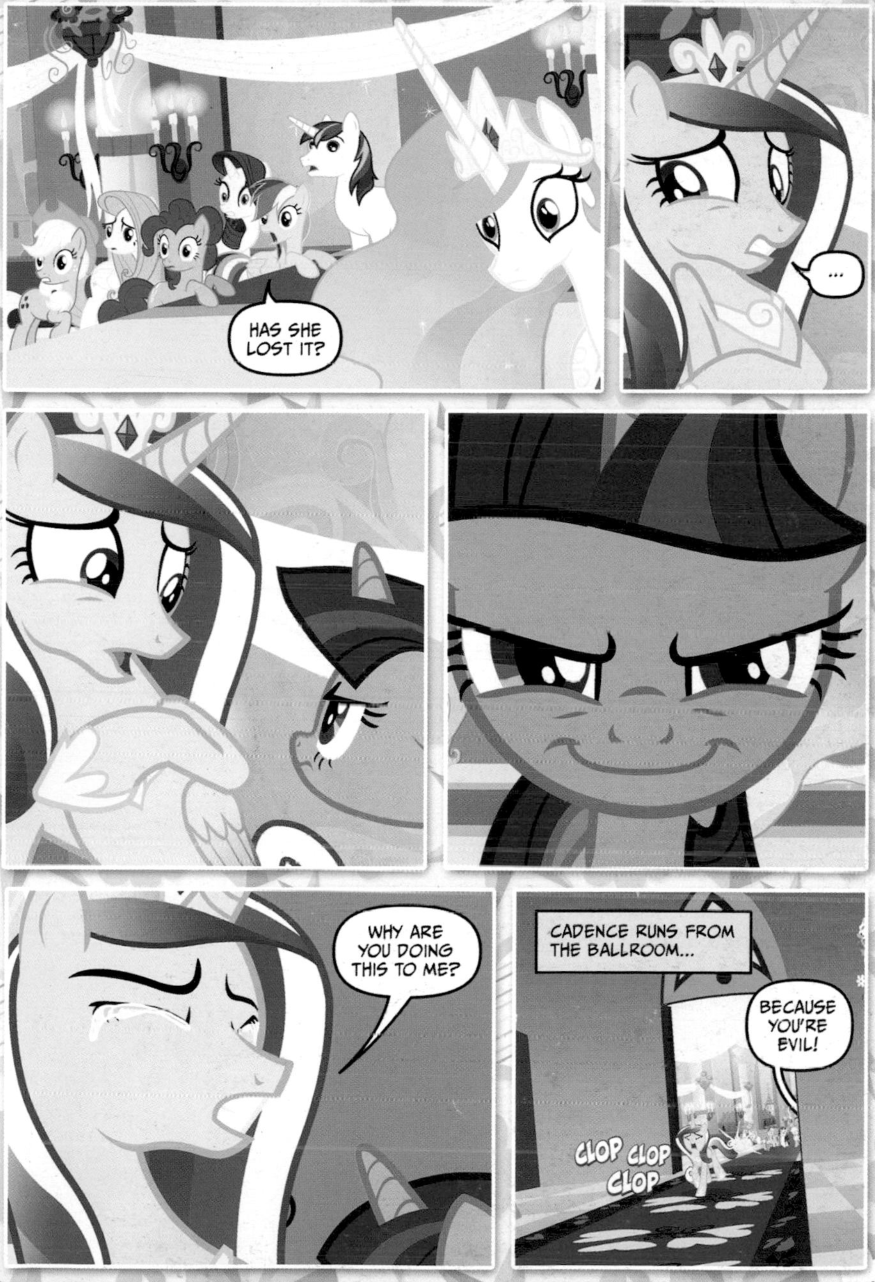
HAS SHE LOST IT?
...
WHY ARE YOU DOING THIS TO ME?
CADENCE RUNS FROM THE BALLROOM...
BECAUSE YOU'RE EVIL!
CLOP CLOP CLOP

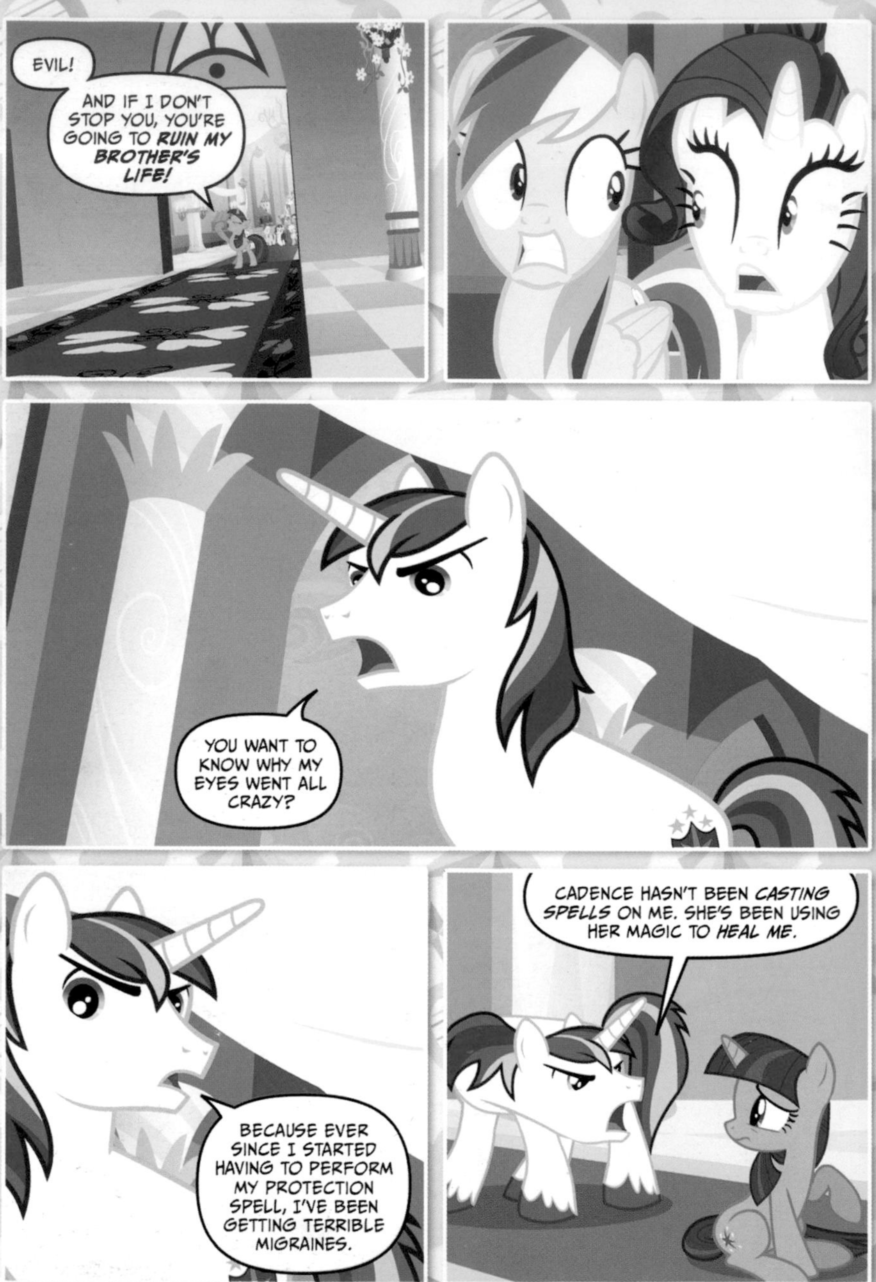
EVIL!
AND IF I DON'T STOP YOU, YOU'RE GOING TO RUIN MY BROTHER'S LIFE!
YOU WANT TO KNOW WHY MY EYES WENT ALL CRAZY?
BECAUSE EVER SINCE I STARTED HAVING TO PERFORM MY PROTECTION SPELL, I'VE BEEN GETTING TERRIBLE MIGRAINES.
CADENCE HASN'T BEEN CASTING SPELLS ON ME. SHE'S BEEN USING HER MAGIC TO HEAL ME.

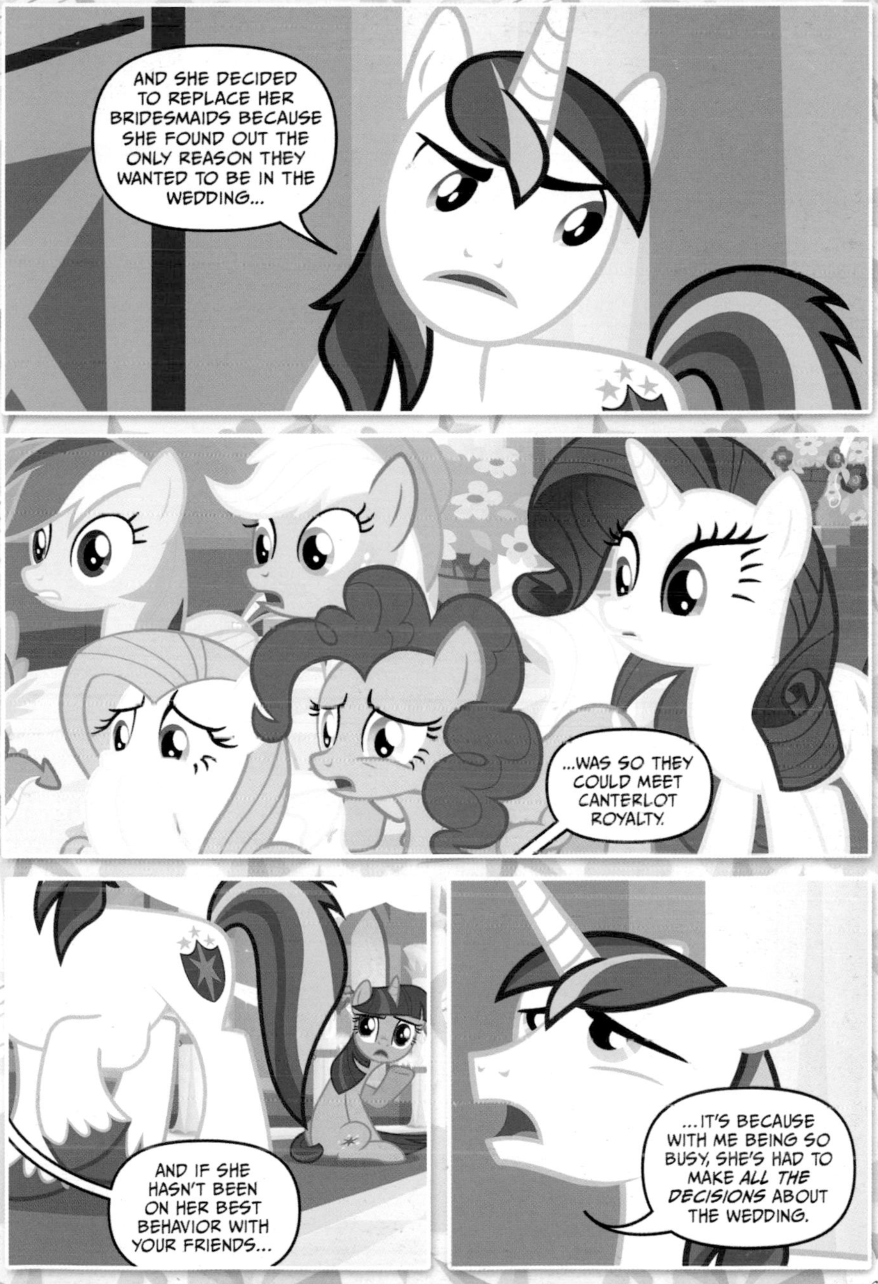
AND SHE DECIDED TO REPLACE HER BRIDESMAIDS BECAUSE SHE FOUND OUT THE ONLY REASON THEY WANTED TO BE IN THE WEDDING...
...WAS SO THEY COULD MEET CANTERLOT ROYALTY.
AND IF SHE HASN'T BEEN ON HER BEST BEHAVIOR WITH YOUR FRIENDS...
...IT'S BECAUSE WITH ME BEING SO BUSY, SHE'S HAD TO MAKE *ALL THE DECISIONS* ABOUT THE WEDDING.

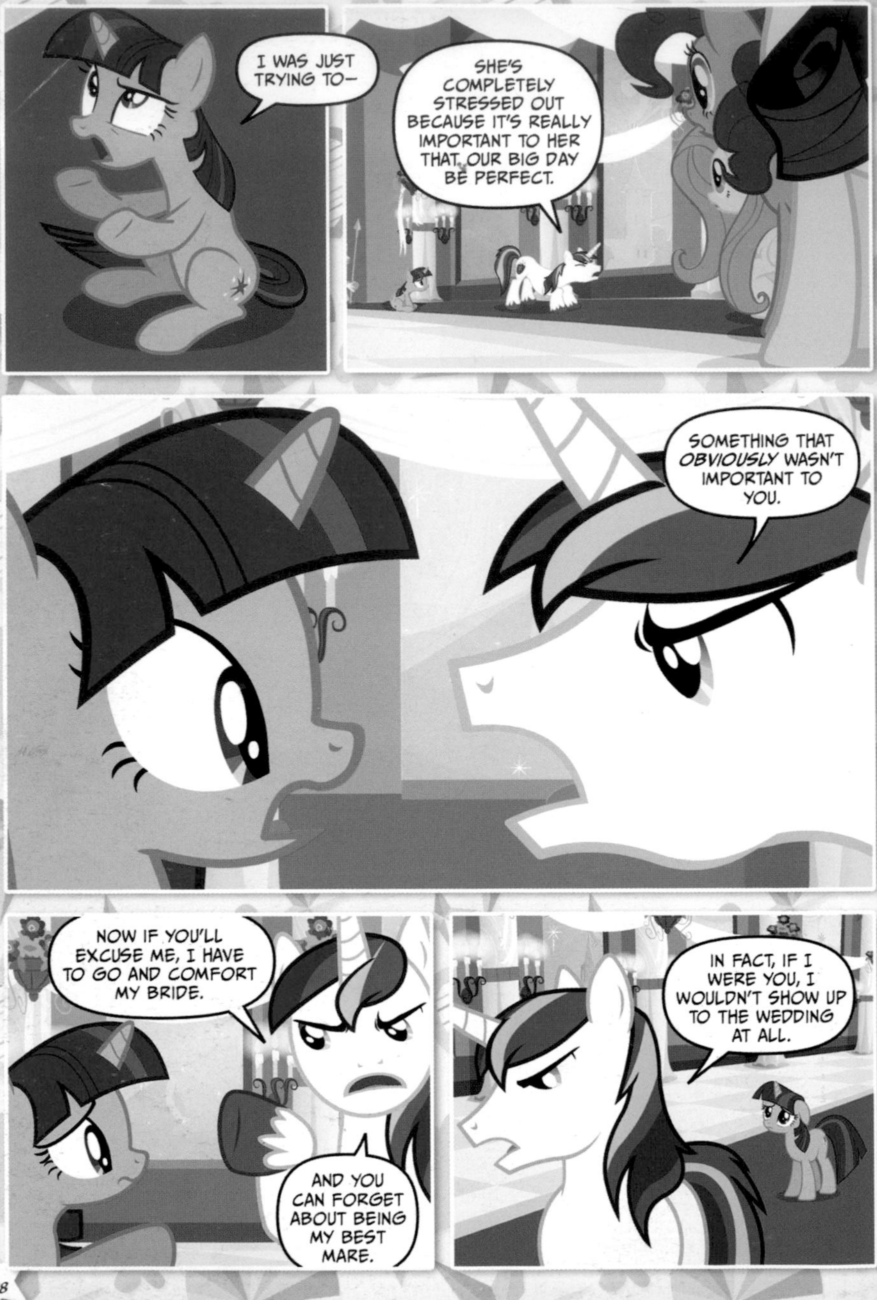
I WAS JUST TRYING TO—
SHE'S COMPLETELY STRESSED OUT BECAUSE IT'S REALLY IMPORTANT TO HER THAT OUR BIG DAY BE PERFECT.
SOMETHING THAT *OBVIOUSLY* WASN'T IMPORTANT TO YOU.
NOW IF YOU'LL EXCUSE ME, I HAVE TO GO AND COMFORT MY BRIDE.
AND YOU CAN FORGET ABOUT BEING MY BEST MARE.
IN FACT, IF I WERE YOU, I WOULDN'T SHOW UP TO THE WEDDING AT ALL.

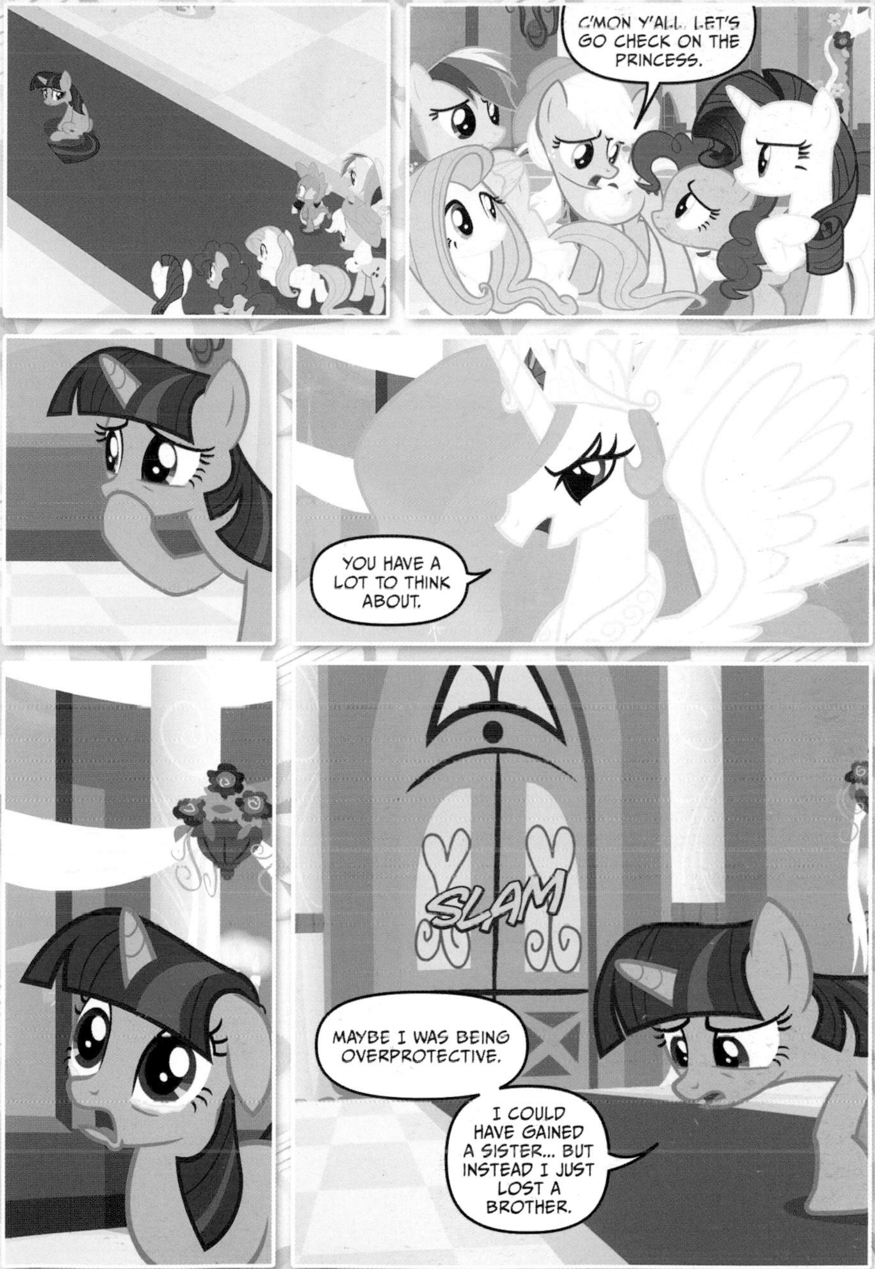
C'MON Y'ALL. LET'S GO CHECK ON THE PRINCESS.
YOU HAVE A LOT TO THINK ABOUT.
SLAM
MAYBE I WAS BEING OVERPROTECTIVE.
I COULD HAVE GAINED A SISTER... BUT INSTEAD I JUST LOST A BROTHER.

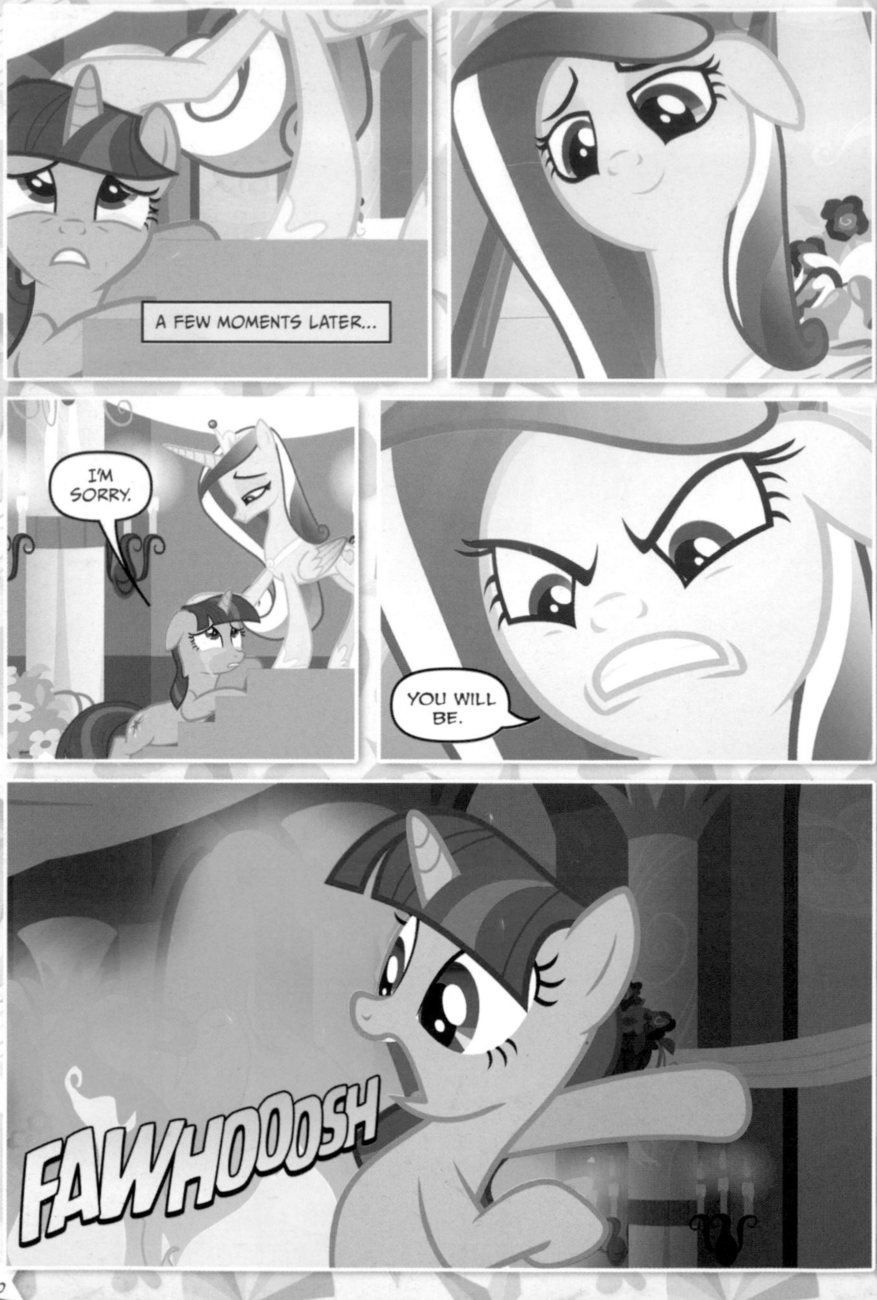
A FEW MOMENTS LATER...
I'M SORRY.
YOU WILL BE.
FAWHOOOSH

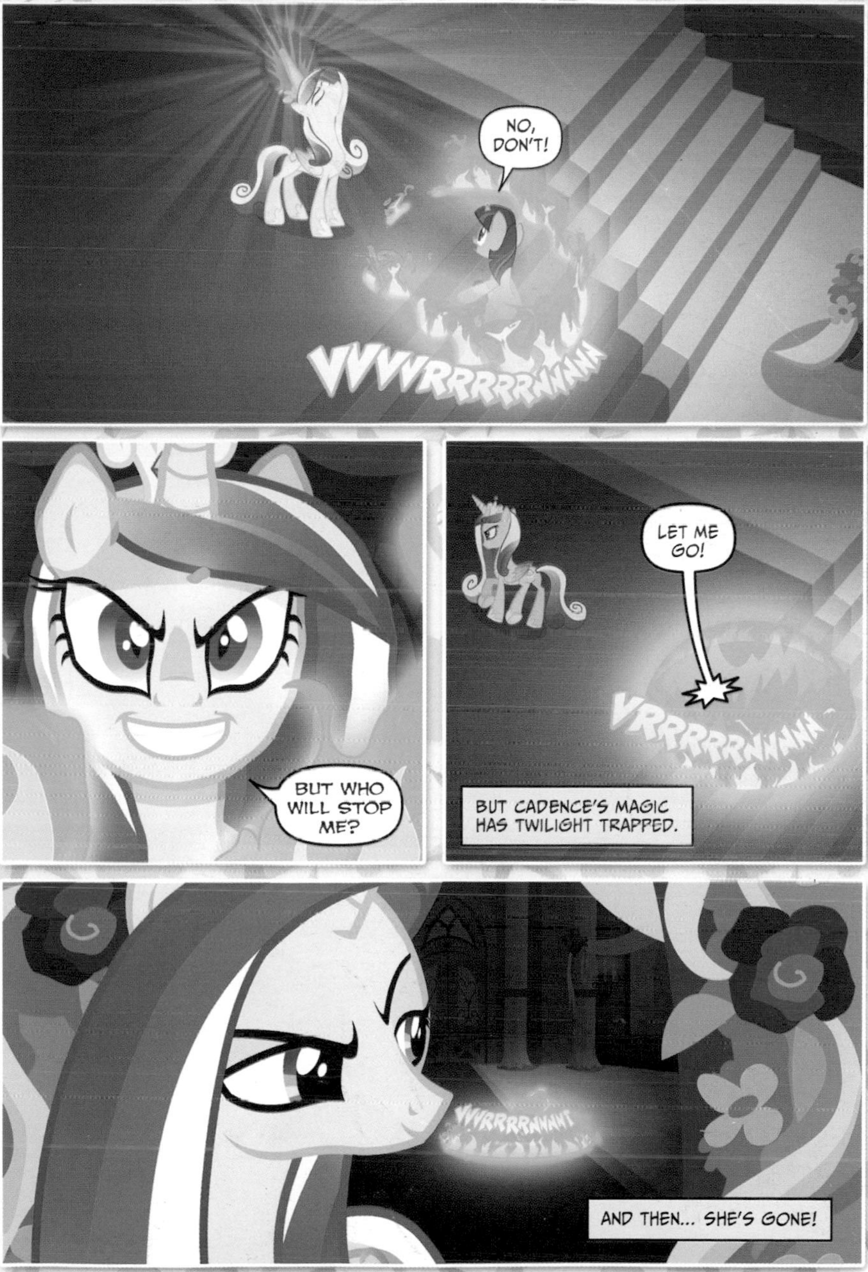
NO, DON'T!
VVVVRRRRRNNNN
BUT WHO WILL STOP ME?
LET ME GO!
VRRRRRNNNN
BUT CADENCE'S MAGIC HAS TWILIGHT TRAPPED.
VVVRRRRNNNNT
AND THEN... SHE'S GONE!

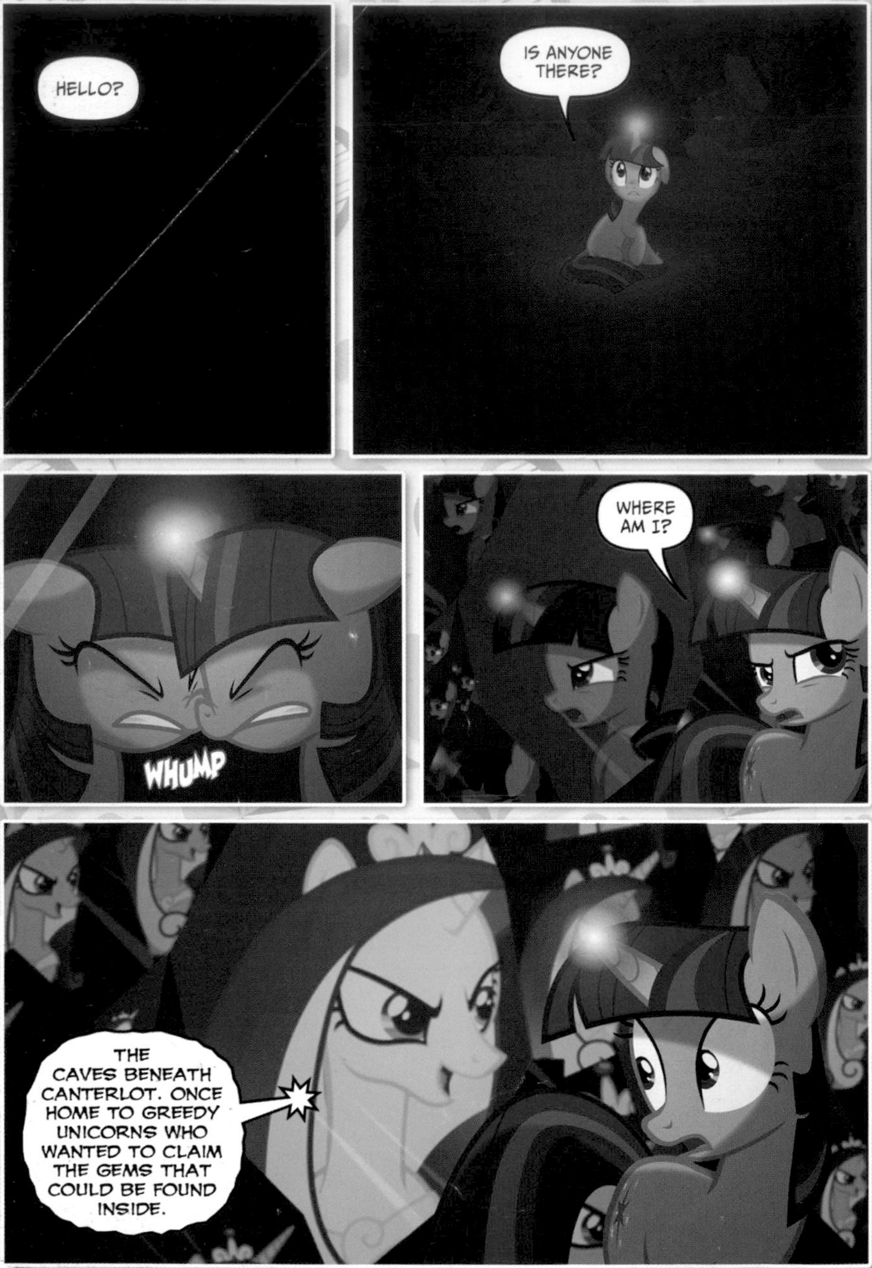
HELLO?
IS ANYONE THERE?
WHUMP
WHERE AM I?
THE CAVES BENEATH CANTERLOT. ONCE HOME TO GREEDY UNICORNS WHO WANTED TO CLAIM THE GEMS THAT COULD BE FOUND INSIDE.

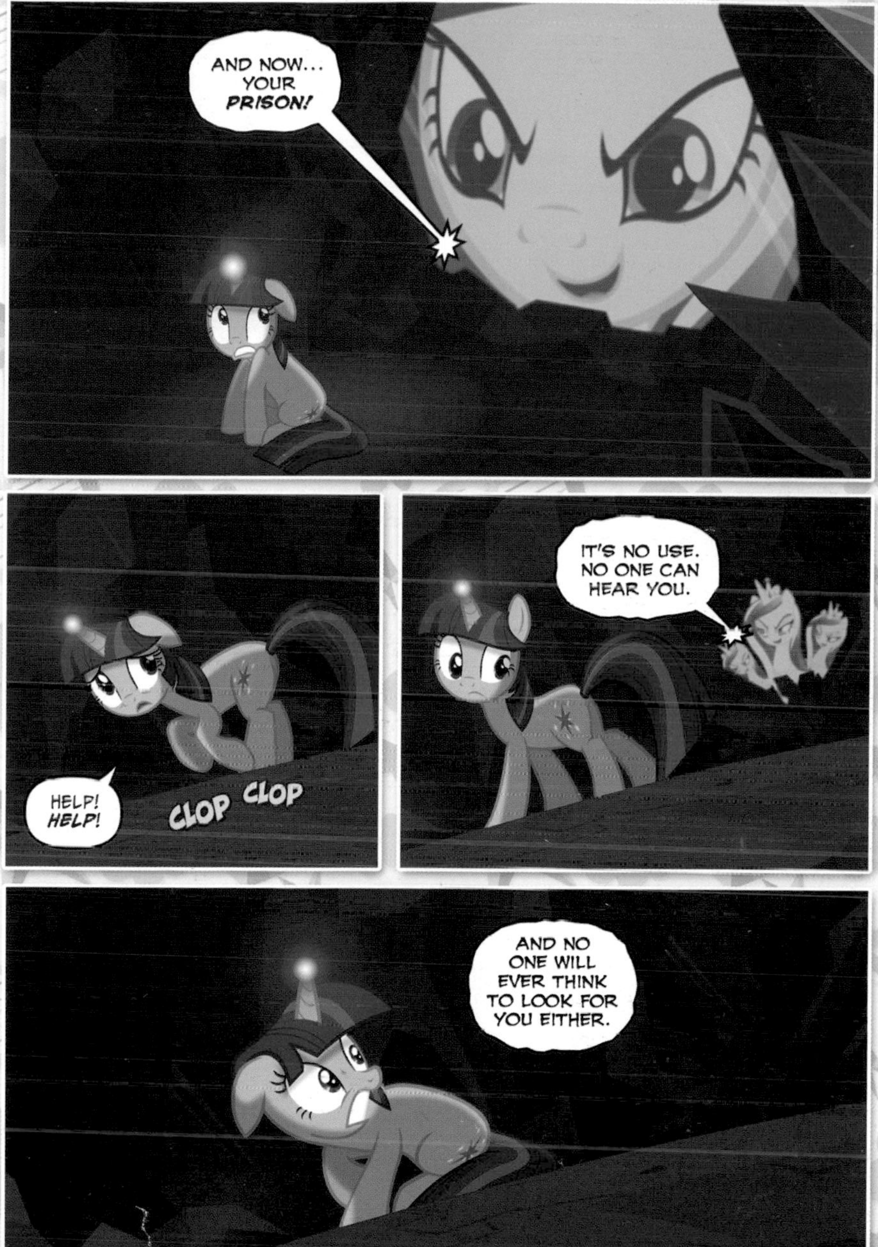
AND NOW... YOUR PRISON!
HELP! HELP!
CLOP CLOP
IT'S NO USE. NO ONE CAN HEAR YOU.
AND NO ONE WILL EVER THINK TO LOOK FOR YOU EITHER.

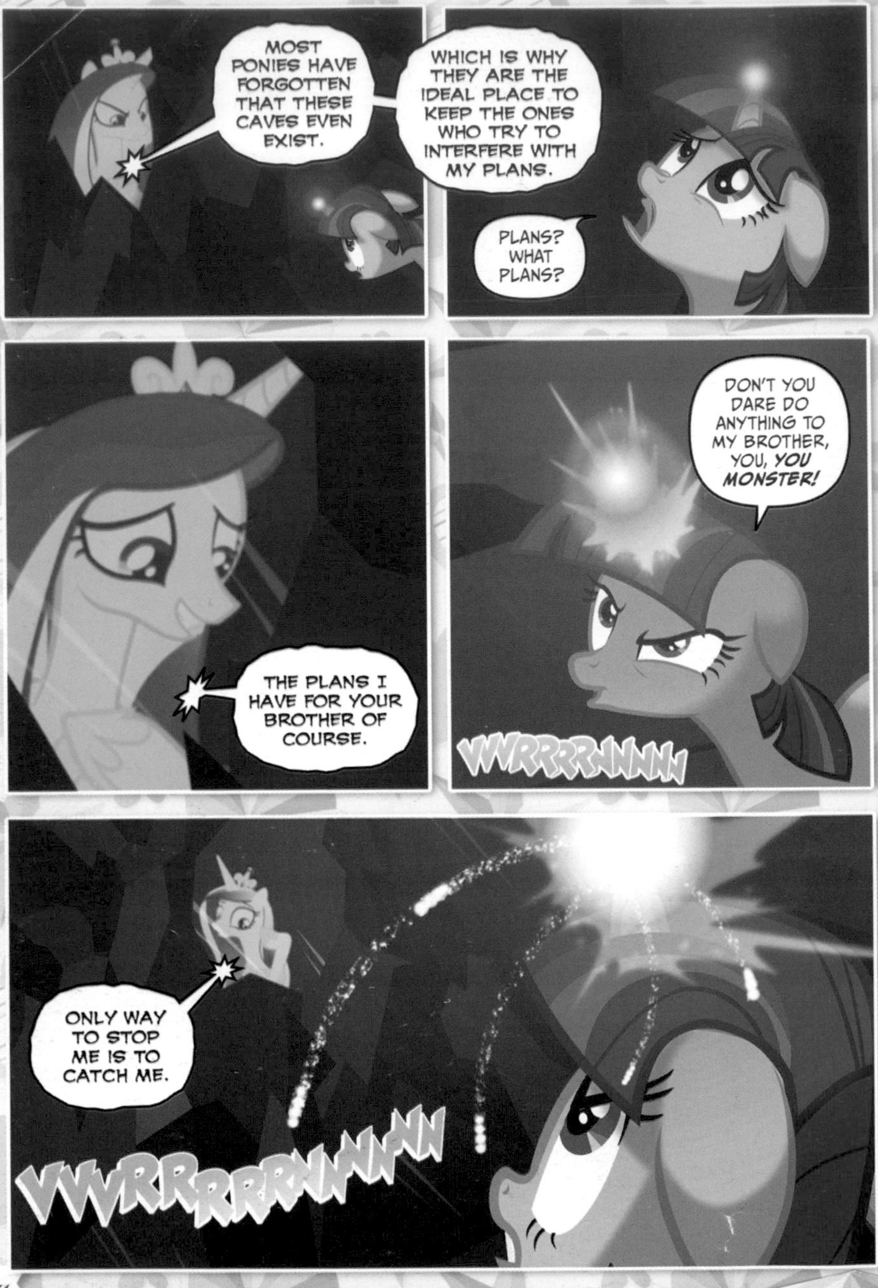
MOST PONIES HAVE FORGOTTEN THAT THESE CAVES EVEN EXIST.
WHICH IS WHY THEY ARE THE IDEAL PLACE TO KEEP THE ONES WHO TRY TO INTERFERE WITH MY PLANS.
PLANS? WHAT PLANS?
THE PLANS I HAVE FOR YOUR BROTHER OF COURSE.
DON'T YOU DARE DO ANYTHING TO MY BROTHER, YOU, ***YOU MONSTER!***
VVVRRRRRNNNNN
ONLY WAY TO STOP ME IS TO CATCH ME.
VVVRRRRRRNNNNNN

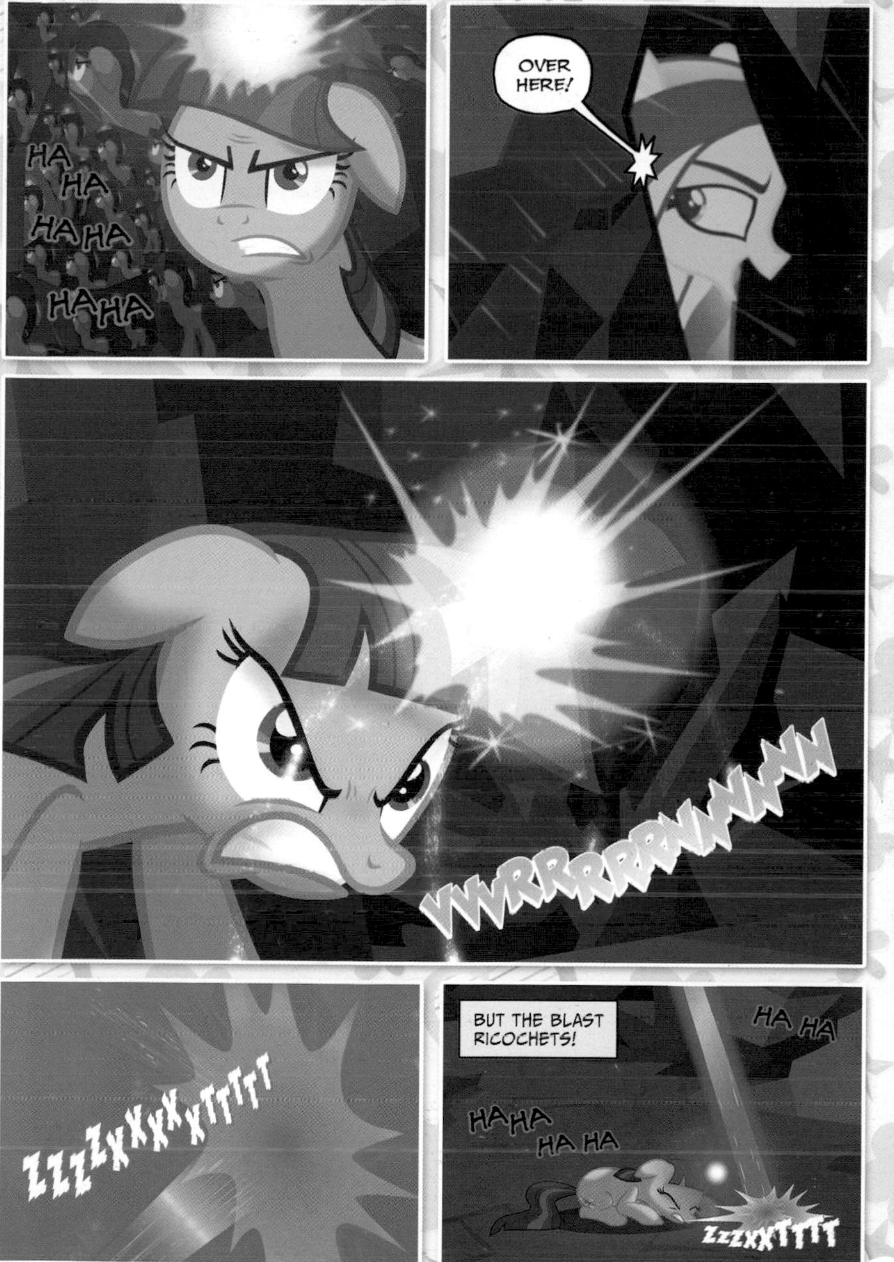
HA HA HA HA HA HA
OVER HERE!
VVVRRRRRNNNNNN
ZZZZXXXXXTTTTT
BUT THE BLAST RICOCHETS!
HA HA
HA HA HA HA
ZZZXXTTTT

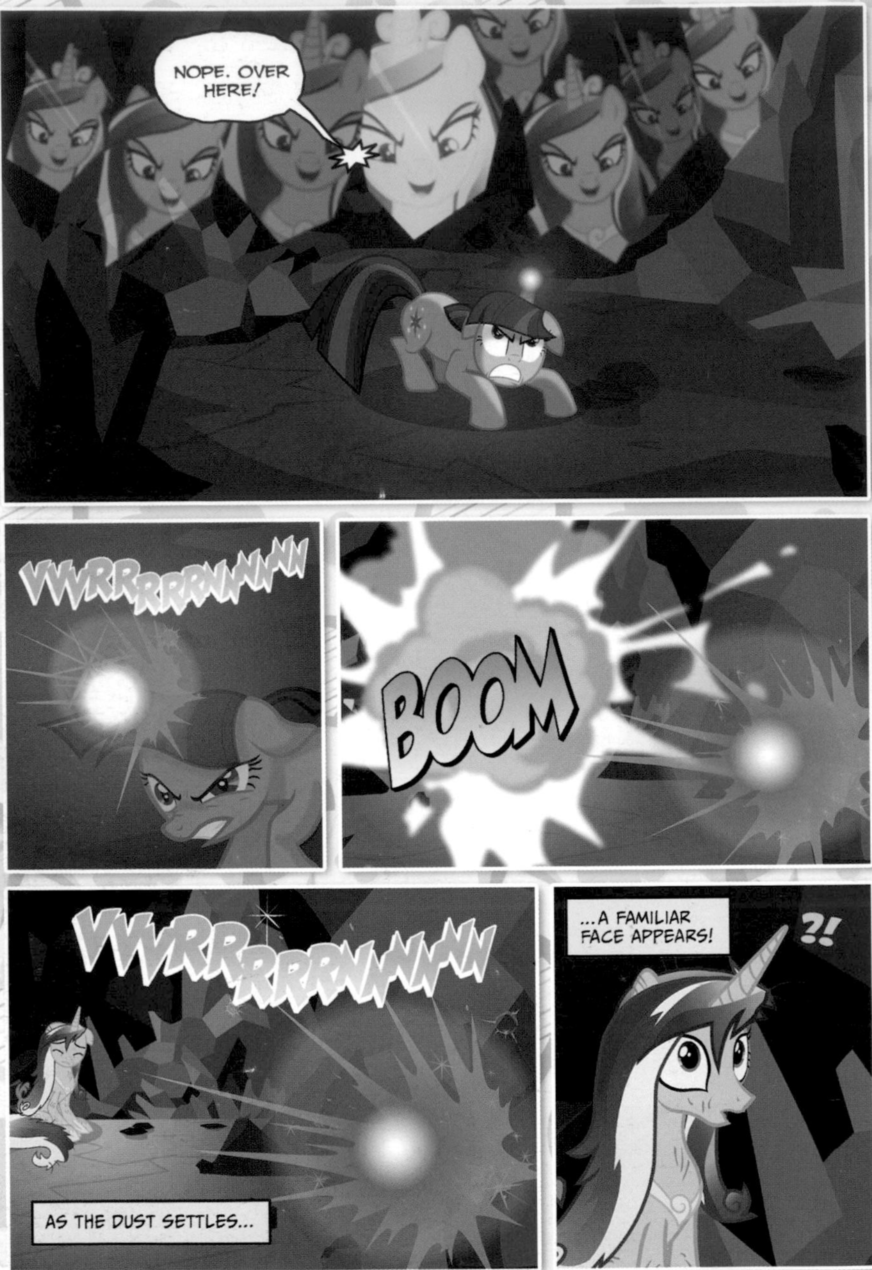

NOPE. OVER HERE!
VVVRRRRRNNNNN
BOOM
VVVRRRRRNNNNNN
AS THE DUST SETTLES...
...A FAMILIAR FACE APPEARS!
?!

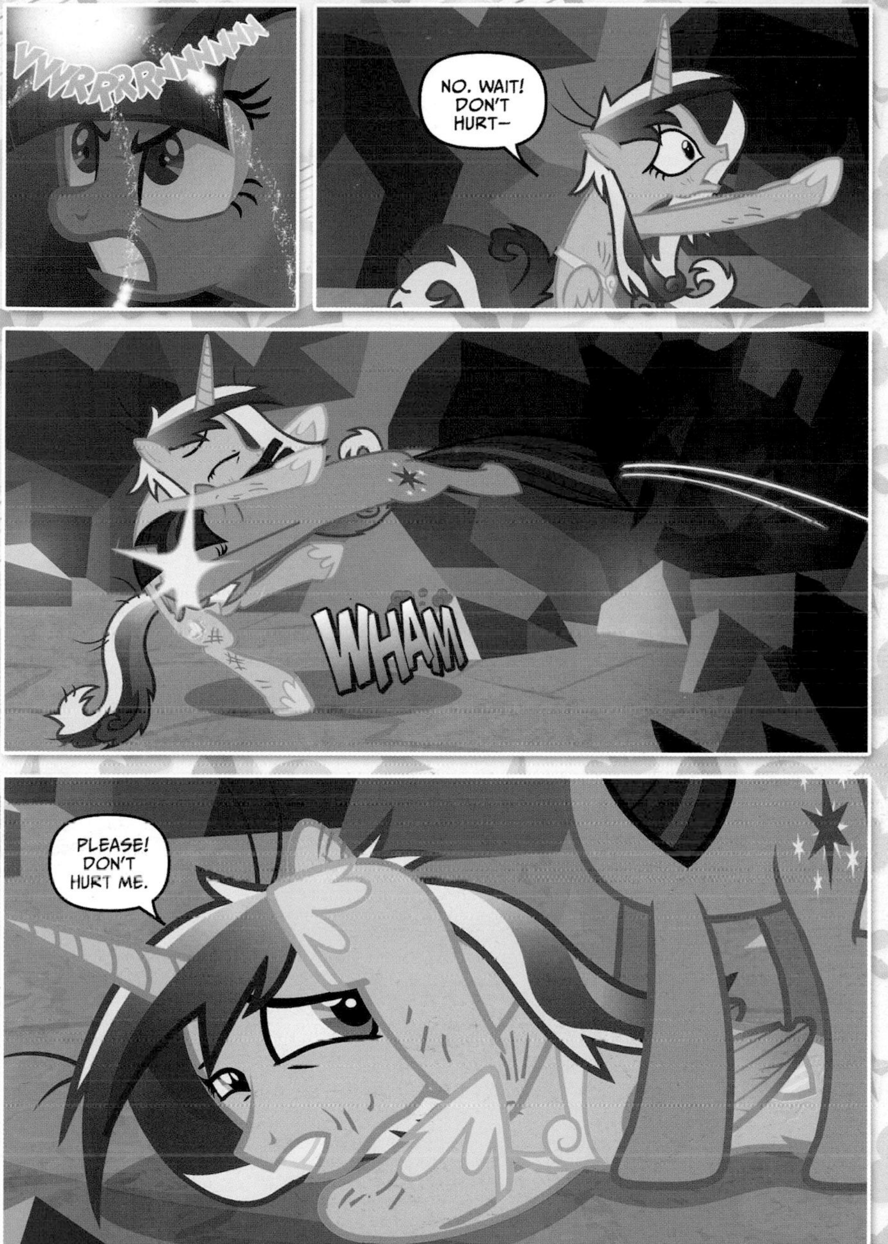
VWRRRRNNNNN
NO. WAIT! DON'T HURT–
WHAM
PLEASE! DON'T HURT ME.

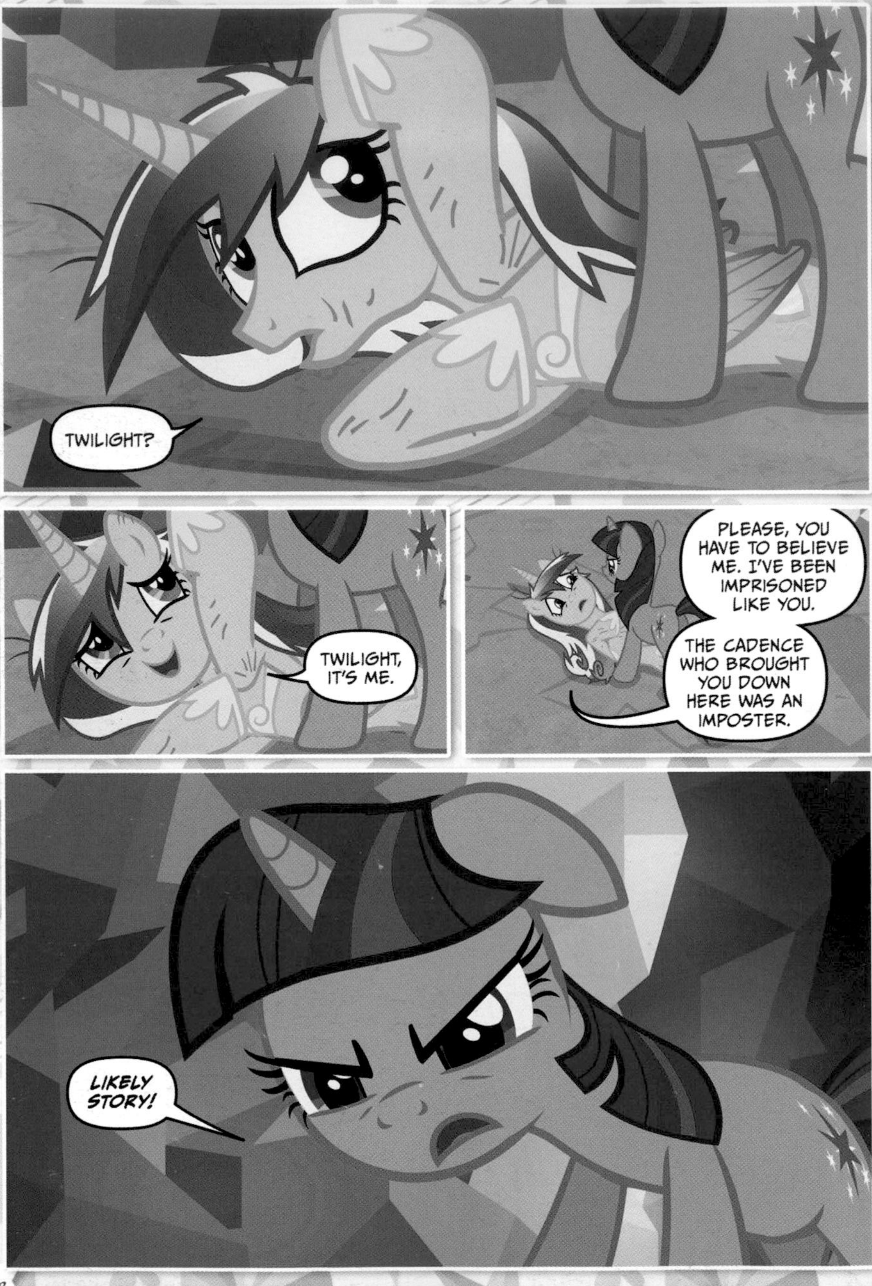
TWILIGHT?
TWILIGHT, IT'S ME.
PLEASE, YOU HAVE TO BELIEVE ME. I'VE BEEN IMPRISONED LIKE YOU.
THE CADENCE WHO BROUGHT YOU DOWN HERE WAS AN IMPOSTER.
LIKELY STORY!

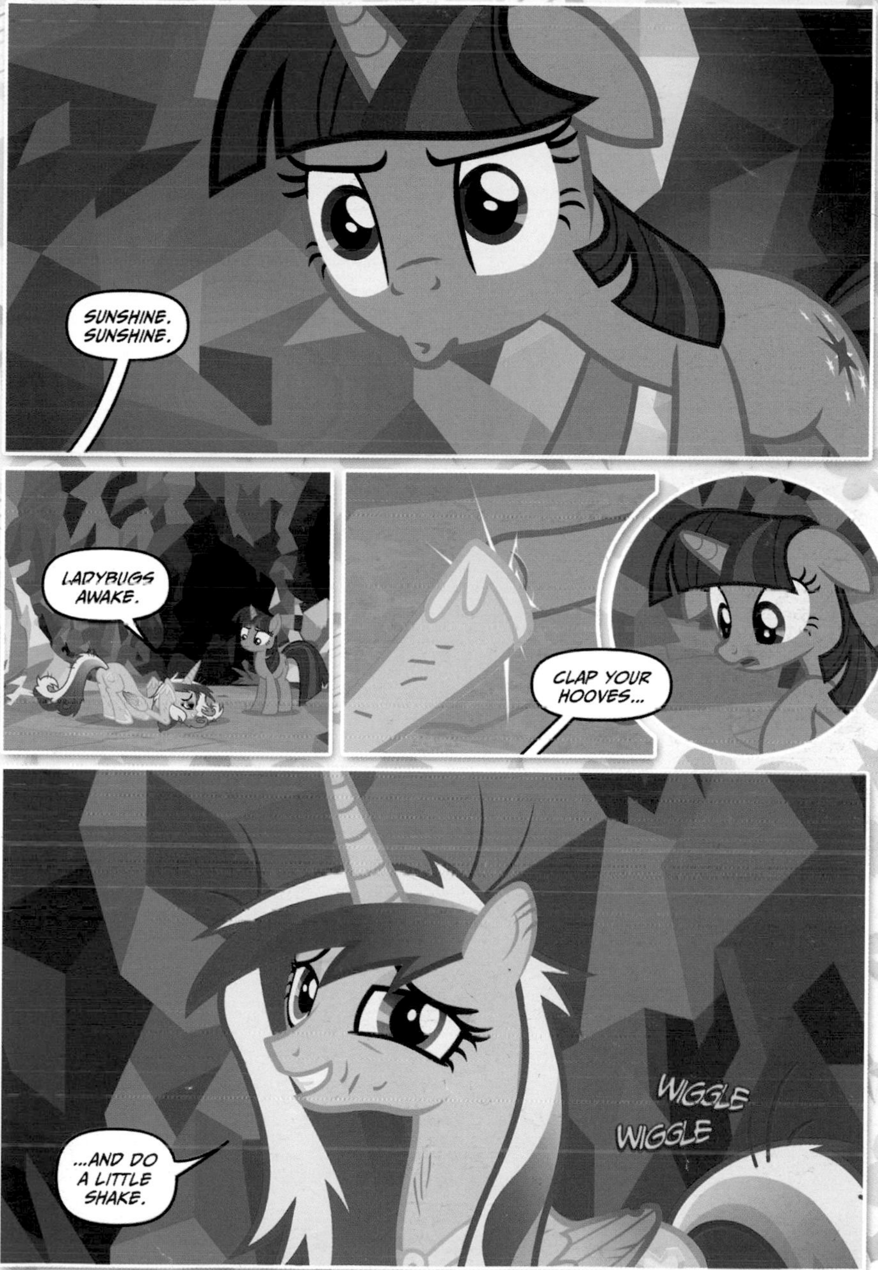
SUNSHINE. SUNSHINE.
LADYBUGS AWAKE.
CLAP YOUR HOOVES...
...AND DO A LITTLE SHAKE.
WIGGLE
WIGGLE

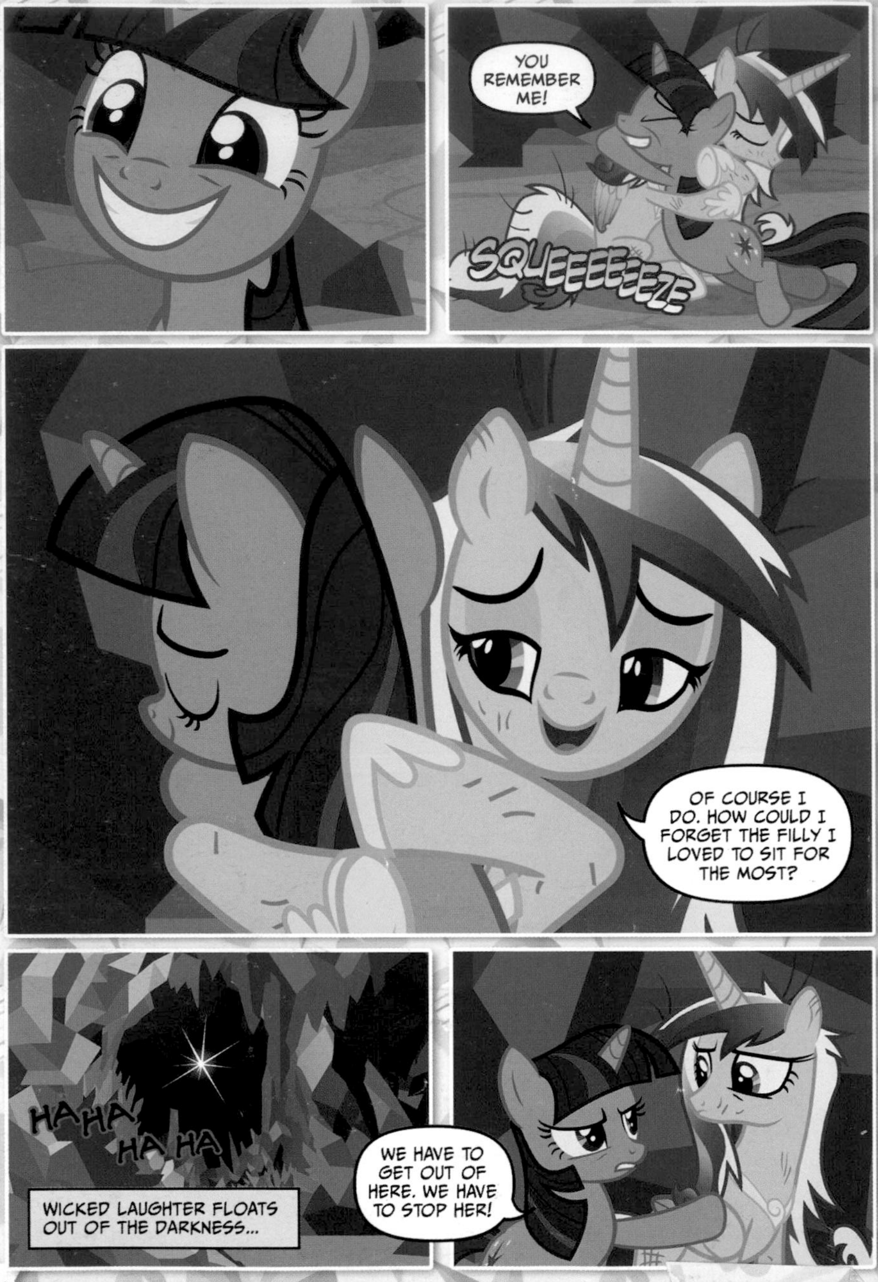
YOU REMEMBER ME!
SQUEEEEEEEEZE
OF COURSE I DO. HOW COULD I FORGET THE FILLY I LOVED TO SIT FOR THE MOST?
HA HA HA HA
WICKED LAUGHTER FLOATS OUT OF THE DARKNESS...
WE HAVE TO GET OUT OF HERE. WE HAVE TO STOP HER!

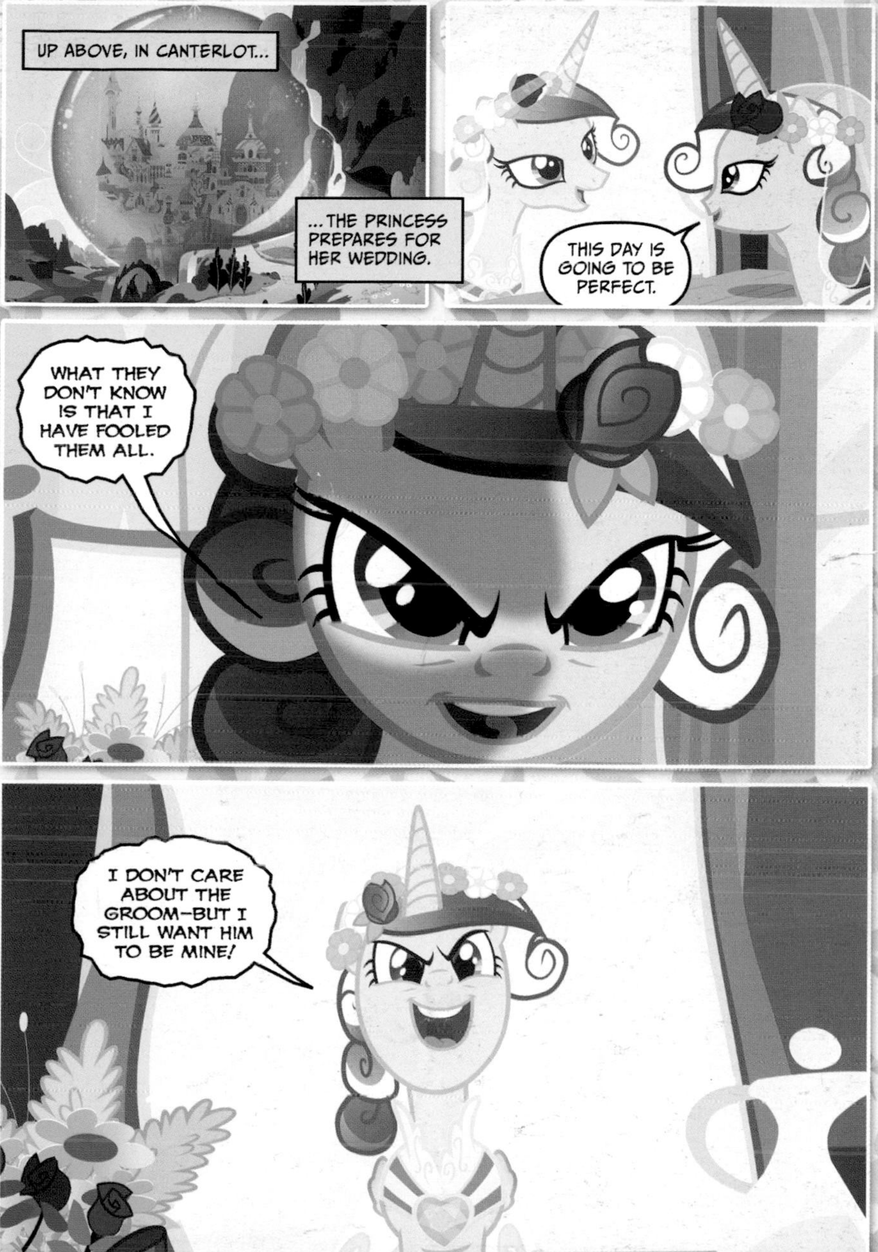
UP ABOVE, IN CANTERLOT...
...THE PRINCESS PREPARES FOR HER WEDDING.
THIS DAY IS GOING TO BE PERFECT.
WHAT THEY DON'T KNOW IS THAT I HAVE FOOLED THEM ALL.
I DON'T CARE ABOUT THE GROOM—BUT I STILL WANT HIM TO BE MINE!

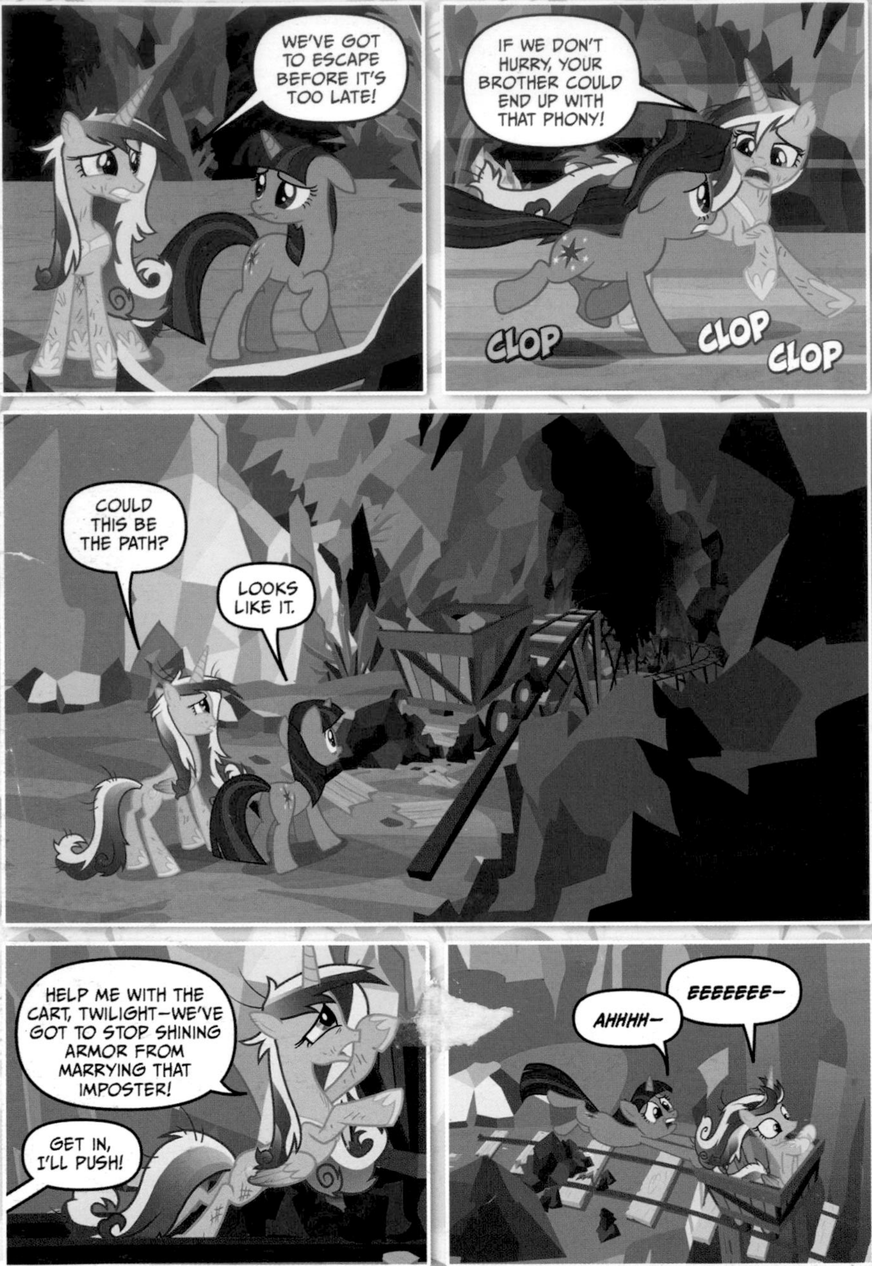
WE'VE GOT TO ESCAPE BEFORE IT'S TOO LATE!
IF WE DON'T HURRY, YOUR BROTHER COULD END UP WITH THAT PHONY!
CLOP
CLOP
CLOP
COULD THIS BE THE PATH?
LOOKS LIKE IT.
HELP ME WITH THE CART, TWILIGHT—WE'VE GOT TO STOP SHINING ARMOR FROM MARRYING THAT IMPOSTER!
GET IN, I'LL PUSH!
AHHHH—
EEEEEEE—

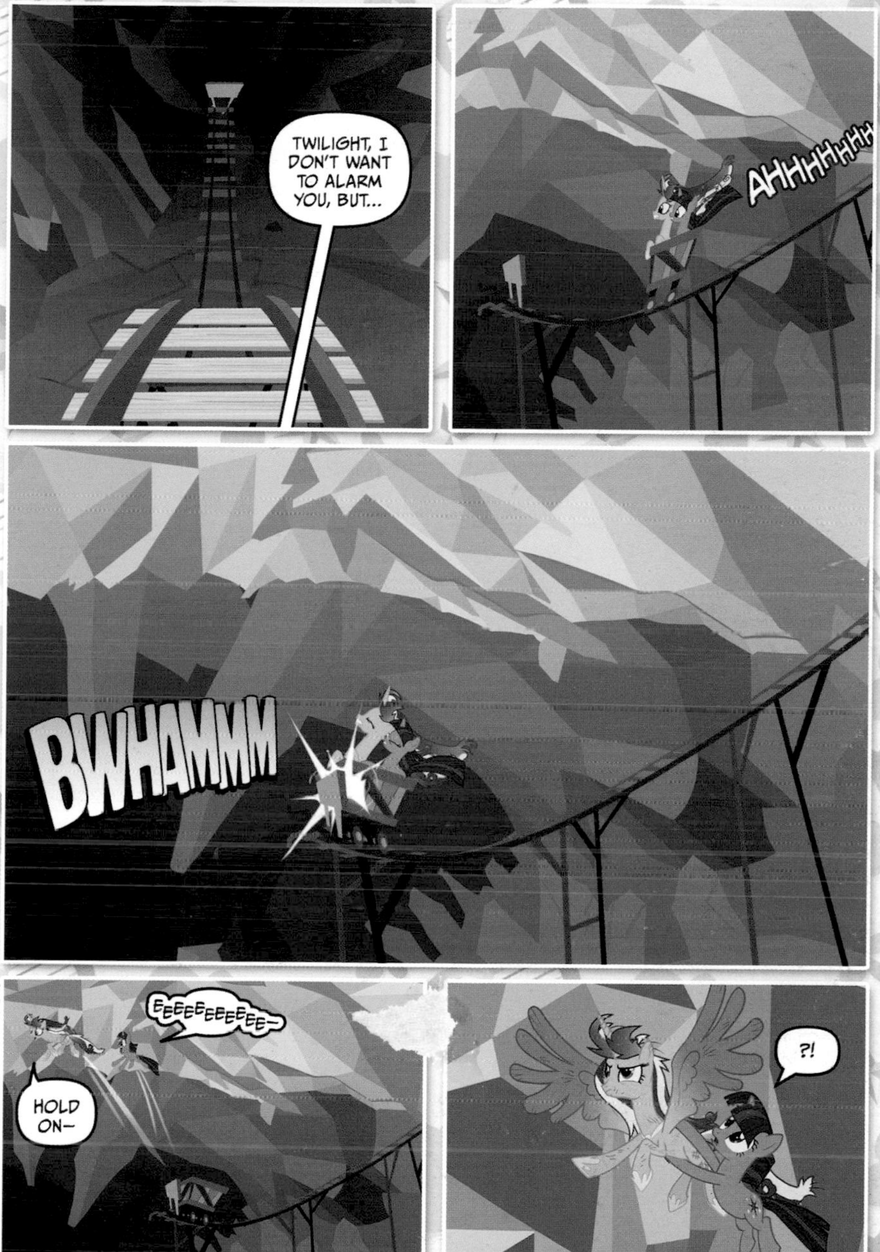

TWILIGHT, I DON'T WANT TO ALARM YOU, BUT...
AHHHHHHH
BWHAMMM
EEEEEEEEEEEE–
HOLD ON–
?!

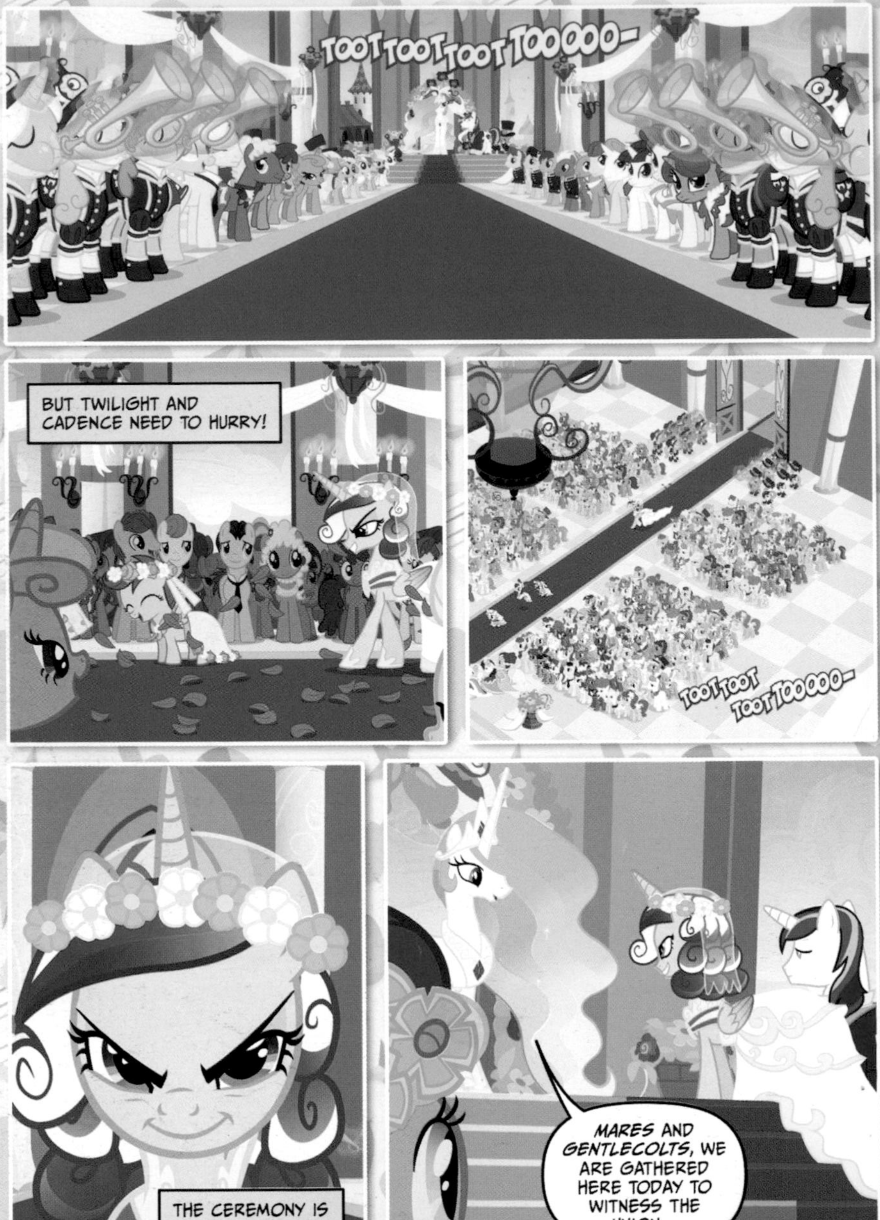
TOOT TOOT TOOT TOOOOO-
BUT TWILIGHT AND CADENCE NEED TO HURRY!
TOOT TOOT TOOT TOOOOO-
THE CEREMONY IS ABOUT TO BEGIN!
MARES AND GENTLECOLTS, WE ARE GATHERED HERE TODAY TO WITNESS THE UNION...

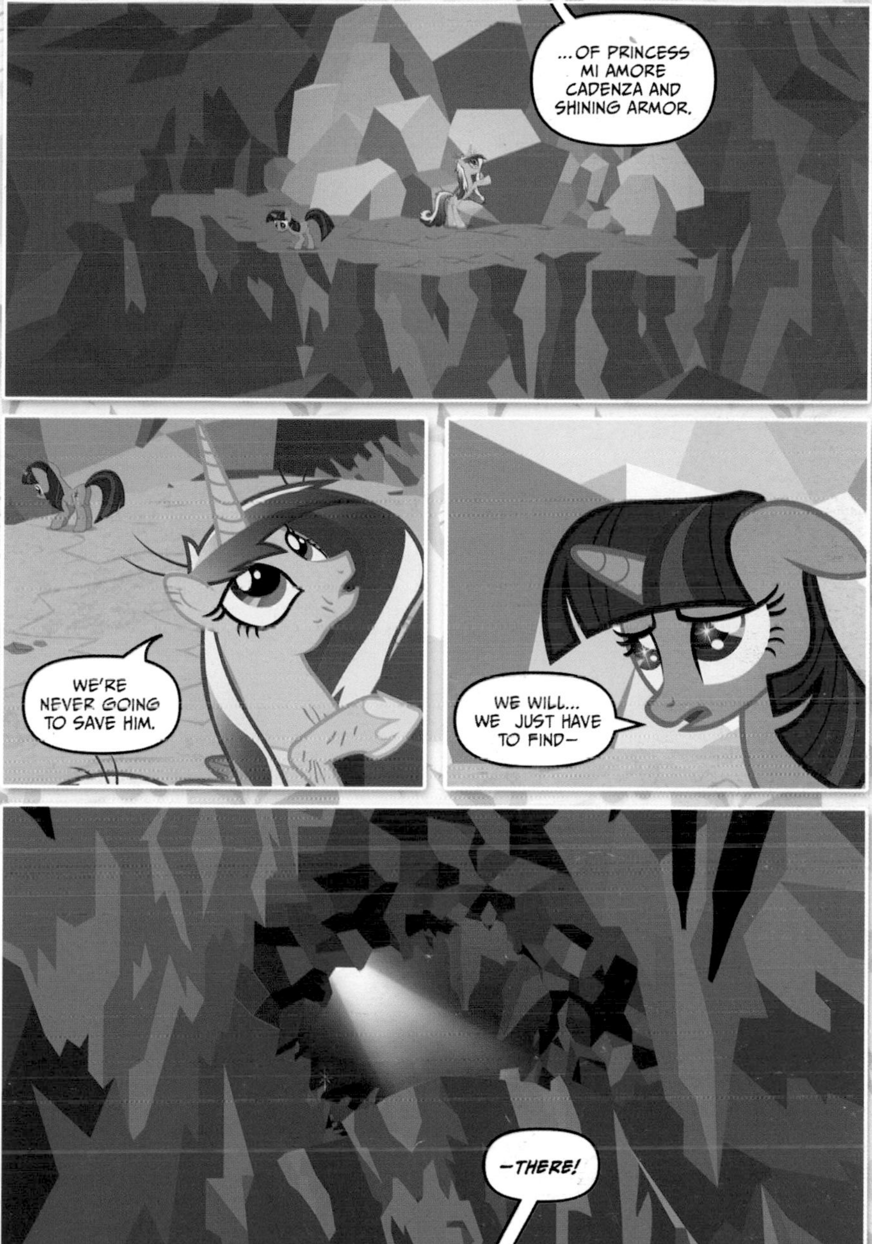
...OF PRINCESS MI AMORE CADENZA AND SHINING ARMOR.
WE'RE NEVER GOING TO SAVE HIM.
WE WILL... WE JUST HAVE TO FIND—
—THERE!

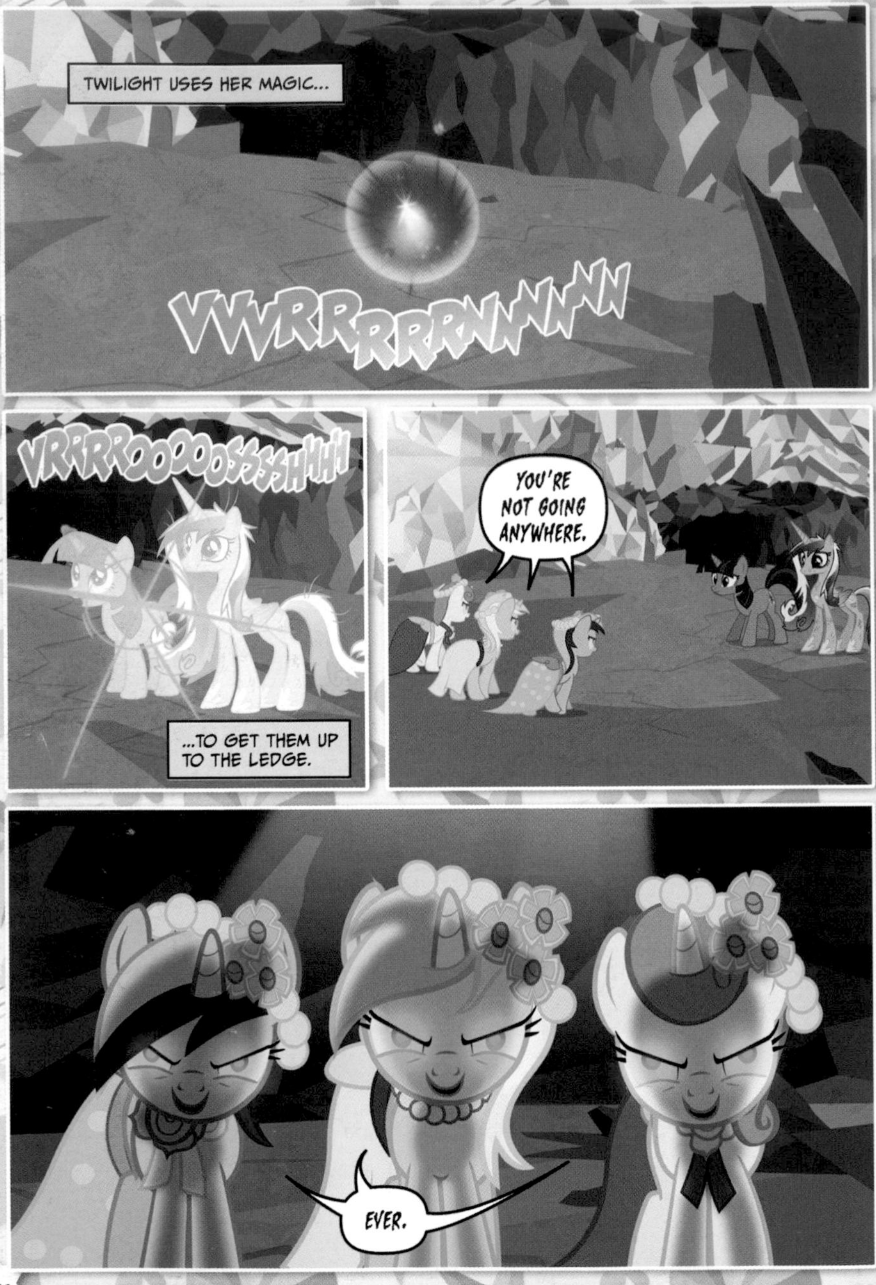
TWILIGHT USES HER MAGIC...
VVVRRRRRRNNNNNN
VRRRRROOOOOSSSSHHHH
...TO GET THEM UP TO THE LEDGE.
YOU'RE NOT GOING ANYWHERE.
EVER.

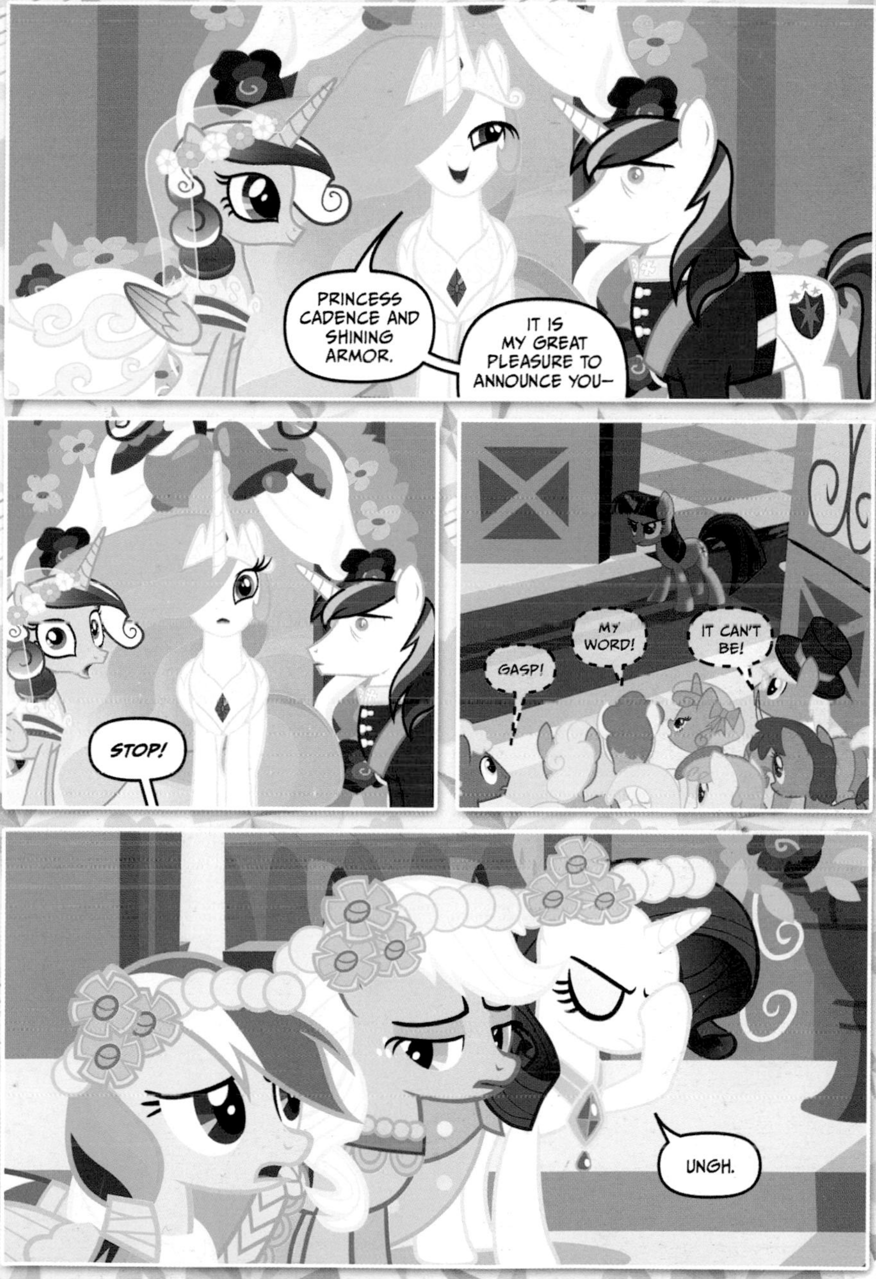

PRINCESS CADENCE AND SHINING ARMOR.
IT IS MY GREAT PLEASURE TO ANNOUNCE YOU–
STOP!
GASP!
MY WORD!
IT CAN'T BE!
UNGH.

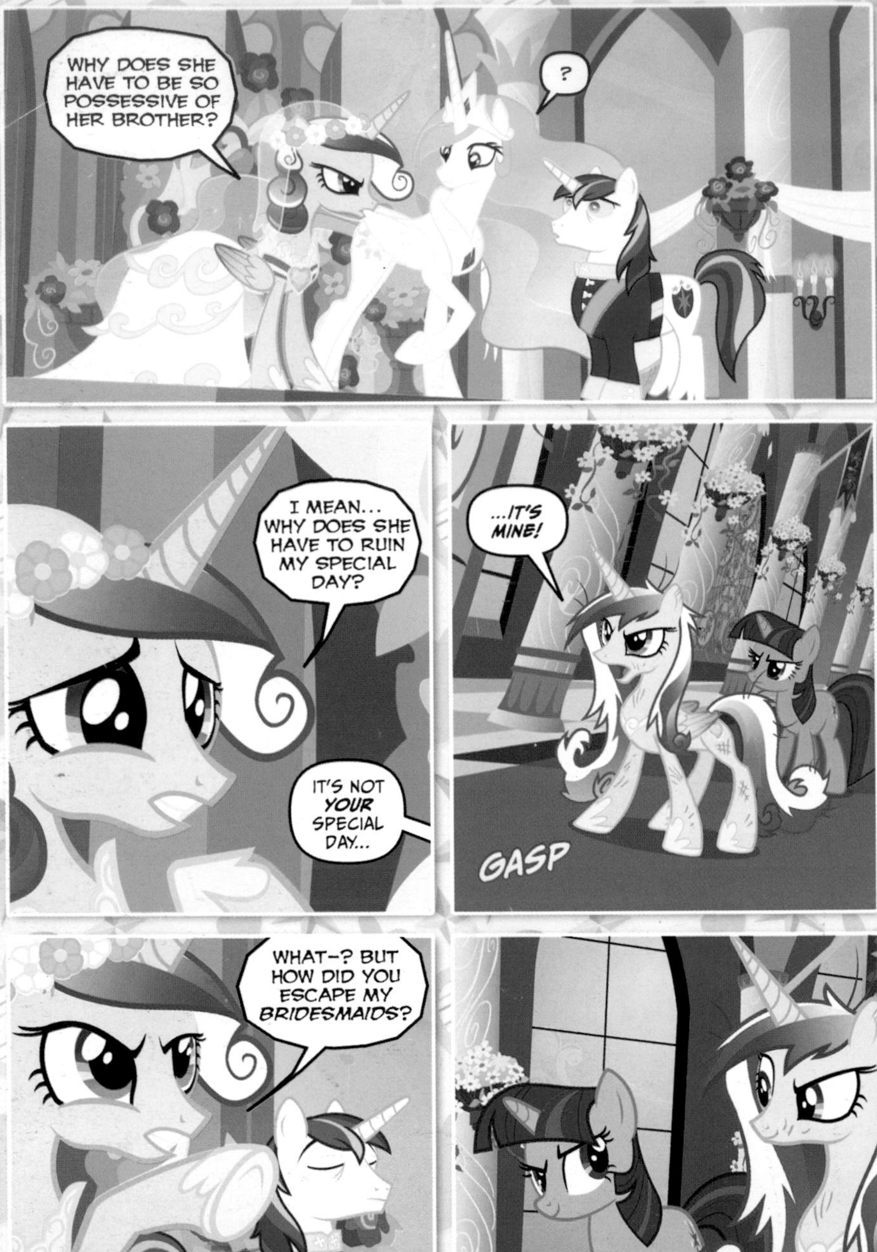
WHY DOES SHE HAVE TO BE SO POSSESSIVE OF HER BROTHER?
?
I MEAN... WHY DOES SHE HAVE TO RUIN MY SPECIAL DAY?
IT'S NOT *YOUR* SPECIAL DAY...
...IT'S MINE!
GASP
WHAT-? BUT HOW DID YOU ESCAPE MY *BRIDESMAIDS*?

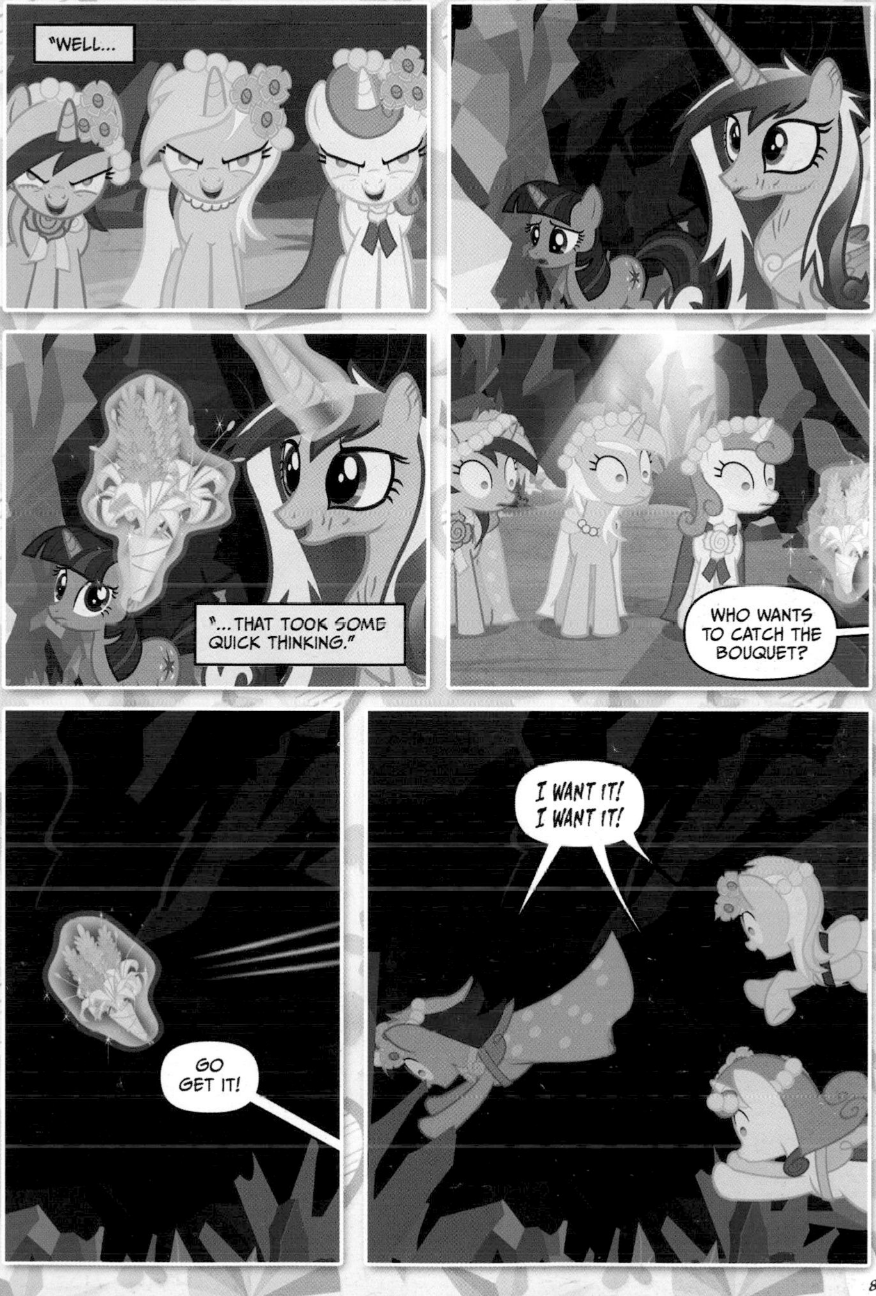
"WELL...
"...THAT TOOK SOME QUICK THINKING."
WHO WANTS TO CATCH THE BOUQUET?
GO GET IT!
I WANT IT! I WANT IT!

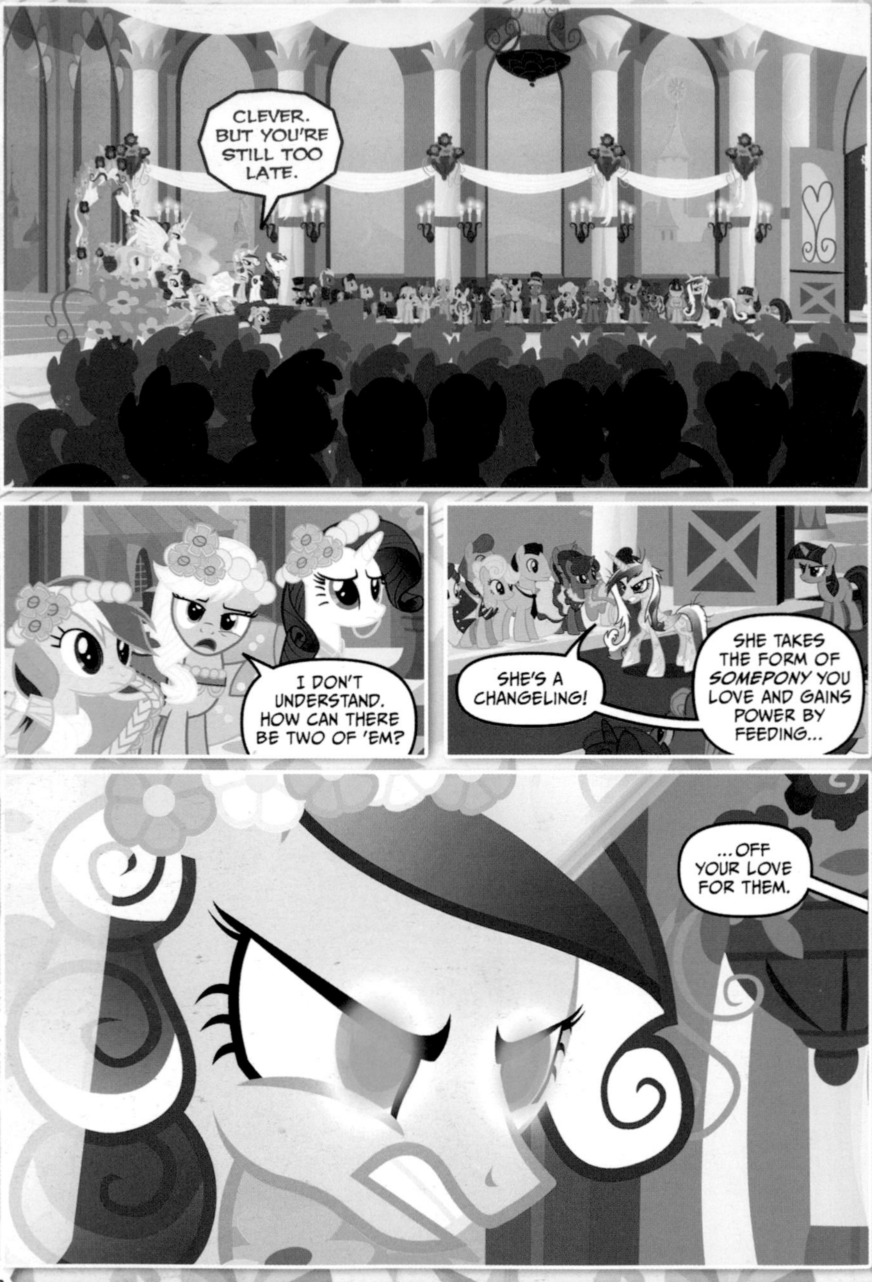
CLEVER. BUT YOU'RE STILL TOO LATE.
I DON'T UNDERSTAND. HOW CAN THERE BE TWO OF 'EM?
SHE'S A CHANGELING!
SHE TAKES THE FORM OF SOMEPONY YOU LOVE AND GAINS POWER BY FEEDING...
...OFF YOUR LOVE FOR THEM.

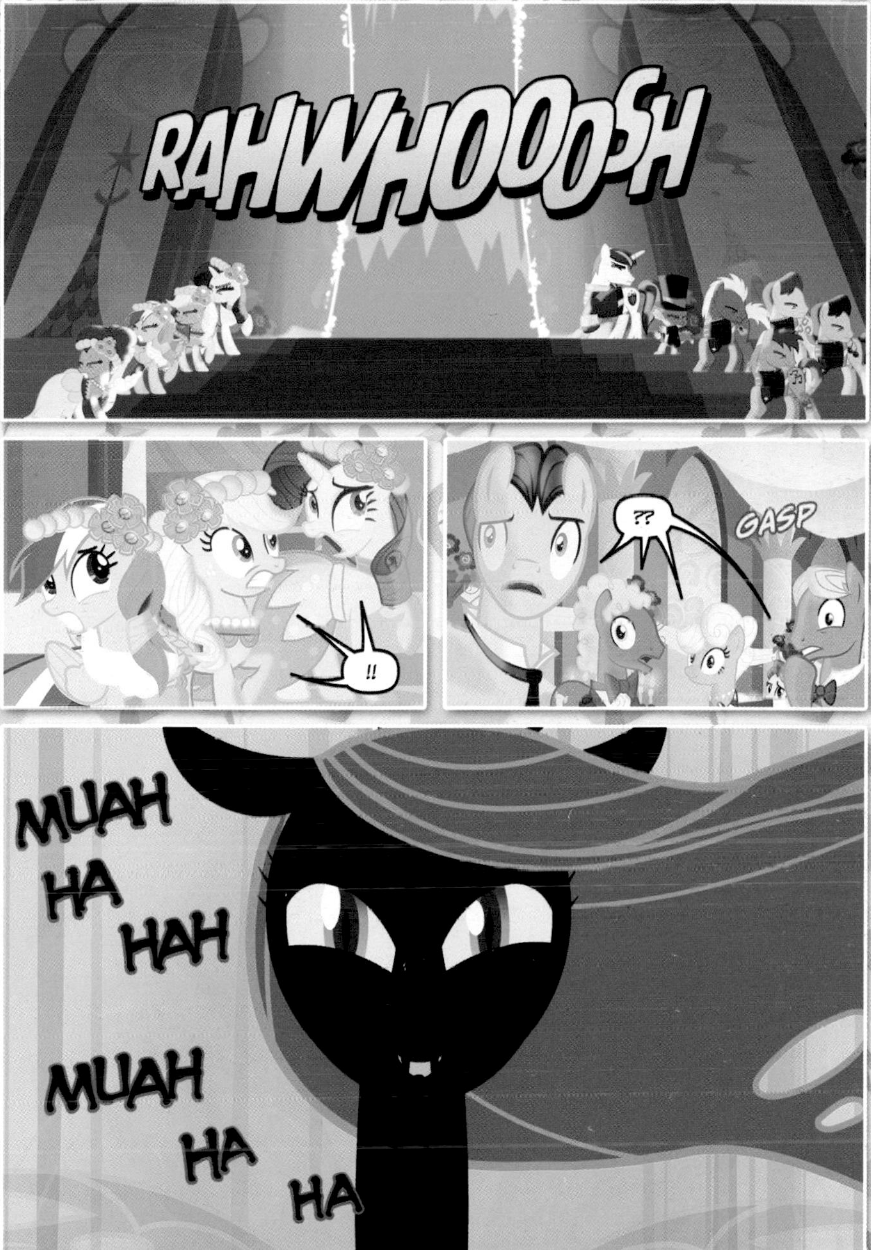
RAHWHOOOOSH
!!
??
GASP
MUAH HA HAH
MUAH HA HA

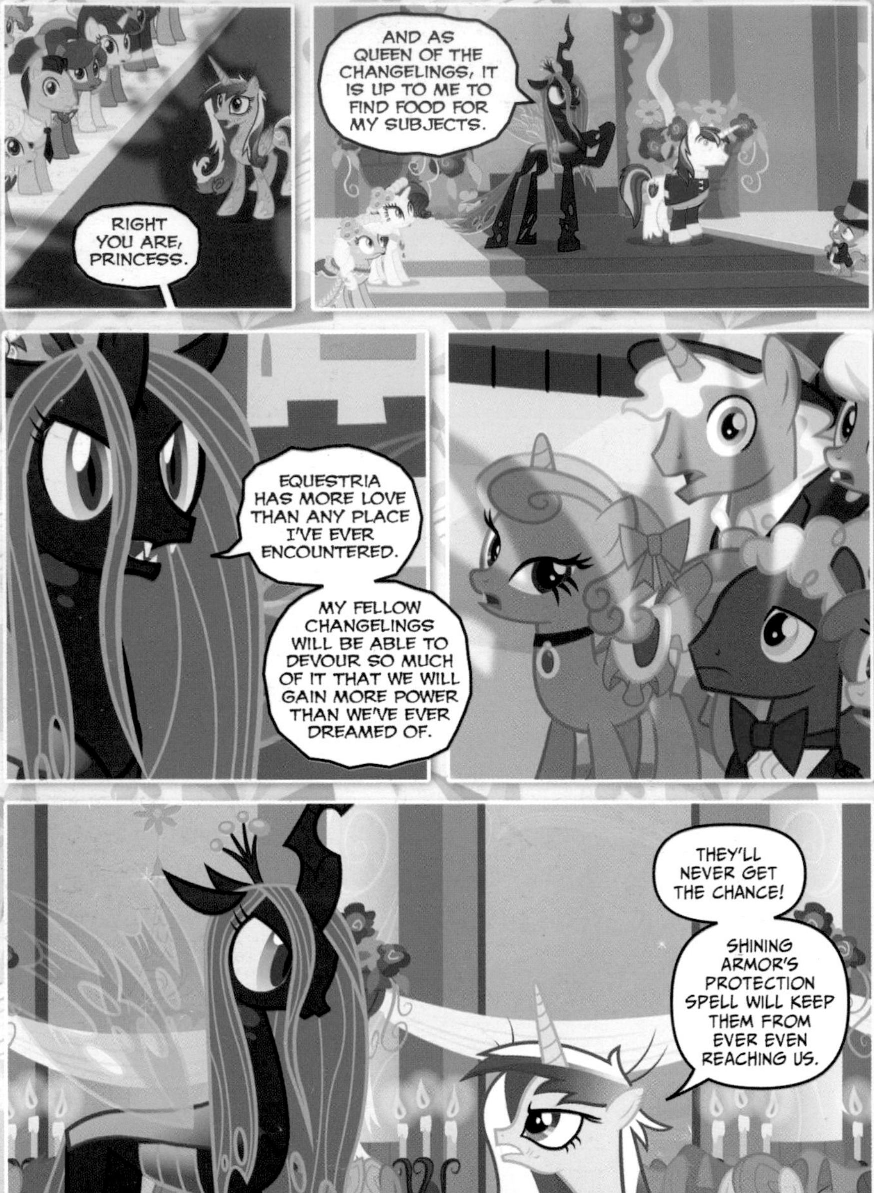
RIGHT YOU ARE, PRINCESS.
AND AS QUEEN OF THE CHANGELINGS, IT IS UP TO ME TO FIND FOOD FOR MY SUBJECTS.
EQUESTRIA HAS MORE LOVE THAN ANY PLACE I'VE EVER ENCOUNTERED.
MY FELLOW CHANGELINGS WILL BE ABLE TO DEVOUR SO MUCH OF IT THAT WE WILL GAIN MORE POWER THAN WE'VE EVER DREAMED OF.
THEY'LL NEVER GET THE CHANCE!
SHINING ARMOR'S PROTECTION SPELL WILL KEEP THEM FROM EVER EVEN REACHING US.

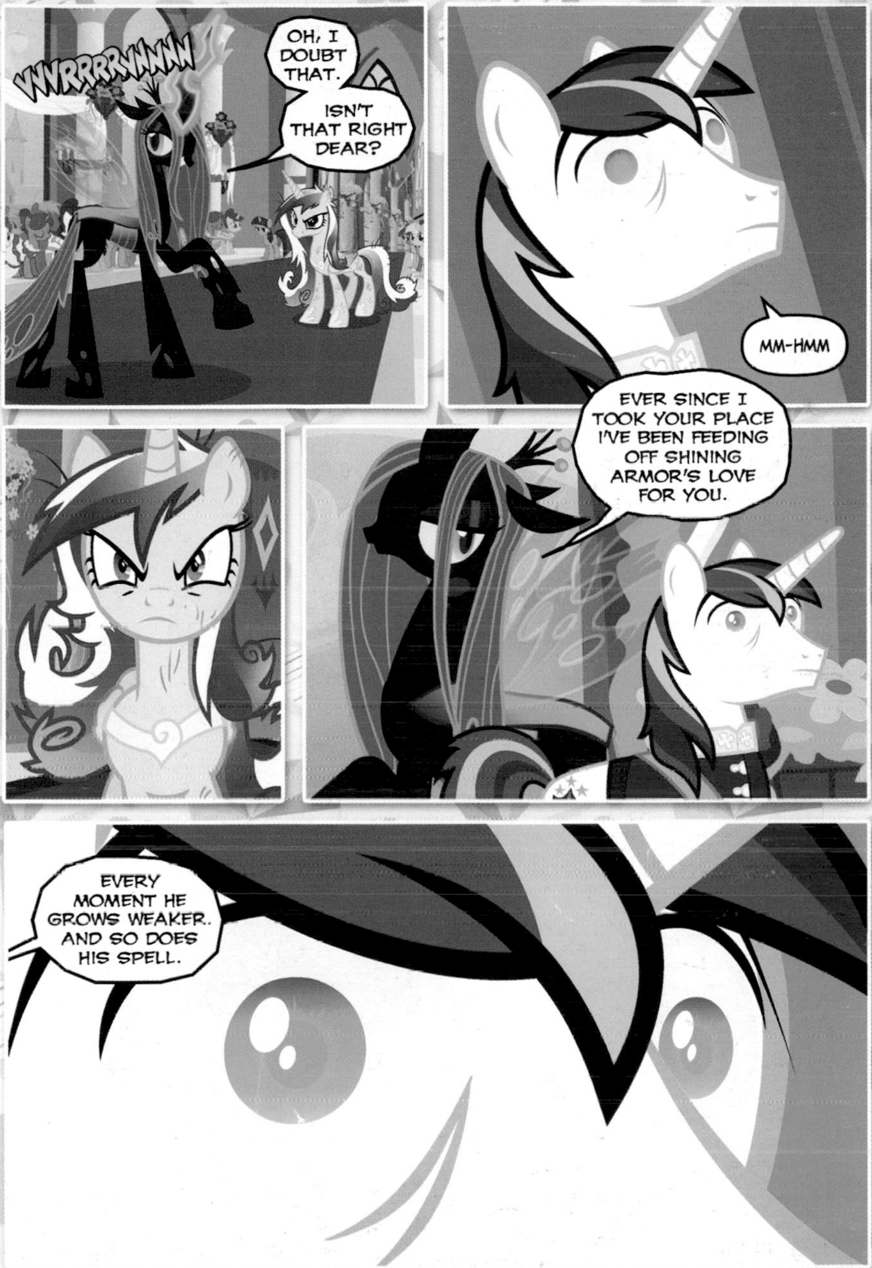
VVVRRRRVNNNN
OH, I DOUBT THAT.
ISN'T THAT RIGHT DEAR?
MM-HMM
EVER SINCE I TOOK YOUR PLACE I'VE BEEN FEEDING OFF SHINING ARMOR'S LOVE FOR YOU.
EVERY MOMENT HE GROWS WEAKER. AND SO DOES HIS SPELL.

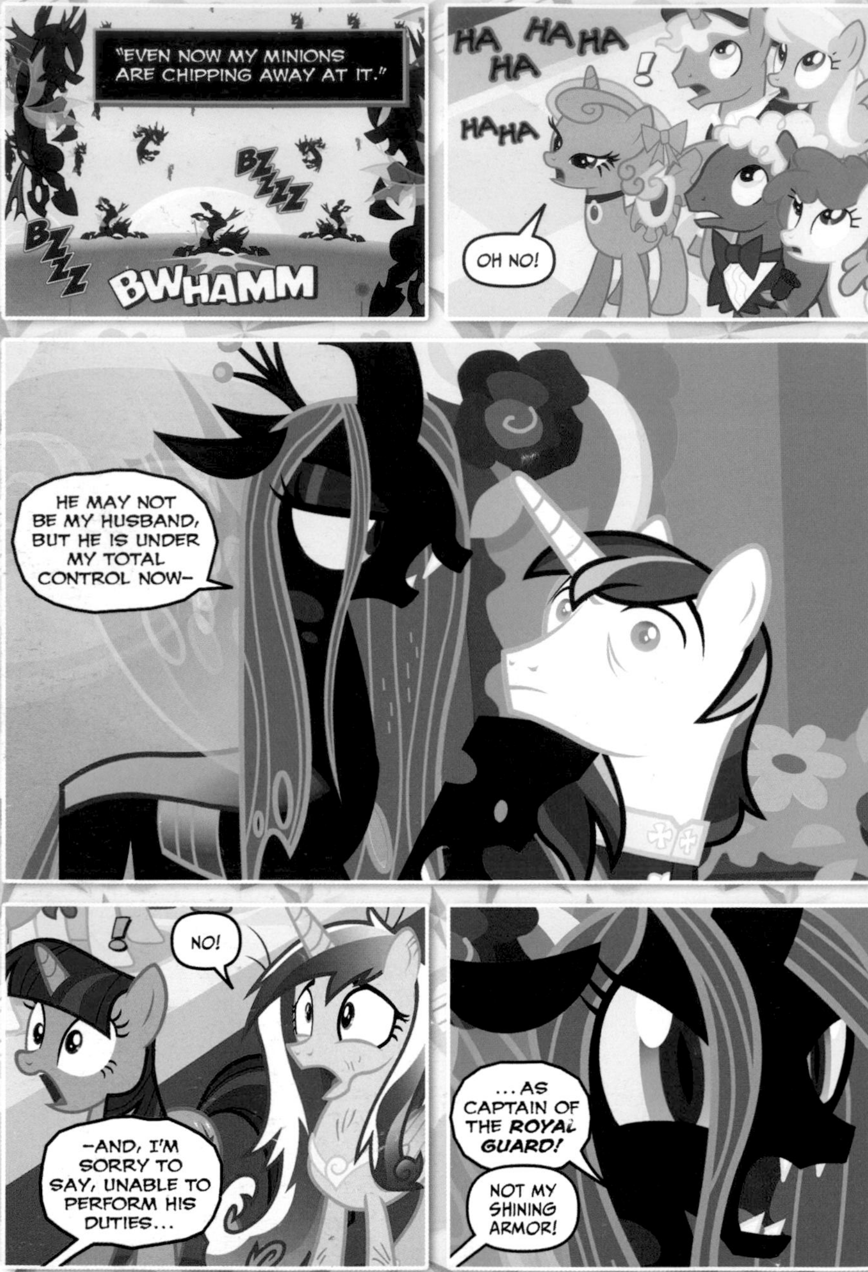
"EVEN NOW MY MINIONS ARE CHIPPING AWAY AT IT."
BZZZZ
BZZZZ
BWHAMM
HA HA HA HA HA
!
HA HA
OH NO!
HE MAY NOT BE MY HUSBAND, BUT HE IS UNDER MY TOTAL CONTROL NOW–
!
NO!
–AND, I'M SORRY TO SAY, UNABLE TO PERFORM HIS DUTIES...
...AS CAPTAIN OF THE ROYAL GUARD!
NOT MY SHINING ARMOR!

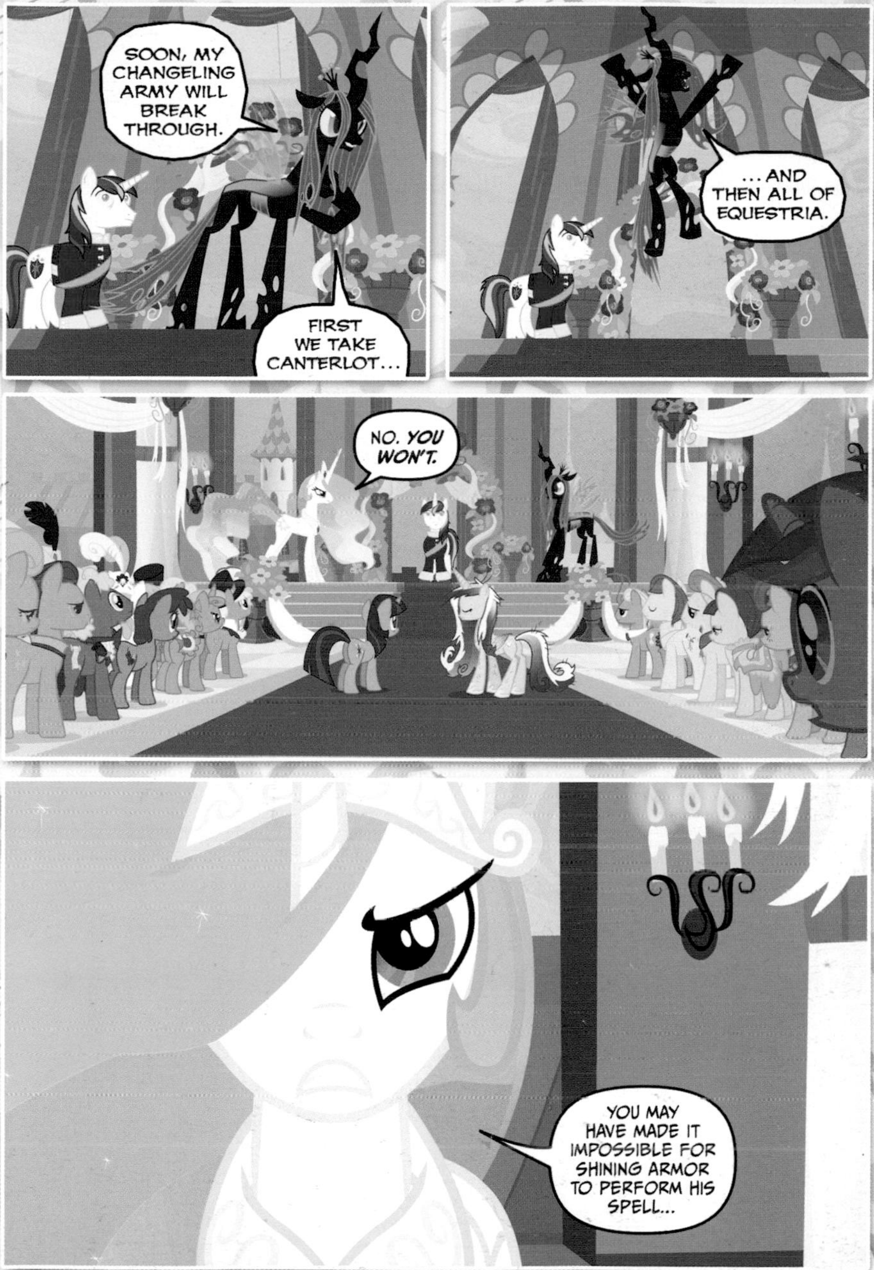
SOON, MY CHANGELING ARMY WILL BREAK THROUGH.
FIRST WE TAKE CANTERLOT...
...AND THEN ALL OF EQUESTRIA.
NO. YOU WON'T.
YOU MAY HAVE MADE IT IMPOSSIBLE FOR SHINING ARMOR TO PERFORM HIS SPELL...

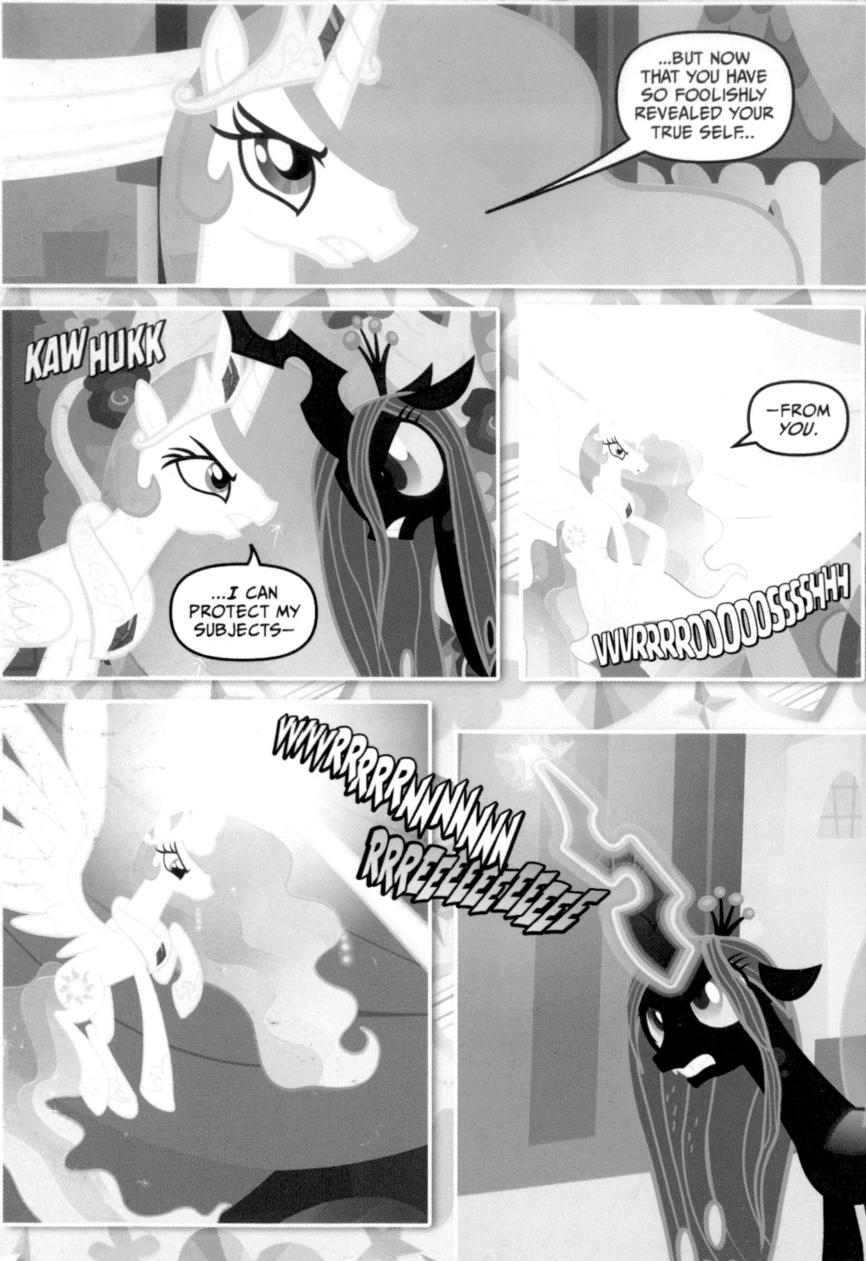
...BUT NOW THAT YOU HAVE SO FOOLISHLY REVEALED YOUR TRUE SELF...
KAW HUKK
...I CAN PROTECT MY SUBJECTS—
—FROM YOU.
VVVRRRROOOOOSSSSHHH
VVVVRRRRRNNNNNNN
RRREEEEEEEEEEEE

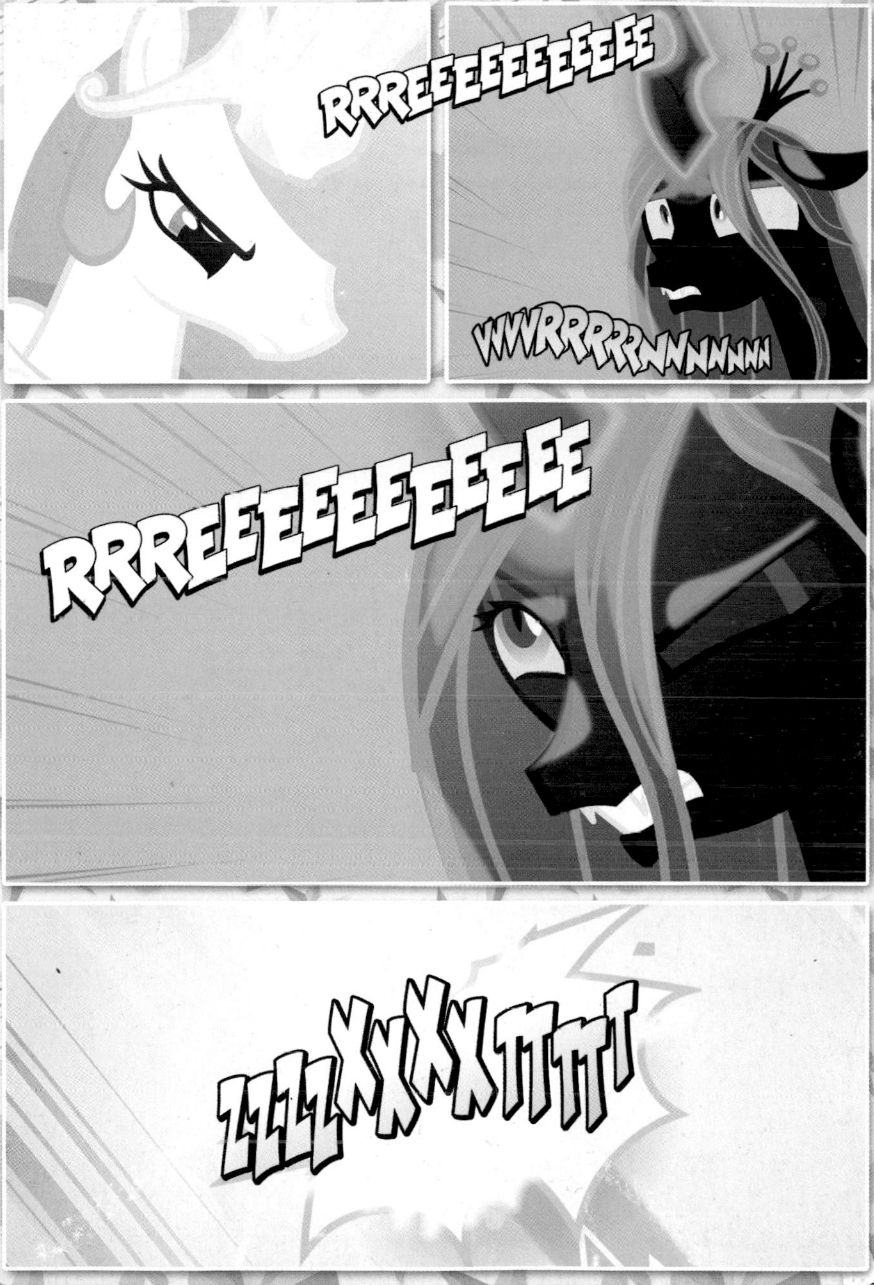
RRREEEEEEEEEEE
VVVVRRRRRNNNNNNN
RRREEEEEEEEEEE
ZZZZXXXXTTTTT

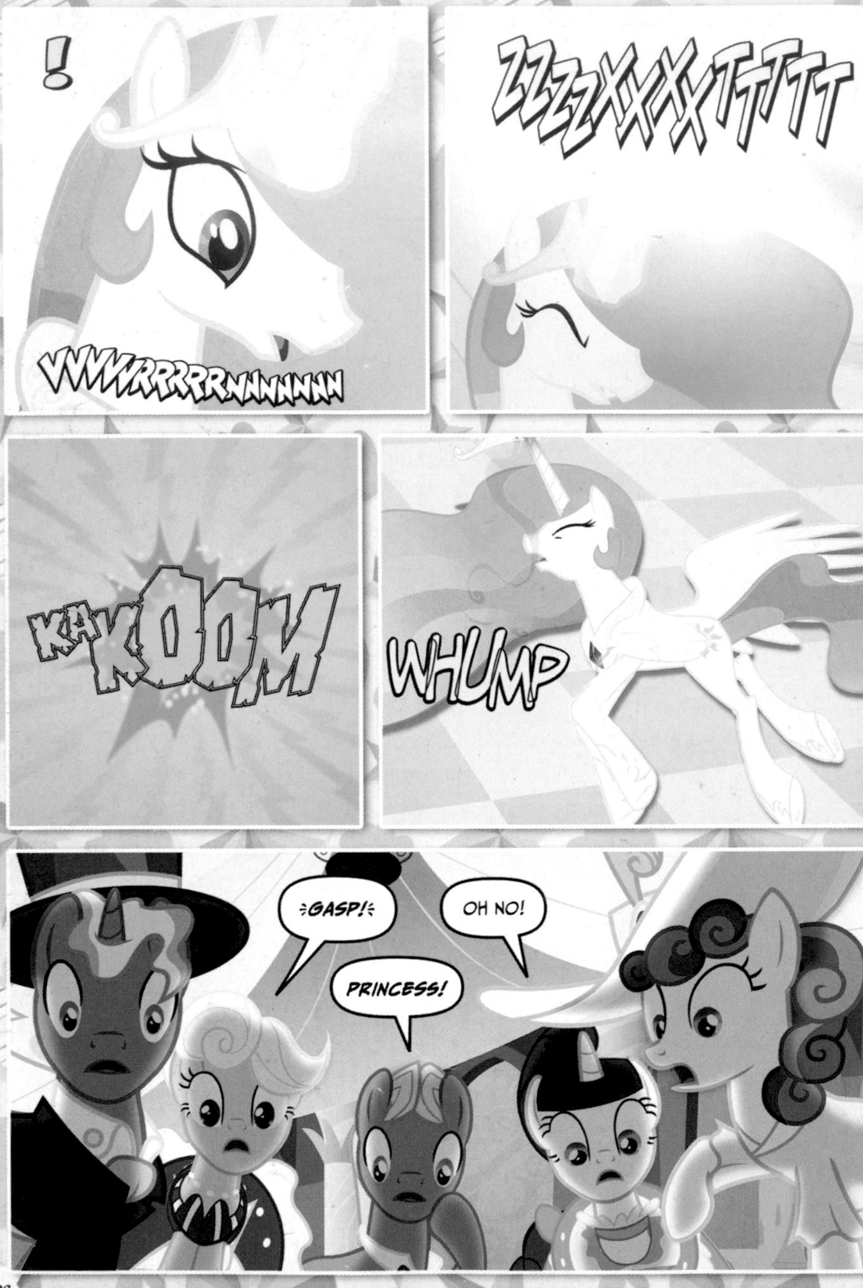

!
VVVVVRRRRRNNNNNNN
ZZZZXXXXTTTTT
KA-KOOM
WHUMP
GASP!
OH NO!
PRINCESS!

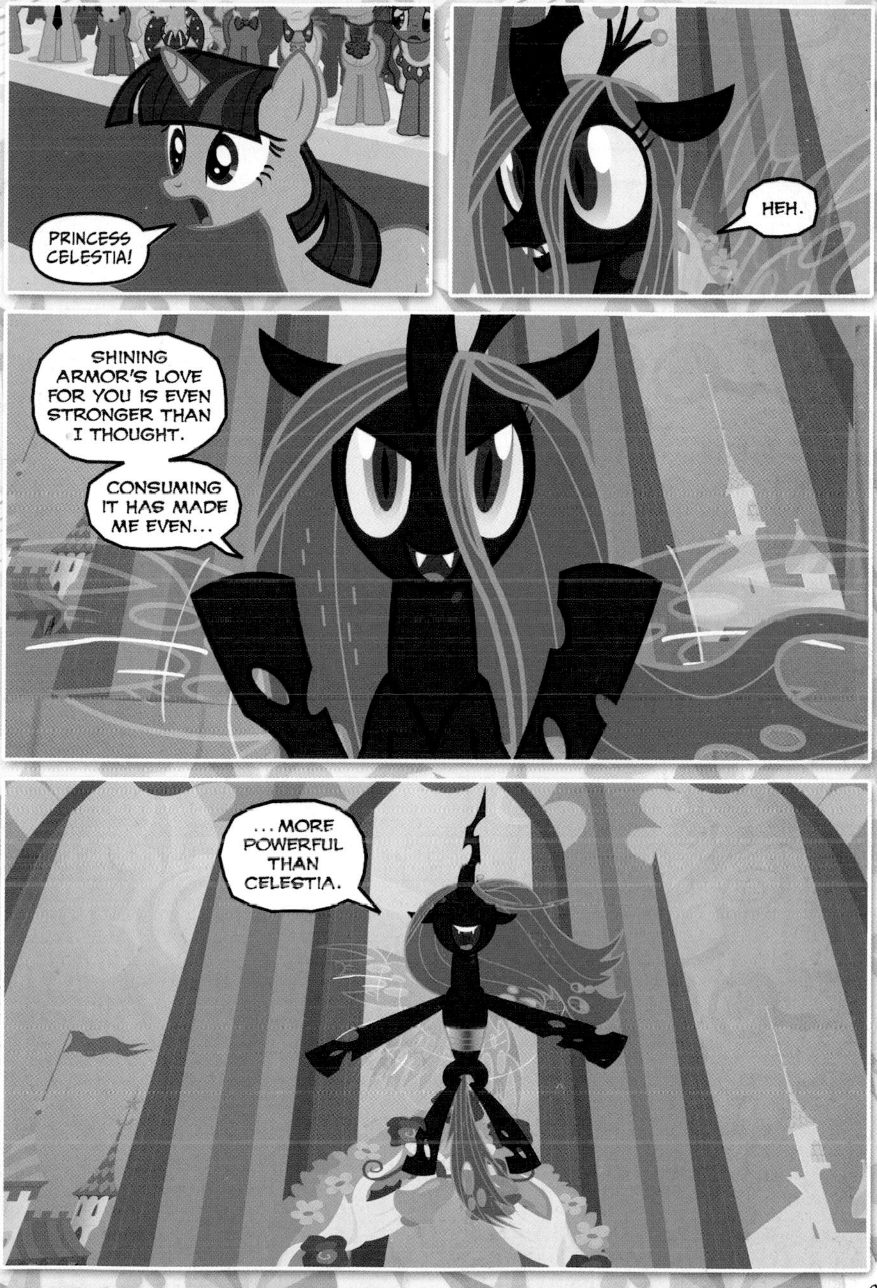
PRINCESS CELESTIA!
HEH.
SHINING ARMOR'S LOVE FOR YOU IS EVEN STRONGER THAN I THOUGHT.
CONSUMING IT HAS MADE ME EVEN...
...MORE POWERFUL THAN CELESTIA.

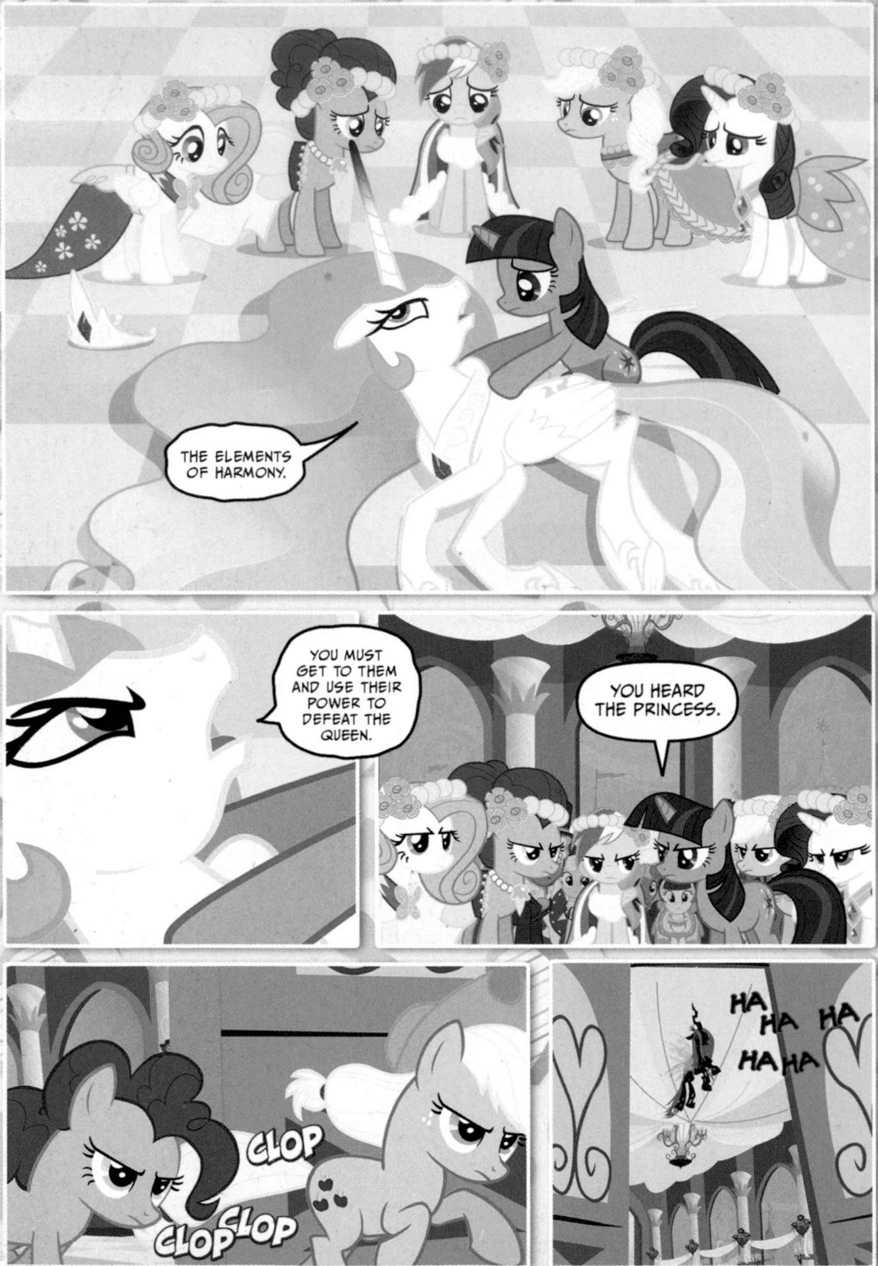
THE ELEMENTS OF HARMONY.
YOU MUST GET TO THEM AND USE THEIR POWER TO DEFEAT THE QUEEN.
YOU HEARD THE PRINCESS.
CLOP
CLOP CLOP
HA HA HA
HA HA

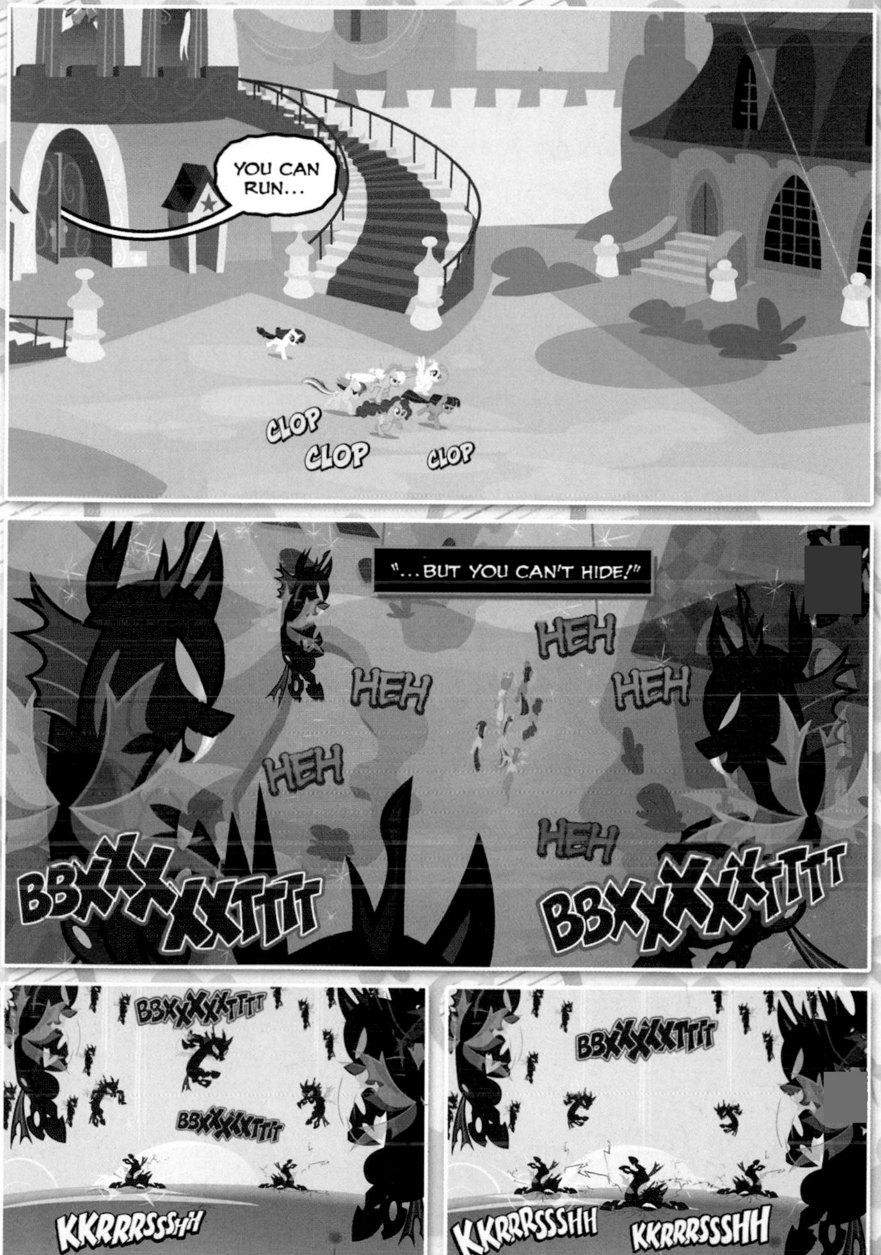

YOU CAN RUN...
CLOP
CLOP
CLOP
"...BUT YOU CAN'T HIDE!"
HEH
HEH
HEH
HEH
HEH
BBXXXXTTTT
BBXXXXTTTT
BBXXXXTTTT
BBXXXXTTTT
KKRRRSSSHH
BBXXXXTTTT
KKRRRSSSHH
KKRRRSSSHH

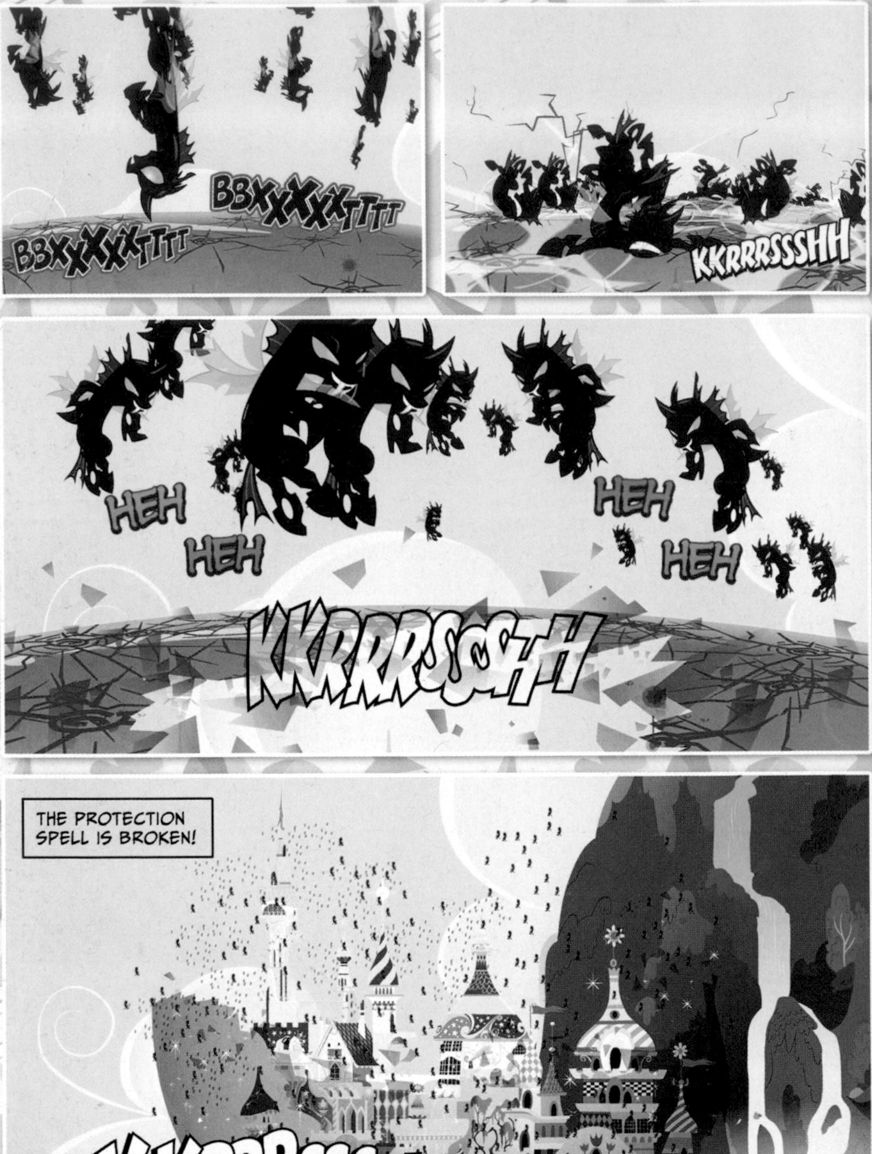
BBXXXXXTTTT
BBXXXXXTTTT
KKRRRSSSHH
HEH
HEH
HEH
HEH
KKRRRSSSHH
THE PROTECTION SPELL IS BROKEN!
KKRRRSSSHH

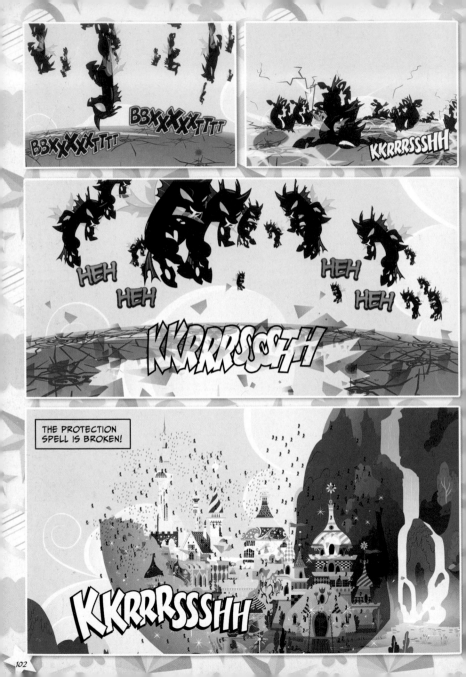

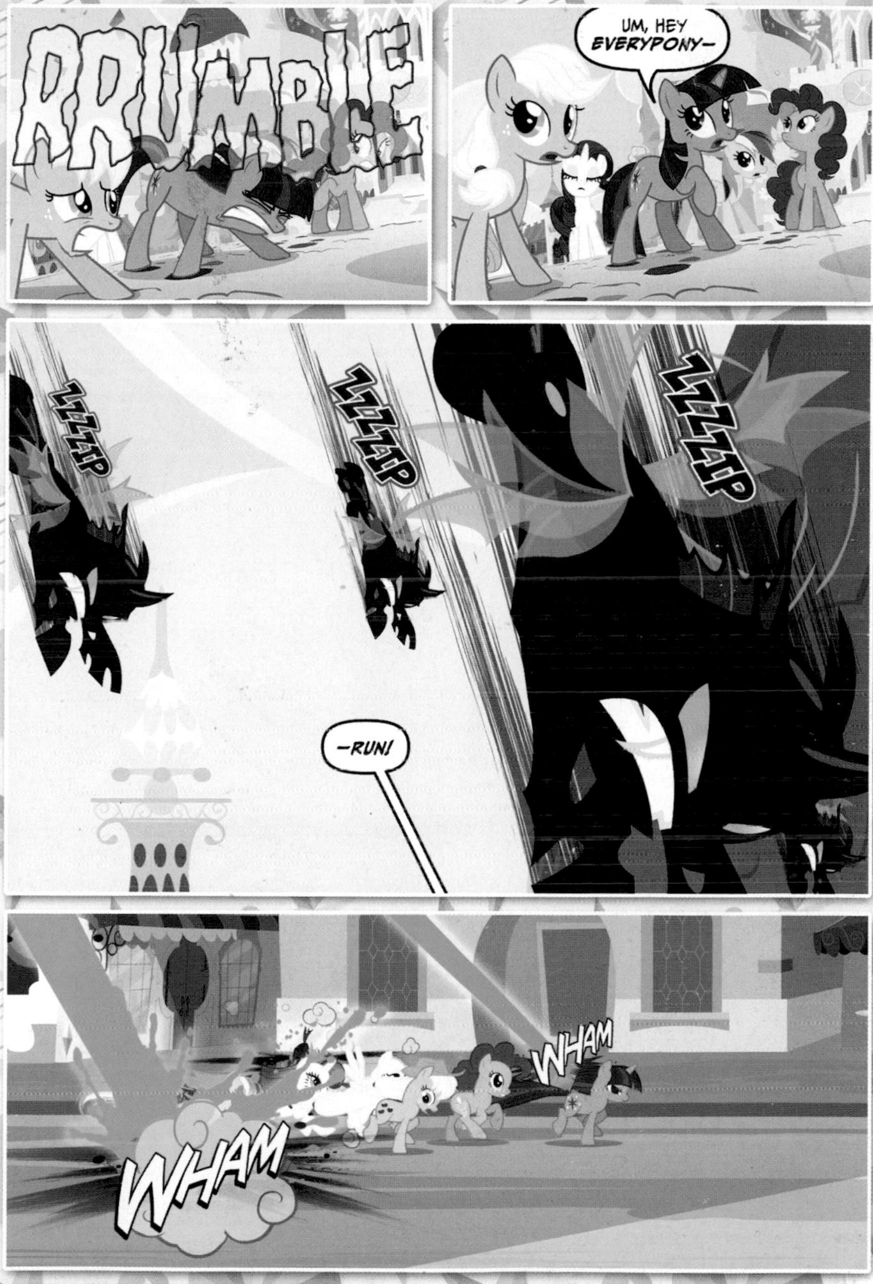
RRUMBLE
UM, HEY EVERYPONY—
ZZZZAP
ZZZZAP
ZZZZAP
—RUN!
WHAM
WHAM

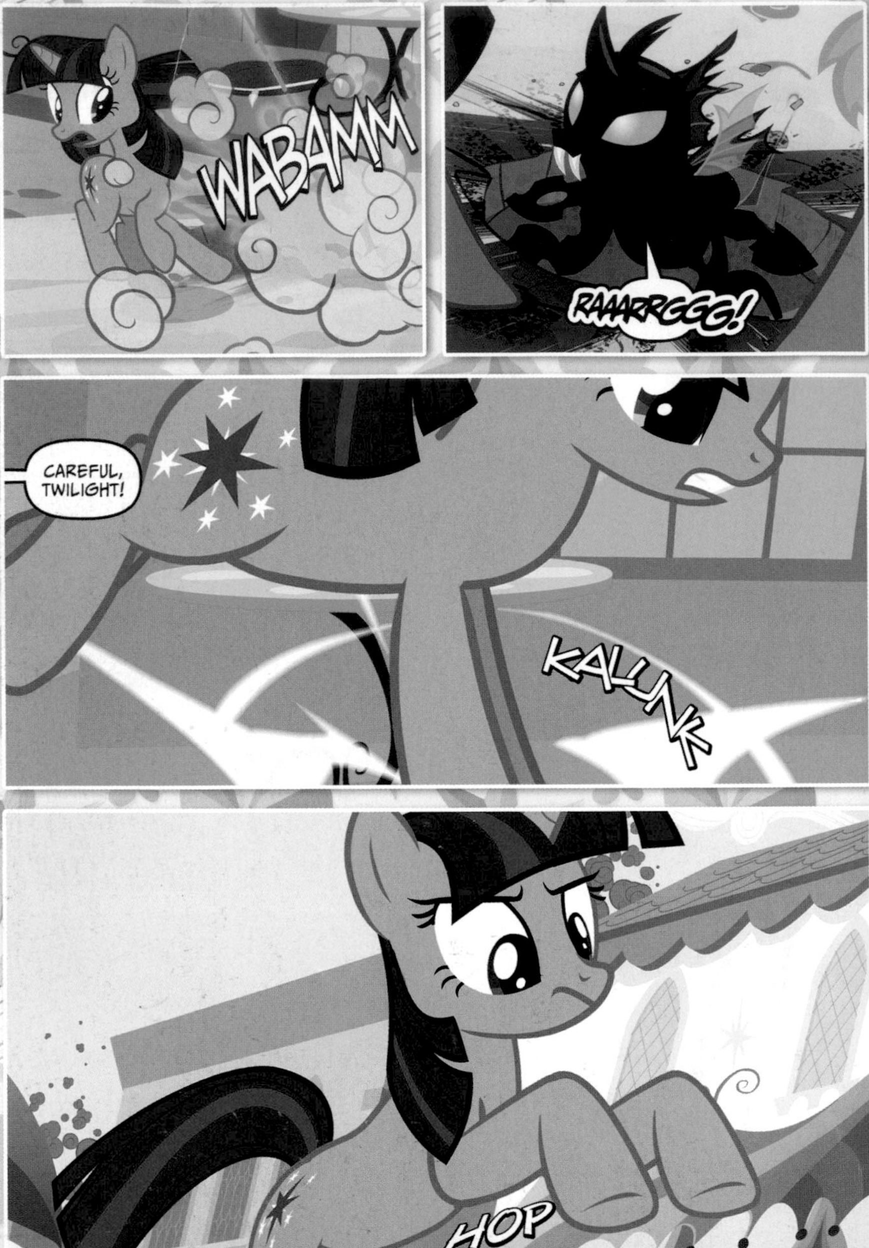
WABAMM
RAAARRGGG!
CAREFUL, TWILIGHT!
KALUNK
HOP

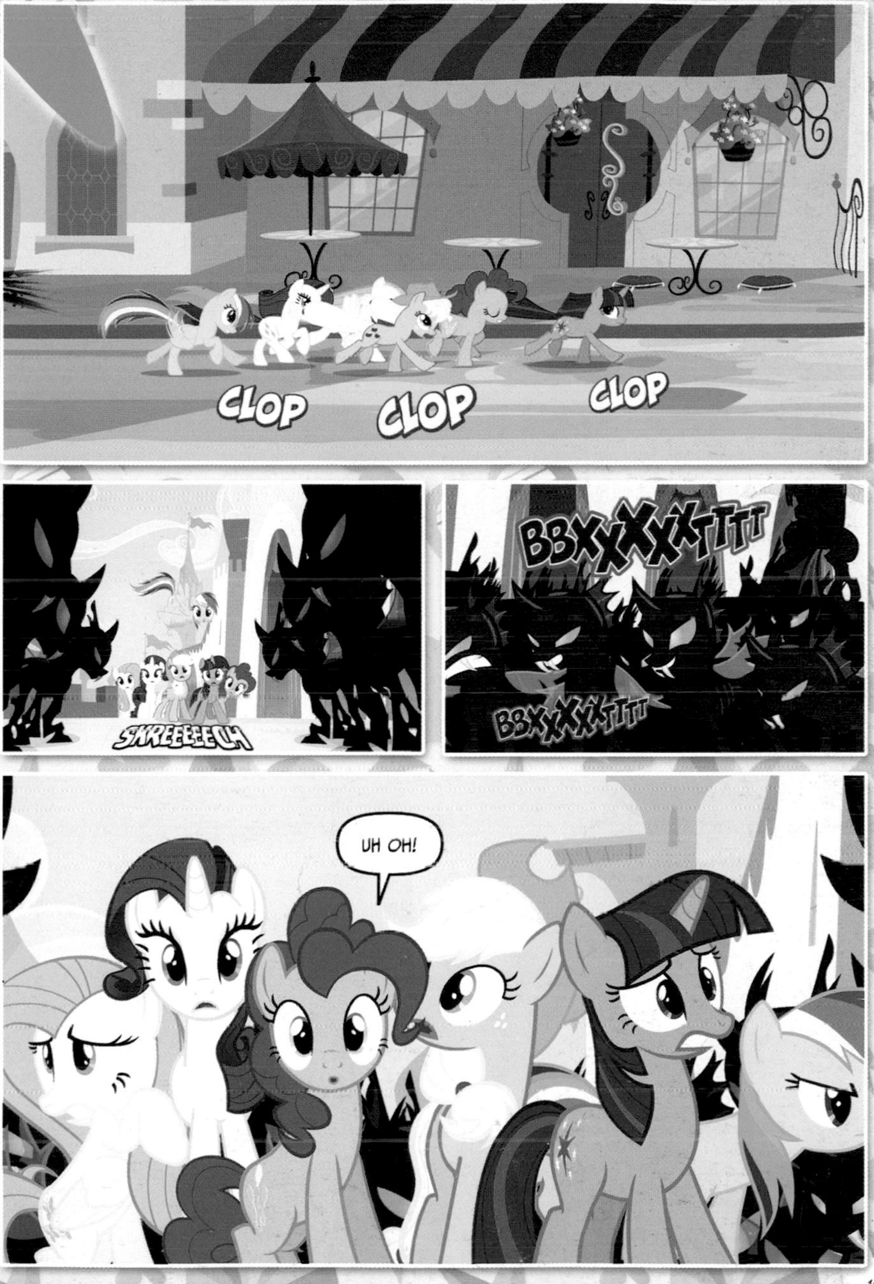
CLOP
CLOP
CLOP
SKREEEEEECH
BBXXXXXTTTT
BBXXXXXTTTT
UH OH!

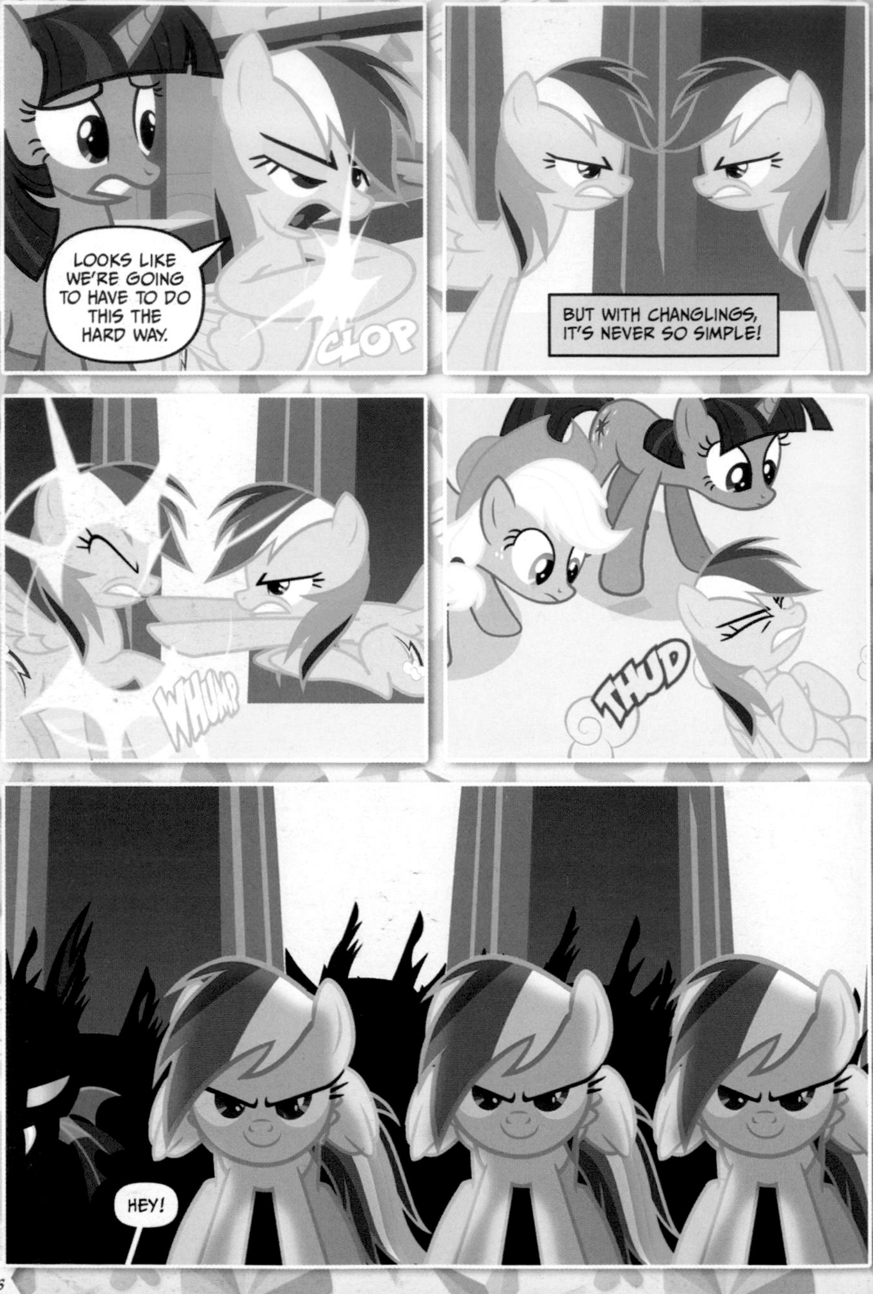
LOOKS LIKE WE'RE GOING TO HAVE TO DO THIS THE HARD WAY.
CLOP
BUT WITH CHANGLINGS, IT'S NEVER SO SIMPLE!
WHUMP
THUD
HEY!

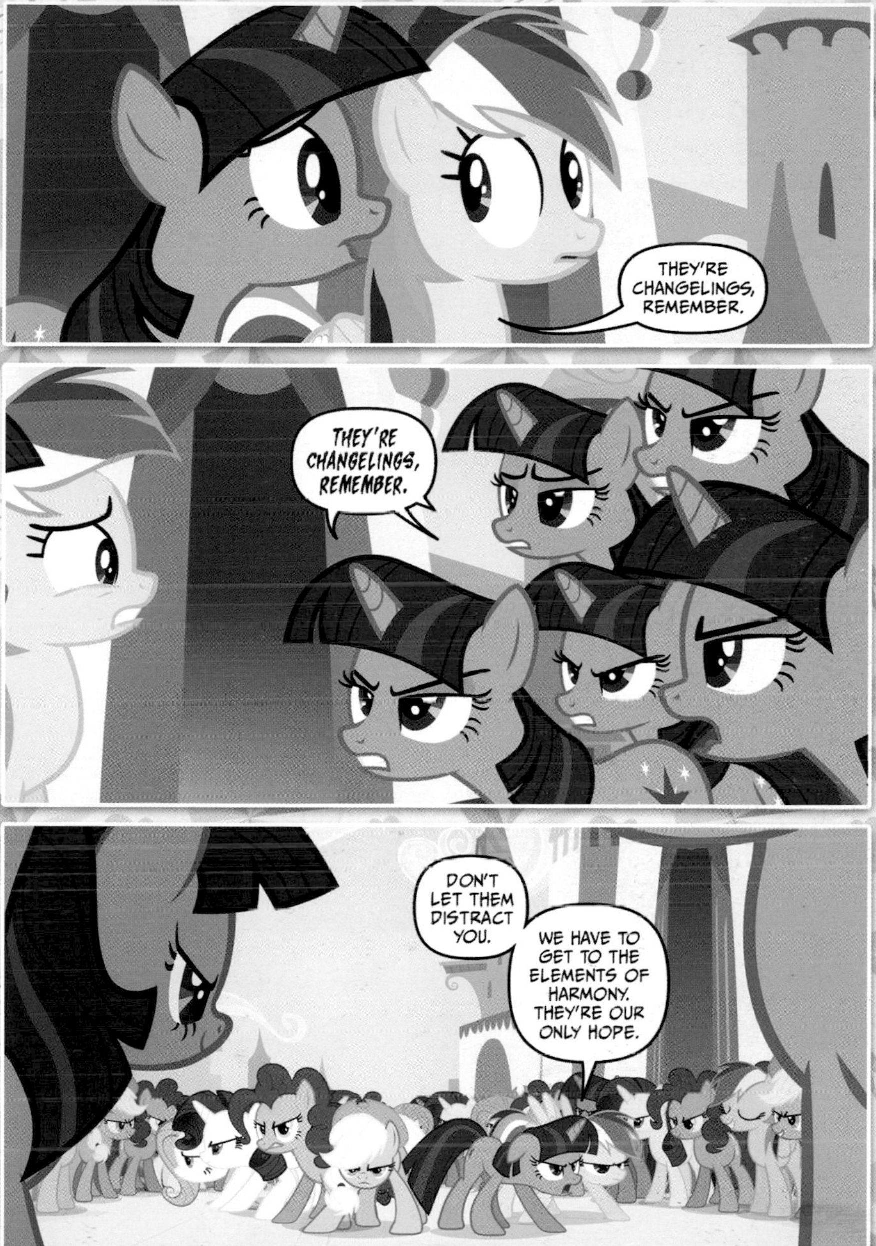
THEY'RE CHANGELINGS, REMEMBER.
THEY'RE CHANGELINGS, REMEMBER.
DON'T LET THEM DISTRACT YOU.
WE HAVE TO GET TO THE ELEMENTS OF HARMONY. THEY'RE OUR ONLY HOPE.

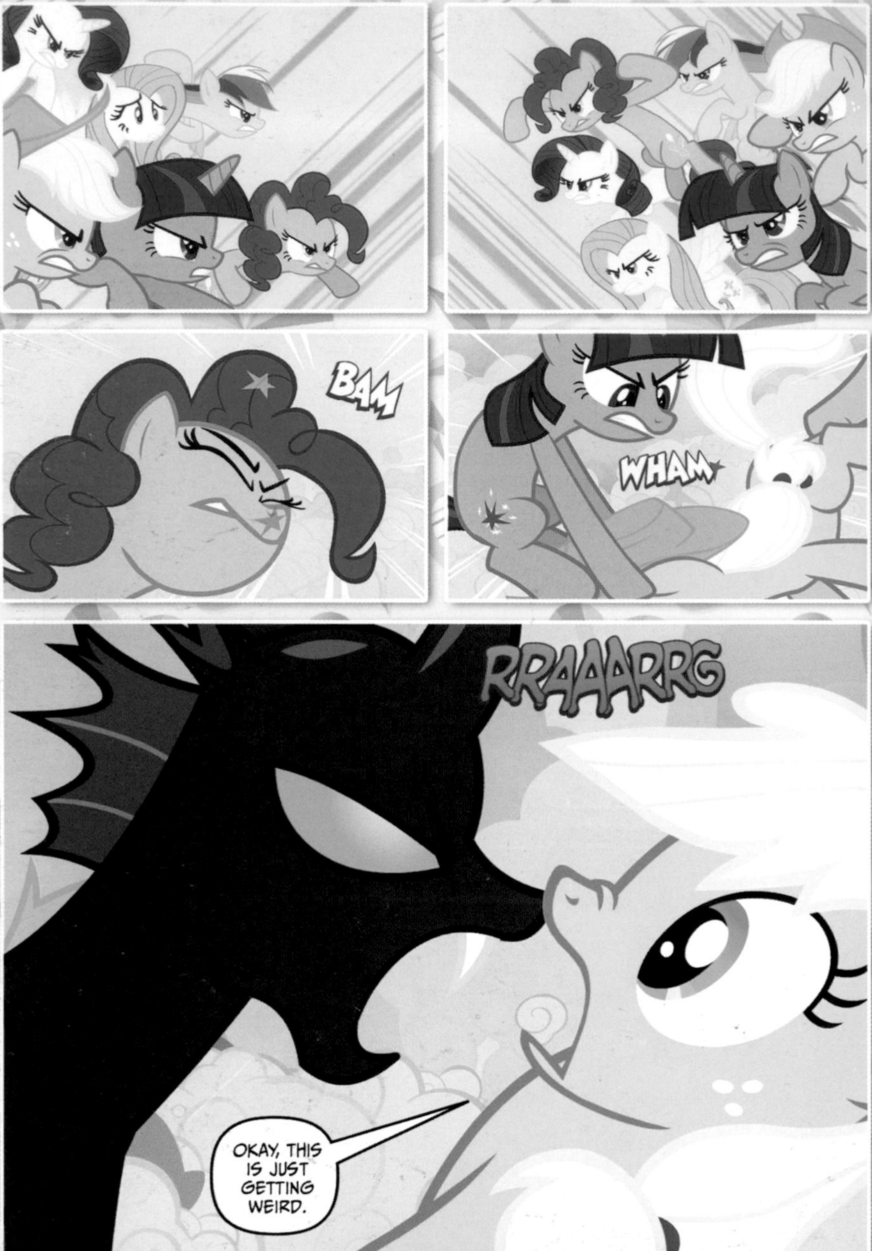
BAM
WHAM
RRAAARRG
OKAY, THIS IS JUST GETTING WEIRD.

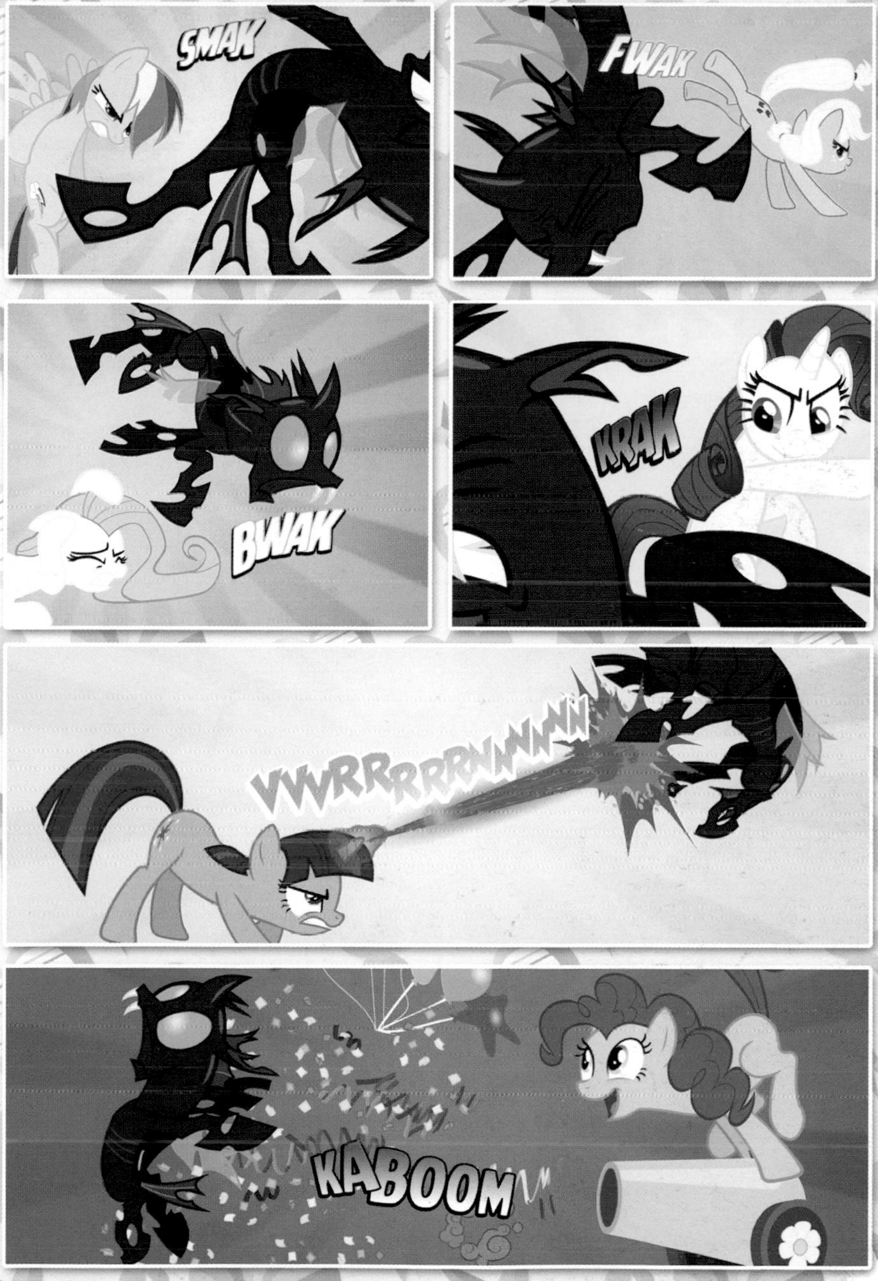

SMAK
FWAK
BWAK
KRAK
VVVRRRRRNNNNNN
KABOOM

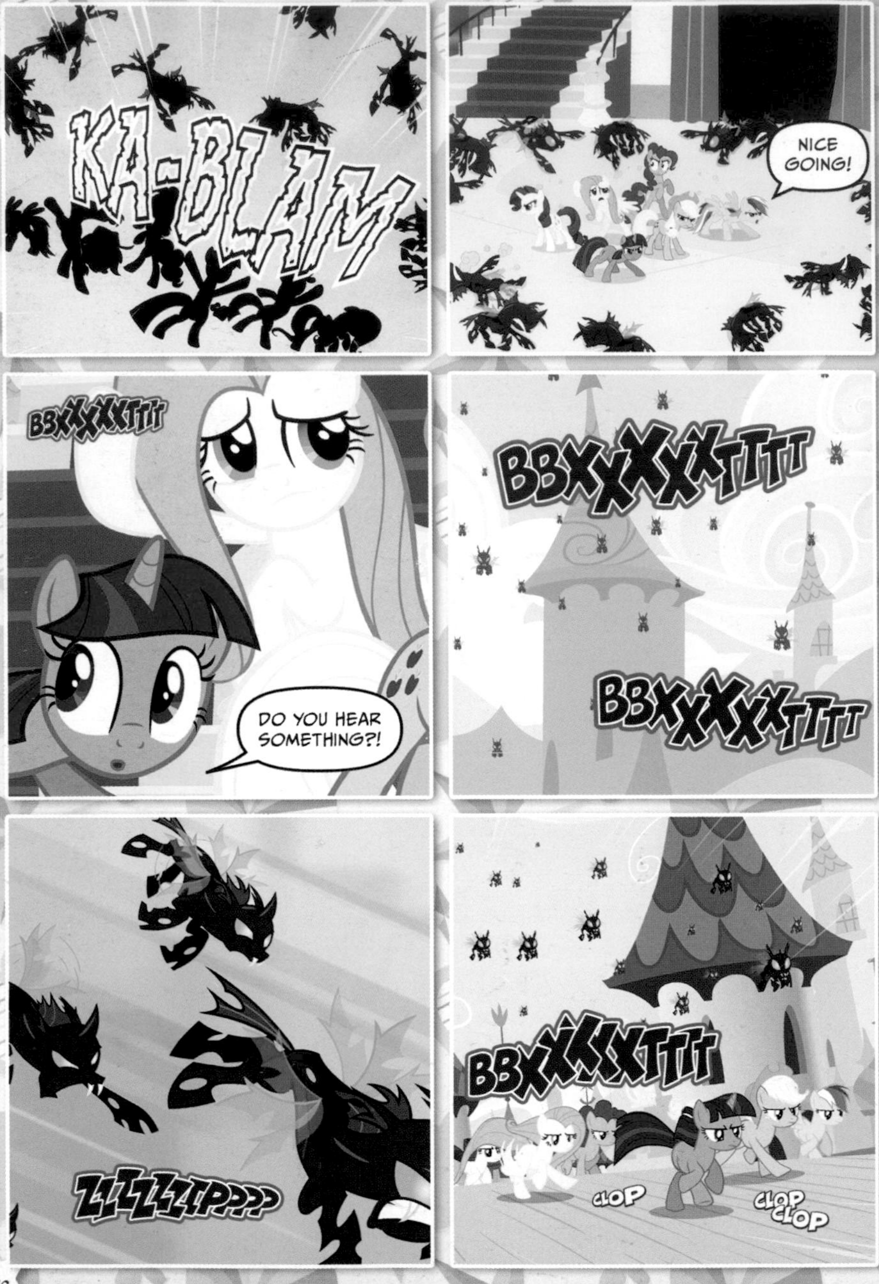
KA-BLAM
NICE GOING!
BBXXXXXTTTT
DO YOU HEAR SOMETHING?!
BBXXXXXTTTTT
BBXXXXXTTTTT
ZIZZZZIPPPP
BBXXXXXTTTTT
CLOP
CLOP CLOP

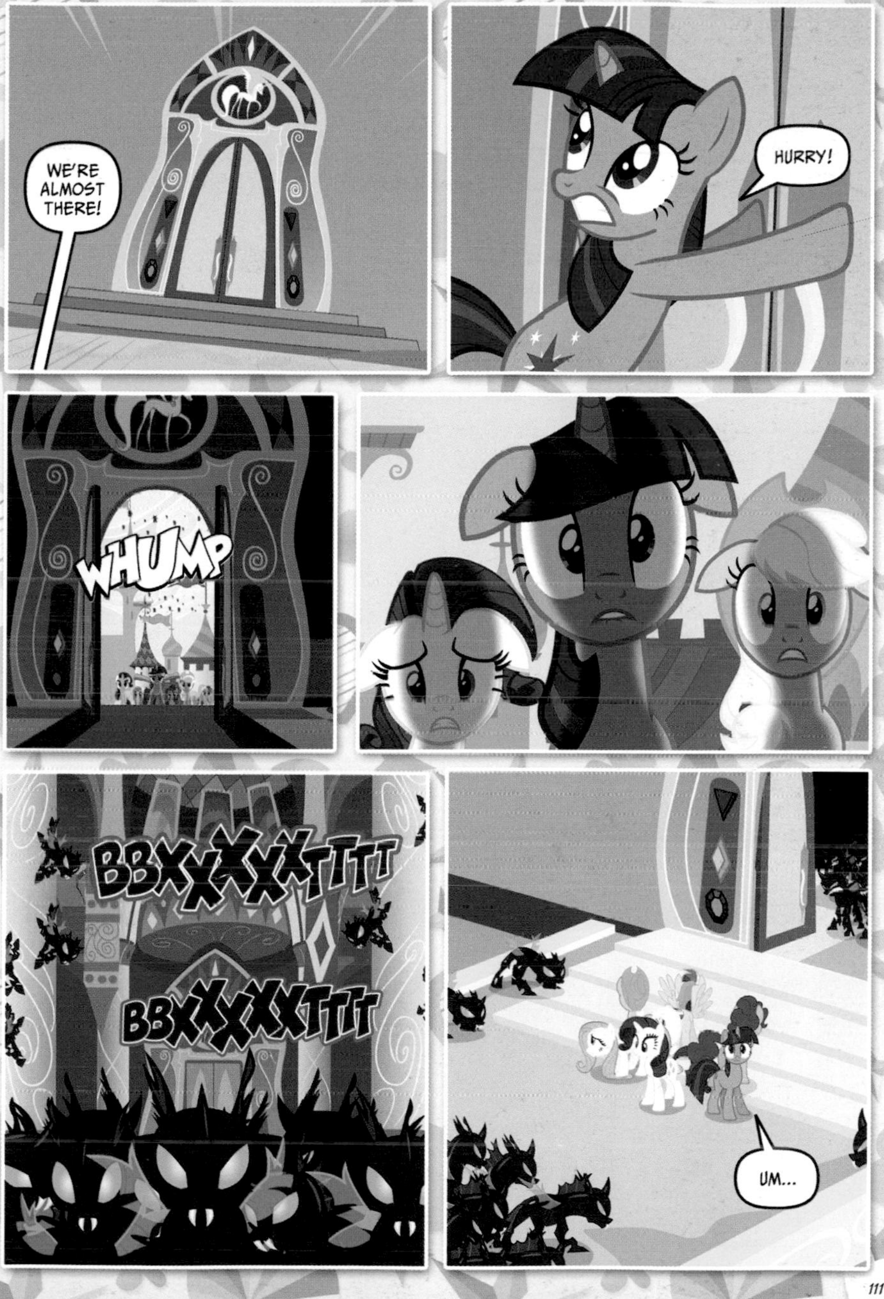
WE'RE ALMOST THERE!
HURRY!
WHUMP
BBXXXXTTTT
BBXXXXTTTT
UM...

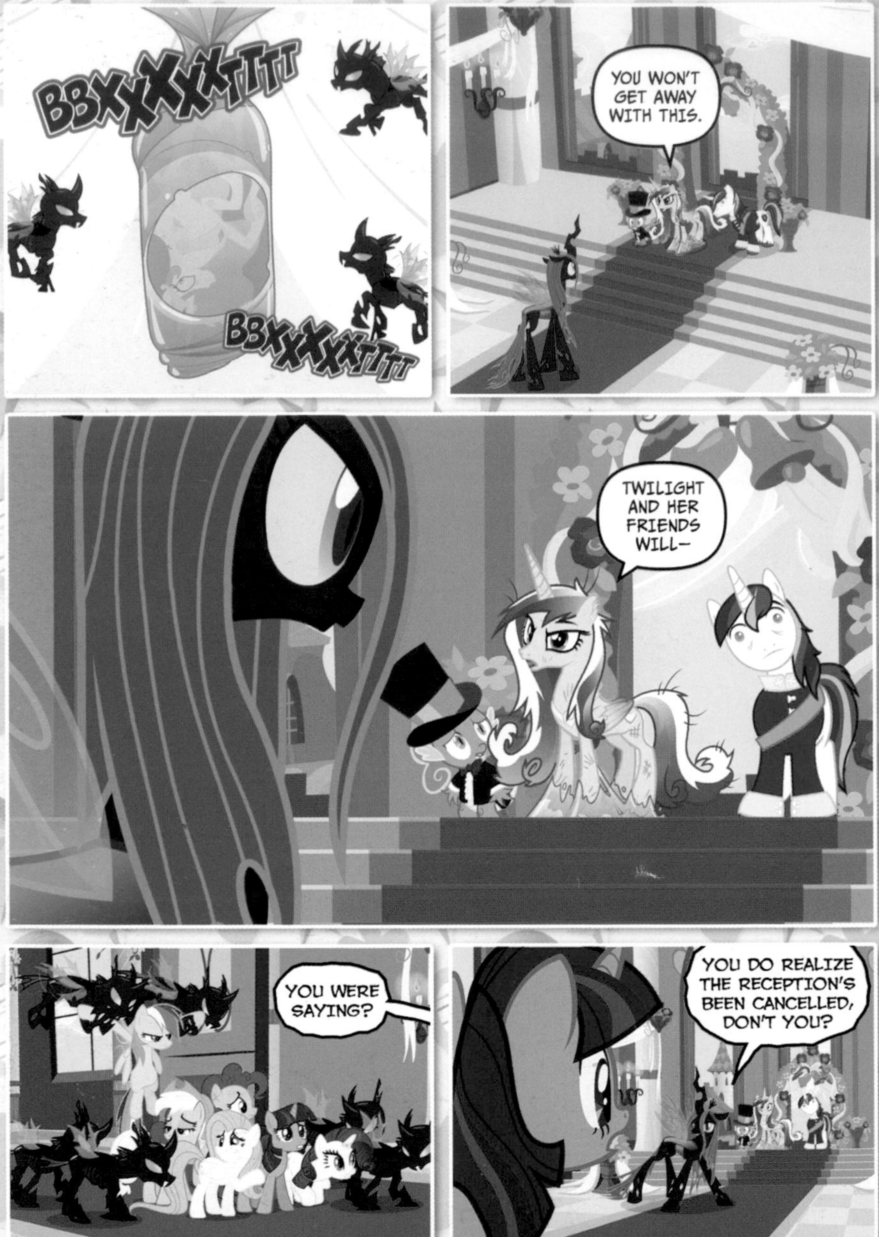
BBXXXXXTTTT
BBXXXXXTTTT
YOU WON'T GET AWAY WITH THIS.
TWILIGHT AND HER FRIENDS WILL—
YOU WERE SAYING?
YOU DO REALIZE THE RECEPTION'S BEEN CANCELLED, DON'T YOU?

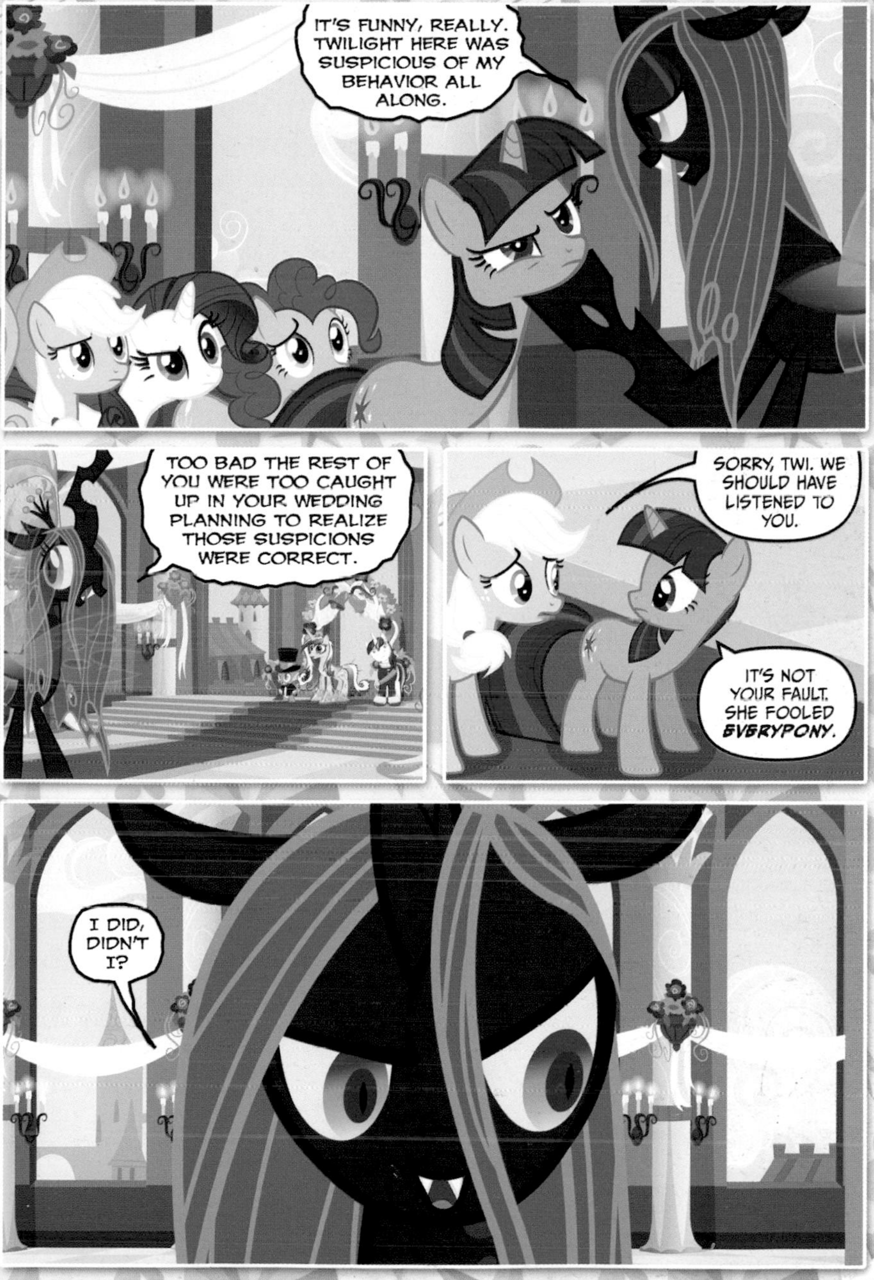
IT'S FUNNY, REALLY. TWILIGHT HERE WAS SUSPICIOUS OF MY BEHAVIOR ALL ALONG.
TOO BAD THE REST OF YOU WERE TOO CAUGHT UP IN YOUR WEDDING PLANNING TO REALIZE THOSE SUSPICIONS WERE CORRECT.
SORRY, TWI. WE SHOULD HAVE LISTENED TO YOU.
IT'S NOT YOUR FAULT. SHE FOOLED *EVERYPONY*.
I DID, DIDN'T I?

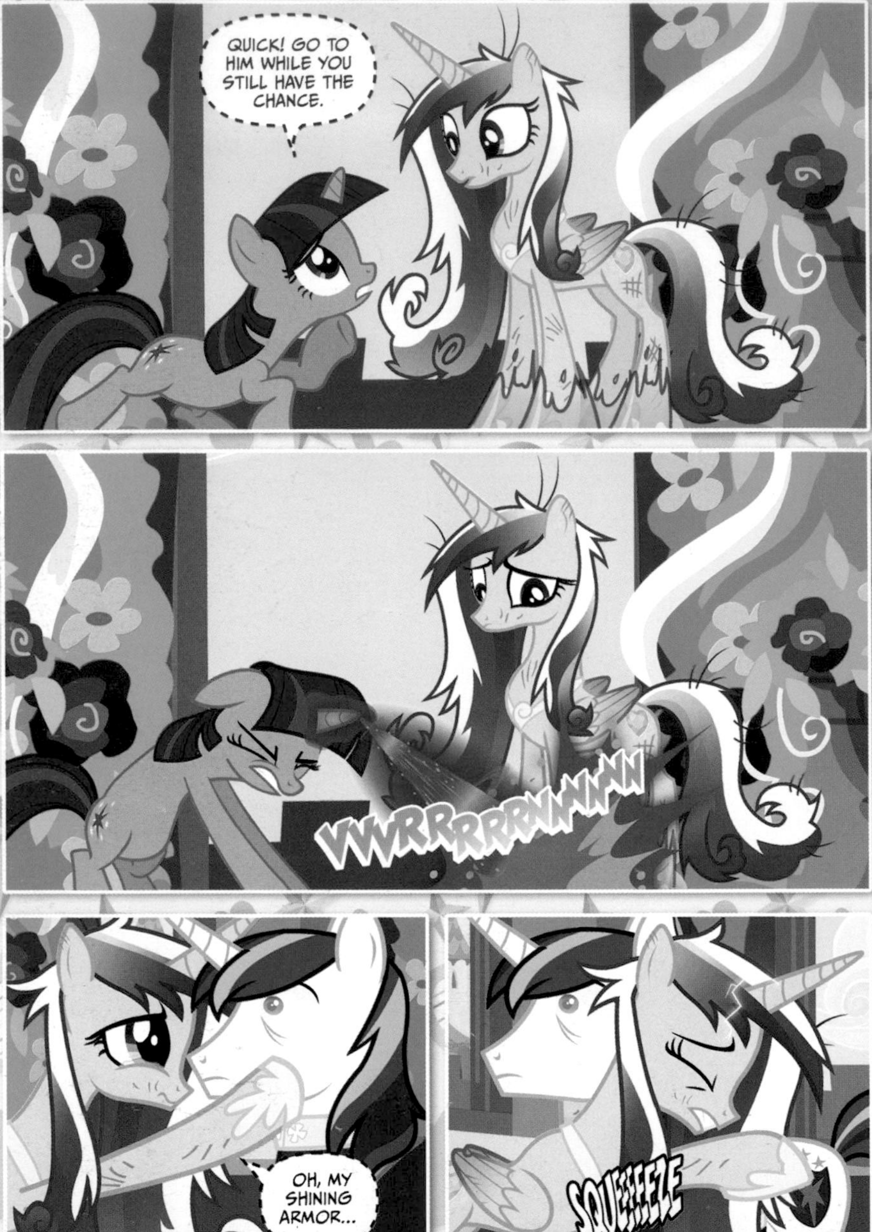
QUICK! GO TO HIM WHILE YOU STILL HAVE THE CHANCE.
VVVRRRRRNNNNNN
OH, MY SHINING ARMOR...
SQUEEEEEEZE

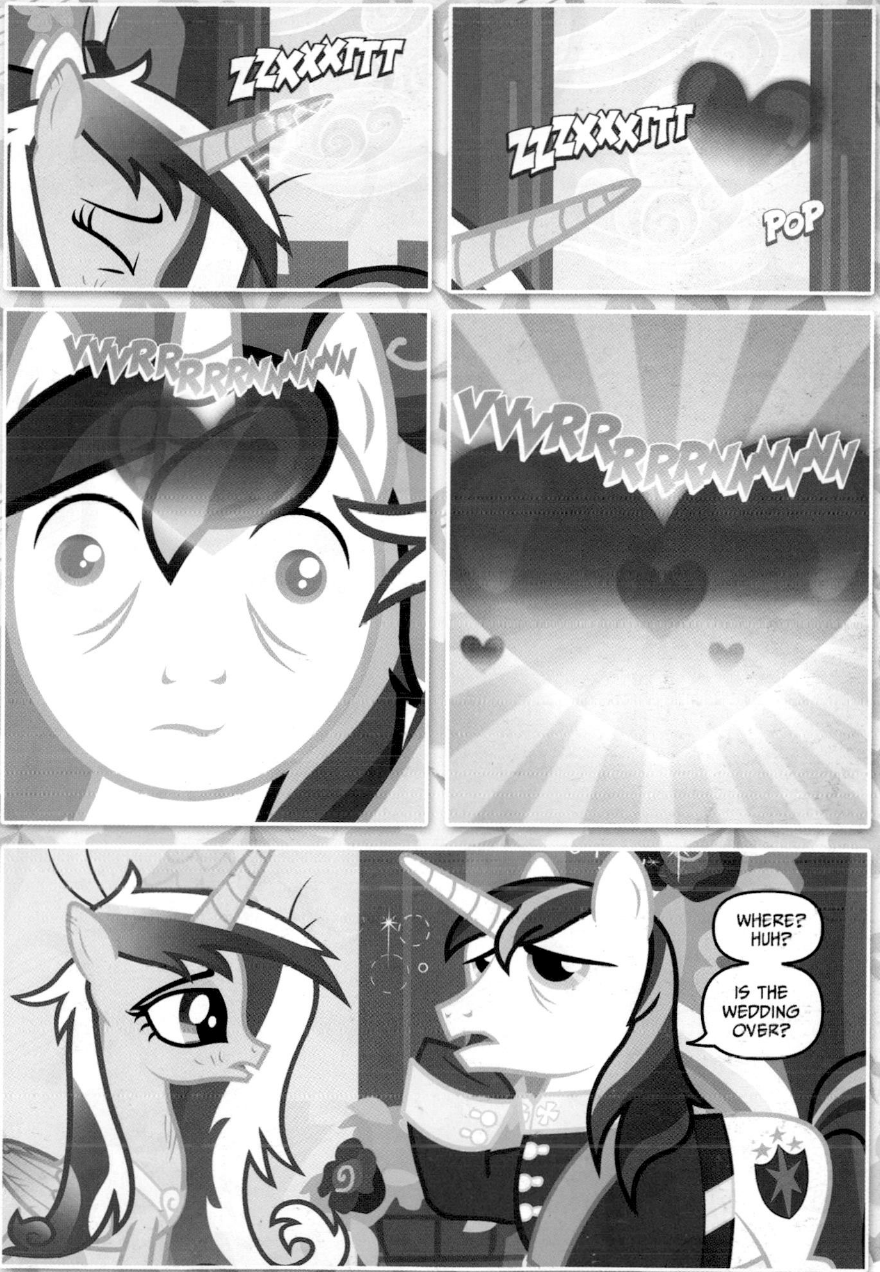

ZZXXXTTT
ZZZXXXTTT
POP
VVVRRRRRNNNNNN
VVVRRRRRRNNNNNNN
WHERE? HUH?
IS THE WEDDING OVER?

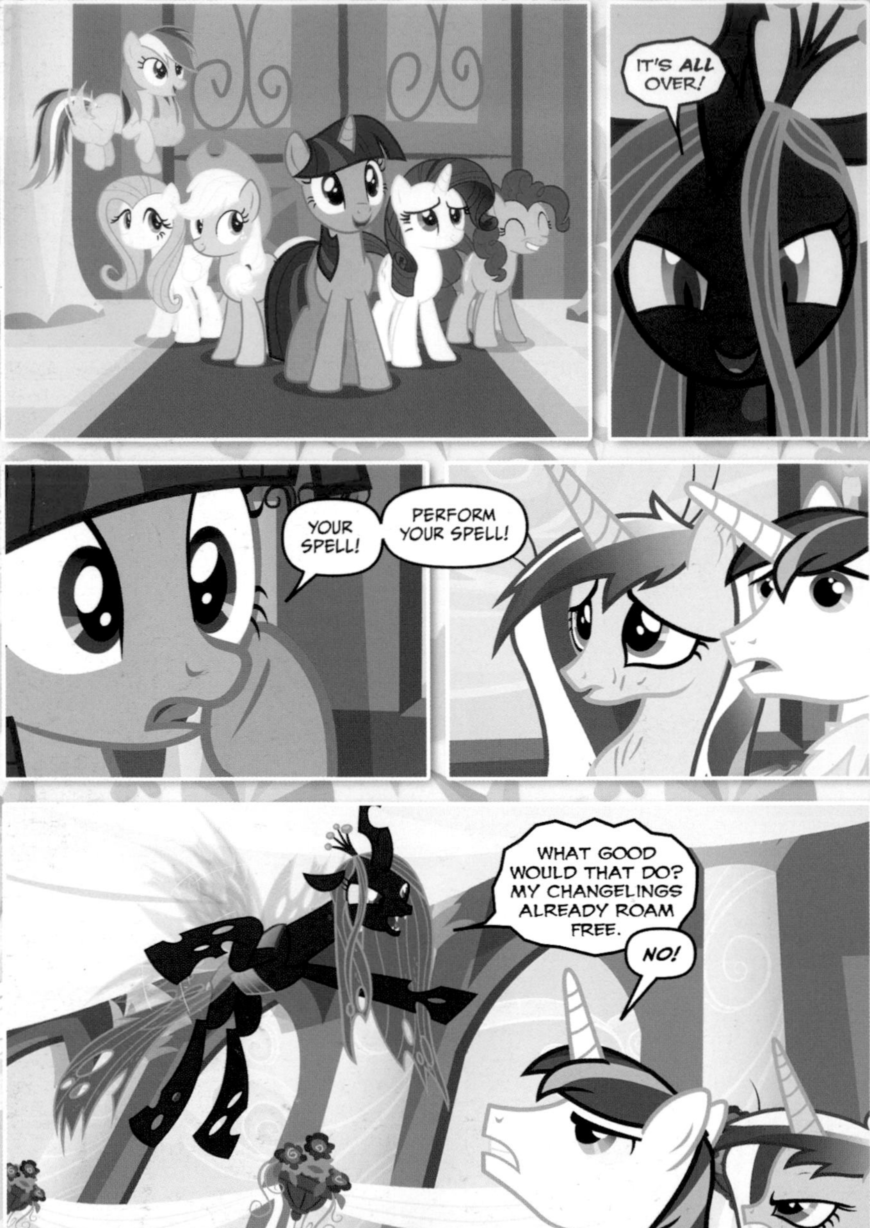
IT'S ALL OVER!
YOUR SPELL!
PERFORM YOUR SPELL!
WHAT GOOD WOULD THAT DO? MY CHANGELINGS ALREADY ROAM FREE.
NO!

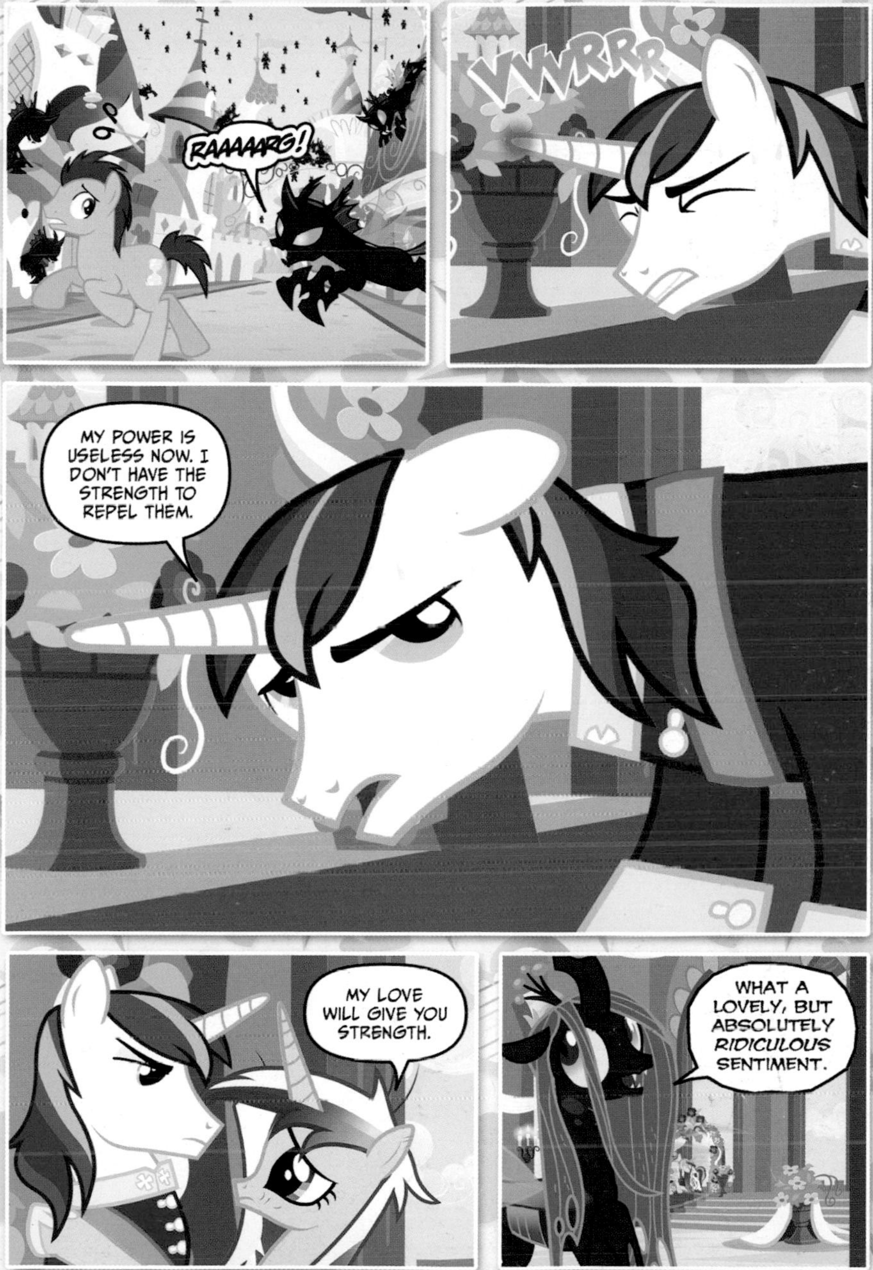
RAAAAARG!
VWRRR
MY POWER IS USELESS NOW. I DON'T HAVE THE STRENGTH TO REPEL THEM.
MY LOVE WILL GIVE YOU STRENGTH.
WHAT A LOVELY, BUT ABSOLUTELY *RIDICULOUS* SENTIMENT.

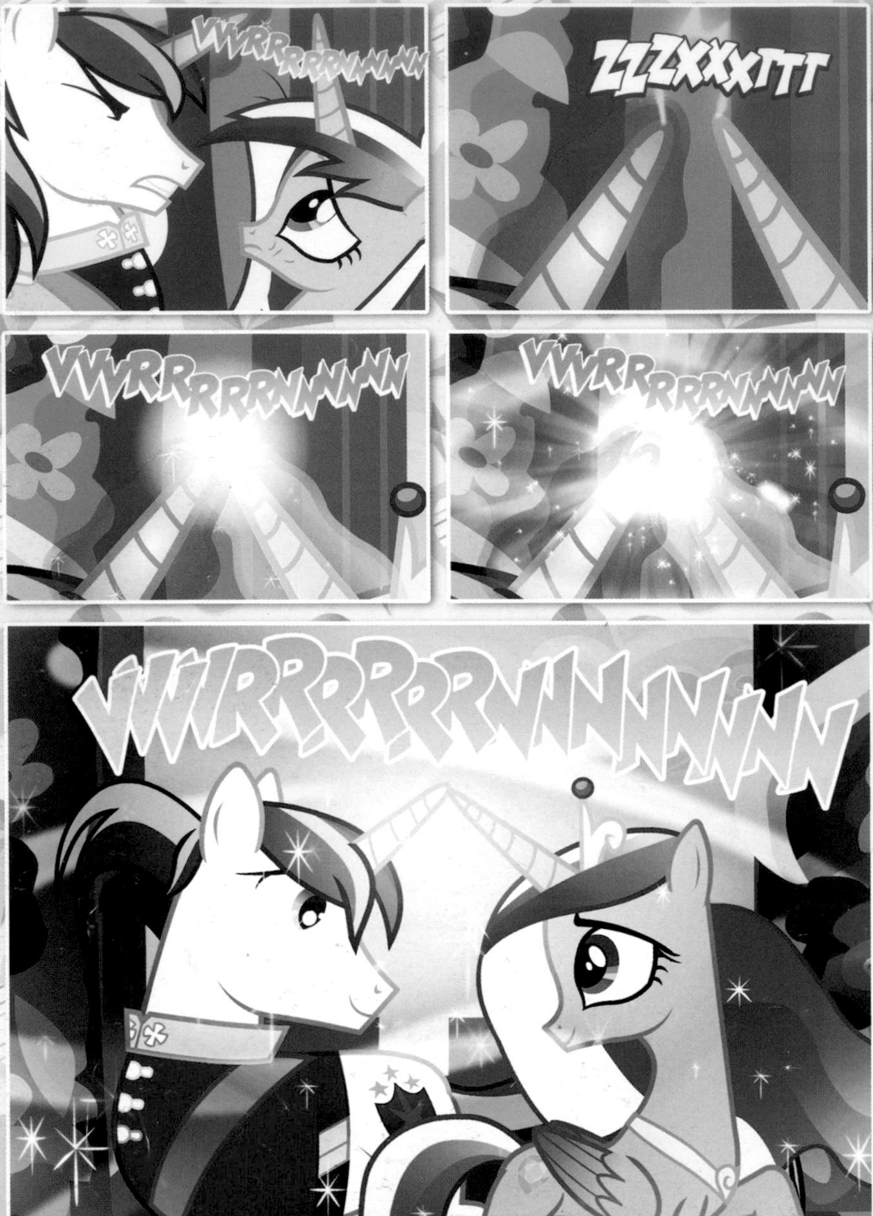
VVVRRRRRNNNNNN
ZZZXXXTTT
VVVRRRRRNNNNNN
VVVRRRRRNNNNNN
VVVRRRRRRRNNNNNNNN

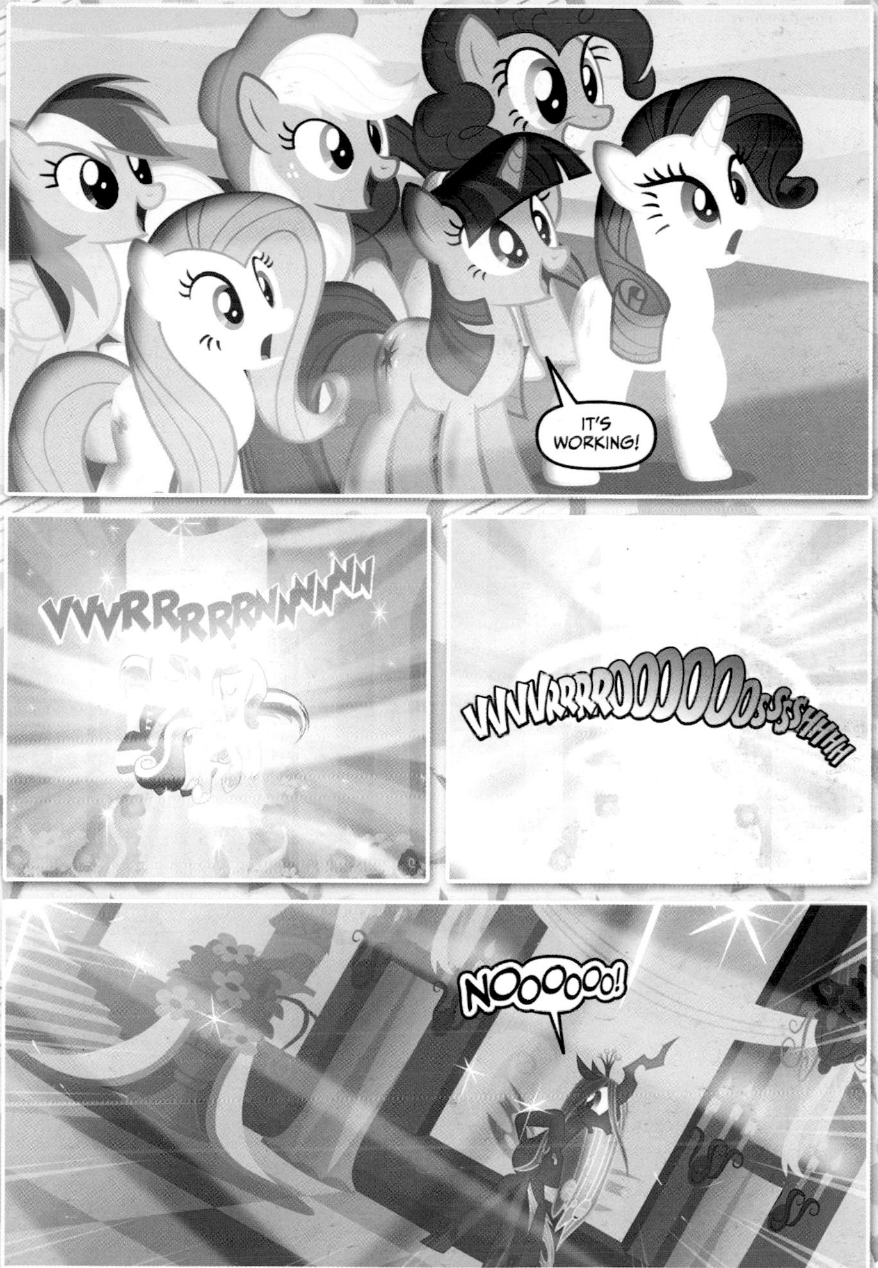
IT'S WORKING!
VVVRRRRRRNNNNNN
VVVVRRRROOOOOOOSSSHHHH
NOOOOOO!

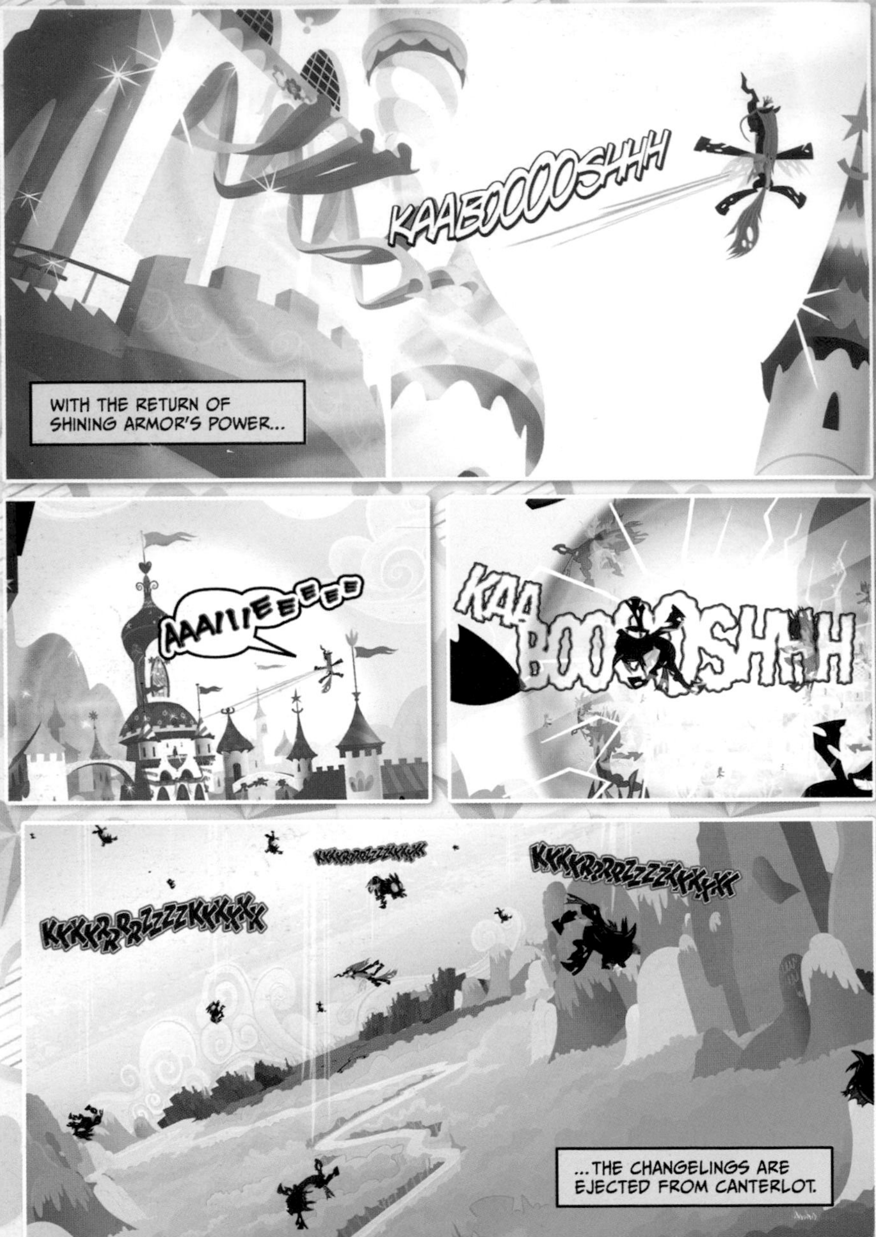
KAABOOOOSHHH
WITH THE RETURN OF SHINING ARMOR'S POWER...
AAAIIIEEEEEE
KAABOOOOSHHH
KKKKRRRRZZZKKKKK
KKKKRRRRZZZZKKKKK
KKKKRRRRRZZZZKKKKK
...THE CHANGELINGS ARE EJECTED FROM CANTERLOT.

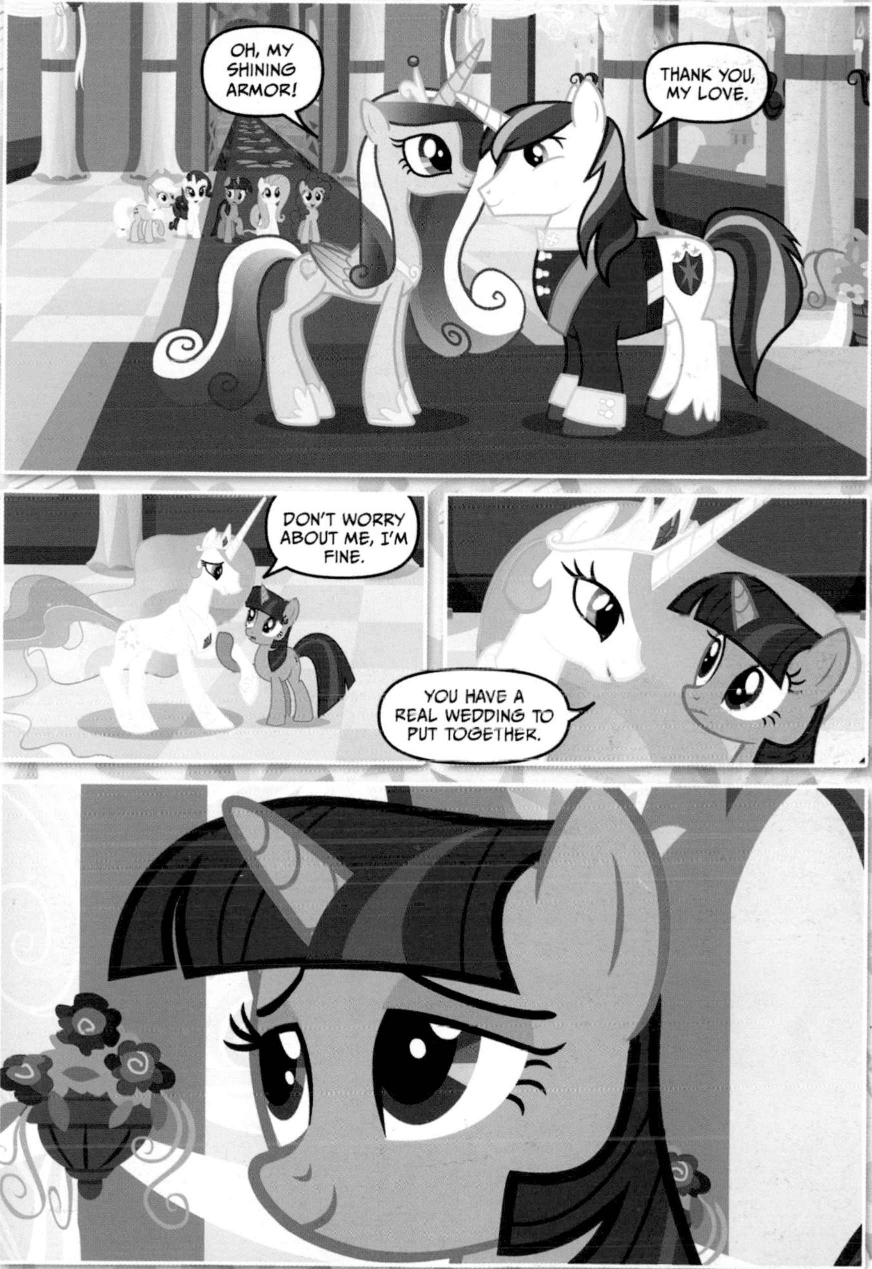
OH, MY SHINING ARMOR!
THANK YOU, MY LOVE.
DON'T WORRY ABOUT ME, I'M FINE.
YOU HAVE A REAL WEDDING TO PUT TOGETHER.

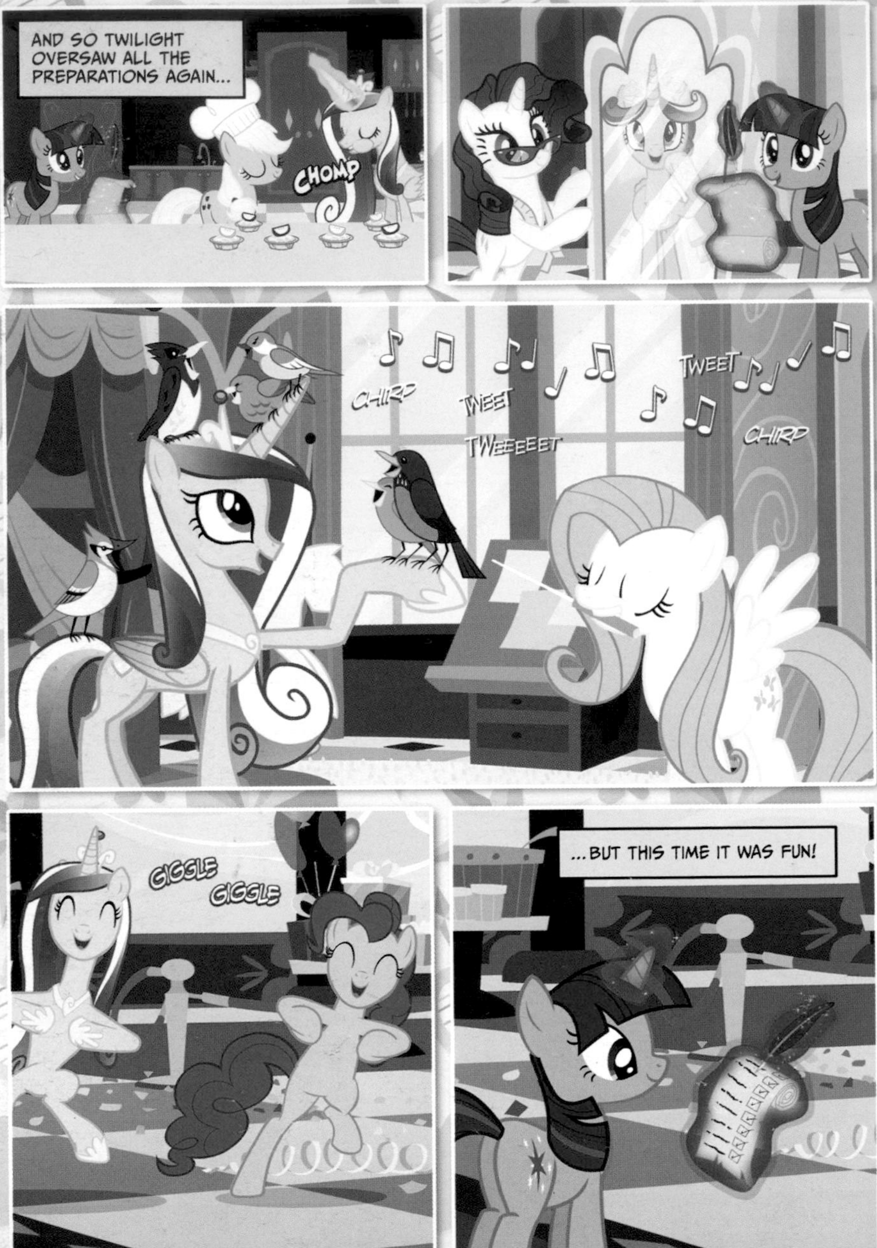
AND SO TWILIGHT OVERSAW ALL THE PREPARATIONS AGAIN...
CHOMP
CHIRP
TWEET
TWEEEEET
TWEET
CHIRP
GIGGLE
GIGGLE
...BUT THIS TIME IT WAS FUN!

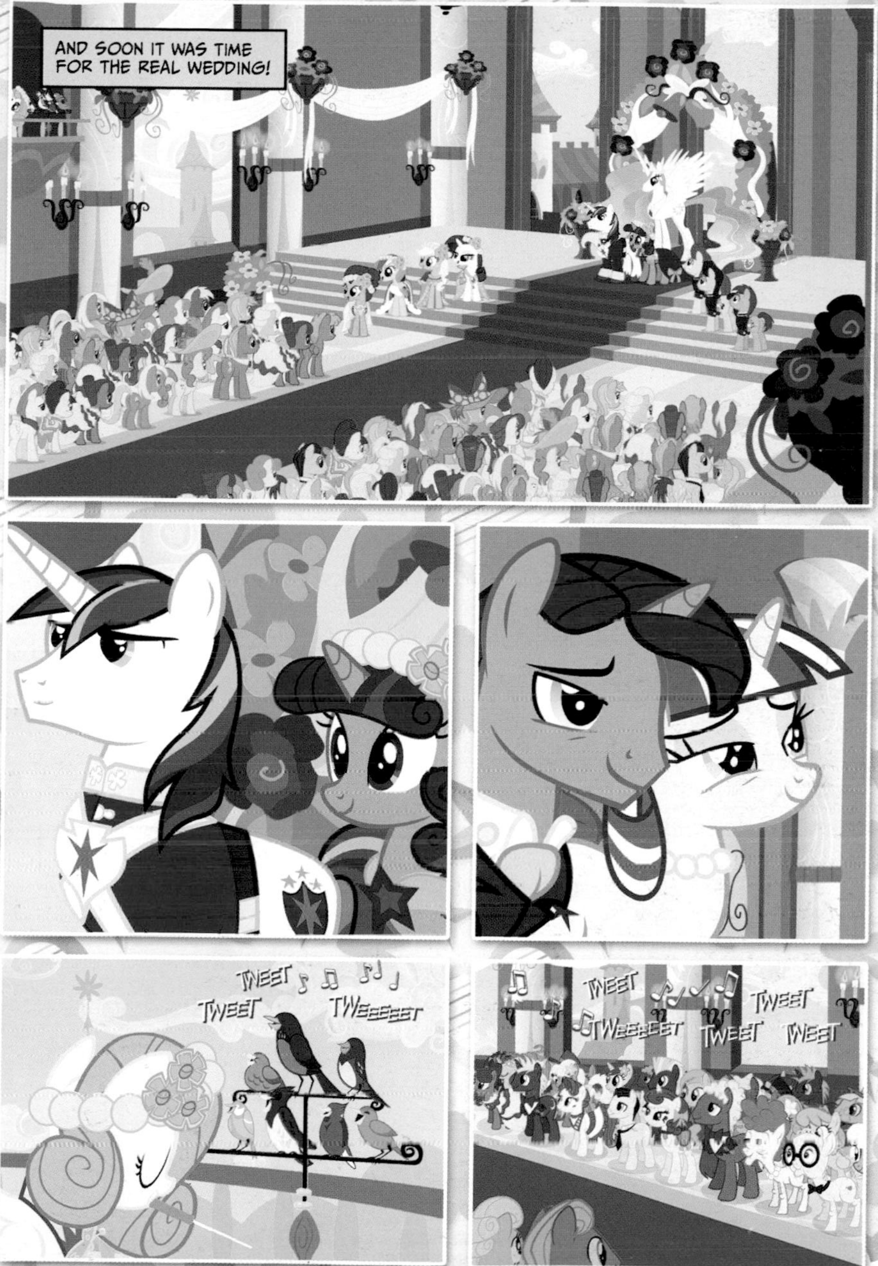
AND SOON IT WAS TIME FOR THE REAL WEDDING!
TWEET
TWEET
TWEEEEEET
TWEET
TWEEEEEET
TWEET
TWEET
TWEET

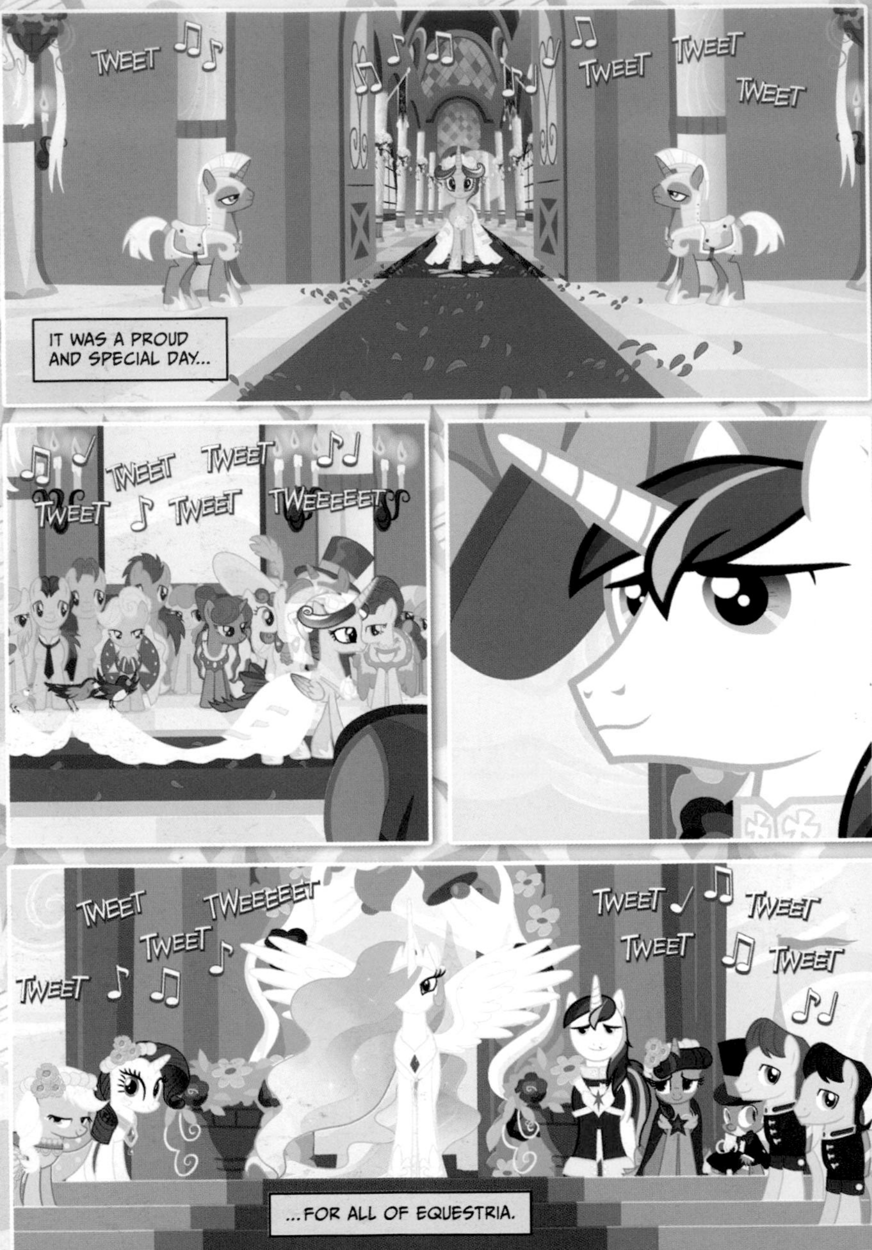
TWEET
TWEET
TWEET
TWEET
IT WAS A PROUD AND SPECIAL DAY...
TWEET
TWEET
TWEET
TWEET
TWEEEEEET
TWEET
TWEEEEEET
TWEET
TWEET
TWEET
TWEET
TWEET
TWEET
...FOR ALL OF EQUESTRIA.

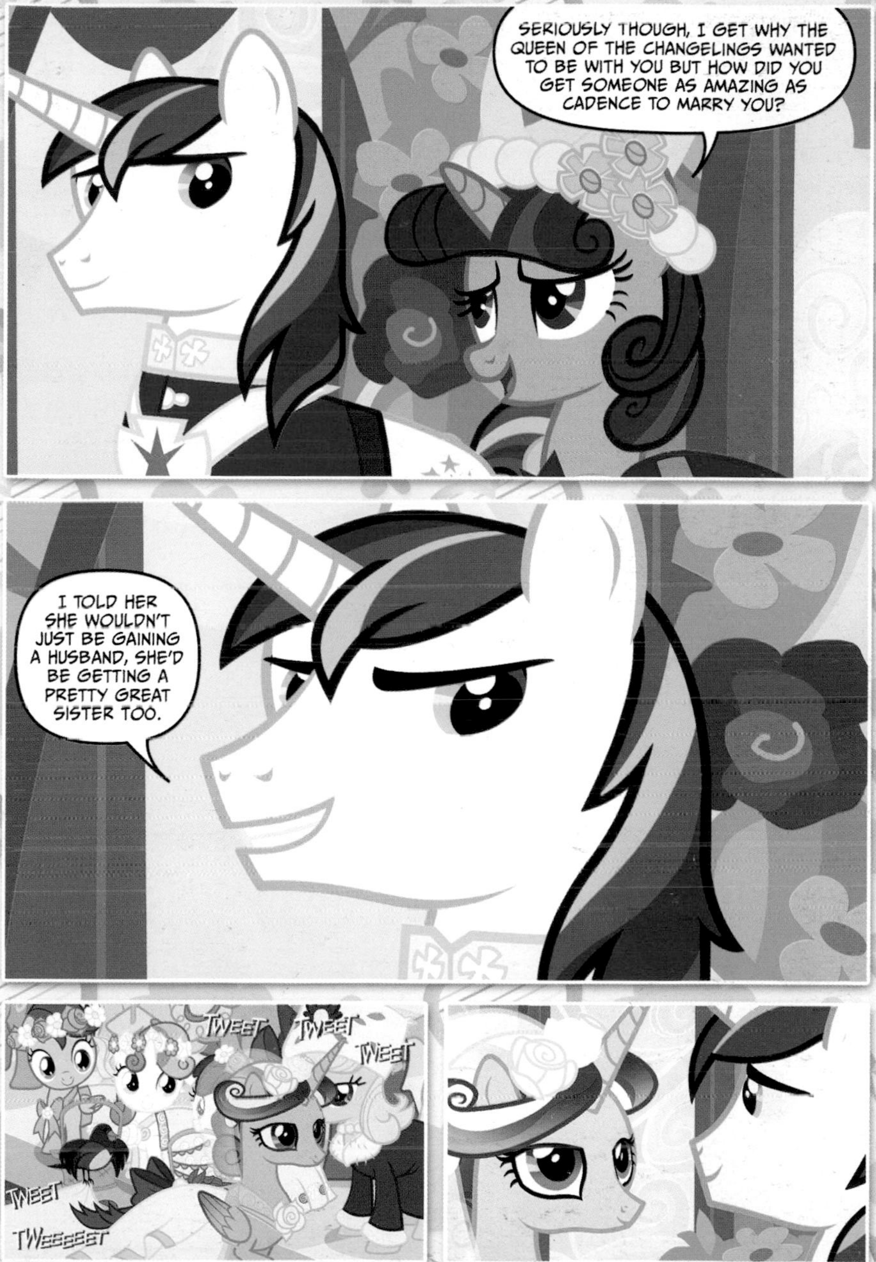
SERIOUSLY THOUGH, I GET WHY THE QUEEN OF THE CHANGELINGS WANTED TO BE WITH YOU BUT HOW DID YOU GET SOMEONE AS AMAZING AS CADENCE TO MARRY YOU?
I TOLD HER SHE WOULDN'T JUST BE GAINING A HUSBAND, SHE'D BE GETTING A PRETTY GREAT SISTER TOO.
TWEET
TWEET
TWEET
TWEET
TWEEEEET

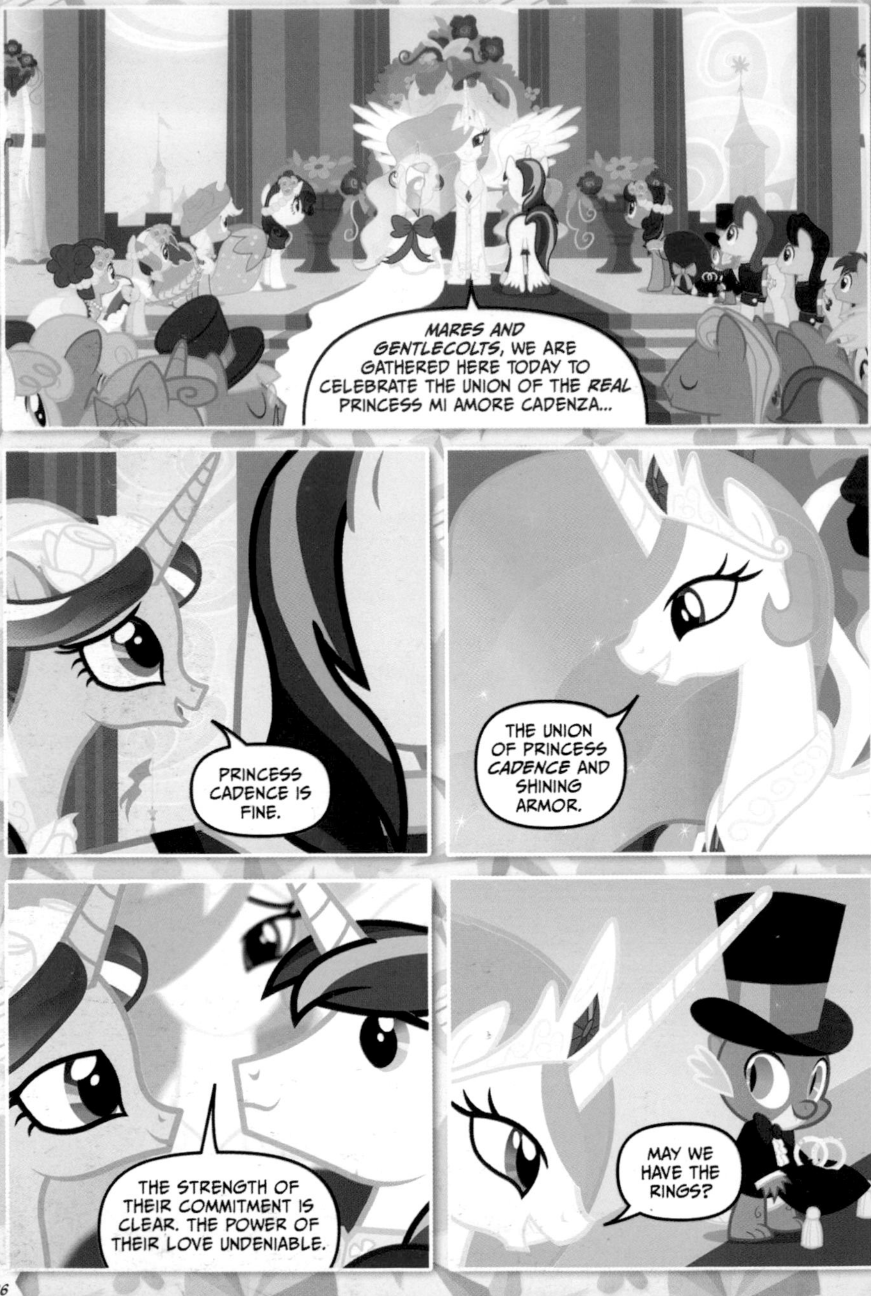
MARES AND GENTLECOLTS, WE ARE GATHERED HERE TODAY TO CELEBRATE THE UNION OF THE REAL PRINCESS MI AMORE CADENZA...
PRINCESS CADENCE IS FINE.
THE UNION OF PRINCESS CADENCE AND SHINING ARMOR.
THE STRENGTH OF THEIR COMMITMENT IS CLEAR. THE POWER OF THEIR LOVE UNDENIABLE.
MAY WE HAVE THE RINGS?

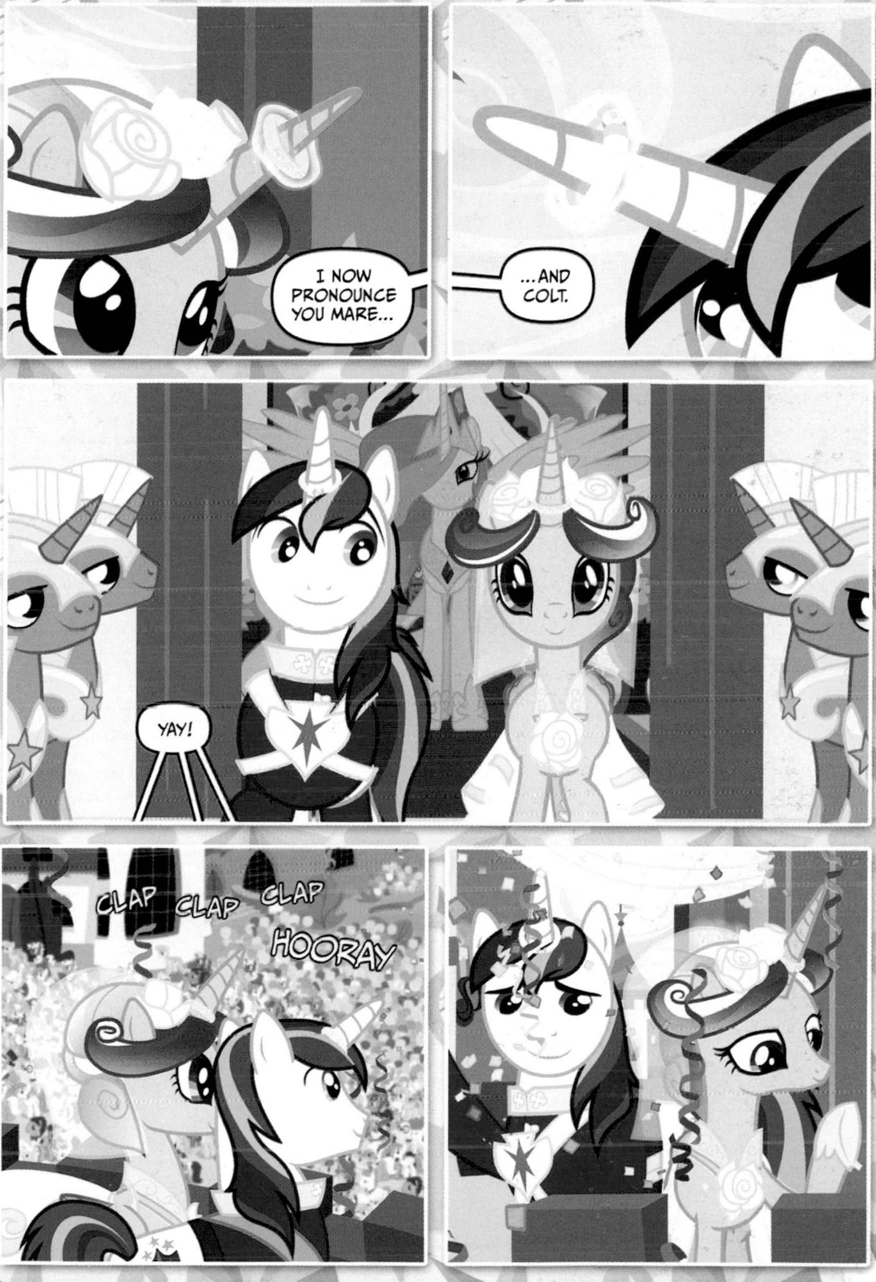
I NOW PRONOUNCE YOU MARE...
...AND COLT.
YAY!
CLAP
CLAP
CLAP
HOORAY

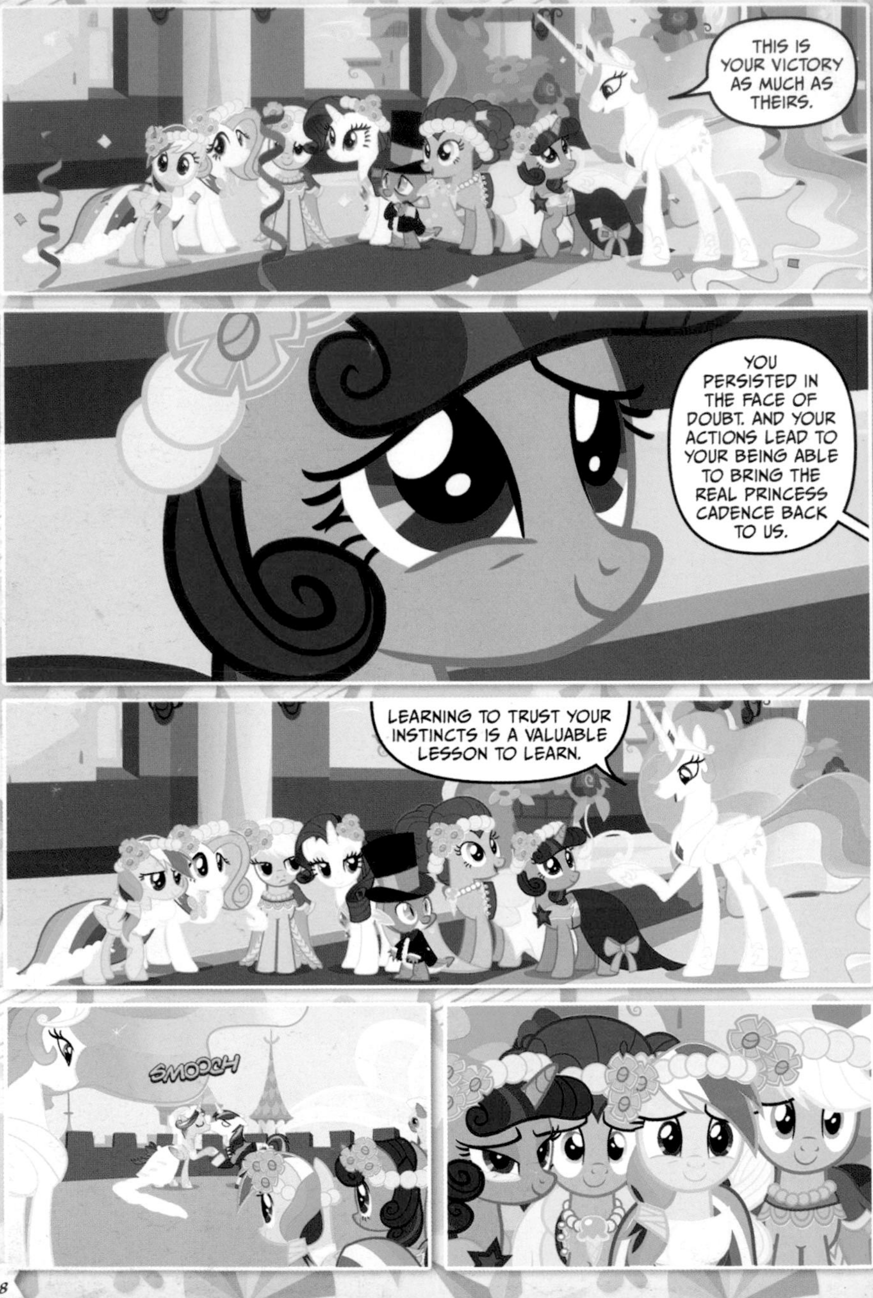
THIS IS YOUR VICTORY AS MUCH AS THEIRS.
YOU PERSISTED IN THE FACE OF DOUBT. AND YOUR ACTIONS LEAD TO YOUR BEING ABLE TO BRING THE REAL PRINCESS CADENCE BACK TO US.
LEARNING TO TRUST YOUR INSTINCTS IS A VALUABLE LESSON TO LEARN.
SMOOCH

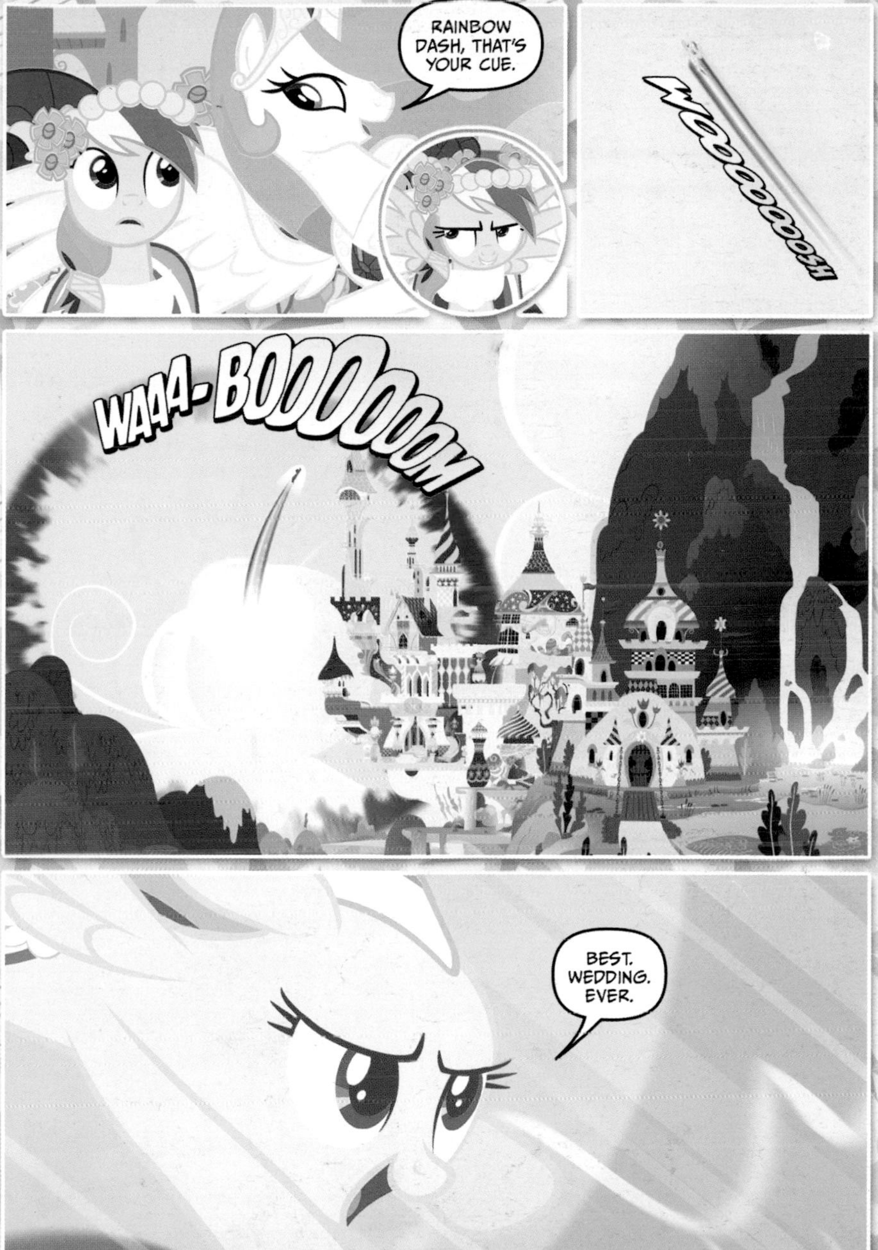

RAINBOW DASH, THAT'S YOUR CUE.
WOOOOOOOSH
WAAA-BOOOOOOM
BEST. WEDDING. EVER.

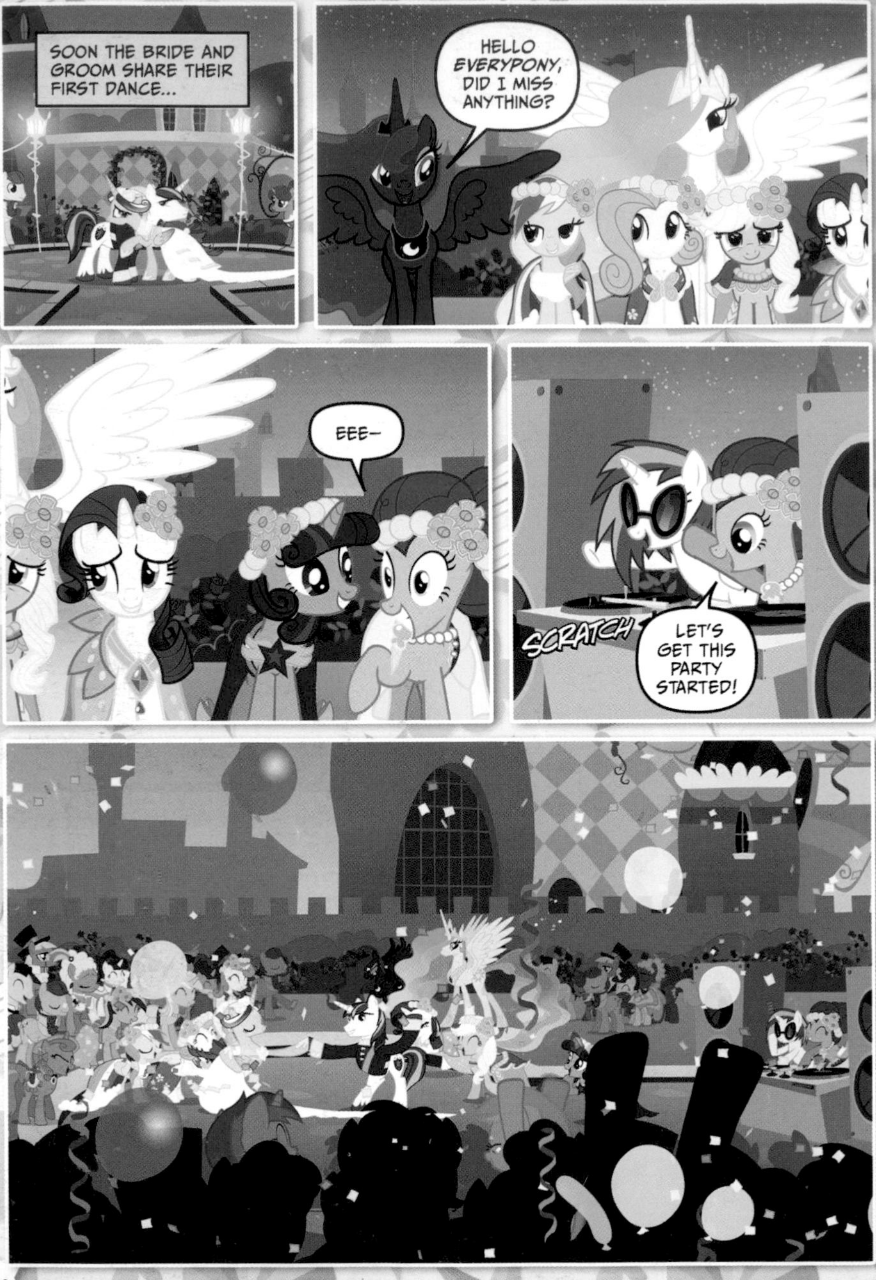
SOON THE BRIDE AND GROOM SHARE THEIR FIRST DANCE...
HELLO EVERYPONY, DID I MISS ANYTHING?
EEE–
SCRATCH
LET'S GET THIS PARTY STARTED!

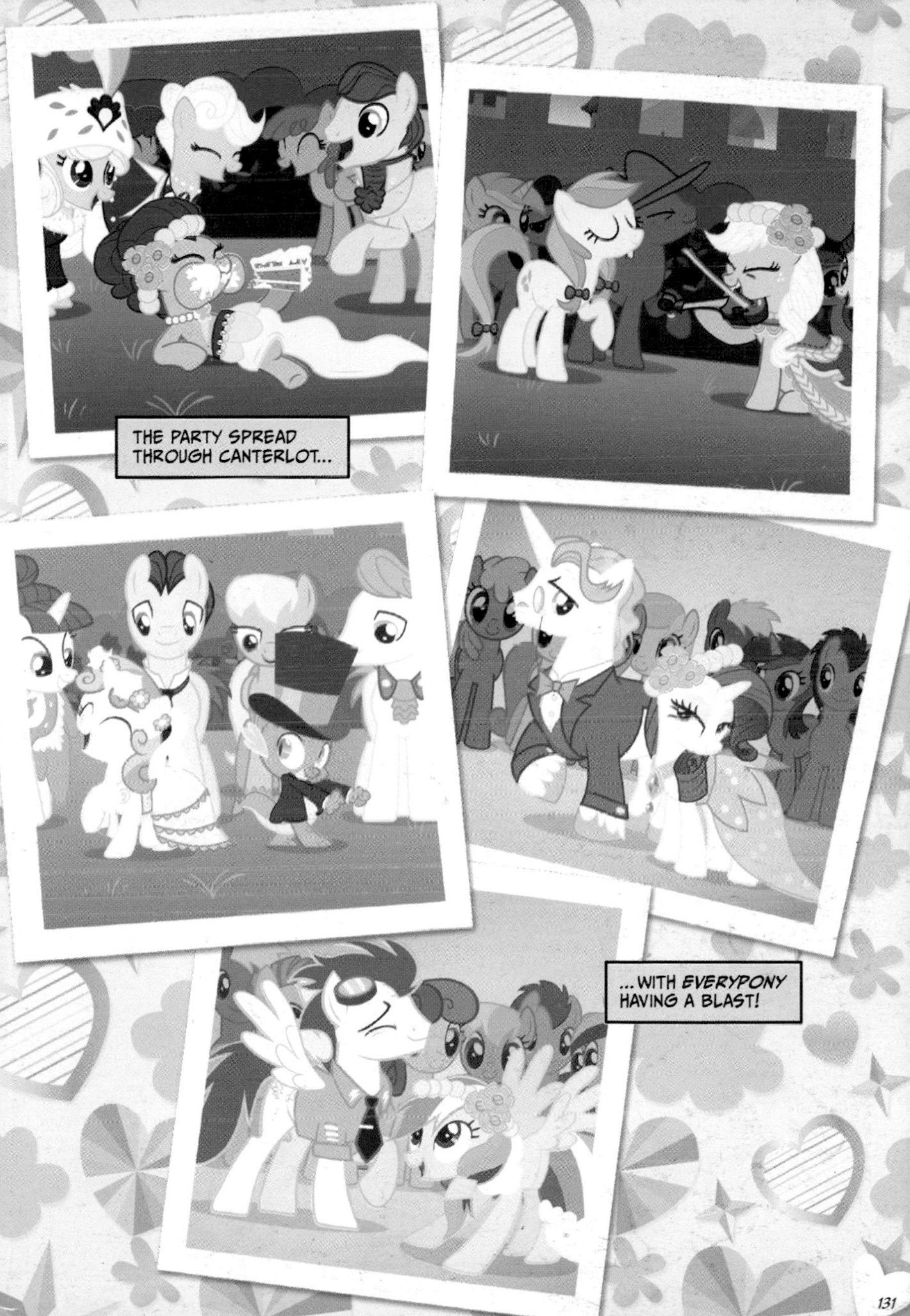
THE PARTY SPREAD THROUGH CANTERLOT...
...WITH *EVERYPONY* HAVING A BLAST!

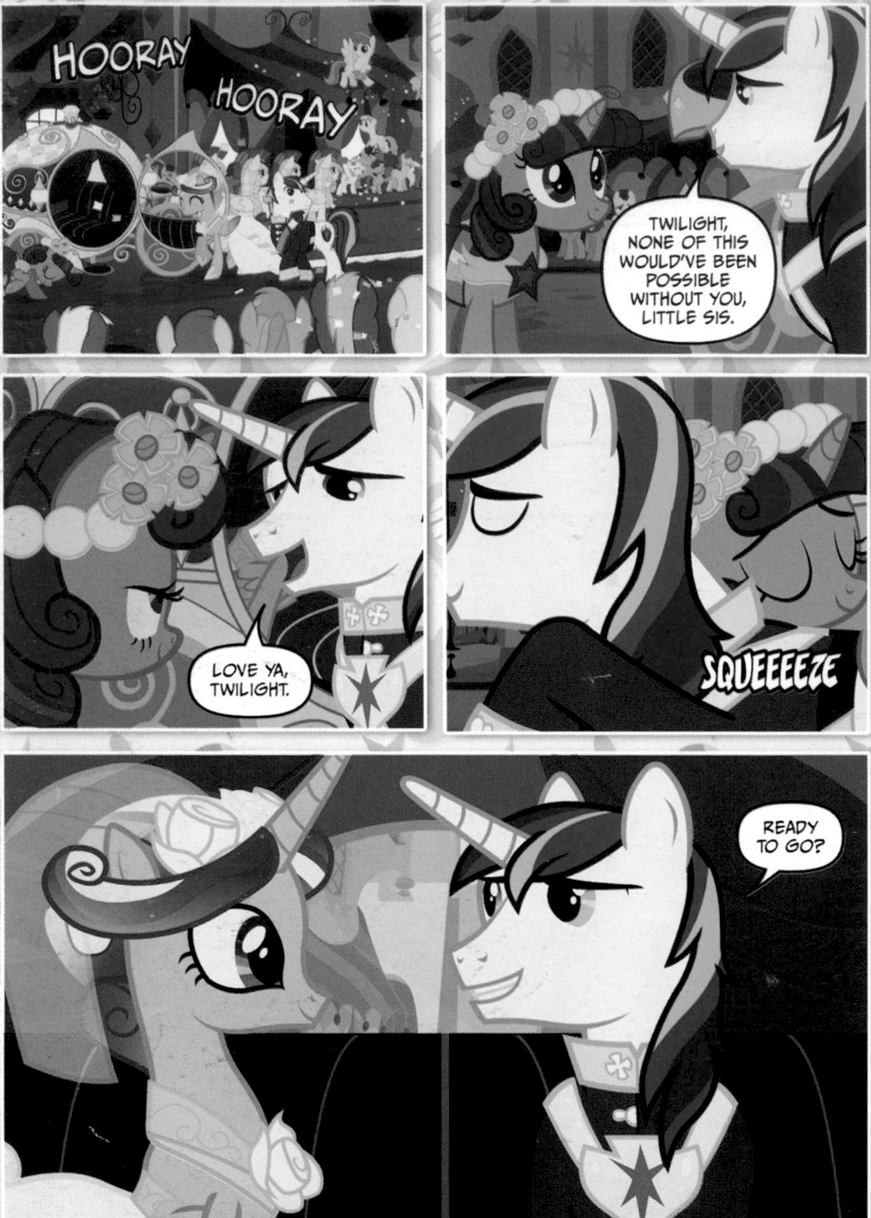
HOORAY
HOORAY
TWILIGHT, NONE OF THIS WOULD'VE BEEN POSSIBLE WITHOUT YOU, LITTLE SIS.
LOVE YA, TWILIGHT.
SQUEEEEEZE
READY TO GO?

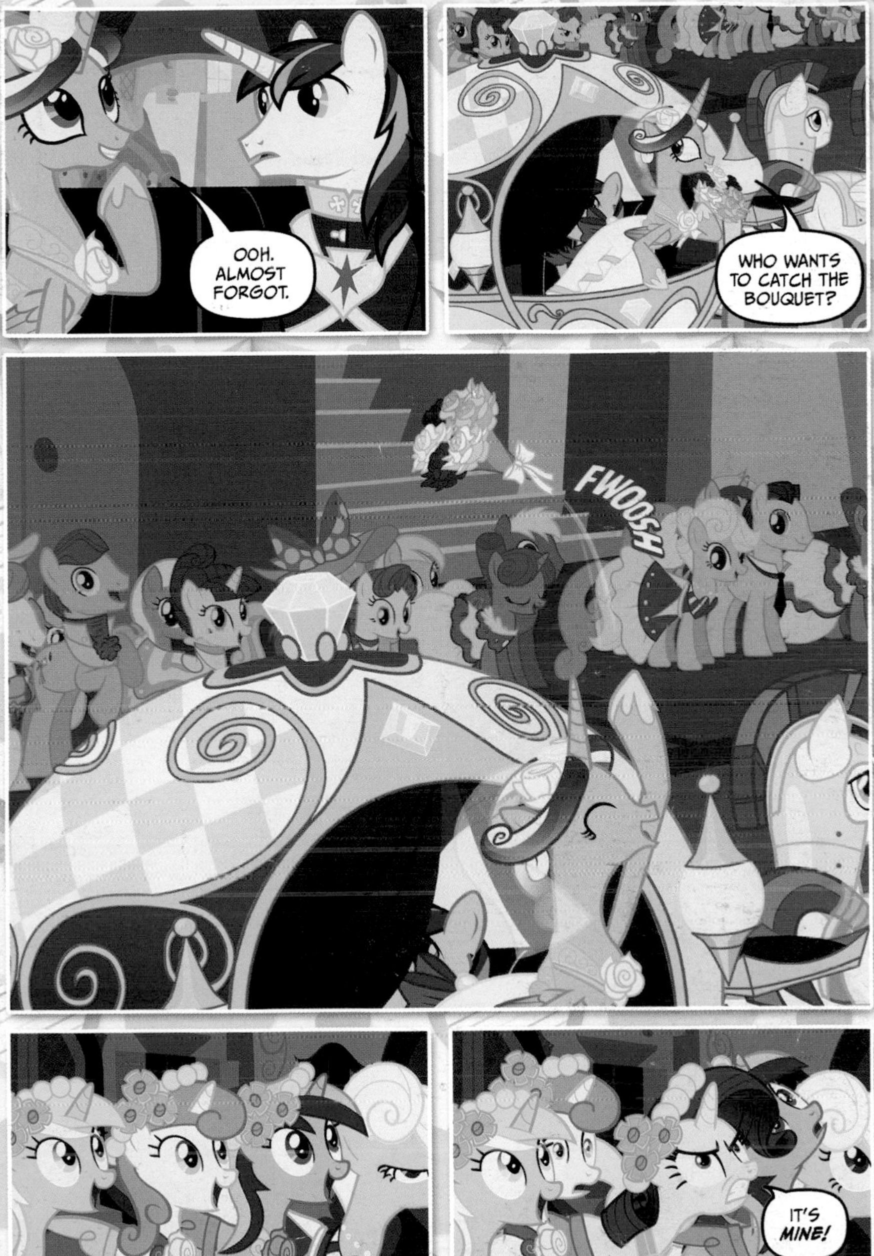
OOH. ALMOST FORGOT.
WHO WANTS TO CATCH THE BOUQUET?
FWOOSH
IT'S MINE!

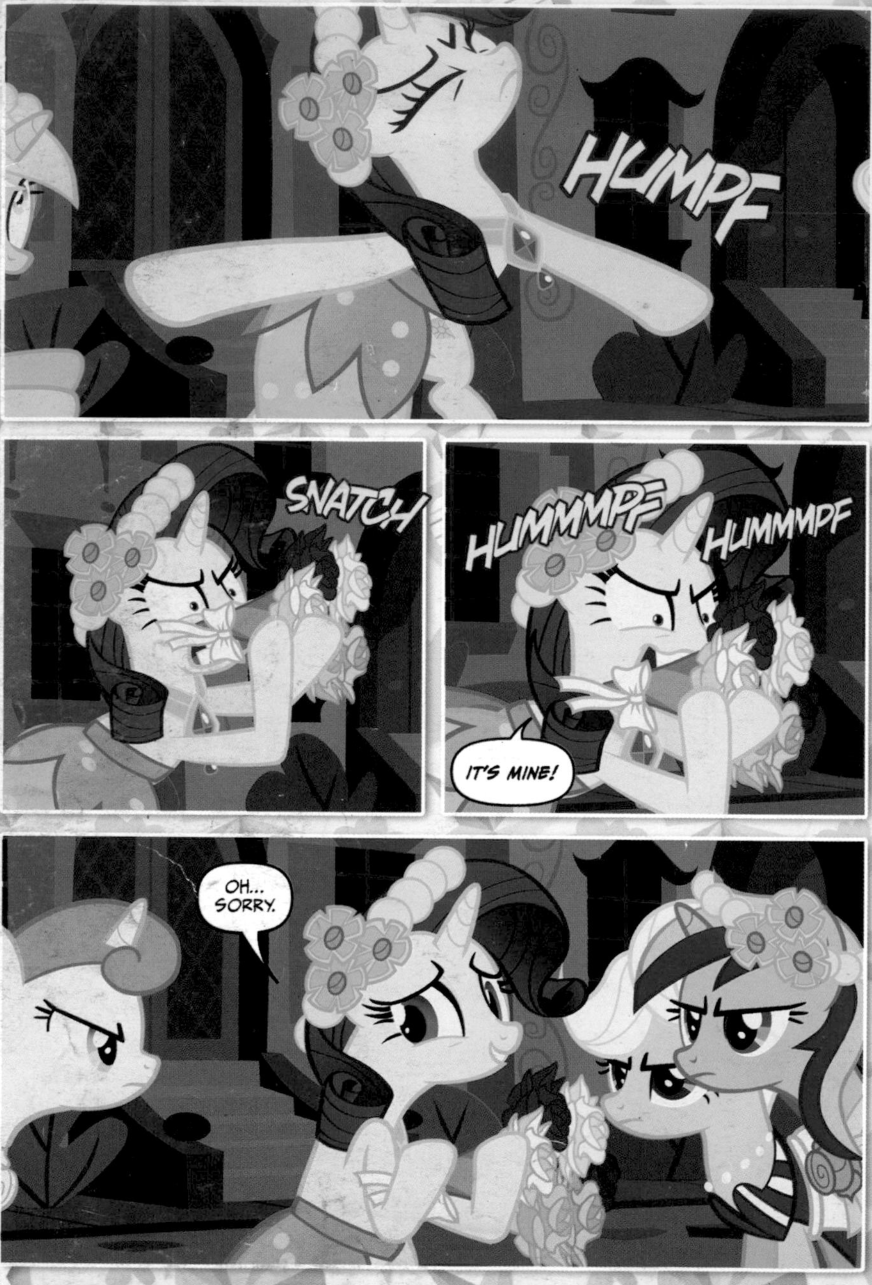
HUMPF
SNATCH
HUMMMPF
HUMMMPF
IT'S MINE!
OH... SORRY.

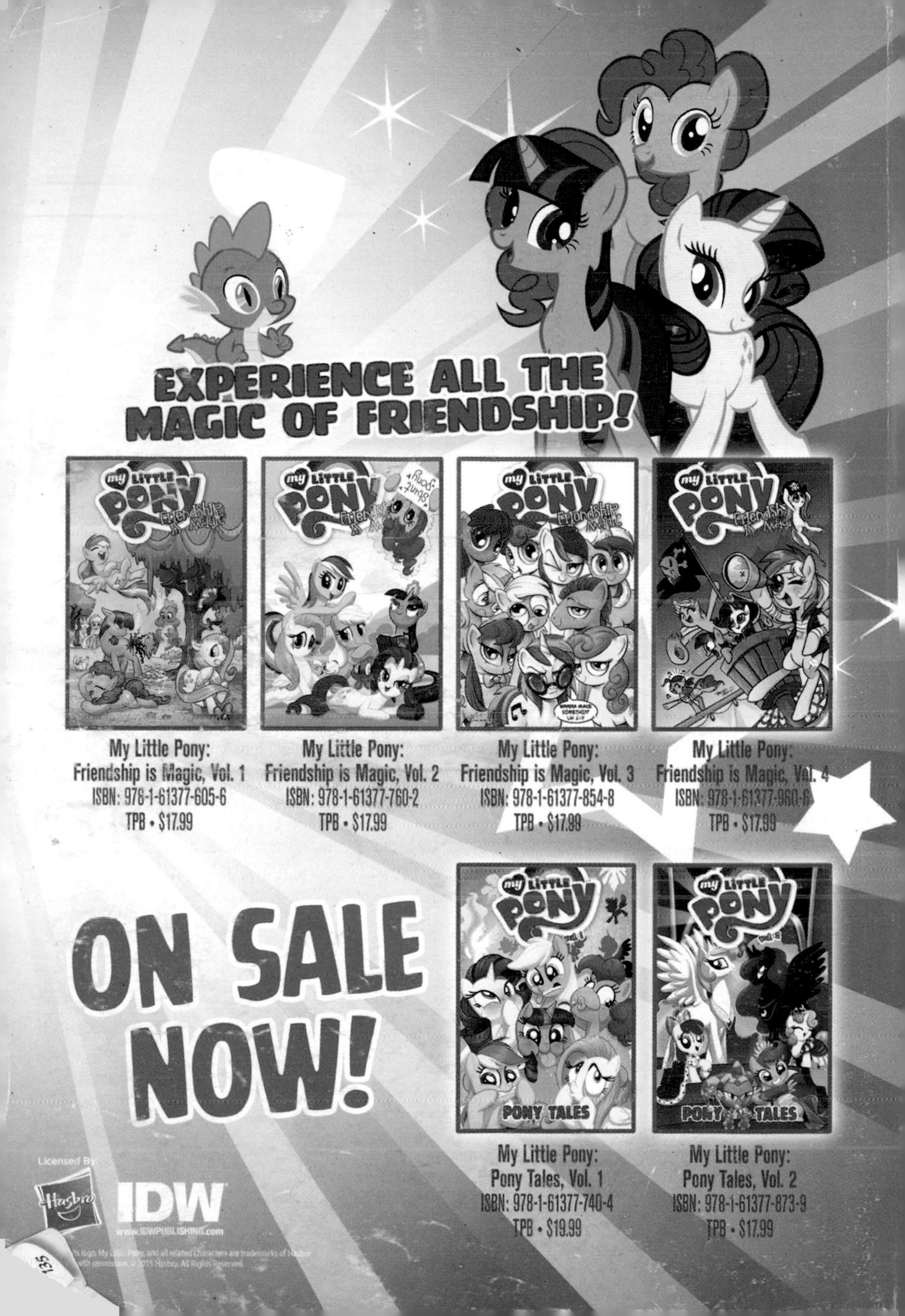
EXPERIENCE ALL THE MAGIC OF FRIENDSHIP!
My Little Pony: Friendship is Magic, Vol. 1
ISBN: 978-1-61377-605-6
TPB • $17.99
My Little Pony: Friendship is Magic, Vol. 2
ISBN: 978-1-61377-760-2
TPB • $17.99
My Little Pony: Friendship is Magic, Vol. 3
ISBN: 978-1-61377-854-8
TPB • $17.99
My Little Pony: Friendship is Magic, Vol. 4
ISBN: 978-1-61377-960-6
TPB • $17.99
ON SALE NOW!
My Little Pony: Pony Tales, Vol. 1
ISBN: 978-1-61377-740-4
TPB • $19.99
My Little Pony: Pony Tales, Vol. 2
ISBN: 978-1-61377-873-9
TPB • $17.99
Licensed By:
Hasbro
IDW
www.IDWPUBLISHING.com
ts logo, My Little Pony, and all related characters are trademarks of Hasbro
with permission. © 2015 Hasbro. All Rights Reserved.

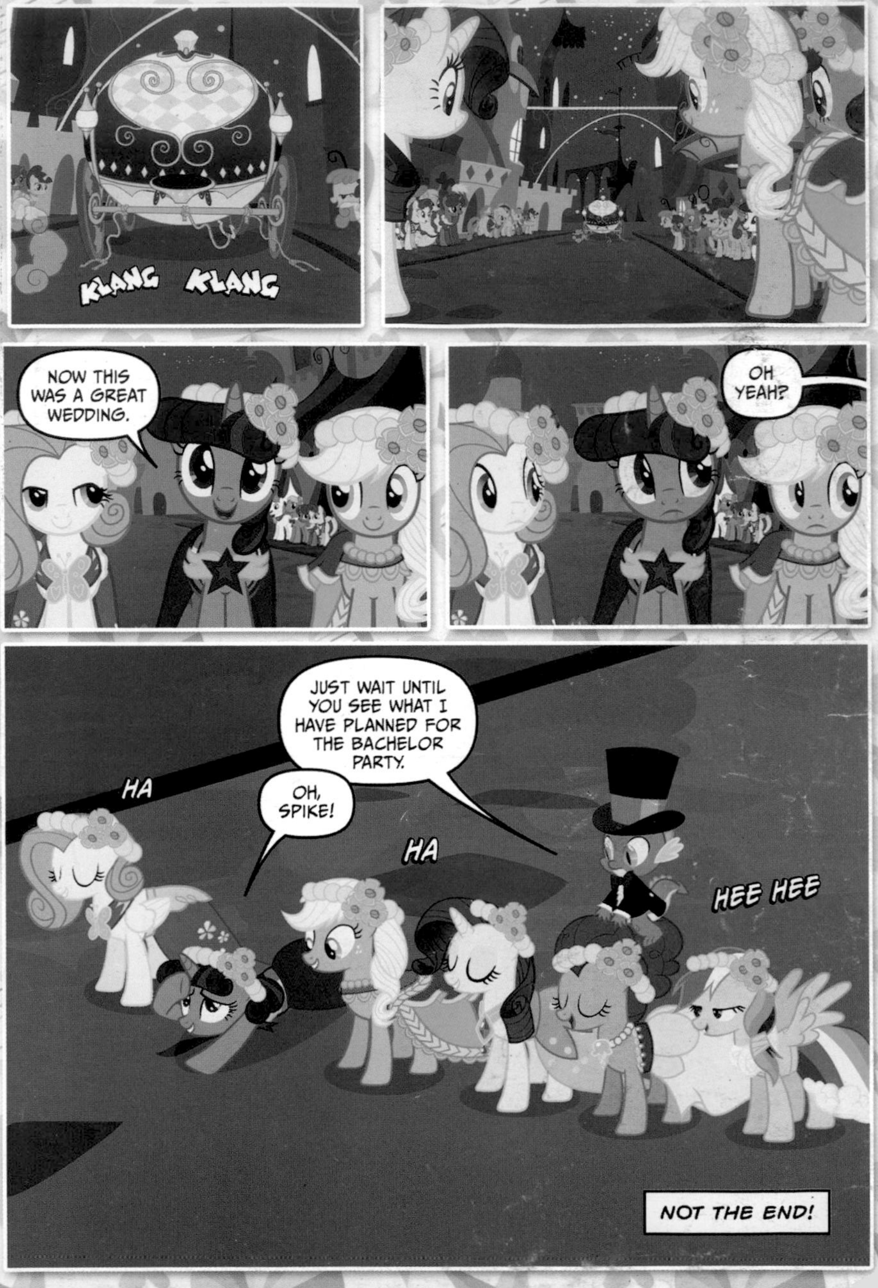
KLANG KLANG
NOW THIS WAS A GREAT WEDDING.
OH YEAH?
HA
JUST WAIT UNTIL YOU SEE WHAT I HAVE PLANNED FOR THE BACHELOR PARTY.
OH, SPIKE!
HA
HEE HEE
NOT THE END!